Drummer in the Dark

Drummer in the Dark

T. DAVIS BUNN

Doubleday

New York   London   Toronto   Sydney   Auckland

WaterBrook Press

Colorado Springs

PUBLISHED BY DOUBLEDAY
a division of Random House, Inc.
1540 Broadway, New York, New York 10036

DOUBLEDAY and the portrayal of an anchor with a dolphin are trademarks of
Doubleday, a division of Random House, Inc.

WATERBROOK and its deer design logo are registered trademarks of WaterBrook Press,
a division of Random House, Inc.

This book is copublished with WaterBrook Press, 2375 Telstar Drive, Suite 160,
Colorado Springs, CO 80920, a division of Random House, Inc.

This novel is a work of fiction. Any references to real events, businesses, organizations,
and locales are intended only to give the fiction a sense of reality and authenticity. Any
resemblance to actual persons, living or dead, is entirely coincidental.

Library of Congress Cataloging-in-Publication Data
Bunn, T. Davis, 1952–
Drummer in the dark / T. Davis Bunn.—1st ed.
p.   cm.
1. Debts, External—Developing countries—Fiction.
2. Debt relief—Developing countries—Fiction.
3. Developing countries—Fiction.   I. Title.

PS3552.U4718 D78 2001
813'.54—dc21   2001028363

ISBN 0-385-49616-8 (Doubleday)
ISBN 1-57856-390-9 (WaterBrook)

For Mason and Mary Williams,
who walk in law and grace

WHEREVER businesssmen gather the talk turns to the present prosperity in America; how long it will last, and what will follow it. Periods of prosperity like the present always have one accompaniment. Always it happens that a considerable number of people think this particular prosperity will not end, that there will never be another panic or another depression. They are always wrong. They will be wrong this time.

—*New York Herald*, November 27, 1925

Introduction

IN 1993, certain hedge funds and investment banks active in foreign exchange caused a run on the British pound. One hedge fund alone netted over three billion dollars profit from sixteen hours of trading.

In 1998, foreign exchange traders attacked the currencies of seven Asian nations. Five countries entered economic meltdown as a result. In a subsequent speech before the United Nations, the President of Malaysia condemned the world's foreign exchange traders and the hedge fund operators. He called them "marauding pirates."

In 2000, the new pan-European currency, the euro, came under attack. According to official reports, supporting the euro against foreign exchange traders has already cost American, European, and Japanese central banks and taxpayers over ninety billion dollars.

Recently the former director of Germany's central bank said that a sustained assault on the American dollar was "only a matter of time."

Because the international foreign exchange and currency derivatives markets are the least regulated of all major exchanges, their exact size cannot be stated. But the most widely accepted estimate places current market volume in excess of three trillion dollars.

Per day.

Drummer in the Dark

PROLOGUE

LIBERTY PARK was a block-wide strip of palms and patchy grass stretching from the Melbourne hospital to the airport's border. The park lay a mile from the high-rent district fronting the Intracoastal Waterway, and was bordered by Florida retirees who couldn't afford beachfront prices. Local residents loathed the park. By day, the place was empty and baking. By night, the druggies and the pros took over. The noise, according to newspaper reports, was inhuman. In the two years since Wynn Bryant had sold his business, cashed in his corporate chips, and built his Merritt Island home fourteen miles north, he had successfully avoided giving the park a second glance.

This steamy March afternoon, Wynn watched his sister from the safety of his air-conditioned Audi. Sybel Bryant Wells, wife of Florida Governor Grant Wells, stood by tables laden with a meal for the homeless. A cluster of reporters hovered by the opposite side of the road, shooting pictures of how the governor's wife celebrated her birthday.

Six years earlier, when his fledgling high-tech company had racked up its first major deal, Wynn had offered his sister her heart's desire. He was twenty-eight at the time and flush with his first taste of success. The years leading up to that point had been fairly savage, and much of his early survival had been due to Sybel's strength. This birthday offer had been Wynn's attempt at payback. Sybel's husband was then a lowly state legislator with lofty ambitions, and money had been tight. Whatever she wanted for her birthday, Wynn had offered to give her, that year and every March to come. If he could afford it, it was hers. Sybel's response had shocked him speechless.

Wynn locked his car and crossed the street. His offer had reaped one voyage for each of Sybel's birthdays, except the year his wife had become deathly ill. He had traveled to Guatemala, El Salvador, and Haiti. They had helped build an orphanage in a tiny Baja village, where San Diego was a myth lost beyond clouds of dust and diesel fumes. They also took a frostbitten journey to Canada's Hudson Bay, where the alcoholism rate equaled winter unemployment—sixty-five percent of the adult population.

But these memories were not what now made the simple act of crossing the street a journey into battle. A month earlier, Sybel had called and asked the impossible. Wynn had silently hung up the phone. Click and goodbye. They had not spoken since. Last week Sybel had sent him a postcard saying simply, Liberty Park, Melbourne, Two pm. Sybel had a habit of growing very terse when things did not run her way.

Sybel was now talking with a slender priest in dark suit and clerical collar. Though she and Grant were Baptist, she maintained close relationships with many churches involved in homeless care and crisis centers. She was also a staunch supporter of a Catholic movement called Sant'Egidio and attended their mass or evening prayers whenever she could. This raised conservatives' ire on both sides of the Christian divide, a fact that granted Wynn bitter satisfaction. Such ammunition was useful whenever she pressed him about his own lack of belief in anything beyond the galling vagaries of life.

Sybel glanced up at his approach, grabbed two empty garbage bags, and headed over. "Give me a hand, will you?"

He kept his arms at his sides. "I'm not going back to Cairo."

"Take the bag, Wynn."

"I'm never going back. You of all people should have known not to ask."

"Those reporters are watching." She thrust the bag into his hand. "And that's not why I asked you here today."

He fell into step beside her. "It was still wrong. You should never have brought it up."

Sybel approached a trio of bearded men sprawled beneath a Florida oak. Their hands were gnarled as the tree's branches, their faces stained by life on the road. "Did you gentlemen get enough to eat?"

Wynn's ear caught the difference then. Usually Sybel came alive at such times. Sybel had a special way with those who had lost their own voice. Normally she could melt all within range, draw smiles from people hard as upright stones. Even the young girls, turned old by the users and the wolves, would sometimes emerge from their shells and speak with her, revealing traces of their blinding pain. Sybel's presence was that compelling, her music that soft.

But not today.

Sybel jammed more soiled paper plates into her bag and walked on. Between groups, Wynn asked, "What's wrong?"

"Everything."

Sybel shared Wynn's dark good looks, and people usually assumed they were far closer in age than the eleven years actually separating them. Sybel had a long neck and a river of dark hair, braided now into a rope thick as Wynn's wrist. But where his eyes were clouded gray, Sybel's were jet black and as direct as her opinions. Normally she was poised, determined, and ferociously independent. Her smiles were seldom bestowed and always genuine. This tight worry was new and a matter of concern.

"Is it Grant?" When she responded by punching more trash into her bag, he asked, "What is it this time?"

"Maybe it comes with age. Maybe he doesn't have the energy to hold onto the lies any more." She glanced blindly around the sunlit park. "No, not lies. Just the things that don't matter as much as he always pretended."

"Why don't you—"

"Our meeting today isn't about me and Grant." Sybel drew him behind a cluster of palms, blocking them from the feeding station's curious eyes. "It's about you."

"I'm doing just fine, Sybel."

"You're wasting your life. You're worse off than these tramps." She rattled the bag like a plastic whip. At such times, Sybel defined impatience. "For two years you've been living life parked in a rest area. Your biggest concern is teaching your latest fling how to use the espresso machine."

"I'm not one of your kids, Sybel." His niece attended seminary in Charleston. His nephew, a gangling teenage baseball fanatic, saw the governor's mansion as his own personal date-pulling machine. Sybel had never had much luck with her men.

"That's where you're wrong." She reached for more garbage, the movements slower now, her voice older. "You always have been. Always will be. I worry about you."

"I'm doing okay. Something will turn up."

"It already has." She straightened, but did not meet his gaze. "Do I still get my birthday present?"

"I'm not going back to Cairo. Not now, not ever."

She swatted the words away. "Something else. Are you still offering me anything I want?"

Guarded now. "What is it?"

"Yes or no, Wynn."

"All right. Yes. But—"

"Go see Grant. Agree to do whatever he says. That's what I want for my birthday." The horizon continued to hold her attention. "He's in Orlando. The Grand Floridian. He gave a luncheon address, he's meeting some campaign donors this afternoon, then we're having a little family gathering this evening. Then I'm leaving for eighteen days in Ecuador. Alone."

"I could come, Sybel."

"I'm not inviting you. Grant is expecting you at five. Which gives you time to go back and put on a tie."

"It's eighty-seven degrees, and I haven't worn a tie in almost two years."

"And a jacket. Dark is best." She halted further protest by finally turning his way, giving him a look all her own. "This is part of the deal, Wynn. Go. You have to be on time."

THE DRIVE into Orlando was the usual trip down nightmare lane. The Winter Park exit crawled by, elongated by four years of memories, all that had come before his wife had died of rheumatoid arthritis. A strange killer, the first doctor had told him, in a voice so detached Wynn could have strangled the man with his own stethoscope. It attacks the lungs and suffocates the patient slow as a python. Almost like going to sleep. After Winter Park came the University Science Park, where Wynn and his two technopartners had almost gone under five times in seven years before finally hitting the golden button. Wynn had spoken to neither man since the buyout. One had accused him of going public too early, the other of selling too low. Now they tinkered in vast private labs and dreamed of another moment in the sun. But without their previous hunger or Wynn to drive them, they were just another pair of embittered millionaires with too much time on their hands.

The Grand Floridian was Grant's kind of hotel. The lobby was built on a series of broad steps like a layered stage. The governor's security detail had cordoned off the high left platform where Grant Wells now sat enthroned on a striped silk sofa under glaring television lights.

Wynn spotted the obligatory aide, a stunning brunette with clipboard and earpiece and miniskirted business suit. She stood not quite to one side, clearly loving the attention as much as Grant. Wynn approached and gave his name, accepted the brilliant smile and the news that Grant was running a little behind schedule. He then retreated to the lobby's opposite corner.

Wynn could not help but color the moment with memories of what had come before. His parents had taught at the American University of Cairo. Days before his sixth birthday, both had died from an illness or poisoning. Perhaps Sybel had discovered which, but she knew better than to discuss anything about that place and time. Nineteen months after their return to America, Grant Wells had been swept utterly off his feet by Sybel's beauty and fire. Sybel had accepted Grant's marriage proposal with two conditions: she would continue at university, and Wynn would move in with them. Grant had been running his father's Ocala electronics store at the time, sitting on the town council and chafing with pent-up ambition. What Grant had thought of an eight-year-old severely traumatized brat invading their married bliss, he never said. Already Grant had shown a politician's ability to mask his inner workings.

"Mr. Bryant?" The brunette gave him another highly public smile. "The governor will see you now."

Wynn kept a pace back so as to watch the movement of those patterned blue stockings. Grant's new aide walked like a two-legged snake. "When did Grant pull you from the typing pool?"

"Three months ago." A toss of the head. "And it was from Emory."

As they crested the top step, Grant rose and saw off his last appointment. Stopwatch accuracy. Grant approached with grin and hand outstretched. "Where you been hiding yourself, sport?"

"Here and there." Wynn gestured back to where the press remained corralled. "Shouldn't you see to them first?"

"Can't." He led Wynn over to the divan. "Besides, they're eating and drinking on my tab. Something you'll learn in this trade. Keep the press fed and watered at all times or they'll pick your carcass like vultures."

"Thanks, but lessons like that I can definitely do without."

That caused Grant to smile. "I take it Sybel didn't tell you why I wanted us to meet."

"*You* arranged this?"

"Oh, she planted the seed, I'll give her that. Credit where credit's due. Three, four months ago, back when old Hutch had his first stroke."

A faint niggling went off at the back of Wynn's mind, like a fire alarm in a distant room. "Congressman Hutchings has suffered a stroke?"

"She didn't tell you a thing, did she. You don't have one idea what's aimed straight at you."

Grant was blunt-spoken, tall, fleshy, and not particularly attractive. In his younger days, he had possessed such a simple worthiness that most people had overlooked his evident flaws. These days, however, he showed a gratingly false bonhomie. His gaze was that of a fish mounted on a wall—bulbous and dead. Wynn had continued to support his campaigns, however, with gifts aimed not at Grant but at Sybel. Since Sybel always refused anything for herself, Wynn remained one of Grant's largest soft-money donors. "You didn't have to arrange all this just because you need more funds, Grant."

"That's not it. Not this time." Grant leaned forward. "I want you to come work for me. In a manner of speaking."

"Not a chance." It was the kind of offer made for Wynn to turn down. "Tallahassee has more hot air than a blast furnace. I'm happy where I am."

"Wasn't talking about Tallahassee. Hutch had a second stroke last week. A real giant killer. He's down, he's out, he's history." Grant slung his arm across the sofa back, hugely satisfied with his news. His battles with Graham Hutchings were legendary. "The press has just gotten wind that Hutch has officially resigned. We need to have our candidate and the special election date all set and ready to go. With Congress split right down the middle, there's not a moment to lose."

Wynn wanted to refuse point-blank, but his promise to Sybel glued the words down deep.

Grant's smile broadened. "She's caught you, hasn't she. Hooked you, dragged you to shore, left you flapping in the sand."

"I hate Washington."

"Sure you do. But you've never seen it from inside the club. Makes all the difference. This time you won't be a tourist with his face mashed tight against the glass. You'll be an insider. Washington will be *your* town." He was expansive now, with the power of knowing the battle was all but won. "Here's the deal in broad strokes. You'll run unopposed, just like old Hutch did in the last election. Our party's got a dead-solid lock on this district, and everybody knows it. Our choice is the people's choice, and that's final. I'll throw some bones to the opposition so they don't complain about either the speed or the selection. Already spoken to their head man, he's been after me on a water-rights bill. The man wanted it bad enough to let us push the election forward. Only voters who'll show up on polling day will be the party faithful."

"You're rigging the election?"

"That shows how much you know about politics in the modern age. Nothing's rigged about this deal. Just highly lubricated, is all. This election will pass without more than a couple of headlines in the local rag. You'll make the rounds, shake the hands, eat a few rubber chicken dinners, smile for the cameras on polling day, and be off to the big city."

Wynn sat buffeted by his sister's wiles. "I don't have any choice."

"Not if you're a man of your word like I've always thought." Grant waved at someone Wynn could not see. "Two quick points before we do the press come-on. First, I'm making a run for the Senate in the next election. I want you to back me."

Wynn's ears were filled with the noise of crashing waves, as though the ocean had moved seventy miles inland. He watched the lovely aide pass out printed sheets to the gathered press, helpless to halt the tide.

"Second, and I hope you're listening because this is critical, Hutch has been backing a piece of legislation that's raised hackles all over the state. Called the Jubilee Amendment. We want you to be our man on the spot and kill this thing stone dead."

"I can't do that." Wynn took small satisfaction in having something to refuse. "A point up front. I'm not your man. I go up, I look everything over for myself, and make up my own mind."

Grant forced his game-face back into place. "I like you. Always have. You're too good-looking for a hard-scrabbling boy, but you've done well by what you had. So I didn't have any mind to tell you this, sport. Rumors have started floating around town about some tricky financial dealings. Insider trading, confidential information about the sale of your company, Bermuda banks, the works."

"Remarkable timing."

"That's how things are. It ain't just rain, it's a hurricane." Grant tapped Wynn's knee. "Here's how it's going to play. You're heading up for eighteen months of the Washington high life. When I launch my Senate run, you're going to come out for me whole hog. Then you can retire down here to your fancy-pants waterside villa and have folks call you congressman for the rest of your days." Another tap on his leg. "And in the meantime you're going to make sure that the Jubilee Amendment is choked to death."

Wynn had nothing to say, which satisfied Grant immensely. He rose and lifted Wynn with him, motioned to his aide, and smiled as the press surged forward. Wynn flinched but held his ground. He said nothing, just stood and let his brother-in-law proclaim how stunned and honored Wynn was by the nomination. To the accusation of rampant cronyism, Grant countered with Wynn's success as a businessman and his staunch backing of the party. The questions and the cameras' square black eyes and the lights all struck at Wynn for maybe ten minutes, maybe five hours. Then he was shaking Grant's hand and staring the man in the eyes, knowing he was beaten, trapped, and more scared than he had been in years.

Grant clapped him on the shoulder, hugged him close for the cameras, and said, "You start tomorrow."

1

Monday

JACKIE HAVILLAND slipped off the headphones, swiped her hair back into place, and rose in stages. Nine hours in the stenographer's chair had left her kinked as a puppet with its joints glued together. She was one of nine women working at the long table, split into cramped myths of privacy by waist-high partitions. The woman to her right looked up and said, "Got us a bridal shower today. Can't get better than the fables of fresh starts, if you're looking for an excuse to party."

"Can't." Jackie's brain felt mushed by another day of listening to court-sanctioned surveillance tapes. "Busy."

"Yeah, right." Neva had a way of huffing a laugh with every part of her body except her face. "I'll give you busy. Give you so much busy you won't know which way is up. Not for days."

Jackie recognized the tone from Neva's phone-scolding of her children. There were three under the age of ten. No daddy. The man had been a Triple-A mechanic until the year before last, when he had walked around a broken-down car on I-95 and a rain-blinded trucker had carried him a hundred and twenty feet. One moment a family, the next just another blues riff. Jackie slung her bag and started down the aisle separating their table from the next. "See you tomorrow."

"Take it from me, girl. You got yourself a bad case of the lonelies. Ain't but one cure for that, and you won't find it sitting in front of your TV." Neva leaned a heavy arm on the partition and pointed at Jackie's desk. "Look there. Got just the one picture, and the boy's been gone over a year now."

"I'm fine."

Jackie took the stairs to the ground floor, chased by their chatter and all the dirty little secrets she had overheard and transcribed. The agency put on a good front downstairs. The name was etched into a crystal tower splashed by an encircling fountain. Big lobby, lovely receptionist, guards, rotating cameras, oil paintings, and recessed lighting in the chambers used for meeting clients. The company specialized in high-tech surveillance, industrial espionage, deep background checks. There was a world of difference between the downstairs chambers and Jackie's arena. Even the music was different—classical below, lite rock where fifty hourly workers sat crammed into a windowless cubicle ninety feet to a side. Jackie had taken the job when her brother became ill the last time. Its only asset was flexible hours—so long as she clocked a fifty-hour week, nobody cared when she came or went. Preston had died fourteen months ago this weekend, another victim of living with his afterburners constantly lit. Since then, Jackie had basically been marking time. Holding on to the here and now meant at least pretending to some final tie with the only man she had ever really loved.

The company's parking lot baked and blistered beneath an April sun. The Orlando afternoon stank of diesel and asphalt and the sullen summer ahead. There was nothing on the horizon that hinted of wind and an excuse to chase the storms Jackie lusted after. She walked to her gas-guzzling Z-28 with its sailboard roof racks and the license plate that read WND-DANCR. A gift from her brother, a relic of the days when money had seemed endless. Back when paying for her graduate school had been a source of pride and joy to them both. Back before Preston had lost it all—job, future, money, health, life.

The car's interior was an oven set on high roast. Jackie cranked the motor, hit the AC, turned up the radio to blot out the voices in her head. Everyone who worked in the agency's boiler room listened to Orlando's time warp to the seventies. Not that looking backward was any brighter than the way ahead. It just held fewer surprises.

An arm in a pinstriped shirt and gold Rolex reached down and tapped on her passenger window. Jackie assumed it was a boss and began forming a generic excuse for whatever she'd done wrong, the man leaned over and showed her shades and a nervous smile. When she opened his door, Jeff slid inside and asked, "Hot enough for you?"

"What are you doing here?"

"More like early August than the week before Easter. Hear it's hitting a hundred tomorrow." Jeff wore the narrow, insect-eye shades popular with the high-income tribes. "How've you been, Jackie?"

"Okay." Jeff was an associate with Orlando's biggest law firm, a dedicated work-hard, play-loose survivor. They had dated occasionally, back in easier times. Before she had hooked up with her ex-fiancé and had her desire for male companionship surgically removed. Jeff's firm was a big user of her company's services, and she still saw him now and then, slipping in and out of the downstairs chambers. Reminding her with his little smiles and quick patter of just how far she had fallen. "Do you have a client out here?"

"Sort of. Look, my Beamer's a lot cooler than this tank. Why don't we emigrate?"

"I'm fine where I am."

"Sure. Great." A flickering glance behind them, then, "Actually, I'm here because a client wants to hire you."

"Tell him to come in through the agency's front door."

"Not the agency. You. And it's a her."

"Who?"

"The client. She asked for you specifically." More than the heat beaded sweat on his forehead and upper lip. "This has to be on the sly. No paper trail, no notifying your bosses."

"Then it can't happen. I never sat for my license." She'd been studying for her private investigator's licence since Preston's demise but had never taken the exam, mainly because she had gradually come to accept just how much she loathed the work. Talking about it now only revealed how little progress she'd made on any front.

"It doesn't matter. My guess is, she already knows."

"I'm not interested in taking on outside work. Sorry."

"Just go see her, okay?" He pulled an envelope from his pocket. "A thousand dollars if you'll drive to Boca Raton and talk with her."

"Get out of here."

"Straight up. A thousand bucks. Just drive to the Boca Beach Club and hear what she has to say. Will you do it?"

The money was already spent before she reached for it. Forget the overdue bills. A thousand bucks was a third of the way to a next-generation wave jumper. "So who's the client?"

"You'll find out when you get there. Just give your name to the Boca gateman and go inside. She'll find you."

Jackie resisted the urge to tear open the envelope. She still had a shred of class left. "This is beyond weird."

"Tell me." The rapid swipe of his face almost masked his scouting to either side. "I'm pulled off a major case, given the most bizarre instructions of my life, sent out here to camp at your office and wait. No phone, no paper trail, and don't be followed."

"What can you tell me about—"

"Nothing. I don't know a thing more." Jeff pushed open his door, scanned for watchers, said, "See you around."

THE BOCA BEACH CLUB was one of those Fantasy Island–type places, something everybody heard of but few ever saw. Certainly nobody in Jackie's present circle. The club was a beachside palace of sandstone, mock coral, and six-hundred-dollar rooms. The three restaurants were off limits to all but club members and hotel guests. Jackie pulled up to the stone gatehouse and gave her name to the sharp-eyed guard. The inner drive was lined with frangipani and hibiscus. Beyond the emerald lawn, yachts rose higher than the emperor palms. The Z's powerful rumble sounded blatantly rude as she halted by the colonnaded portico. The valet approached hesitantly, probably wondering why the guard had let a job applicant use the front entrance.

Jackie checked her reflection in the car window. She had stopped by home just long enough to don an outfit from happier times—gray silk slacks, Magli pumps, sleeveless cotton blouse one shade darker than the slacks, black linen jacket with the sleeves hiked to her elbows. Jackie handed the valet her keys and the requisite buck, and headed inside.

"Ms. Havilland?" An older woman in tennis whites and a cashmere cardigan rose from the settee by the entrance. "I'm Esther Hutchings. Thank you so much for coming."

"You have a persuasive way of asking."

"I've reserved us a table on the veranda."

Jackie followed her across the reception hall, a vaulted chamber with fifty-foot domed ceilings interspersed by Gothic arches and chandeliers. "Some place."

"Mizner designed it." When Jackie did not respond as expected, she added, "He is the architect responsible for the Florida Spanish style. You find a lot of it here in Boca and in the older communities around Miami."

Pearls. The woman should be wearing pearls, plus one of those frilly outfits made for tea and doilies and servants in dark suits. Esther Hutchings carried herself impossibly erect and spoke as though each vowel were individually polished. "My only regret is that our family didn't hold on to its old Boca estate. Mizner's heir designed it. My father sold it to a developer for a perfectly ridiculous sum. To his dying day he claimed he didn't know the man intended to tear it down and build one of those atrocious beachside hotels."

Jackie blinked as they entered the rear atrium, both from the sudden light and from the view beyond the floor-to-ceiling windows. The bay sparkled a million-dollar blue, the oleander blossoms offset a manicured lawn, and every moored yacht dwarfed her garage apartment. The veranda was enormous and empty, their table made intimate by mirrored pillars and man-size Oriental vases.

"I've ordered us tea, I hope that's all right." Esther Hutchings halted by a pair of chairs pointed dockside and a low table buried under linen and silver. "I believe that chair has the nicer view."

The nearest vase held orchids in purple cascades. Through the royal growth Jackie caught sight of her reflection. Her hair, a rich blond streaked lighter by salt and sun, showed the three months and counting since her last cut. Hastily applied makeup did not mask the burn to her nose and forehead. Her eyes, always her best feature, held wide-open confusion.

"Shall I pour?"

Jackie slipped off her jacket and draped it over the chair back. "It's your show, Mrs. Hutchings."

"Yes. Very well. To the business at hand." Esther Hutchings leaned back in her chair, the tea untouched. "My husband is a United States congressman. Or rather, he was. Recently he suffered a second stroke. A debilitating one. I've traveled down for a much needed rest. At least, that's the reason I'm telling the rest of the world."

Esther Hutchings paused as another couple entered the atrium. The woman was a pastel silk mirage, the man a product of surgical design. A waiter appeared as if by magic, informed the couple that the entire veranda had been reserved for a private party, then just as silently disappeared.

When they were alone once more, Esther Hutchings continued, "Before his stroke, my husband led a battle to set restraints upon Wall Street and the international banks. Now there is a smear campaign to destroy his name and all he stood for. I want you to track down whoever is behind this."

"This is a joke, right?"

"Do I appear comical to you, Ms. Havilland? Last week, my husband's replacement won a special election. Wynn Bryant is his name. A truly despicable man. I wouldn't be the least surprised if he was behind this smear campaign."

"Mrs. Hutchings, I'm sorry about your husband." Jackie chose her words carefully. "But all this belongs to a totally different world from the one where I operate."

Esther Hutchings revealed an ability to sneer with polite loftiness. "Perhaps there is something about your present employment that you find utterly captivating?"

"At least it's real."

"So is this." Esther Hutchings belonged to a bygone era of grand dames and rigid authority and people who jumped at her behest. Jackie's disregard for how things should be left her flashing fire. "I insisted on our meeting here because this club is *private*. There are few places where a public person can be both open to visitors and closed to prying eyes. I am being closely watched, Ms. Havilland. My husband's foes are determined to ensure that every shred of his life's work be turned to ashes."

A thousand bucks, Jackie reminded herself. She reached for her cup, took a tepid sip. At least the view was nice.

"I have made very careful inquiries and am convinced you are ideal for this job. At age twenty-seven, when your brother could afford to support you both, you began graduate studies in international finance at the University of Florida. Then your brother, a hedge fund trader and high flier in the currency markets, became seriously ill. You dropped your studies, returned home, and nursed him through a year-long illness that stripped away all your combined savings before finally—"

"That's enough." Having this stranger spout her secrets in these absurd surroundings seriously rattled Jackie's cage. "I'm out of here."

Esther Hutchings restrained her with one tense hand. "No one would ever suspect us of having any connection. Which is vital if we are to succeed."

"Let go of my arm."

"One thing more. My husband was convinced that Pavel Hayek and his group are the driving force behind the opposition to financial reform."

She froze in midflight. "What?"

Esther Hutchings pulled a manila envelope from her tennis bag. "Just do me the kindness of looking over these documents. I've enclosed a contract as well. If you agree to help me, sign one copy and forward it to my lawyers. The first payment will be sent to you immediately." When Jackie made no move to take the package, Esther slipped it into her hand. "I urge you to view this as a matter of vital importance."

"This meeting is over." Jackie left the veranda, crossed the lobby, and reentered the reality of a tropical afternoon.

She handed the claim check to the valet, took a couple of hard breaths, and stared out over the palms at a torrid sky. Unlike this fairy-tale castle with its emerald lawns and mountains of fragrant blossoms, the real world held broken dreams, men who lied, and families that fractured and never healed. What right did Esther Hutchings have to taunt her with such a bruising reminder of everything that was not hers?

Jackie paced to the shaded line where the portico's shadow was sliced by the sun. Her idle hands opened the packet and pulled out a series of documents fronted by the contract.

"Ma'am? Excuse me, is this your car?"

She blinked in confusion at the valet standing by the Camaro's open door. Jackie handed him a bill without even checking the denomination and slipped behind the wheel. Then she read the figure typed onto the contract's payment line a second time. She looked up at the valet who was waiting to shut her door, and declared, "This can't be right."

2

Wednesday

NEWLY ELECTED United States Congressman Wynn Bryant checked his watch. In precisely nine minutes he would be back inside the longest day of his entire life. And it was scarcely one in the afternoon.

Scattered across his desk were the remnants of a sandwich his secretary had brought up, and position papers on fourteen urgent matters that yesterday he had not even known existed. He licked the mayonnaise from his fingers and sifted through the seven he had not yet read. The previous weeks had been a whirlwind of cameras and meetings and people and chatter. Wynn had clocked over three thousand miles and never left the district, always accompanied by a party staffer. Election day had found him too numb to care, even when the local press had declared him just another of the governor's lackeys with their interchangeable names.

After meeting yesterday with his regional office staff back in Melbourne, Wynn had caught the last flight to National and gone straight to the Willard—according to his travel agent, the best hotel within walking distance of Capitol Hill. It was a grand old place, full of Federalist grace and lofty heights and gilt. As good a place as any to call home for a while.

This morning, his entire Washington staff had been present to greet him. Everyone seemed highly intelligent, motivated, sharp, and far more aware of the business of politics than he would ever be. Even his secretary had a degree from Princeton. After a brief run-through of pending business, much of which Wynn had not understood, a staffer had walked him to the Capitol via the underground tunnel system. While inside the concrete maze, Wynn noted dozens of faces that had the vague familiarity of news flashes. All he could think was, sooner or later he was going to have to ask all nine staffers their names again. The aide had guided him into the House chamber, pointed him to Hutchings' desk, wished him luck, and departed.

The swearing-in had proceeded swiftly. A few other members had stopped by his desk, shaken his hand, welcomed him to the club. That's what they called it, or some did. The club. They had all seemed impossibly at home with the place and the proceedings. One had even mentioned how his own desk had once belonged to Samuel Adams. Wynn had seen little beyond the pomp and circumstance and the sea of faces in the visitors' galleries. He sat and let the process wash over him for an hour or so, then rose to his feet, exchanged nods with the Speaker, and returned to his office overland. He doubted he could even find the tunnels, much less navigate them. Springtime in Washington meant tulips and cherry blossoms, mint-green trees and wind too cold for a supposedly southern city. The flowers were obviously for the tourists. No one else paid them any attention.

He had arrived in his third-floor office to the sound of ringing phones. They never seemed to stop. He had taken nine calls back to back, the last from the state secretary of commerce with regard to an upcoming bill. Wynn had duly taken notes and then lost the page. These had been followed by two subcommittee meetings. Thankfully, nobody seemed to expect him to do more than show up, look through his papers, and shake a few hands. He had returned to his office and demanded time for a solitary lunch. His chief of staff had immediately brought in the stack of position papers for him to peruse. A little light reading to go with his chicken Caesar roll.

Two minutes.

His suite of offices were quietly efficient and never silent. C-Span crooned the political equivalent of Muzak, a constant background drone. The outer office was tightly involved in work he did not know enough to question. Perhaps it was just their way of welcoming him, everyone occupied with something critically important. But Wynn didn't think so. Their message seemed clear enough; he was an interchangeable cog. No matter who sat in his high-backed leather seat, the business of power would keep rolling along.

Tension hummed in time to the overhead fluorescents. The office furniture was a hodgepodge of styles and decades. His secretary possessed a tiny alcove behind the reception counter. His chief of staff, a singularly unattractive man with the Florida cracker name of Carter Styles, had the only other private office, attached to the back of the reception area and possessing a much-envied dirty window. The suite's other room contained five cramped staffers.

Wynn's own office was comparatively luxurious. It boasted a rich blue carpet, two paneled walls, built-in glass-fronted display cases, and a less shopworn desk. A burnished state seal hung over the doorway. State and national flags stood to either side of the big windows behind him. From a collection of photographs on the trophy wall, Hutchings brooded worriedly over the governor's choice of replacement.

Wynn was examining Hutchings' expression when the phone rang. He glanced at his watch. Right on time. He saluted the former congressman with the receiver and announced for himself alone, Guilty as charged. "Yes?"

"Jackson Taylor is on line three."

"Who?"

An incredulous pause. "Mr. Taylor, Congressman. Chairman of the party."

"Oh. Right." No doubt this would become another tidbit to pass around the office. Further evidence of his utter ignorance. "Fine."

"And Senator Trilling's office called again. The third time today. They say it is imperative that you spare the senator fifteen minutes."

"Can I fit it in?"

This was clearly a more appropriate question. "There are no votes scheduled for this afternoon's session, Congressman."

"Book it." He glanced at the pile of embossed cards by his phone. "Are all these invitations for me?"

"Yes sir." A slight lilt came to her voice. "Apparently word is out about your arrival."

The pile was a half-inch thick, the engraving expensive, the titles and the places awesome. "Anything I should pay particular attention to here?"

"The one on top is a reception tonight. To greet the new British ambassador."

Certainly better than returning to his empty hotel rooms. "Would you call and say I'll be there?"

"Yes sir. And the White House just called. They ask if you could please stop by today at four."

"Does this happen every day?"

"Sir?"

"Never mind. Line three, did you say?" He punched the button before she could respond. "Bryant."

"Wynn Bryant, as I live and breathe. You probably don't remember me. I'll bet a boatload of tarpon you don't have the first tiny idea who you're talking to."

"The only Jackson Taylor I know couldn't have caught a tarpon with a stick of dynamite and radar. If that Jackson Taylor has landed this job, then it's time I packed up and went home."

"No you don't, son. No you don't. We need you too much up here." A professional's voice, polished as a putting green. "Can you spare me ten minutes?"

"You got it."

"Have your people point you down here, but leave the dogs at home. Time for a little one-on-one."

PARTY HEADQUARTERS held an intensity similar to his own office, the staffers hustling about putting out their own five-alarm fires. Wynn gave his name and was ushered into the chairman's outer office. He'd scarcely had time to seat himself before a familiar voice said, "Wynn Bryant. I swear, politics makes for some strange bedfellows, don't she?"

Jackson Taylor approached with hand so outstretched the fingers looked splayed backward. "When I heard Grant was putting you up for the job, my first thought was, whoa, don't know if I've got it in me to go another fifteen rounds against this man." He swallowed Wynn's hand in a beefy grip. Up close Taylor smelled of some expensive fragrance and shone with a dedicated golfer's tan. "Then I recollected the face and the stories and I thought, shoot, Grant's done caught himself a winner here."

Taylor turned to include the pair of people emerging from his office, an elegant older gentleman and a young aide. "Last time I saw this man, he was walking off with fifty-eight and three-quarter million of my dollars."

"You got off light," Wynn said, unable to hide the remembered burn. "The judge was going to cook you."

To the elegant man in the doorway, Taylor went on, "Little bitsy company down Orlando way, first thing I ever heard of them was how they were busy suing us in federal court. Old Wynn here claimed we'd been engaging in unfair competition."

"Which you had." Bribery and commercial extortion to prevent their clients from using Wynn's newer products, not to mention encroaching on Wynn's patents. Wynn's company had been bought out as part of the settlement.

"Water under the dam, old son." Jackson Taylor gripped Wynn's arm, giving him a power massage. "You got rich in the process, am I right or am I right."

"Didn't get a nickel that wasn't ours."

The older gentleman spoke with the bored nasal twang of old New England money. "Sounds like you two have a number of old battles to discuss, Jackson."

"No time for that. We got too many wars in the right here and right now. Don't we, Wynn."

"We'll leave you to it, then." The gentleman started forward, trailed by his aide. "Good to see you again, Jackson. Congressman."

"Appreciate the check, John. You don't know how much it means, counting on people like you in our hour of dire need."

Wynn watched Taylor give the gentleman a two-handed farewell, then allowed himself to be ushered inside. To his left was the most amazing power wall Wynn had ever seen. There must have been a hundred photographs, including five different presidents. "I think some of those people are dead."

"Don't let on." Taylor motioned him into a chair. "You take coffee?"

"I'm fine, thanks." To his right, a trophy case held every party memorabilia known to man, most of it gilded. On its top, a full-winged eagle came in for a sterling silver landing. "This is some place you've got here."

"Yeah, it's all Washington." Jackson Taylor had formerly been CEO of a Fortune Twenty company, one division of which had been the largest competitor of Wynn's own firm. "How about this now. The two of us sitting here, talking like two old buddies ready to take on the world."

"Never thought it would happen," Wynn agreed. "None of it."

Taylor leaned forward. "We are allies, aren't we, old son?"

Wynn found more warmth in the gaze of the deer mounted on Jackson's wall. "Like you said, Jackson, I got rich off the battle."

"There you go then." He leaned back, satisfied. "My secretary's made you a list of critical issues coming up. And some related files. You want me to messenger them over?"

"Sure. Don't know when I'm going to read them, though."

"Yeah, this place will bury you in paper if you let it. Have your staffers give them a look-see, hit the high spots for you." The smile resurfaced. "Talked with the boys. Wanted you to know we're ready to bankroll your next election."

"I'm just a caretaker, Jackson. In and out in eighteen months."

The grin broadened, creasing the tanned skin around his dead eyes. "Give the town a few weeks. This kind of power has an infectious quality. Besides, you're our kind of man."

"What kind is that?"

"A fighter and a winner. I've heard how you handled yourself through the election, tossed in the deep end and swimming hard. I've seen enough to know you're a natural for politics."

"Is that what you wanted to meet with me about?"

"Partly. Mostly I wanted a little face-time, find out how we're going to get on." The eyes tried for warmth. "I think we're gonna do just fine, don't you?"

"Swell." Wynn started to rise. "Thanks for having me over, Jackson."

"Don't mention it." The chairman rose with him. "Tell me something, Wynn. You got any plans for the Jubilee Amendment?"

"All I know is, Grant wants to see it killed."

"Not just Grant, old son. Not by a long shot." He offered his hand. "That mean you're going to vote it down?"

Wynn accepted the meaty handshake, spoke carefully. "The governor stressed to me how important it was to have this item killed."

"Stomp down with both feet, bury this snake in the dust." He guided Wynn toward the door, massaging his hand so hard the bones ground together. "Any plans for housecleaning in your office?"

Wynn broke the grip with a downward shove. "I just got here, Jackson. Give me a break."

"A word to the wise. Nobody around here'd be sorry to see Carter Styles sent packing. The guy was a buddy of Hutchings from back home, and he's been a mistake from the start. One businessman to another, Carter is a liability you don't need. He's offended too many people, and for no good reason."

3

Wednesday

WEDNESDAY MORNING Jackie sipped tea from a mock Ball jar, the kind with a handle. The clear glass revealed a wildflower yellow too beautiful to hide inside a mug. She had been up long enough for any more coffee to be offensive, but she was no closer to answers. She stepped out her front door and reveled in a wind strong enough to shove her around. Her garage apartment was surrounded by Florida oaks now turned cross and agitated. She took a deep breath and tasted a faint trace of something found only within sea-laden storms. Jackie liked to think it was a remembrance of liberation and times that still lay easy on her soul.

She was drawn back inside by a ringing phone. It was Neva, the closest thing she had to a friend at work. "I must have tried to reach you a dozen times yesterday. Me and the boss both. Your phone stayed busy the whole time."

"Sorry, I was on the internet." Hooked into the web, searching for clues. This after spending most of the previous night going through the information Esther Hutchings had given her. The preliminary review had been sketchy but compelling. As a member of Congress, Graham Hutchings had made numerous inquiries into the uncontrolled and increasingly rampant activities of the international currency traders and hedge funds—the subject of Jackie's unfinished thesis. Hutchings had documented occasions when the funds had wreaked havoc with national economies. He specifically named several huge funds that had played these currencies like chips on a roulette table. The list of investment banks and hedge funds was almost smothered in hand-written notes, but the top name made Jackie's blood run cold. Hayek.

She had then gone on-line and searched out data on specific activities. She had not been looking for answers so much as keeping her hands busy while her mind tried to fit itself around this new juncture in her life. She used several search engines, their names springing up from the past, painful as splinters to her heart. All the work she had put into her own research, all the hopes, all the despair at having to push it aside when Preston became ill and the money ran out.

The final site she stumbled upon had been locked behind e-barriers, requiring her first to request entry and then download a questionnaire. The queries had reflected a group who were either very serious or seriously frightened. Her last act before logging off at one o'clock in the morning had been to send a preliminary response, introducing herself.

"I should have called in," Jackie told Neva. "But to be honest, I didn't know what to tell you."

This was not Neva's problem. "You better have a serious case of the never-get-overs, girl. Else I'm supposed to ask where you want us to mail your final check."

"I've been offered another job."

Neva brightened. "Always said you were too good for this grind. Doing what?"

"Investigation."

"You got your license and you didn't tell me?"

"I don't need it for this."

"So tell."

"I'm being offered a ton of money by some rich old lady. She's given me this fancy contract, calls me an independent consultant. Wants me to check out something related to my studies." Neva was the only person at work who knew the whole tale of Jackie's former life, and about her brother. Not to mention about her ex-fiancé, Shane, the ultimate destroyer of dreams. "I wish I knew what to do."

"Wait, let me work on this a minute. Somebody's come by, offered you a job that'll get you out of this hole, and says they'll pay you a heap of cash. And you've spent all day hanging in between?" She gave Jackie a chance to come back, then said, "What am I missing from this picture?"

"Come on, Neva. How often do things like this happen without a serious catch?"

"All the time, girl."

"Not to me. This looks like just another chance for life to stab me with what I see but can't ever have."

"So you're turning it down?"

Jackie wanted desperately to return to the safety of aiming low. But she was bored to tears with life and aching for change. She had not realized how much until the sleepless hours before dawn, lying there with the darkness illuminated by her fears. "You know what my problem is? I want things too much. All it takes is a tiny glimpse of everything I've never had, and I go up in flames."

"What kind of answer is that?"

She was saved from further confessions by a knock on her door. "Hang on a second." She set down her phone and walked over to where a UPS delivery man stood outside her screen door. "Can I help you?"

"You can if you're Ms. Havilland." When he held up his packet she realized it was ringing. "It's been doing this for the past thirty minutes. Maybe it's a bomb."

"Right." She unlatched the door, signed his electronic clipboard, and accepted the package. "Rid the world of a pair who really matter."

She ripped the pull-tag, reached inside, came up with an ultraslim cellphone. She pushed the button and raised it to her ear. "Hello?"

It was the frosty matriarch from Boca Raton. "Where are you?"

"Standing in my doorway, staring at a delivery man's dental work."

"They promised delivery at nine. It's almost half past. If I pay for a service I expect precision."

"We run on Florida time down here. That's something all the money in the world can't change. Hold on just a moment." She walked back over to her other phone and told Neva, "I have to go."

"Tell you what. I'll speak with the man, remind him of how you walk on water round here. See if maybe he'll give you enough time to check this thing out."

"I don't know what to say."

"Just go find some good luck for both of us. And keep in touch, you hear?"

She set down one phone, picked up the other. Cradled it a moment. Wishing for more clarity than the day offered. Beyond her front window the trees rocked and shuddered beneath a steadily growing wind. "All right."

"I tried all yesterday to reach you."

"My place only has one line. I've been on it trying to research your problem."

"There's a sealed envelope in this packet. Open it, please." As

Jackie tore open the envelope, Esther went on, "Your first payment, as promised."

So much money. The slip of paper should have weighed a ton, pulled earthward by the ballast of temptation. "Why pluck me out of the unknown?"

"Your questions are becoming repetitive, Ms. Havilland. I wish to hire someone who will remain utterly bought and utterly secret. Have you signed the contract?"

"Not yet."

"Time is of critical importance here."

"I'll decide today."

"Very well. There is a handwritten slip in the envelope."

"I have it." A foreign sounding name and a number. Washington area code.

"A second contact, in case I can't be found. To be used only for matters of critical urgency." A pause, then, "I suggest you move on this while you still can."

Jackie dithered for a time, cleaning her cramped three rooms while struggling with an already tumultuous day. Her garage apartment was carpeted in a ferocious orange shag. The wall air-conditioning units banged and wheezed, the plumbing clattered, and her refrigerator belonged in a museum. But her tiny back porch was a roofline haven, as far from her dead-end world as she nowadays expected to travel. She moved back to her dinette table, its scarred surface lost beneath the Hutchings papers. But she had no stomach for further work, not with the go/no-go decision swinging like a pendulum blade. Her eye was caught by a printout she had made the previous evening. The region's loose-knit clan of wind surfers had circulated a map of the present storm with a time and place to meet. Jackie rose from the table and dressed for a day that might have some meaning after all.

TAKING THE BEELINE EXPRESSWAY from Orlando to the coast, Jackie crossed I-95 and the bridges splitting the Florida mainland from Merritt Island, then pulled onto a tiny spit of sand and saw grass. A half-mile across the northern waters, cruise liners rose from Port Canaveral like clownish mountains. Beyond them, a shuttle had been pulled from Kennedy's Vehicular Assembly Building and was settled onto the launch gantry nearest the Intracoastal Waterway. The shuttle's stubby wings stood in resolute serenity, ready to defy all the elements and arguments as to why it could never fly.

As she unloaded her gear, a cluster of storm jumpers pushed shouts and invitations her way. Jackie knew all their first names, but few details more beyond cars and boards. The pirates among them had hit on her once or twice, then accepted her turndowns with buccaneer grins and the shrugs of those with more chances than time. She was respected because she came for most of the heavy blows and handled herself with the fanaticism of one who lived for such events. Jackie waved at the group but did not approach. Today was not one for their clubby atmosphere and single-minded tales of flight. She wanted nothing more than abandon.

She rigged her sail, tied the boom storm-taut, and stepped her mast. She went back to the car for the storm harness, which she slung about her shoulders and cinched between her legs so that the hook dangled just below her rib cage. She drew her hair tightly into a band, pulled the daggerboard from her trunk, locked the car, and dragged the board across the shore.

Jackie smiled at the hoots from those already back and standing weary along the roadside, and pulled her board into the kicked-up bay. The water was warm as a brackish bath. Even at knee depth the wind pushed up sparkling froths, which her blood answered with an adrenaline champagne all its own. She slid the daggerboard home, hefted the boom, tested the fore foot strap. She took a couple of little ready-jumps, feeling the wind impatient to pluck her away. She gave all her weight to the boom and the board, then rose up so swiftly she had to shout, knowing it was a day of promise and speed. She slipped her back foot into place, felt the swooping rush, and gave into the only oblivion that had ever worked for her.

The board was no longer clunky and two generations out of date. It was a chariot pulled by spendrift stallions, and she a woman who knew no earthly bonds. She flew so fast the board scarcely touched the wave crests, her solitary wing searching for that last tiny thrust that would break her free entirely and send her shooting away from all the impossibles of a life she had been forced to call her own.

Mainland to her right and Merritt Island to her left, she accelerated until passing homes and stands of water-bound green all became shades of speed. She hooked the harness ring on to the boom and leaned farther back until her body was as billowed as the sail, two arcs joined by impossible balance. With each little wave jump she was drenched anew in water warmer than the wind. She felt her fingertips and the tip of her ponytail trace across the wave tops, and became more intimately connected still to her partner in this dance. From behind there came a hooted shout of approval. Glancing around, she saw an upside-down mate leaning upon his mast rope with one hand, trying to right himself from a spill, his other hand a fist over his head as he screamed to her an instant's fame.

Downwind where the island ended and the water broadened, the waves became frothy sloping catapults. Jackie raised herself back up, unleashed the harness hook, and began steering with body movements and fractional adjustments of the sail. Her clenched fists searched through the boom for the faint quiver of coming gusts. She took the measure of each blow, reaching for the invisible fist. Abruptly a new feather of strength pressed against her sail and her cheek. She angled slightly east, aimed for the highest of the waves ahead, crouched further, timed the approach, then jumped and shouted with the effort. The wind joined with her own cry, shrieking up almost a full octave, willing her into the wild gray sky.

She flew. Time halted then. Her cry became a silver thread reaching out with the raucous force of a gull, weaving its way into the heart of the storm, a call of hope and thrill and pain. She willed the moment to go on forever, never to return her to a waterborne world. She splashed down in a hard landing, the sail dipping and drenching, which meant she had to sail on long enough to lose the water-weight before searching again. Then she found another invisible fist and aimed for the clouds and the universe of eternal storm.

Jackie flew as far as the next causeway, which meant a two-hour push tacking back upwind. The water was largely empty, save for a few other lightning-fast storm jumpers, several sailboats throwing heavy wakes and rigged for blow, and one motorboat. She circled back behind one of the uninhabited marsh islands and took shelter in a cove overhung by palmettos and wild palms. A trio of stalking herons watched from the white-sand beach, gray heads turned so they could all give her a resentful one-eyed glare. She lowered the sail to the water, seating herself so she could watch the waves be trimmed and topped by the blow. She dropped her eyes to her board, inspecting the frayed seams along the daggerboard and the rusty repair screws she had put in herself to reinforce the foot straps. The check on her dinette table represented the first money since her brother's death not marked before it arrived for meeting the day-to-days. But in this haven of wind and light, she knew it was not the lack of answers that worried her. It was the fear of finding nothing more than another false freedom.

A pod of dolphins swam into the tiny cove. The surrounding green offered a sliver of calm water not more than fifteen feet wide. Breezes filtering through the mangrove and palmetto and silver palm sent tiny shivers across the sheltered waters, out to where the bay joined with a froth-covered sea. The dolphins lumped up and wheezed their gentle breaths, circling around two tiny fins that signaled the presence of babies. The bayside species was smaller than their ocean kin, and more comfortable with humankind. They nosed about, rubbing bellies upon the soft white bottom sand, whistling their shy chirrups, offering quick notes of water-borne inquiry. How was she? Confused, was the answer. Frightened by the prospect of waking up again. Awash in memories of former times.

There had indeed been other chances, given only to be stripped away. A father who let his wife drive him off, leaving little Jackie screaming for him to stay, or else take her with him. Those pleas had resulted in years of vicious torment from a hyperjealous mother who prized her wounds like medals. Jackie had survived by living to protect her little brother, a golden-haired seraph too sensitive for the best of this world, much less able to survive alone their mistake of a mom. Preston had prevailed because Jackie had sheltered and bolstered. He had never been one for people or words, but his mind had gobbled math the way another might devour mystery novels. In school he had thrived on calculus and uncertainty theory, subjects that left Jackie utterly cold.

When Preston accepted a job with the Hayek Group, she had worried without understanding why. When the money had started pouring in, she had grown truly frightened. But Preston had found a place that justified his talents, one so all-consuming he could ignore the past they both loathed. Preston had risen among the ranks of traders until she could no longer argue against his choice. She had finally given in to his enthusiasm, accepted his money, and revived her own dream of returning to graduate school. All the while, she remained troubled over the waters where Preston now swam. She studied international finance in hopes of delving the tides and the currents and identifying the sharks before they devoured him.

And then Preston had introduced her to Shane Turner.

Jackie was in the process of tossing that particular memory to the wind when she noticed the motorboat. It was the same one she had seen earlier, and now that she was focused upon it she had the impression this was not its first pass around her island. The man at the wheel fastened upon her with a pair of binoculars, a ludicrous act considering the turbulence. Jackie rewarded him with an appropriate gesture, then rose uncertainly to her feet as the boat veered and headed straight for her. The dolphins whistled a warning and disappeared.

Apprehensive and utterly isolated, she began pulling her mast from the water. Her position in the cove was suddenly very hazardous, out of other storm sailors' sight, in a wind strong enough to drown out her screams.

Jackie gripped the boom and swept the sail about, seeking a pocket of wind to cast her away. But the trees and untamed shrub were too effective a wind block. She was about to give up and fling herself into the water when the motor craft swung broadside and the man shouted across, "Are you JackieH at Juno.com?"

The query was so ludicrous she let the boom fall without thinking. "What?"

"JackieH at Juno.com!" He was young and his voice high-pitched. More than that she could not tell over the motor's idling roar. He was ridiculously muffled in a floppy fishing hat pulled low, sunglasses, and a windbreaker with the zipper pulled up to his chin. All she could see clearly were his pale nose and mouth. And bone-white hands that knew nothing about holding a boat steady. "Is that you?"

When she gaped and nodded in response, he cut the motor with the boat still broadside to the chop. It was an expensive rental, an overpowered OMC inboard-outboard. He was far enough beyond the cove's shelter for the next wave to almost pitch him headlong over the side. Jackie found herself relieved by his evident alarm. "Start your engine and put it one notch above idle, then steer directly into the wind."

As he fumbled and struggled to follow her instructions, she settled back onto her board. "Now back into the cove, no, don't turn the boat around, just put the boat into reverse."

But the young man showed no desire to approach any closer than where he was. Instead he left the motor running, oversteering and unsettled by the chop. Over the wind and the motor he called, "Why are you interested in certain people and companies?"

Again she had no choice but gape in reply. The young man expected nothing more. "You're already in danger! There's only one way to survive, are you hearing me, JackieH?"

"Yes."

"Keep searching under your current internet address and find nothing. Then take on a second name with a different server system and use another name as both ID and payee."

She thought she detected an accent but couldn't be certain. "Why?"

"Use a secure phone for your hookups. Your home line is either tapped or will be soon. When you're established, go to the website Trastevere." He spelled it out. "Can you remember that?"

"Who are you?"

"This is *vital!*" His shriek carried the strain of more than the present tempest. "Trastevere website. Leave me a message." He paused for a moment, pressed the sunglasses up tight to his nose, continued, "Address it to the Boatman."

"Wait. I need to know—"

But the young man revved the motor and blasted away, almost tumbling over the back of his seat in the takeoff. Jackie was left to the isolation of a confused and storm-tossed day.

4

Wednesday

WYNN ARRIVED at Senator Trilling's office still fuming over his meeting with Jackson Taylor. It did not help matters to find the ranking senator from California housed in chambers that were positively palatial compared to his own. "Congressman Bryant?"

"That's right."

"Kay Trilling. Are you alone?"

"Is there a problem with that?"

"As far as I'm concerned, no. But few people in elected office go anywhere around here by themselves." Her tone was so clipped the words sounded razored. "There's always the risk of being caught and compromised, or having the press claim you said something you can't deny."

"Which means I've just made another beginner's blunder." Not bothering to keep the bitterness from his voice.

She bobbed her head, perhaps to hide a smile. "This way, please."

Trilling was black, rail-thin, extremely well dressed, and tough. She led him into her private office, shut the door, and continued, "I miss Graham Hutchings terribly. Personally as well as politically. We were in a prayer group together. I don't suppose you'd be interested in joining us."

"Excuse me?"

"Never mind." She gestured to her associate, a handsome silent man with the aquiline features of an Arab or North African. "This is Nabil Saad, an intern seconded to my office by the World Bank."

Evidently the senator commanded a more senior staff than a mere congressman. "I had the impression you wanted to speak to me about something urgent."

"That is correct. Hutchings and I were to have worked together on a Conference Committee. I don't suppose you know anything about this."

"Not a thing."

Little worry lines invaded her polished image, creasing out from her mouth in rays of subsurface strain. "This is not good. The committee is a joint House-Senate group intended to reconcile two conflicting versions of the same legislation. There is a big appropriations bill coming up, very critical to both sides, over a thousand pages to cover."

Wynn sensed the room's tension converging about him. Two pairs of eyes, one feminine and Western, one dark and very Arab, carefully measured his reaction. Trilling went on, "One of the issues we intend to cover is known as the Jubilee Amendment."

"Right." So this was more of the same. Everybody probing, looking for the deal. Making sure he was bought and paid for. "Of course."

"You've heard of it, then."

"All I know is, a lot of people want to see this thing dead and gone." Wynn rose to his feet. "Whoever appears next on your list, tell them I've already gotten the message."

"I don't understand."

"Oh, I think you do. Now if you'll excuse me, I've got a lifetime of catch-up waiting back at the office."

Trilling did not rise so much as uncoil, her lips pursed so tightly now the creases ran up both sides of her nose. "Quite frankly, Congressman, I find your manner disappointing. This is a critical issue."

"Aren't they all."

"Don't you even want to know where we stand?"

"Couldn't care less."

She moved swiftly, blocked the door with her body, and hissed, "I don't know who you think you are, mister, but a warning to the wise. I've dined on upstart freshman from both chambers for years."

Wynn jerked on the doorknob, giving her a choice to move out of the way or be knocked flat. He said in parting, "I've always despised politicians who've grown slick as bazaar salesmen."

"I'll make sure you regret your attitude and your words both."

"Not near as much," Wynn replied, already crossing the outer office, "as I regret being here at all."

□ □ □ □

WYNN REENTERED THE SUNLIGHT, still smoldering. He searched his pockets and pulled out his cellphone, then grew angrier still at how natural the action was. He had not used one since his wife died, not since the sale of his company, not since his last day in court. All three soul-wrenching blows had come in the same month, and in that order.

He and Dianne had been filing the separation papers when she was taken ill. Wynn had returned home and played the dedicated husband for eleven grueling months. Esther Hutchings, Dianne's closest friend, had been one of the few who had not approved of his actions. Of course, nothing Wynn could do would ever have been proper in Esther's eyes. She had loathed him with undisguised bitterness, and at Dianne's funeral had publicly accused him of causing his wife's death. Two weeks after the funeral, Jackson Taylor had finally made a firm offer for Wynn's company. Wynn had never thought making money could be so hard, never understood all the warnings about the price of success. Not until the day he had signed the documents, then turned up in court to hear his attorneys announce they were dropping all charges. Wynn had found himself wishing there were some way to shout his denial. He had walked away from the courtroom a free and solitary man, with utterly nothing to fill his days or his soul's gaping wounds. Swearing then and there he would never care so much for anything ever again.

"Congressman Bryant's office."

"It's me. Wynn." He stepped back into the shadows of the Senate office building. "Who in our office is handling this Jubilee Amendment?"

"I believe Carter is holding those files."

"Perfect." He glanced at his watch. "I'm headed over to the White House now."

"Your meeting's been changed to the OEOB."

Wynn started to ask what that was, then decided he'd rather reveal his ignorance to a taxi driver. "Have Carter meet me in the lobby."

He clicked off, then dialed another number from memory. He still had some fury to vent, and his sister was scheduled to have arrived back from Ecuador that morning. Her convenient absence throughout the campaign had rankled deeply.

"The governor's mansion."

"Is Sybel Wells back yet?"

"Who is calling?"

"This is her brother, Wynn."

"Of course, Congressman. She arrived about three hours ago. I believe she's in her office. One moment, please."

A pair of clicks, then, "Wynn? I was going to call you tonight—"

"What have you gotten me into here, Sybel?"

"Just a moment." She spoke in low tones to someone else, then, "All right. What's the matter?"

"I'm trapped up here in Washington. I'm drowning in bureaucratic garbage. Everybody is an enemy with an agenda I don't understand."

"Not everybody."

He hated her calm, tight control. "Jackson Taylor is here, Sybel."

"Of course he is. He's the chairman of your party."

"He asked to see me. Just to make sure I'd drop the Jubilee Amendment. You know what that is?"

"Certainly."

"Did you also know Grant ordered me to kill it?"

"Grant told you that?" A pause, then, "So that's why he didn't fight my idea any more than he did."

"Wait, it gets better. Grant threatened me, Sybel. He said he'd go public with our funds transfer—"

"Stop right there." It was her turn for panic. "You're a congressman now, do you understand me? You're calling the *governor's mansion.*"

"All right. Fine."

"I'll deal with Grant. You deal with Washington."

"I don't think I can." A wrenching confession.

"Deal with it, Wynn." Revealing her core of stainless Sybel steel. "I've got to go."

THE DRIVER was from Outer Slombonia and drove a taxi that smelled like an imported camel. But even he knew what OEOB stood for, or at least he took off as soon as Wynn repeated the letters. Only they soon became caught in a long, simmering Pennsylvania Avenue traffic jam. Wynn glanced at his watch and saw he was soon to be late for his first appointment with White House personnel. He leaned forward to repeat, "OEOB?"

"Is Old Executive Office Building just there." A swarthy finger pointed at the appendage attached to the White House's right side. "You are walking maybe, yes?"

"Absolutely." He paid and started hoofing it down the sidewalk. Someone should hand out a booklet to all incoming politicians, he mused, something entitled Welcome To The City That Will Eat You Whole. He glanced at his watch, started sprinting.

The OEOB was the kind of building Wynn might have enjoyed researching for a couple of days, entering only when he could greet it properly. This had become a habit of his in the first empty days, studying up thoroughly before diving into any new experience. The OEOB's exterior invited that kind of study, a palace of age and dignity, an appropriate home to federal power. But Wynn was running to somebody else's schedule now. He took only a moment to stand with a group of tourists, gasping for breath and combing his hair with his fingers while they flashed their video cameras. When they moved on, so did he.

Carter Styles was in the lobby waiting for him, and for once the man looked right at home. The lobby was utterly without charm, a monument to just how awful a job bureaucrats could do. Take one incredibly beautiful building and remodel the entry with a plywood security desk, steel-reinforced doors, and institutional gray-green paint. Fill the stone-walled chamber with echoes of self-important people, clanging metal detectors, ringing phones, and crashing security locks. Light it poorly with asylum-style hanging fluorescents. Welcome to the machine.

Carter Styles displayed a charm as paltry as the lobby's. He showed his driver's license to the guard, gave the name of their host, passed his briefcase through security, and marched Wynn down a high-ceilinged hall. All without speaking a word to his new boss.

The President's gophers were a pair of quietly intense midlevels. A young man in an ill-fitting suit and checked wool tie met them in an outer office as cramped as Wynn's, and led them into another tight cubicle. Only this one had an utterly awesome view of the White House, seen through the brushwork of new leaves. As Wynn gaped, the trio exchanged tight little smirks.

"We're so grateful you could grant us a few moments of your time, Congressman. Why don't you have a seat over here." The spokesperson, Harriet something, was a tightly unattractive package with burning hazel eyes and a bulky knit suit. "Could we ask you what you have planned for this weekend and the Easter recess that follows?"

"I've got a little catching up to do."

"We were wondering if we could ask you to represent the administration at a pair of international finance conferences." The woman's preppy tone managed to turn the request into a slur. "Apparently Congressman Hutchings was an official sponsor of both events. The first one takes place this Saturday in College Park, that's about an hour's drive from here. Congressman Hutchings was pressuring the President to attend. But you must already be aware of this."

Wynn resisted the urge to turn and glare at Carter. "Is the President going?"

"Unfortunately he has meetings scheduled at Camp David. The Treasury secretary is also involved. The President thought you might make a natural replacement."

The young man spoke up. "You're no doubt aware of the Easter Conference. The Jubilee 2000 assembly in Cairo has been one of Hutchings' pet projects for over a year."

"He's deluged the entire city with papers on this subject," the woman agreed.

Wynn said slowly, "Cairo."

The woman registered surprise. "You weren't aware of this?"

Carter pointed out, "This is the congressman's first day on the job."

"It's no big deal, Congressman," the young man said. "If you refuse, it won't cause an international crisis."

"As far as this administration is concerned, the debt-relief issue is dead in the water," the woman agreed. "Something we never could get Hutchings to understand."

"Obviously the President wouldn't expect someone fresh on the Washington scene to drop everything and fly off to the ends of the world," the young man added. "Especially for a non-starter like debt relief. We were told to sound you out. Nothing more."

"The College Park Conference is equally back burner," the woman agreed. "According to our read on the situation, attendance will be limited to the sort who don't matter."

"We're doubtful it will even get a mention in the national papers."

"Anything the press considers below the event horizon definitely is not going to raise this administration's flags."

Wynn rose to his feet. "This has been most enlightening."

The young man said, "So we can tell the President you won't be attending?"

"College Park sounds fine." If for no other reason than to do the opposite of what this snide pair expected. He headed for the door, not caring whether Carter was with him or not. "Cairo is definitely out."

Wynn passed through the dismal lobby and rejoined the tourist hordes, just another Washington suit. When Carter caught up Wynn demanded, "Exactly when were you planning on telling me about all this?"

His chief aide shot back, "You made a big mistake back there. And it cost us."

"Would it be too much trouble to put me in the loop here?"

"Big mistake." Carter stopped on a relatively quiet stretch of sidewalk and glared at his new boss. He was unattractive in a distinctly Florida cracker manner—piggy eyes, curly reddish hair going patchily bald, sizable gut. Utterly un-Washington in appearance, wearing a rumpled blue blazer, button-down Oxford shirt, stained tie, pressed chinos. "You missed out on a chance to score by asking for something in return."

"That's what was behind this, they wanted to size me up?" The slow burn intensified. "I'll do better next time."

Carter snorted and turned away. "That was your one and only. You've now been dismissed as somebody who'll be gone before you matter."

"I'm not through here," Wynn said, his voice sharp enough to command Carter's full attention. "What's going on with this Jubilee Amendment?"

"What difference does it make? You're just a caretaker, right?"

"I want to know."

"Don't bother. It's totally over your head." Carter's sneer finally surfaced. "Eighteen months of embassy parties and scoring with the power groupies, and you're extinct."

Wynn watched in amazement as the man walked away, dismissing his own boss as he would a bad smell. Unbelievable. Wynn no longer cared whether the party chairman had an ulterior motive for wanting Carter Styles gone. The man was definitely history.

But before Wynn could call him back a second time, his cellphone sounded. He watched Carter's departure as he said, "Bryant."

"Good afternoon, Congressman. Might I please ask where you will be tonight?"

The voice was male, but lilting with softness and foreign vowels. And utterly unfamiliar. "Who is this?"

"Libretto is my name. Father Libretto. I bring very best wishes from your sister." He had the brisk cheeriness of one utterly alien to Wynn's new world. "A newly arrived man of power such as yourself, surely you were planning to join Washington society at one place or another this evening."

"I don't—"

"Consider it a request for information passed by your dear sister, Sybel."

Wynn answered numbly, "The British embassy."

"An excellent choice. Until tonight, then." The phone clicked dead.

5

Wednesday

COLIN READY logged off his main computer, a final act that occurred only when he was leaving for the day or going upstairs. One dimension of reality suspended to make room for another. Points of convergence altered across space and time. Colin hesitated a long moment, then decided there was no alternative but forward motion. He left the safety of his cubicle, padded down the long line of fluorescent caves, waved his pass at the electronic doors, and entered the maelstrom.

Once strictly a magnet for kids hunting mouse ears and Sleeping Beauty dunce caps, Orlando was now enduring ravenous expansion and the fastest service-sector growth in the United States. Many large New York companies were either relocating south or sending down their peripheral operations. The lure of cheap land and hourly wage rates sixty percent below those in the Big Apple proved too hard to resist. Schwab was the latest Wall Street defector, now running a huge campuslike operation near Winter Park and employing over two thousand people, most of them techies.

Farther south, in the former no-man's-land between the airport and the Kissimmee sprawl, another series of collegiate buildings housed the Hayek Funds Group. With fewer than nine hundred employees, Hayek was small by Schwab standards. Yet Hayek had moved not only its ops center but the whole shooting match—funds management, bonds, derivatives, foreign exchange, international corporates, everything. The move made *Wall Street Journal* headlines for over a month, because this was the first U.S.–based hedge fund that saw no need for a substantial Wall Street presence. Some called it an indication of Hayek's personal power, a man so good at his job that the money would follow him to Patagonia if required. Whatever the reason, Hayek was now the largest hedge fund and currency trader based south of the Mason-Dixon line.

Orlando's recent influx of computer-driven companies had resulted in a sudden dearth of specialists. High-tech headhunters swooped about like vultures over roadkill. Salaries had risen. The search had moved farther afield, then farther still. Which was how Colin came to be there at all.

The Hayek Group's trading room floor was a windowless box, three-quarters of an acre in size. Three hundred desks. Two glassed-in balconies. The wall clocks now read a half hour past Wall Street's closing bell, and the place stank of tension and money and deodorant-tainted sweat. Couriers scurried. Traders shouted and gestured and cursed and attacked their boards. The room was littered with paper shreds, remnants of that day's kills. Normally Colin fed upon the floor's energy. The buzz, as much as the money, was why he stayed around. The trading room was an incredible high, like working inside a war zone without the flak. At least, it had been so before his personal universe had tracked upon a dark and deadly orbit.

Eyes followed Colin's progress along the back of the trading room floor. He was an enigma, the techie granted access both to the floor and the people upstairs. He was called upon whenever traders' hardware glitched and was almost always able to offer a quick solution. He was known to be soft-spoken, almost apparition-like, and available when needed. One day he had simply appeared out of nowhere; the next he was indispensable. And that accent. One moment southern, the next foreign as warm red beer.

Colin entered the elevator and used his pass to access the penthouse. In truth, Hayek's offer had rescued him from the dicey realm of gray-market e-theft, scamming money as a sometime game designer, but mostly living for the forbidden rush.

Colin Ready was a white-hat programmer, a former hacker now working for the people he had formerly sought to break and enter. Colin studied his reflection in the elevator's polished brass doors, saw a man in his late twenties with a narrow build and smooth ageless features, a weak mouth, mousy brown hair, and the eyes of a corpse. No outward sign of techie mania. No pager, no palm-pilot, no bottle-bottom glasses. Trembling slightly now, but extreme nerves were standard in forays to the penthouse.

Colin entered Hayek's outer office and squinted against the glare.

His cubicle was two rows removed from a window, and here the afternoon light branded his eyeballs. The senior secretary knew him so well by now, she did not even ask if his errand was urgent. Nothing less would have brought Colin upstairs. He seated himself and waited with the suppressed tension of one who knew he was the bearer of vital data.

Colin's father was British, his mother a true Georgia fireball. After years of legendary battles, they had finally split when Colin was eight. Which had left him spending summers in Leeds, winters wherever his mother happened to be wed that season. For years he had lived with the knowledge that he was born to solitude, his only friends fenced beyond electronic barriers of his own creation. Once there had been another, Lisa, a truly chaste woman so far as computers went. The impossible love. He had lost her earlier that spring, and now his heart lurched with a permanent limp.

"Mr. Ready?" The senior secretary was a narrow-faced woman turned old by her work, with eyes that only feigned feelings, and not well. "Mr. Hayek will see you."

Now that he was here, now that the time had come, Colin had difficulty finding the strength to rise and cross the palatial expanse. But the secretary was holding open the twenty-foot doors. So he took a hard breath and pushed himself forward, into the inner sanctum. Mentally he reviewed the array of armaments he had prepared for just this moment. The warrior ready to battle giants and win the invisible prize.

The chairman was seated at his polished boardroom table. To enter the conference alcove meant crossing two silk Isfahans and passing the boat-sized stinkwood desk, the pair of Monet oils, and the bronze Rodin nymph dancing by the corner silk sofa set. The alcove was separated from the office proper by sliding shoji screens with frames not of paper but mother-of-pearl. The conference area itself had glass walls with lakes and green beyond. Computer screens shone everywhere, silent projectors positioned so that wherever the chairman sat, all he had to do was glance up and instantly be fed the market's constant spew.

Colin stood by the alcove entrance, waiting for the chairman to look up and motion him forward. The atmosphere was more subdued than the trading floor itself, yet far more intense. Around the table sat a group from the trading floor, including Eric, the closest Colin had to a friend among the traders. They circled the paper-stacked table like sated pumas around a fresh kill.

Pavel Hayek himself was not attractive, but his visceral power was so obvious the man's physical attributes meant almost nothing. Today he wore a double-breasted blue blazer with the fancy crest on his pocket. The chairman was a trim late fifties, with even features, softly accented English, and perfect grooming. His gold ring matched the crest on the doors and the wall behind Colin, a crowned phoenix rising from burning brands. Colin had done some checking on Hayek, as much as he dared. Enough to know the man's rumored royal heritage was genuine. The guy actually was a prince. Which meant he lived up to his nickname, the King, in more ways than one. At least, that was what most people called him around here. It was only beyond the Hayek compound that one heard his other nickname, Elvis. No one doing business with Hayek dared use it, even in jest.

"A half-billion dollars in new long-term capital is a big mouthful." This from Alex, the firm's senior foreign exchange trader. "How much time do we have to lay it out?"

"Not long." Hayek was very tight with his words, measuring them like gold. The man was known for having no capacity for small talk. None. "A few days at most. And directed exclusively at the foreign exchange markets."

"You want us to lay out half a big one, only in forex derivatives?"

"That is correct."

Alex had a trader's ability for rapid assessments. "You want to make the market sit up and take notice, is that it?"

Hayek seemed pleased by the appraisal, but said merely, "This could be the beginning of a very large fresh inflow."

"How big?"

"Large enough for us to consider establishing a second fund." He stifled further comment with one upraised hand. "That we shall leave for later. Thank you all."

Hayek waited for the minions to depart. Only Jim Burke, Hayek's second in command remained behind. Hayek did not invite Colin to sit. "Yes?"

"Someone is hunting again. I thought you would want to know."

"Hunting?"

"Using Congressman Hutchings' data, apparently. Asking the same kind of questions."

King and courtier exchanged a silent communication before Hayek demanded, "You are certain of this?"

"Yes."

"Tell me how."

"I inserted a target, a source any new hunter would go after. They'd have no choice but to reveal themselves in the process."

"You are referring to the internet?"

"The web. Yes."

"Go on."

"The site automatically inserts a rogue program into the hunter's computer system. I can then go in and search for data."

The chairman asked his senior man, "Do you understand what he just said?"

Jim Burke was both a trader and a nerd, a serious combination. He was also, in the eyes of those who worked for Hayek, a walking fruit-loop. There was a lot of personal weirdness within the hedge fund world. The business routinely attracted those with meager people skills. But Jim Burke took this infirmity far beyond any logical boundaries. Among the Hayek force, Jim Burke was known as the Unabomber.

Burke replied, "I think so, yes."

Colin held out a sheet, despising the revealed tremors. "This is from my initial scan."

Burke reached forward. "I'll take that."

The chairman waited as his squire surveyed the paper. Burke looked up and said, "This could be a red flag."

"Then check it out thoroughly." Hayek turned back to Colin. "You too. Can you get back into his system?"

"Her," Burke corrected, still scanning the data. "Apparently it's a woman. A local. Jackie Havilland."

Colin replied, "Every time she logs on, my insert will instruct her computer to download all new files."

"I want to know everything."

Colin was utterly grateful to find both the words and Hayek's iron glare directed at his number two. Burke offered, "I'll put the new men on this."

"Immediately," Hayek commanded. "This very afternoon. There is not a moment to lose."

6

Wednesday

BY THE TIME Jackie returned home, clouds and the setting sun cast a pastel gauze across the sky. The windswept day was so replete and the evening so gentle, she was almost prepared to dismiss the Boatman. His bizarre tales of foreboding and mystery were just too far removed from the same old, same old.

The borderlands of Winter Park contained some of Orlando's oldest homes. Three blocks off U.S. 50, there existed a time warp of Florida oaks and two-story wraparound verandas and squeaky sash windows. Her particular treetop haven was a former servant's apartment set above a derelict shed. The main house was a renovator's dream—three floors of Victorian peaks, rotting porches, and peeling paint. The owner was Millicent Kirby, a widow who probably belonged in a padded cell. But the old woman was as attached to the house and the neighborhood as Jackie, and had a terror of being sent off somewhere to rot away alone. Jackie pretended the only reason she did Millicent's shopping and arranged for gardeners and an occasional maid was because she didn't want new owners to cast her adrift as well.

The muscles of her upper body quivered with a satiated hunger as she unstrapped her board from the roof of her car. Her legs scarcely held her aloft as she carried her gear into the shed. The surrounding trees bade a rustling farewell both to the departing day and storm. The nightly chorus of owls and cicadas sang an invitation to stick with the tried and true, the safe, the easy.

Then she noticed the figure standing by the big house's back window.

Jackie had never seen Millicent remain in view so long. Even the monthly housekeeper claimed to see only a flitting wild-haired figure who danced from room to room, always just out of sight. Jackie studied the motionless figure holding up the curtain so that her hyperthin frame was visible. Jackie pointed a silent question up the stairs and was granted a single nod in response.

She hefted a serrated repair knife from her tackle box, then took the outside stairs as quietly as she could. The first sight of her door hanging drunkenly on one hinge pushed a soft groan from her gut. Jackie turned back to Millicent and shouted, "Call the police!"

The woman did not move. Jackie grimaced with understanding. There was nothing the police could do if the robbers were gone, which they had to be if Millicent was still there and letting her proceed. And the old lady wanted no truck with anyone who might threaten her isolation. Police meant social services, and they would only lead to windowless confines and nurses with needles. Jackie gripped her knife tighter and entered the maelstrom.

Her place was thoroughly trashed. All the cupboards were emptied, all the remnants of her life stirred into a bitter caldron. She stepped carefully, moaning from the pain of recognizing small items, things prized by her alone. It was only when she realized much of the plastic crunching underfoot formerly belonged to her brother's computer that she came close to breaking down. All her files were gone.

She walked downstairs, crossed the lawn, and was met by Millicent opening the back door. The gray head remained pointed determinedly downward. In all the time Jackie had lived there, Millicent had never once met her eyes. Through rage bordering on anguish, Jackie asked as gently as she could, "Did you see them?"

"Heard them first. Shouting. First inside, then when they left. Big men. Angry."

"How many?"

"Angry men." Millicent's eyes tracked up and to the side, then down and away, searching for safety in a world far more insane than she would ever be. "Two first. Then another. When the third man went inside the shouting started. Bad words."

"Would you recognize them again if you saw them?"

"Too many words for three men. But just three. First two gray men. Then one blue. I counted because I knew you'd ask."

Jackie sighed and patted the woman's bony shoulder. Up close Millicent smelled like her house, mildewed and ancient. "Thank you. You did just fine."

Jackie crossed the unkempt lawn, climbed the stairs, and reentered her former haven. She spent hours searching for what had not been trashed. Nothing seemed to have been taken—no surprise there, as there was little of any real value. The intruders seemed to have been intent not upon robbery so much as mayhem. Jackie wept tears made fiery because they remained internal, as she mourned mementos of a life that had become almost a myth.

She sorted through the shredded papers until she came up with a pair of Washington names and numbers. The phone had been ripped from her wall and the tiny cellphone was missing altogether, so she walked to the corner booth to call Esther Hutchings. At least she was likely to offer a sane note, if not sympathy. The robot-voiced answering machine fitted the anonymous night. Jackie left a terse message, then dialed the second number. If this did not qualify as an emergency, nothing did.

The phone was answered before the second ring. "Yes?"

"Is this Nabil . . . I'm sorry, I can't read your last name."

"Who is speaking?"

"My name is Jackie Havilland."

"This name I do not know." The voice was male, deep, and resonated with an accent she did not recognize. Perhaps Arabic. The man also sounded very suspicious. "How did you receive this number?"

"Esther Hutchings gave it to me."

"Ah. Then you must be the mystery woman."

"My apartment has been broken into and everything destroyed."

"Which proves we were right in telling Esther not to take this course. She has only increased the danger to us all."

Whatever Jackie had been expecting, it was not this overt hostility. "Can you get a message to her, please? They stole my cellphone and tore my other from the wall."

When she stopped, the man said impatiently, "Yes? That is your message? Then I suggest you call the phone service and not Esther."

"Look." She took a deep breath. It would be too easy to unload her anger on this voice. "Give me a break here, all right? I've just come back to a house that looks like a demolition site. I'm not thinking straight."

A pause, then, "This I can understand. Very well. I will call Esther for you and say they came. And when you were not home they left you a warning."

The matter-of-fact tone both unsettled and attracted her. "I need to ask you something."

"Yes?"

Jackie searched for some question that would help uncover all the man was not saying. "Esther supplied me with typed notes annotated by hand, I assume from her husband."

"Another grave error."

"I need to know who made those handwritten notes. Some of them refer to people I can't identify, and—"

"Anyone with half a brain would know the honorable gentleman would himself be writing notes on his personal documents."

"How interesting." Acid rose to etch her words. "Seeing as how Graham Hutchings was apparently writing with both hands, and the left-handed notes show definite feminine traits."

The deep voice showed its first trace of hesitancy. "Feminine. Yes. A researcher and dear friend helping Graham with his work."

"Friend, foe, or morph, I don't care. I just want to talk with her."

"So would I," the voice replied mournfully. "Oh, so very much. Alas, my dear friend was there when they came with her warning. You understand what I am saying to you?"

"Not exactly."

"My friend was caused to fall from a building in Washington. That was their warning to her. So now all our questions must be directed toward the grave."

7

Wednesday

THE BRITISH EMBASSY was a brick-and-glass wart rising from the leafy expanse of Massachusetts Avenue. Everything wrong with sixties architecture had been gathered together and planted amid the massive oaks and sycamores. Wynn passed through the metal detector and gave his name to the receptionist. An older woman standing along-side the table responded instantly, moving forward, offering her hand. "An honor that you would join us, Congressman. I am Audrey Port-man, the ambassador's personal aide. I know he is anxious to meet you."

She did not lead so much as direct him from alongside. Midway across the floor, she murmured for his ear alone, "Perhaps I should mention, Congressman, the two ladies and the gentleman in the far corner, the ones watching us."

As far as Wynn could tell, every eye in the room stalked their progress. "Yes."

"British journalists. The two ladies represent the *Guardian* and the *Independent* respectively. The gentleman, however, represents the *Sunday World.*"

He caught the warning tone. "I should avoid him."

"We refer to such tabloids as the rags, Congressman. And with good reason."

She managed to insert herself into the group surrounding the ambassador, drawing Wynn along with her. "Excuse me, Lord Vinson, might I have the pleasure of introducing Congressman Wynn Bryant."

The gentleman was as polished as his aide, and as well briefed. "Of course, Congressman. What an honor to have this opportunity to add my own personal welcome. You are recently arrived to this fair city, I believe."

"Just yesterday."

"Then you are even more the newcomer than myself. Perhaps you have not had the pleasure of meeting our esteemed companions." Lord Vinson made swift progress around the circle. Wynn shook a dozen hands, met as many measuring gazes, felt himself invariably coming up short.

"I see you have not yet found yourself refreshment." The ambassador steered him away from the others, a single step taking them beyond earshot. He signaled a passing waiter and said, "I have long been an admirer of your predecessor. Had the occasion to meet him, twice in fact, when Graham was over attending symposiums in the City."

Wynn accepted a glass, sipped at a liquid he did not taste, and guessed, "The Jubilee Amendment."

The ambassador's eyes gleamed. "So nice to know you share our interest, Congressman. So very nice. Perhaps you would be so kind as to join us at the residence for dinner. I assure you, the chancellery is a far more pleasant environ than here. And more private." A hint of a smile, a nod, and the man was lost in the swirling throng.

Before the crowd could sweep Wynn up again, however, another man was standing in front of him. He appeared so smoothly he revealed a lifetime's practice at slipping into tight spots. "Congressman Bryant, I am Father Libretto. We spoke this afternoon by phone. What a pleasure it is to meet you, sir. A pleasure indeed. Sybel speaks so fondly of you."

Though Wynn was surprised to face the slight man in the dark suit and Roman dog collar, this time he was also ready. "Before we get started on whatever you came to say, first tell me about the Jubilee Amendment."

Father Libretto smiled, revealing teeth as neat and compressed as the rest of him. "Sybel warned me not to make the world's mistake of dismissing you as inconsequential. She said you had been a fighter all your life. Once you locked down on a goal, she told me, you were satisfied with nothing less than the ultimate prize."

"The Jubilee Amendment," Wynn pressed.

"Read your files, Congressman. They have far more information than what I can give you before someone else walks over and sweeps you away. Read the pages neatly typed by your staff. Resist the temptation to dismiss this as nothing more than the ramblings of a passionate and tragic brother in Christ."

"You mean Hutchings?"

"I mean, Congressman, that this is more than a question you have presented here. This is a *choice.*" The priest noticed someone coming up to join them, and adroitly moved up alongside Wynn, turning them together so that the newcomer met a wall of two joined backs. "We are a group wanting to do more than just survive, Congressman. We are joined by the call of God. We seek to hear the voice of those who have been robbed of speech. We seek to give life to ourselves by giving hope to others."

"You're not making any sense."

"Of course not. And so long as you continue to ask the wrong questions, Congressman, so long as you seek to remain safe and observe everything from the comfortable distance of power's mountaintop, you will not understand anything. You have ears, but will not hear; eyes, but will remain safely blind." The gentle voice had not risen in tone, yet there was a new passion at work, as forceful as it was gentle. "I am not here tonight to answer your questions, Congressman. I am here to beg you to *wake up.*"

"I don't understand a word you've just told me."

"Do not permit yourself to lose this opportunity to find true wealth. Do not." A small hand gripped his arm, a hasp locking out all but the gentle words. "When you wake up at night, Congressman, alone and desperate despite the world's assurance that you have everything anyone could ever dream of, I urge you to heed the unheard voice. Sybel assures me that you can be the one we need. We seek another fighter, Congressman. We need another friend. And in return, all we can offer you is work and strife and possibly a lifetime's worth of frustration."

The priest made to turn away, then added quietly, "Oh, and passion. I neglected to mention that, did I not. The passion of a quest worth the day and the night and the day, until the moment when the day is no more."

WYNN WANDERED AIMLESSLY through the room, shaking innumerable hands, mulling over the priest's mystery, until he spotted her. This particular woman could not have approached unseen. Not a beauty like this. If he had been comatose and she had advanced from behind, he would still have noticed. She was that striking.

Serious hair. That was his first thought. A rich cinnamon, and long enough to tease her shoulders like caressing fingers as she walked. A designer suit whose skirt was cut high to show off million dollar legs. Body undulating smoothly, almost hidden by the cutaway jacket. Eyes huge and a mere shade browner than her hair. She stopped before him and announced, "I believe I've waited long enough, don't you?"

"Excuse me?"

"I couldn't possibly race up the first moment you arrived and fling myself at your feet."

He smiled. Not at her words, but her accent. It was English and Oxbridge and rich, as perfect a match as her jewelry, understated and utterly appealing. "Why not?"

"Oh, come now, Congressman. Even a newcomer like yourself is aware of the dire situation facing a single unattached woman in Washington. Nine to one is the current ratio. Appalling situation, really, they should pass a law. I was considering some awful act, like flying to New York for a wanton weekend. And then here you come, sauntering in all by your lonesome." She had a way of framing the words as if she were tasting them. "That sounds utterly brazen, doesn't it. I'm so ashamed I really should turn and flee. But I dare not. I might never have another such occasion."

Wynn waved his glass at the room. "It doesn't bother you that the entire hall is watching us?"

"Well, of course they are. The latest addition to the Washington power set is a handsome widower and as unattached as a prince from my childhood fairy tales. His first night in Washington, and already he's snagged by a K Street lobbyist." She offered a long-fingered hand. "I'm sorry, I've not even introduced myself. Valerie Lawry."

"A pleasure." And a relief. The priest had already been relegated to the realm of unwelcome night visitors. "What did you say you were?"

She gave a delighted laugh. "Oh, Congressman, this is just too rich."

"Call me Wynn."

"Wynn. I had heard the name, but it was too perfect to be real. It sounds positively drawn from the days of President Hoover. I can see the caption now, Win With Wynn, all draped with bunting and patriotic balloons."

Wynn wished for something intelligent to say. But her perfume and her looks and her eyes were a potion that robbed him of what little sense he ever had. "You're a lobbyist."

"Indeed so. K Street is home to the most expensive of our breed. The hottest guns for hire."

"Who are you representing tonight?"

"No one, good sir." She reached out a hand, as though wishing to touch his arm, then thinking better of it. Instead she traced a finger down the outside of her sweat-beaded glass. "Tonight I am merely hunting prey."

A senior official of the British embassy inserted himself at that point. Wynn did not hear the name, scarcely saw him at all. The man's flushed cheeks and fruity laugh revealed he was as hard struck by Valerie as Wynn. She took the opportunity to move a single step closer to Wynn, permitting him to feel a trace of her heat, showing the intruder the unified front of a couple together. The man got the message and, with a diplomat's ease, passed over a card and departed.

Valerie stepped back a little, but not as far as before, using the intruder as an excuse to draw them slightly closer. "I confess to an ulterior motive."

"Name it."

"Oh, you should never be so swift to agree to anything in this town, good sir. Tit for tat, that's the name of the Washington game. Work everything to your ultimate advantage." She grazed his arm with her jacket, scalded him with a look. "Whatever I ask, you should ask for more in return."

He watched her take a slow sip from her glass, eyes never leaving his. "Information."

This was not the response she had been expecting. "I beg your pardon?"

He started to ask about the Jubilee Amendment, decided he would first read the file. Besides, the priest and his words did not fit into this scene. "My staff."

She lowered her glass. More guarded now. "Yes?"

"I can't get a handle on their response to my appointment. They were respectful, alert, and didn't seem to care."

"Not the least bit worried about impressing the new boss, you mean."

"That's it exactly."

"They are power addicts." The diction more precise now. "Washington draws them like the mother lode. They will do their job, work eighteen-hour days, and if you don't get along, just move on. I know of numerous unfilled places among the two Houses, chiefs looking for experienced staffers. There is no time to train newcomers, you see. No time for anything."

"So all my staff have worked in other congressional offices?"

"Congress, committees, two have pulled stints in the White House. All but one are Washington old-timers."

"Carter Styles," he guessed.

"Very good, Congressman. I must be very careful not to underestimate you."

"How do you know these things?"

"It's my job. I have a file on every congressman, senator, senior staffer, cabinet member, and White House flunkey. Every one of them needs to be tracked and identified. What they are passionate about, which issues they could be flexible over, where they go, who their allies are."

"It sounds like I could learn a lot from you."

"So much. So very much indeed."

Wynn was intrigued by the way this woman switched from business to intimacy with a look, a word, a tip of her tongue tracing the edge of her teeth. "You had some request of your own?"

"Graham Hutchings was a professional acquaintance. I have long wanted to go by and pay my respects, but it's not a journey I wish to make on my own. I was wondering if I might possibly impose."

"You don't want me."

"Oh, Congressman . . ." Valerie finished with a very pretty smile.

"No. Really." Utterly serious now. "Esther Hutchings and I are enemies from way back."

"Then this is the perfect opportunity for you as well. You must go by and pay your respects, Wynn. Listen to me. I know this town. You've been appointed to replace a man who has been debilitated by his work. A visit is required. It is the absolute minimum in decorum. What is the worst that could possibly happen?"

"She might gnaw my head off."

"I doubt that very much." This time the hand did come to rest upon his arm. "Now you really must regale me with the tale of this bad blood. I positively thrive on such gossip."

"Not a chance in this world."

From coquettish to serious in the span of one breath. "Go, Wynn. Do this thing. Or you will be buried by people unearthing the tale and spreading it far and wide. Embellished, inflamed, and made immeasurably worse."

He accepted his defeat by finishing his drink and setting the glass on the tray of a passing waiter. "All right."

"Excellent. Shall we say six-thirty Friday?" She graced him with a full-wattage smile. "Come now, Wynn. It won't be that bad. And afterward I'll offer you a fine dinner somewhere. My treat."

As she walked away, Wynn caught sight of the priest slipping through the exit. The little man did not necessarily look his way, perhaps he just glanced at the room as a whole. But it was enough to repaint the evening a darker shade and turn Wynn's idle longing to dust.

8

Thursday

JACKIE AWOKE to a skyless dawn. She stretched muscles made doubly tired by hours of frustrated cleaning, and stepped onto her tiny balcony. Somewhere close overhead the firmament was swallowed and gone, replaced by a seamless gray nothing. No wind, no sound, nothing to mask the humid heat or the din already rising from the awakening city. One look was enough to confirm that the weather perfectly suited her plans for the day ahead.

Her reflection in the single remaining fragment of her bathroom mirror looked grim and weary. She prepared camp-style coffee, boiling water in a battered pot, then pouring it directly over the grounds in her only intact mug. As she sipped the bitter brew, Jackie surveyed the final three bags of formerly precious trash.

The apartment was utterly bare. Every scar and yellowed seam was revealed, every fray and stain in the carpet, every fabrication of a life precariously stitched together. Jackie felt more than exposed. She felt violated.

Jackie dressed in her standard mourning garb—black calfskin boots, black jeans, black T-shirt, black velvet hair ribbon. She did not need her shredded wall calendar to know the date. The monthly routine was branded upon her soul with a lifetime's acrid heat.

She closed her flimsily repaired door and carried the last of the trash bags downstairs. As she walked down the drive, a voice called from out front. Jackie carried the bags with her, both because they were in her hands and because it would be a genuine excuse to leave.

Millicent's doctor asked her, "You all right?"

"Fine." At least she was not damaged where it showed.

"Millicent said something about wolves in gray jackets."

"I was burglarized." She glanced at her watch, not because she was late, but merely to show she had things to do.

The doctor gave no indication he had noticed. Now that he was semiretired, Dr. Crouch fought to slow all the world to his own pace. He was old enough to remember when house calls were expected, and too stubborn to change. "You call the cops?"

"There wasn't anything stolen. Just wrecked. And you know Millicent."

"She didn't want to open the door for me, thought maybe a social service type was hiding behind a tree." He frowned at the bags. "You still ought to file a report."

She gave a noncommittal shrug. "How is Millicent?"

"Crazy as a loon. But other than that, not too bad. You still doing her shopping?"

"Twice a week. Today, in fact."

"Get her some Cream of Wheat. Had to hide her bottom dentures. Looks like her gums are infected again." He stared at the sagging empty porch. "She moved her mattress and bedsprings into the front parlor."

"All by herself?"

"Sure didn't get any help from me. Millicent says there's less moonlight on the street side, which means the beasts don't howl so loud."

"She told me the burglars were cursing something awful," Jackie replied, hating how she had caused the old lady to worry.

"She keeps the downstairs rooms clean as a whistle, is all I know. She takes her medicine and she dresses herself, in a manner of speaking. 'Course, the way things are now, yellow leg warmers with a neon green cocktail dress and black sneakers might be high fashion."

Jackie started toward the curb. "Let me know if I need to do something for her."

Crouch called after her, "Know what Millicent told me this morning? You're a good daughter. I said she could take that right to the bank."

Jackie dumped her load with the other bags and lengthened her stride back to the Camaro. Crouch's words merely darkened the day's already bitter cast. She backed down the drive, ignoring the doctor's hesitant wave. The motor rumbled deep-throated taunts all the way to her mother's nursing home. Good sister, daughter, student, fiancée—all the lies she had watched crumble, all the energy lost to pretending it didn't matter.

The nursing home's front door expelled the harsh scent of industrial cleanser. The place was extremely Catholic and packed with religious ornaments and nurses in the white headdresses of the full-on devout. Jackie had come here because it was the only Medicare bed available when her mother had suffered the stroke. Now she counted it as one of the luckiest days of her life. Nobody else would have put up with her mother for this long.

Like many of the home's staff, the manager was Ghanaian, stoic, and quietly sympathetic. The heavyset woman rose from her desk and beamed a welcome far too genuine for this place. "Miss Jackie, what you doing here so early? I didn't expect you before lunchtime."

"I've taken a couple of days off work. Thought I'd come over before things got busy."

"If I had me a day free, sure to goodness I wouldn't be spending it here."

Jackie started grimly for the stairs. "How's Mom?"

"She's drinking her own bile and dying just as fast as she knows how. Same as always." Knowing dark eyes followed her departure. "Don't you go be doing the same, mind."

AFTER JACKIE'S FATHER had dumped them, her mother had gone through a series of bad jobs and worse men, finally landing as a waitress at a HoJo's on Route 50. The place had been so rough she would seldom let her children come in for the free meals offered to all employees' families. And there she remained, right up to the moment Preston struck it rich and rented her a fine little place on a lake. Their mother had never acknowledged the gifts, for that would have meant also accepting that a man in her life had done something good.

Jackie let herself into her mother's room. The upper half of her mother's bed had been slightly elevated. Evelyn Havilland lay there inert and pale. Eyes closed. Chest hardly moving. Face slack. Taking revenge on life and everyone she had ever known by shutting them out. Jackie carried the chair over from its station beside the opposite wall, seated herself by the bed, and waited.

"These people do everything they can to hurt me." The mouth scarcely moved. The eyes never opened. "You satisfied now? You should be."

"Hello, Mom. Would you like something to drink?" Jackie picked up the plastic cup from the bedstand and saw it was empty. "Let me get you some water."

Evelyn Havilland said nothing more until Jackie had fitted the plastic straw into her mouth and let her sip. "A decent daughter'd have gotten me out of here. Found me a place with people who know how to do things right. But not you. Oh no. Too much trouble, finding your own mother a decent place to breathe her last."

Evelyn turned her head then, just a fraction. Far enough to shoot her daughter a glimmer from shadow-filled eyes. "Probably just as well you didn't try. You'd only have made a mess of it anyway."

Jackie found a fly buzzing about the room to focus her attention upon. It was a trick she had used since childhood. A dust mote in sunlight would do. A sound from beyond the room. Anything to keep from being opened and penetrated.

"I always knew it would come to this. Lying here waiting for the end, looking at a daughter who's wasted every chance she's ever had." Pausing now, building up the venom. "And every man."

A bad day. Sometimes Jackie could slip in, spend an hour beside the inert figure in the bed, exchange no more than a few words. Converse only with her memories and all the old pain. Such days were a delight compared to these, when she was forced to remember how she never had the chance to be young.

"Not a day goes by, I don't regret the horrible mess you made with Shane. I adored him, you know." Another pause to refill the fangs. "Didn't even learn about it from my own daughter. Oh no. Shane had to be the one to come and tell me you'd run away. I couldn't believe it even then. Told him no daughter of mine would be that stupid."

Jackie rose and picked up the chair. Deliberately she placed it back against the wall. There to wait another month for the only visitor her mother had. She masked her movements as she did her thoughts. Wondering what her mother would do if she lifted the chair and swung it down upon her head. Thank her, probably.

"You're going to see your brother's grave now, I suspect. What a loser he turned out to be. The ultimate disaster. Just like his father. Hung around just long enough to ruin my life. Never could take the bad times, neither of them." Evelyn swiveled her head back up, closed her eyes. "Don't have a daughter, don't have a son. All that sweat and worry for nothing. Might as well not have lived."

"Bye, Mom." Jackie left the room without a backward glance. Her work here was done.

JACKIE SPOTTED THE TAIL while she was buying flowers. It was mostly the way the man stood and stared at her. Then she noticed the car, and something sparked inside her brain; he had been following her since the nursing home. She'd never been involved in a surveillance job, but while working around the office she'd learned the signals. Jackie checked in both directions but could not identify another suspicious car or tracker. She glanced back in time to see the man lock his car and hurry across the street. That was definitely an amateurish move, letting her spot him beside his wheels.

She paid for the flowers and headed through the cemetery gates. Just inside she turned and faced him full on. The man knew he had been spotted, there was no disguising it now. But to her surprise, he did not duck back or head down a side lane. Instead he merely stood there, hands bunched together by his belt buckle, and waited. She continued along the gravel path, warmed by the thought that this might be one of the men who'd trashed her apartment. It was enough to grant the day a momentary reprieve. She would love to meet those guys, give them a piece of whatever was available and heavy.

The cemetery was packed with mourners and gardeners. Jackie made the turning down the now-familiar lane and glanced back. He was still there, yet showed nothing to suggest either hostility or threat. What he looked like was a Latin hunk. Olive complexion, early fifties, extremely well groomed. Clothes with a European cut, shoes so well polished they reflected like black mirrors. The day was an oven set on wet-bake, yet he walked in jacket and tie. He held to a respectful distance, a professional mourner waiting for her to show him the proper place to grieve.

The problem was, she had no interest in sharing this part of a lousy day. So she checked to make sure there were a couple of gardeners nearby, then walked straight up to him. "You want something?"

"Forgive me, Ms. Havilland. I have no wish to disturb you in this hour of communing with your brother."

She recognized the voice instantly. Not Latin at all. Arab. But just as handsome up close. "You're that guy. The Arab on the telephone. Esther's emergency contact."

"That is correct." He bowed slightly, a gesture as formal as his tone. "Nabil Saad is my name. I am Egyptian. Again, forgive this intrusion. But we needed to meet. And the contact required someplace more private than your apartment."

She took a moment to inspect him, trying to get a handle on this sudden appearance. Nabil Saad was not tall, standing only a few inches above her own five-seven. Flecks of silver decorated the dark hair at his temples and crown. He wore a jacket of tiny gray-and-black herringbone. It looked incredibly expensive, probably silk. White-on-white shirt, black gabardine pants, perfectly knotted silk tie. Face both hard and soft, eyes liquid and black as night. And calm. Standing and accepting her inspection in silence.

Jackie said, "Excuse me, I'm a little confused here. Last night I got the impression you didn't want to have anything to do with me."

"My objections had nothing to do with you personally. But Esther Hutchings had no right to hire you as she did, without our approval. Nor did she ask permission to give you my name."

Jackie hoped her confusion did not show. "But she did."

"Indeed so. Esther has never been prone to listen to anyone when her mind is made up. And now you have been attacked, and you have my name. Esther needed to make contact with you. Esther's file spoke of this monthly pattern. I elected to come meet you myself."

"So there's this file on my private life that's been passed around?"

"You must forgive us all, Ms. Havilland. Such intrusion is not excusable."

"I totally agree."

"And yet we are faced with an impossible situation. Lives are at stake."

"That friend you mentioned on the phone last night?"

"She was like the daughter I do not have." Nabil Saad's features opened to reveal an ocean of sorrow. "Our cause was her life's work. Yes. Her passion. And it killed her. Of that I have no doubt."

Jackie found herself unwilling to press further. Not when his pain so closely resembled her own. She found herself wondering what it would be like to care so passionately about a cause, or have someone else carry such grief for her own passage.

She used her flowers to gesture along the lane. "You mind excusing me?"

He gave another of his gracious half-bows and showed the incredible wisdom to say nothing further. Instead he merely walked to an empty stone bench.

Jackie pretended she did not feel his presence as she rounded the curve and halted by the all-too-familiar patch of green. She settled her flowers into the stone vase rising beside the simple plaque. Preston's name had been carved into the dark granite, nothing else. No need to add the burden of those too-brief dates. She would never forget the day of his departure or his age. Or how she had failed him.

As ever, the mirror to past mistakes remained imperfect and depressing. She endured it for a respectful period, then allowed herself to turn away. As dissatisfied and aching as ever.

The Egyptian rose at her approach. He seemed to reflect her own tumult, a gift of understanding so potent she found herself unable to remain at a safe distance. The deep melodious voice said, "My family is Coptic. An ancient Christian church, so old it is hard to know where truth ends and fable begins. Forty days we spend mourning over those gone ahead. People gather from all over the globe for the day of burial, then remain for a week and more at the side of those seeking either to heal or drown in grief. Both responses are acceptable to families such as mine."

She felt drawn as much by his sorrow as his words. Nabil Saad kept his face turned toward the corner and the unseen grave. "Alas, my young friend was unable to attend her own funeral. And it was my fault. I used my position to insist that the Washington police not simply dismiss her death as suicide. She was murdered. I have no proof, but still I ordered them to treat it as such. The detectives in charge of the case were very angry. They took revenge in a very painful manner."

Jackie guessed, "They refused to release the body."

"I insisted that the young lady had been thrown from the roof for asking the wrong questions and hoping to make the impossible a reality. The detectives insisted the case would go nowhere, then punished me for this extra work. There were problems with the autopsy, questions of this and that . . ." He waved a dismissive hand, an utterly Arab gesture. "I was left to face her parents and confess that I was responsible for their grieving over an empty coffin."

His gaze was so open and wounded, Jackie could let herself be swallowed and comforted both. "So I must thank you, Ms. Havilland, for granting me this moment in a place of hallowed death."

She looked back down the curved pathway and faced a rising tide of memories. "You've heard the expression, a child too fine for this world? That was Preston. A little boy to the end. My finest memories are all about making Preston laugh. He was my very best friend."

"Come." He touched her with the invitation and a gentle hand upon her shoulder, guiding her back to the stone bench.

Jackie found herself willing to seat herself beside this stranger, though normally she could scarcely draw breath until she had passed the outer gates. "Preston had a brilliant mind. He was a mathematician. He grew up in mind and body, but his heart remained that of a child. Untouched by anything." Jackie halted and focused on something beyond her aching empty universe. After a time, she went on, "Preston specialized in calculating statistical probability. I had no idea what the words meant until he told me. I'll never forget that day. Preston was sixteen and as excited as a man falling in love. Which I suppose was what he had done. He showed me these pages in his book, lines of calculus and a few sentences of description. I remember I told him, there aren't any numbers. I said it as much to make him laugh as because that was what I was thinking."

"And then he went to work for Hayek," Nabil Saad intoned. "And you went back to school."

"Preston worked as a specialist on the currency markets, calculating risk and currency trajectories. I never felt comfortable with his work or his world. But I could not say why."

"It was the natural response of one who loved him with a goodly heart. Love grants one the wisest of vision."

"It was almost enough to study, to grow and search and do all the things I had dreamed of. Still I wanted to put a name to my fears, so I started researching his new realm. I found some very real dangers. But it was never enough to make Preston back away." The remembrances tasted metallic. "Then the work and the life began to consume him. Preston took to drugs like candy. Crystal meth and cocaine, they fueled his fire. That and adrenaline. He just burned up. By the time he finally came back for me to nurse, there was nothing left. The doctors put all sorts of names to it, but I knew and so did he."

"And you stayed with him to the end."

She turned away from the memories and the comforting closeness. She had to, or lose it totally. "Why are we sitting like this?"

"Some of those opposed to involving an outsider asked me to spy on you. I decided there was enough spying already. So I came to introduce myself, and to give you this." He slipped an envelope from his pocket. "Esther asks that you come visit her. Tomorrow."

"In Washington?" She stared at the envelope, but did not take it. "Why doesn't she come back here?"

"There are difficulties. Go and you will see." He settled the envelope into her hand and rose. "I count it an honor to have made your acquaintance, Ms. Havilland. I would even call it a pleasure, were we not so surrounded by remorse."

She stared up at him, amazed at his ability to smile with his eyes and weep with his voice. "Call me Jackie."

He offered his hand. "I agree. Such secrets as ours should only be shared between people who can claim first names."

"I have about a thousand questions."

"If you force me, I will speak. But the secrets are not mine alone, and I would prefer that you first go to Washington."

She thought a moment, then released his hand. He rewarded her with an enigmatic smile of approval. Then she recalled an inept boatman and yet another baffling message. "A guy I met a couple of days ago, scared out of his wits, talked about a website called Trastevere. Does that mean anything to you?"

The shutters came down over those dark eyes. She actually saw it happen. "Piazza Trastevere is in Rome," he said, and took another step back. "It is the site of a movement called Sant'Egidio." The words became his only farewell, as he then turned and walked away. Not really fleeing, but moving swiftly enough to show he hoped she would not speak again.

Jackie found herself willing to let him go. To her quiet amazement, the day now held a strange sense of comfort, and the cloying heat was not altogether bad.

9

Thursday

"LET ME GET THIS STRAIGHT." Eric, a junior trader and Colin's closest friend on the floor, was a tousle-headed young man on the downside of thirty with eyes of his grandfather's generation. He bent over to observe Colin Ready sprawled on the floor by his feet. "You're telling me that my computer doesn't like having coffee poured down its plug holes?"

"I've read the care and feeding manuals cover to cover." Colin continued removing a goop stubborn as old glue. Down here on the floor, among the cables and scraps of abandoned paper, the air smelled pretty foul—old socks, meal scraps, sweat, dead coffee. A human zoo. The underside of the money treadmill. "I've never come across any suggestion that you should kick-start your machine with caffeine."

Eric was like most on the middle rung, inching his way up with strings of good days, only to plummet back to the precipice's edge with a near-fatal trading error. He was also constantly in debt, raising his head above the waters only around annual bonus time. This was a common trait among the junior traders. They pulled in anywhere from sixty to two hundred thou, but their tastes and ambitions were molded by those on the top rung. Senior traders pulled two to three mil, doubling that in bonuses. It was hard to live on peanuts when the senior traders chowed down on filet mignon.

It was a slow morning, a few desultory traders trying to talk up the market, the rest waiting for the world to take its first hit of adrenaline and find a reason to scream. Those nearby watched the screens and smirked among themselves as Eric played with the mutant techie. "Any word on what's happening upstairs?"

Colin did not need to look up to understand the question. The trading room's ceiling was forty feet up. The left and front walls were over-shadowed by glass-enclosed balconies, each about eighty feet deep and a hundred and forty long. One held the special issues department, traders designing and selling their own derivatives. The other had formerly been the domain of middle managers and had been known as the Snake House. But three weeks earlier, the managers had been moved upstairs, one floor below Hayek himself. Now a team of outsiders was working like army ants, installing new equipment. Nobody knew why, or whom it was for.

"I have no idea," Colin replied truthfully. "They haven't let me up on the parapet."

"Oh, Mr. Ready, there you are." The thin-faced guardian of Hayek's inner chamber hurried down the aisle. The traders parted swiftly. She paid them no mind. "I've been looking all over for you. Mr. Hayek's screens have started flickering again."

"Right." Colin slid out. "I'm all done here."

Eric muttered, "What do you and the King talk about? It can't be football."

Colin dusted off his pants, decided not to risk further delay by going back for his jacket. He followed the severe woman through the front security doors and out into the reception area. A pair of gray-jacketed men scowled their way but said nothing. One sat by the front entrance, another stood by the stairway leading to the glassed-in balconies. Colin did his best to follow the secretary's example and pretend they did not exist.

Hayek's secretary did not speak again until the elevator doors had closed around them. "I'm sorry, sir. I didn't know what to say. There isn't anything the matter with his computers that I'm aware of. But when I couldn't locate you, Mr. Hayek grew most irate. He also said to bring you quietly."

Colin started to ask who the muscles in gray were but decided she would not tell if she knew. "It's fine."

The doors opened. "You'll need to wait just a moment please, Mr. Ready. I'll tell Mr. Hayek you're here."

Upon entering the antechamber, Colin found Jim Burke standing outside Hayek's office doors. The Unabomber looked as seriously weird as ever. Today it was a white polyester shirt, patterned black-on-black tie, black pants, railroad shoes. Newly polished crew cut. Prison-type black-rimmed spectacles. This on a man earning serious seven figures, maybe eight. "Morning, Mr. Ready." Jim Burke nodded toward the empty corner chair. "Why don't you have a seat. Mr. Hayek has somebody with him just now."

Three other men sat hunched around the coffee table. One was Dale Crawford, chief of Hayek's security detail, a leather-skinned former policeman from somewhere strange and hostile—Oklahoma perhaps, or the Dakotas. Because of their matching navy blazers, earpieces, and grim secret-service expressions, Dale Crawford's bunch was known throughout Hayek-land as the KGB. The other two men wore the same gray blazers and dark slacks as the strangers downstairs. Only the anger burned more fiercely with this pair. They trained their ire first on the security man, then on Burke, then Colin. Black volcanic gazes taking careful aim.

Burke walked over and settled a hand on Colin's shoulder. He spoke to the gray goons with a raspy slowness the traders loved to mock. "This is one of the good guys. Nod if you understand me. That's fine. Colin Ready is his name. Can you say that? Never mind."

The head of security smirked at Colin's discomfort beneath Burke's hand. Burke went on, "See, we had this problem. Money kept disappearing and we couldn't figure out how. All we knew was, at the end of the month our books weren't balancing." The hand squeezed. Perhaps the man intended it to be reassuring, but Colin could feel his bones grinding together. "Then we had this idea, bring in a man from outside, have him look through all the electronic pathways. Mr. Ready identified the problem, and fast. We're talking days, after we've been at it for three months. More. What did you call it, Mr. Ready?"

"Fractional interest siphoning." Squirming to let Burke know the hand was not welcome.

But the man was not getting the message. Or chose to ignore it. "Mr. Ready designed us a hunter-seeker program. I'll never forget that name. Loved it. And it worked. We found two backroom nerds dipping into the accounts payable, taking a couple of bucks here, a couple there. Did us for six hundred thou. The trouble was, they vanished just before we came for them." A significant pause, waiting for Colin to confess he'd had a hand in warning the pair. The hand squeezing painfully.

"Mr. Ready?" The secretary had never sounded more welcoming. "Mr. Hayek will see you now."

One of the swarthy men tried to rise with him. "Plant yourself back down," Burke ordered, then released his grip and moved a step aside. "See you around, Mr. Ready."

As Colin slipped past the secretary and entered the chairman's office, Hayek pointed him to the chairs arranged by the back wall. "Be with you in just a moment, Ready."

Colin took his seat, not bothering to mask his sudden interest in the woman seated before Hayek. He had seen her before, flashing in and out of private conferences with the King. Someone this stunning attracted notice. Colin had done some checking, discreetly of course. She was a big voice up in Washington, a player in the power game. Valerie Lawry was a lobbyist with one of the K Street firms. She ignored Colin entirely, remaining intently focused upon the man behind the desk. The antique table was big enough to rival oceangoing vessels, easily capable of sleeping six. It suited the chairman perfectly. The woman was saying, "I fail to see the merit behind your actions."

"That is my concern," Hayek replied. "I am simply telling you what needs doing."

Colin stared at his nemesis-boss, and thought of a great cat resting easy, or a god from some mystical age when giants ruled the earth. Hayek's authority was that strong. Colin had spent quite a bit of time around the man, more than anyone else from the back room. He had seen how certain women went for Hayek, and not the ones he might have expected. Powerful women, intelligent and aggressive. Young, old, beautiful and not so; their responses to Hayek seemed spontaneous, visceral. Either they loathed him, wanted to spit toxins and erase him from the earth, or they were attracted so strongly they could hate him and still want him. Hayek seemed to find both responses amusing, and used either to his advantage. Like now, bringing in his tame hacker while he met with the sharp-edged beauty. Playing the hacker and the woman both like pawns.

The woman continued to ignore Colin and told Hayek in her overbearing English accent, "I'm paid to advise you. And my advice is, you're overreacting. I fail to see why anything Esther Hutchings does at this point is of any importance to you. What are we referring to here, a soon-to-be widow hiring a backroom flunkey? From what I've read, Jackie Havilland's experience is limited to a few college classes which ceased over a year ago. She is out of date and utterly unconnected to the issues at hand."

The name pushed Colin up straighter in his seat. Hayek's intense gray gaze shifted over, pinning him down. Thankfully his attention swiftly returned to his other visitor, who continued to scoff, "Not to mention a congressman so green he's never even heard of K Street. This is definitely not worth your time."

The power in the room seemed compressed, or perhaps it was just the hacker's fear at work. Adding electricity to dry powder, waiting for the explosion. But Hayek remained utterly unfazed, saying merely, "I'll be the judge of that. You've got your orders. Start marching to my music."

The woman bit down hard on her response, picked up her purse and briefcase, and left the room without a word or backward glance.

A man who loathed unnecessary words, Hayek merely demanded of Colin, "Any update on Havilland?"

"Nothing of any importance." Colin held to as calm a tone as possible, this close to the flame.

"Explain how you were alerted."

"My bogus source, the place a hunter would be bound to check, automatically inserted a virus into the searcher's computer when she logged on." Sometimes after Colin returned from one of these sessions, his mind would go into random-sort mode, sifting through a myriad of impressions he had not even been aware of at the moment. The way sunlight glinted off the Rodin sculpture, or the glass case of T'ang artifacts, or the painting that watched him, the nymph caught in midflight. All he was aware of at the moment was Hayek's piercing gaze. "The virus included a command to download all file directories every time the searcher logs on. I can then institute a file transfer, which the searcher sees as simply the internet service provider upgrading her software before shutting down."

The chairman reached forward, hefted a silver dagger with a carved crystal handle. "I need a better understanding of this woman. Describe what you know."

This was another strange thing about Hayek, how he would sometimes feed voraciously on the smallest particles of information, and other times sweep away all comments and analyses and data, crashing down with a judgment out of the blue. His staffers called such moments Blitzkriegs, and dreaded the havoc they wrought. What amazed them all, and added to Hayek's mystique, was how incredibly often the man was proven right.

"Jackie Havilland is Orlando-based. A grunt worker in a large private investigations firm. Failed graduate student at the local university. Her brother worked for you."

"I vaguely recall a Havilland. What was his first name?"

"Preston. Resigned for health reasons."

"Of course. A currency analyst, am I correct?"

"Yes." Colin swallowed, then ventured an aside. "Frankly, I'd have to agree with your last visitor. This woman doesn't seem very important."

Hayek lifted his head, getting a fix on him. "Motive."

"She does her banking on-line," Colin stammered. "She's apparently being paid what for her must be a ton of money."

Hayek gave his head a fractional shake, still dissatisfied. Still hunting. "Anything else?"

Colin grabbed at the single shred that came to mind. "She's a windsurfer. A wave jumper. Her computer is filled with images, many of them photographs of herself."

"Former computer," Hayek corrected, his face darkening.

"Sir?"

"Those men outside committed a serious breach of my orders. I requested a search, they turned it into a frenzied attack." Hayek used the crystal dagger to point back to the matter at hand. "This windsurfing. What does it mean?"

"Probably nothing." When this did not satisfy, Colin continued, "I have a buddy who does it. The good ones are fanatics, hands like planks, no fear. They live for days with winds that otherwise shut the seas down. They use their boards like wings."

Hayek mused softly, "Fanatic."

The programmer took the ensuing silence as his signal to leave. But Hayek drew him back around with, "A great deal is riding upon your being right about this nonthreat."

Colin wished only to be away. "Nothing can be getting by me, unless she's writing things longhand."

"Why did the Hutchings woman choose her? Find the motive." The dagger aimed toward the door. "And do so fast."

10

Thursday

WYNN'S SUITE at the Willard looked vastly different at ten-
thirty in the evening. It held the same antique furniture as that
morning, the same chest-high floral display and chintz sofa set and two
tiled fireplaces. Four brass chandeliers bathed the chambers in a false
ruddy glow. An eighteenth-century wall cabinet hid drinks and the entertainment center. The silk wall coverings were in six shades of ivory
and bone. Two oils illustrated carriages along Pennsylvania Avenue, instead of the noisy traffic whose cacophony now filtered through his
windows. Everything was as perfect as twelve hundred dollars a night
could make it. But this time of evening, there was no escaping the bar-
renness.

Wynn kicked off his shoes, dropped his jacket and tie on the bed,
and padded around on carpet as lush and deep as his lawn. The downstairs bar beckoned, but in truth he didn't want another drink. He
wanted whatever could still this restless craving in his gut. No matter
how glorious and history-filled the downstairs rooms might be, he knew
he wouldn't find it there. Not when he couldn't even attach a name to
his longing, other than to call it a desire to be anywhere but here.

He telephoned the Florida governor's mansion, using the private
line that connected directly into their living quarters. When his sister
answered, he asked, "Are you alone?"

"It doesn't matter. This is still not—"

"I know, I know. I just want to talk. Where's Grant?"

"In a meeting downstairs. Power brokers up from Miami. He could
be gone for hours. Just a minute." The phone was put down. He heard
the rattle of earrings being set into an ashtray. A long high-pitched zipper. A rustle. Then the phone was lifted back. "All right."

He settled into the sofa. "I'm having trouble with my staff."

"What did you expect?" No acid tonight. Just a lightning-fast response from a woman with all the brains and political savvy one head could hold. "You know how much a Washington staffer earns? Less than your former secretary. They live six to an apartment, as cramped at night as they are in your office during the day. These people are up there earning slave wages either because they love the power or because they're committed to a cause."

"So why don't they seem to care about me?"

"You're the one using the revolving door of elected office. Not them. They're in this for the long haul." She gave him a chance to come back for more, then demanded, "Now tell me what's really on your mind."

"I am drowning in things I don't understand."

"So learn. If you want. It's your choice, Wynnie. You can do what your staffers tell you, sleep through your committee meetings, show up on the floor only for the votes, find yourself a trustworthy limo driver, become the darling of the Washington party elite. You can jump right onto the social A-list if you want, you know. It's all there for the asking."

"Either that or work myself to death." Thinking of Graham Hutchings and dreading another confrontation with Esther. Wishing he had not agreed to go.

"You can't have both." This was Sybel at her best. Seeing with the crystal clarity of one who had never forgotten a single lesson, who knew every debt owed, every favor unpaid. A woman who had been born for the position of queen. "Your staff will teach you, if you want. If you can make them believe you really and truly care."

"Someone suggested I should pay my respects to Graham."

"Who told you that?"

"A lobbyist I met last night at the British embassy reception. She said the visit is a necessary protocol up here."

"It's good advice, Wynnie. Take it."

"You know what Esther thinks of me."

"Nobody said this would be a cakewalk. Just get it over with. In and out in fifteen minutes. Quicker than a visit to the dentist."

"Your friend was there last night. Father Libretto. Who is he?"

"You just said it. A friend." Noncommittal. Giving nothing away. "You can't have enough friends up there, Wynnie. Believe me."

"How did he get into the reception?"

"Every active priest is considered an emissary of the Vatican. The Vatican has an embassy in Washington. I imagine he requested their assistance."

"Is he working on this Jubilee thing?"

A sigh. Nothing more. But a signal just the same. "Are you sure you want to know?"

"What I know," Wynn replied, "is I keep asking simple questions and receive nothing but a runaround."

"All right. I'll spell out a few things for you. Father Libretto is one of the leaders of a group called Sant'Egidio."

"You work with them."

"So do a lot of other people. They have two objectives, neither of which interests you in the slightest. They seek to feed the poor, and they promote world peace."

"And this ties into Jubilee?"

"Wynnie, listen to what I'm saying. If you're going to follow the cocktail circuit, if you're going to do as Grant told you, then none of this matters. Don't worry yourself about it."

"What's the big secret here, Sybel?"

"There is no secret. It's just . . ." His big sister seemed at a loss, which seldom happened. "The Jubilee Amendment was Graham's passion. But it did not begin with him. It's a world movement to write off all the third world's outstanding debt."

He waited. "That's it?"

"I told you, Wynnie. It doesn't concern you. Not unless you first make a choice. A hard one." A note of pleading entered her voice. "You've spent the past two years tightening down the clamps on your life. Drawing the walls ever closer. Caring for less and less. I've tried everything I know how to get you to open up again. I pray for you, Wynnie. Every night. That something will come along and make you wake up before it's too late. That you'll open your eyes and recognize there's a purpose and a calling that needs you as much as you need it. I know you better than anybody else on earth, and I know how much you have to offer."

It was Wynn's turn to pause. His sister had been religious all her life, a product of being eleven years older and knowing their parents that much longer. He knew their parents had been very religious. It was one of the first things that ever came up when anyone spoke of them.

Their faith. Their caring. Their passion. Their calling. Sybel had spent a lifetime living up to their memory in her own special way, caring first for him, then for Grant, and always making time for her causes. Building homes for the destitute, feeding the poor, funding free medical clinics, promoting daycare centers in marginal neighborhoods, speaking up for people with no voice of their own.

Wynn had responded differently to the challenge of parents who were no longer there. They had left him at five, a tender age to be burdened with the loss not just of his family but his entire world. Wynn had rebelled. He took refuge in fury, until the relatives who took in the orphaned siblings threw up their hands and threatened them with foster care. Sybel was by this time in her first year of college. Grant was seven years her senior, completing his final year of law school—law review, number one in his class, most likely to succeed, good family, the works. And totally in love with Sybel. She agreed to marry him on the one condition that he make room in their new home for Wynn. She had been equally up front, equally tough, with her baby brother. Behave or leave, one chance, that's final. Wynn had behaved. As had Grant. They had never become true friends, but peace had reigned. And Sybel had never let go of her faith.

"That's what this is all about?" Wynn demanded. "A religion thing?"

"You don't just wake up one day and start caring for people you've never met," Sybel replied. A hint of defensiveness to her words. Or perhaps it was desperation. "First you learn to recognize your Maker, call him by name. Let him redirect your vision and your direction. He must be the one to show you how to care, how to open up, how to live for something more than just yourself."

Old words, concepts he had heard from her a hundred times before. Given new force by the current situation, swimming against tides that threatened to drown him. "So this is the big choice."

She caught the tone. Sybel shut down in one harsh breath, becoming as tired and drained as he had ever heard. "Just go to bed, Wynnie. Wake up tomorrow, the sun will be shining, the people will be calling, everyone bowing and scraping and happy for whatever you want to give. Just forget we ever talked. Tomorrow will be full of all the good things you've always dreamed about."

"Sybel, wait, I didn't—"

But she was already gone.

11

Friday

COLIN READY checked his monitor clock. Again. Fifteen minutes to his scheduled meeting with the King. Though there was no move on the Havilland front and everything else seemed in good shape, he was apprehensive. Merely entering Hayek's presence left him exploring the edge of chaos. And today there was something more. Colin detected a difference to the techie chamber's machine-processed air. There was nervousness beyond his own, a current strange even for this place. He rose and poked his head outside the cubicle's padded walls. The techies' central corridor was empty save for the normal wind-down noises of people preparing for Friday departures. Then he caught a hint of something behind him, a tempest brewing beyond the locked trading room doors. He returned to his desk, logged off, and headed out.

There were two ways to Hayek's penthouse. Since the compound's side entrance was used mainly by backroom peons, their elevator rose only as high as the fourth floor. It was then necessary to navigate through the twisted passages of accounting and take the stairs up the final flight. But Colin's work had earned him a trader's passkey, which meant he could slip through the unmarked security-coded door, cross the trading room, and take the front elevators directly to the realm of clouds and rain.

He slipped his key into the magnetic slot and entered bedlam. He counted five different battles raging at various points around the trading floor. Edging along the back wall, Colin was pleased to see that his hypersensitive radar had been giving accurate readings. Friday afternoons were usually fairly soporific, the only action coming from traders desperate to balance impossible positions. Today was ground zero.

Normally Colin considered such energy to be a serious kick. Today, the mothlike existence so close to Hayek's flame left him shaken and separate. He found himself forming dialogue for Lisa Wrede, the young lady who had never agreed to visit this world, and who in fact had wanted nothing more than to draw him away. He had often tried to describe the manic power of such unbridled avarice, wanting her to see how laboring in this secret realm was for him a major league rush. Lisa had responded with either loathing or pity, two great potions for inciting quarrels.

To Colin's right, the spot desks took up by far the largest section of the floor, as Hayek was a huge player on the international forex markets. Forex was the standard way to denote all foreign exchange dealings. Each desk was assigned one or two specific tasks—dollar-mark, yen-mark, franc-pound, and so on. Each trader answered to a senior trader, who was assigned a certain amount of daily bread. Usually a senior trader handled between a half and three-quarters of a billion dollars in outstanding debt at any given time. Each junior trader under him or her was assigned a lesser amount, depending on seniority and track record. A junior trader was also licensed to trade up to a certain amount without looking for the senior trader's approval. This amount was usually granted in ten-million-dollar increments. A trader's limit was raised or lowered depending on his record of profitability and was reassessed every other week. Limits were reviewed more frequently only if the trader moved close to the ax. When a trader carried a loss situation for too long—say, forty-eight hours—or went over his loss budget at evening closedown, that trader was history.

Next to each top trader sat an assistant, there to ensure all trades were recorded and confirmed by accounting. The assistants were all young wannabes, learning the ropes and waiting like vultures for the ax to fall. Their constant hunger was a huge reason why the trading floor remained one of the tensest working environments on earth.

This afternoon the forex action was focused two rows away from where Colin stood. A junior trader shrilled, "I think somebody's trying to push Canada around! I've got three back-to-backs for fifteen each!"

Such sudden moves happened occasionally in late-afternoon trading. A big guy might select what felt like the day's weakest currency and seek to push the nervous Nellies into panicking before the closing bell.

Which was why Alex, the spot market's senior trader, was on his feet, riding his staff hard, using his voice as a whip. "Buy forty-five!"

The junior trader hesitated. "The price has just pumped up a hundred points."

A hundred points was a full cent, a huge rise for one afternoon. Enough to draw Colin over to Eric's desk, where he could watch the action with someone in the know. Alex retorted, "It's a bluff. Hit the bid."

The trader handling the Canadian dollar desk was a young woman unused to the frantic muscle hitting her now. She shrilled the words, "I'm offered forty more!"

Eric sat and swiveled his chair around, back and forth, pumping out the energy, watching the scene like he would a favorite movie. Eric's desk handled dollar-euro, a thousand miles from this afternoon's action. Eric said to the trader on his right, "Five hundred says she enters meltdown before the market closes."

"You're on."

Eric leaned back, said to Colin, "You want some of the action?"

"I'm just a lowly backroom boy," Colin replied. "I'll just sit and watch, thank you."

Alex shouted back to his junior lady, "Buy forty."

"Ninety more! And another fifty!"

"Do it all!" The senior trader had sweat rings from his arms to his belt. No surprise there. If he was wrong, if this was a legitimate swing and not a late-afternoon gamble, this would be his last day on the floor. Every trader had a loss limit over which he or she could not stray, at least not for the end-of-day postings. Any time a trader approached the limit, especially this close to the week's final bell, he entered angina territory. "Who's the seller here?"

"No word."

Alex searched out a stray idler, pointing at the woman next to Eric. "You! Find out!"

The subordinate jammed knuckles, speed-dialing broker contacts.

Colin asked, "Shouldn't you be busy?"

"My markets have gone to sleep," Eric replied. He inspected his boards with idle satisfaction. "I'm a half mil up on the day and counting down to the first frosty glass. I'm gold."

Alex yelled, "Give me something!"

The trader next to Eric replied, "I've got my number one broker in Canada on the horn. She says it's definitely not Ottawa."

If it was the Canadian central bank effecting a move, all was lost. The senior trader hesitated, then ordered, "Hit the bid."

The junior trader's hair was a rat's nest. Her glasses slid along her sweat-slicked nose like a ski slope. "They're offering another fifty! And I've got sixty more coming from nowhere!"

His voice belonging to an adrenaline junkie, Alex ordered, "Hit them all."

There was a moment's breathless wait, a hush made stronger by all the noise that had come before. All the traders sat and watched the screens. The young female trader stared at Alex, searching frantically for the assurance that Monday she'd still have a desk. Then Eric stabbed a finger at his central screen and shouted along with two others, "Canada's falling!"

"How far?"

"Fifty, no, seventy-five."

"Down ninety!"

"I've got a buyer at a hundred off!"

Alex collapsed into his seat. "Sell it back. Clear the decks."

Colin glanced at his watch and reluctantly headed for the front door. If only he'd had the chance to share this scene with Lisa. He'd have explained how traders had no vested interest in the big picture. Traders could show no remorse for how their actions affected lives beyond this tightly enclosed world. Trading rooms didn't have windows so the outside universe had no way of disturbing the flow. So far as this world was concerned, if outside events were positive, traders made their bucks. If people got offed and dreams were crushed along with national economies, traders made different bucks. So long as the money rolled and markets moved, up was down and down was up.

Only Lisa was gone and there was only himself to entertain. But since everyone else was chattering, why not join in, in his own quiet way.

COLIN WAS BACK DOWNSTAIRS inside five minutes. The duration of his stay at the top of Everest was not the surprise factor here. Meetings with Hayek never lasted very long. But today Hayek's secretary had immediately ushered him inside, without the customary wait to remind him of his lowly grub status. Hayek had then grilled him about the Havilland woman. For a man controlling multiple billions to spend this much time on a lowly peon was beyond bizarre.

The downstairs front lobby was Friday-evening calm. Across from the elevators, the receptionist sat behind her desk buffing her nails. The pair of sofa sets flanking the front windows were empty, as was the carpeted stairway leading up to the trading room balconies. That was another strange thing about recent developments—how every day spawned more gray-suited goons unable to speak decent English.

Beyond the security doors, the trading floor was in cleanup mode. As soon as Colin appeared, Eric and his boss emerged from a cluster of spot traders and walked over. "The man goes upstairs just another electro-nerd," Eric taunted. "He comes down a stud muffin."

Colin stared at the one trader he might class as a pal. Eric's words made no more sense than Hayek's. Discordant random acts were becoming one solid mass, tearing through everything in its path. "What are you on about now?"

"Power, my man. Access. Fresh data. The keys to our world. They've been slipped into your mangy paw and you don't know enough to know you've been remade in the master's image."

"And you," Colin replied, "are seriously twisted."

"Absolutely. But it's still true." Eric leaned closer still. "The hoodoo beauty in Records was breathing hot over you, my man. Tell me you know who I mean."

"Mandy," Colin said. She was the talk of the entire Hayek team. A redheaded Popsicle with a polar glower. "That is nothing but myth and dangerous fabrication."

Alex broke in, pointing toward the empty balcony. "Your confabs with the King wouldn't have anything to do with the new realm up there, would it?"

"Not a hope." Colin turned his gaze upward. The parapet was empty for a change, the workers gone for the weekend.

"Come on, you can tell your old pal," Eric goaded him. "Word is, Hayek's bringing in a load of fresh meat. Fitting them out with data he's not sharing with the rest of us. You know what that means?"

"Yes." Colin understood the looks now. They saw him as part of a new threat.

"It means we're finished," Alex said. From this range the senior trader had the pungent odor of an electric fire. "The first in the know takes home the bacon. The rest get the street."

"I don't have any idea what's intended," Colin replied. Both traders responded with tight-eyed distrust. "Look, I don't know any more than you do."

Alex said, "So what is it exactly that you discuss with the King?"

"Fire walls. Security. The same as always. Only right now they're extremely amped about something. They're giving a ridiculous amount of attention to what anyone else would call smoke in the wind."

"They think somebody is breaking into our system?"

"I'd stake my life the shields are intact. My guess is they're planning something new. Something extremely large." Colin looked up at the mysterious parapet. "We're talking galactic war here."

Alex scratched his chin. "Could be this new fund Hayek mentioned a few days back. But why put them in a separate cage?"

Eric mused, "Wonder if this has anything to do with the gray goons we've got wandering around outside."

"I have no idea." Colin smarted over suddenly being classed as a foe. "But I'm fed up with the present state of affairs, I can tell you that."

Colin exited the trading floor by the front doors. The receptionist had packed it in for the week, and the foyer was empty. Checking out the upstairs balcony was a random act of madness, but he did not care. Actions like this used to drive Lisa crazy. But he had always enjoyed the odd moment of reckless abandon. He liked to call them the nerd's alternative to extreme sports. They were usually done on-line, but not always. Like now. Lisa had loathed these exploits, calling them acts of a forfeited life, indications of all the wrong turns he took inside himself. Colin had hated it when she began talking like that. But now she was gone, and the imaginary argument was all he had left.

The carpeted stairwell curved around the elevator shaft, rising to a newly formed antechamber. The air conditioner sighed softly. There was no other sound.

"In for a penny," Colin whispered, and pushed through the glass doors.

The balcony offices and the partitions were gone. The open space was now fitted with three rows of state-of-the-art trading desks and ergonomic chairs. Colin did a slow sweep of the room, stunned by the realization that they must have rewired the company's system so that all these new operations would be routed outside existing channels. Otherwise he would have noticed the traffic. He announced to the empty chamber, "This makes no sense whatsoever."

He walked over to the outer wall. The glass was so thick he could not hear a sound from the scene below. Heads popped up, gawking at him. But Colin had no answers for them. The mystery had only heightened.

With no notice or warning, Colin was abruptly hefted by the back of his shirt. He would have protested, but his throat was being sliced by his collar riding up and cutting off his wind. He was pulled back a fraction, then slammed cheek first into the glass wall.

A deep-chested grizzly voice roared in his ear, but the words were so mangled by a strange accent Colin heard only the anger and the force. Colin used one hand to try and pull his collar far enough from his throat to take a decent breath, and the other to pry his face from the wall. He might as well have attempted to lift the Hayek building.

The assailant pulled him back once more, far enough for Colin to see the imprint of his face in the glass. As the gray-jacketed goon started swinging him forward again, Colin tried to protest but could only manage a strangled "Aack." Then he was mashed flat once more. A bug on the windshield of life.

A voice from behind them demanded, "What's going on here?"

The goon spun Colin about, Colin's toes barely brushed the floor. He now faced Dale Crawford, head of Hayek's security team. Colin could hear the awful sound of his own choking and felt his chest burning with need. He tried in utter futility to pry off the iron-hard arm. Another moment and he was going to pass out.

The goon shook him like a puppet and growled his mangled version of English. The blue-suited security man moved forward. "This is one of the old man's chosen." To Colin, the security guard went on, "You're not permitted up here, Mr. Ready. This area is strictly off limits."

The goon growled something further and shook Colin so hard his teeth rattled in his skull.

"I said let the guy go." Just as the periphery of Colin's world began to blur, Crawford stepped forward and chopped down hard on the goon's arm.

Colin was unable to break his fall. His legs were little more than water and gossamer casings. He lay on his side and took the sweetest breath in his entire life, and struggled to his knees. Coughed. Wiped a string of dribble from his mouth. Coughed and breathed again. Looked up.

The blue suit was nose-to-nose with the goon. "You don't like it, why not take a piece of somebody who bites back."

The goon in gray roared and waved his fists. Crawford stayed in tight. "Guys like you make me puke." Without taking his eyes off his adversary, the security guy said, "You better clear on out of here, Mr. Ready."

Colin stumbled to his feet. One hand searched for whatever support was closest, the other held his throat. He stumbled from the room and blundered down the stairs. When he pushed through the trading doors, he endured gaping stares from the crowd that had watched his humiliation. Eric rushed over, took his arm, and helped him back to his cubicle. Colin's meager consolation was that nobody on the trading floor would ever again doubt on which side of the line he stood.

12

Friday

ON THE FLIGHT from Orlando to Reagan National Airport, Jackie found herself thinking of a list she and Preston had made, back when the money had first started coming in. Jackie had been pulling in about two and a half thousand a month, working overtime every chance she got, while Preston somehow crammed six years of school into three and a half. Preston had been too busy for girls most of the time. And Jackie despised how guys had assumed a girl with a high school equivalent and night school credentials would pant when they spoke the magic words, Porsche and a gold card.

Then Preston had gone to work for Hayek. His starting salary had been no great shakes for that industry, forty-six thou and change. For the next five months Jackie had pressured him, using every possible argument for him to quit that crazy job and go for something normal. She had wanted him to go back to school for his doctorate. She could support them for another couple of years, no problem. Then Preston had come home with his first bonus check.

She had arrived back from work and found him seated at the kitchen table. The house had been dead quiet, her brother's face waxy. He had explained how he had made a couple of bets for Mr. Hayek, predicting how the market was going to swing. He had insisted the pound was overvalued and sterling was going to plummet. He had convinced Hayek he was right, even when his calculations had gone directly against the chief trader's bets.

Jackie had seated herself across the table from her brother and repeated the one word, "Bets."

"Listen to what I'm telling you, Sis. I used this model I've cooked up and identified a clear disparity in the market. So I argued my case, and Hayek backed me. He told the senior trader to put a hundred and fifty down on my trend assessment."

"A hundred and fifty what?"

"Million dollars." The words were spoken with the ease of one utterly disconnected from reality, so calm Jackie's heart lurched for them both. "And we won. Big time." Preston pushed the envelope closer still. "It's my bonus check. Go on. Take a look."

The check was too big to fit inside that slender little envelope. Seventy-nine thousand nine hundred and twelve dollars. Jackie looked at her brother, wanting to tell him to take it and quit, put the tainted money to some decent use. But he was beaming now, happier than she could ever remember seeing him. "How did he get these numbers? I mean, twelve dollars, why not just round it up to eighty thou?"

He laughed, the sweetest sound in Jackie's universe. "Leave it to you to pour on the cold water. You know what this means, Sis? We're free."

"We'll be free when you find yourself a real job in the real world."

"You can quit your job. Finally go to school."

That froze her up solid. She could scarcely squeak, "What?"

"You don't think I've noticed how you've listened when I talk about school? Now's your chance to stop living your dreams through me and go for your own brass ring." He reached for the pencil she used to make her shopping lists, pulled the envelope back over. "We'll start a list. Things we're going to do. Not just talk about them. Do. Normal things."

"There's nothing normal about any of this."

"Careful now. You're almost sounding like Mom." He scribbled across the top end of the envelope, and said aloud, "Normal things. First on the list is Sis going back to grad school. Gainesville should do, you can commute, we'll get a house on the north end of town. That's number two. A house."

"We're fine here."

"This place is a dump. A house with a pool. You've been driving around looking at houses and neighborhoods for years." He looked up, pressing her with the eagerness of a kid the day before Christmas. "Come on, help me out here."

She was urged forward, not by her own desire, but his euphoria. "Vacation."

"There you go. Ship or plane?"

"Plane."

"Right. Mountains or ocean?"

"Mountains."

"You got it. Start packing, Sis, we're on our way."

She shook her head slowly back and forth, feeling then and there the unspoken threat, the gnawing worry. *This isn't real,* she thought, almost wishing it was so.

JACKIE STOOD OUTSIDE the Watergate Complex, wondering what to expect. Or pretend to be. She watched four couples emerge through the glass front doors, glittering in evening wear and jewels and musical prattle. Jackie forced herself up the stairs and into the brightly lit lobby. As she waited while the doorman called the Hutchings apartment, she wondered how people could grow so comfortable in their masks they stopped hearing all the lies they sang.

Upstairs, Esther Hutchings was the same woman Jackie had met before, only now she was utterly undone. The poise was shattered, her cashmere sweater heavily stained, her makeup streaked and two days old. "Come in. Sorry, the time has gotten away from me. Graham has had a very bad day."

"It's no problem." The living room was tasteful, the lighting muted, the oils on the wall no doubt original. The carpet was thick as a newly trimmed putting green. The upholstered furniture and the cushions and the silver-clad table were all perfect.

"My husband hates hospitals. He would rather die than go into a nursing home."

"I understand." Double sliding doors opened off the living room onto what had probably been a formal dining room. Paintings also hung on those walls, and additional silver ornaments stood upon other antique cabinets. Only this room now held a pneumatic hospital bed that could be electronically cranked to a hundred different positions. The kind necessary for someone who might never rise again. The back was pumped up so that the inhabitant could stare out over the dusk-washed Potomac. Jackie said, "You don't need to explain."

"No. I suppose I don't." Wearily Esther observed her husband. "He has good days and bad days. This one . . ."

"Hasn't been so good."

"Here, let me take your bag. Would you like something to drink? A coffee, perhaps?"

"Not if it's any bother."

Esther managed a tight little smile. "We keep a fresh pot charged at all times around here."

"A coffee would be great. Black."

"Just a moment." Esther took the back way and disappeared.

Jackie walked to the open double doors. She was not drawn by the figure in the bed so much as the man seated beside it. The visitor was ugly and overweight, and his carrot red hair grew in odd tufts. His shoes were stranded at the end of the bed along with his jacket and his briefcase. He was reading the *Washington Post* with the steady drone of someone who had been at it for quite a while. He did not look up until Jackie's shadow fell on the page. Then he said in greeting, "Graham understands every word."

"I'm sure he does."

"You know strokes?"

"My mother."

"Right. I remember. Esther told me." He offered a hand. "Carter Styles."

"Jackie Havilland. Do you do this every night?"

"My wife wouldn't permit that. Or my kids. I try to make it by a couple of times every week. I used to work for him."

But the look he gave the immobile man with the glittering dark eyes said that Esther's husband had been far more than a boss. And still was.

Jackie's eyes searched the room for something that would explain how a silent man with parchment skin could lie in this bed and command the world about him. How Graham Hutchings could grip this visitor so fiercely he would come and read the paper to a corpse.

A wooden cross hung directly in front of the bed. All the paintings in this room, Jackie now noted, were religious. The one over the glass balcony doors captured her. A figure holding a lantern stood at an ivy-clad door and knocked.

Carter Styles flipped over his paper, but did not resume his reading. Instead he asked, "So tell me what you see."

Jackie sensed Esther moving up behind her and knew the young man's words were some form of test. "The door doesn't have a handle."

"Which means?"

"Either the door was meant to stay shut," she mused aloud, "or it has to be opened from the inside."

Carter glanced to the woman behind her, said nothing. Esther touched Jackie's elbow. "Your coffee is ready."

Jackie nodded to the man in the bed, received a flickering shift of the gaze in reply. She followed Esther back into the living room and chose the sofa that would place her back to the sickroom. She needed to concentrate here.

Esther put the steaming cup on the table in front of her. "My husband was absolutely certain that the American fund managers and the Washington lobbyists were conspiring to emasculate our financial system's oversights and restrictions. Are you aware of the Ecuador currency crisis?"

The bone china was eggshell-thin, the aroma rich enough to shove the sickroom stench momentarily aside. "It happened just as I was leaving school. The professors were all certain it had been orchestrated."

"They were correct. Hayek was behind it."

Jackie set down her cup. "You're sure?"

"Of course not. If I were, we wouldn't be having this conversation. But Graham was certain enough to take this on as his mission in life." Hands unaccustomed to being idle straightened everything in reach—magazines on the table, throw cushions, the edge of the carpet, Jackie's own saucer. "Today's hedge fund operators and the investment bankers who front for them are nothing more than financial gunslingers. The forex traders are the worst of the lot. Of course you know what Soros did to the pound sterling and the financial markets of England."

"Yes." In other circumstances, Jackie would have found the woman's constant plucking and straightening enough to give rise to a good scream. But now, with the mantle of sorrow draped over those strong features, she could not help but reach over and settle her own hand upon Esther's. Showing her that she was not alone.

Esther stared down at the hand covering her own. Misery and fatigue smudged and slackened her face. "You can't imagine what it's like living with a man on a mission. I positively loathed it at times. I was jealous of his cause and everything that kept him from caring for me as much as he did all these other things." She blinked once. Twice. "And now it's all in my hands. Life is such a lover of cruel irony."

Before Jackie could form a response, the doorbell rang. Esther walked wearily to the door, glanced through the security peephole, and murmured worriedly, "Oh no. This is just too much."

Jackie rose to her feet as the door opened. Which proved a good thing, because she definitely did not want to meet this newcomer sitting down. The black woman who entered was as tightly coiled as she was perfect in poise and dress. Navy suit. Pearls. Graying hair done in a carefully clenched helmet. Determined chin, fierce dark eyes. With a linebacker's stride, she crossed the room and planted herself in front of Jackie. The woman demanded in a voice somewhere between alto and angry bass. "Is this her?"

"Kay, not tonight. Please, we've only—"

"I asked you a question, Esther."

She waved a weary hand of introduction. "Jackie Havilland, Kay Trilling."

"I can't believe you did this, Esther. You know Graham would be against it. As I am. *Totally* opposed."

"How did you find out?"

"Nabil called me. He, at least, thought I should know what was going on here."

"If you'd just sit down and hear what I've—"

"I have no intention of being taken in like the rest of you. It was wrong to draw her in, and doubly wrong to bring her here."

"Kay, this has been one of the worst afternoons Graham has had. The doctor was here for hours."

"All the more reason." She spun about. "I want a word with you in private."

"I'll call you tomorrow—"

"Now, Esther."

Esther sought her own fierce resolve but found too little to argue. "Let's move into the kitchen. Excuse us, please, Jackie."

Jackie turned and went back to the other room. Carter watched her approach with a blank expression. She demanded, "What did I miss in all that?"

"Senator Kay Trilling," Carter said. When that explanation was not enough, he added, "Lady doesn't mince words."

"I noticed."

"She and Graham—" He was cut off by the doorbell ringing once more. They stopped and listened for Esther, but heard only an argument rising from the kitchen. And the weak sputter of a cough from the bed.

Carter moved quickly for such an ungainly man. He padded around to the bedside table, shook the cup to make sure there was still liquid inside, then fitted the straw into the man's mouth. The doorbell rang a second time. Jackie asked, "Is it like this all the time?"

"A lot of people miss our Graham." Words spoken in the matter-of-fact tone of someone who lived with that fact night and day. "See who that is, will you?"

13

Friday

WHEN VALERIE CALLED and suggested they meet at the Longworth building entrance, Wynn protested, "I'm drowning in work here. I'm not going to be able—"

"Nonsense," she replied, and cut the connection.

Fifteen minutes later she called once more to announce in dulcet English tones that she was downstairs waiting for him. Wynn sat there a moment longer, hearing nothing save the rise of his own dread.

His footsteps rang empty and forlorn as he padded downstairs and passed the building security. Outdoors he discovered that night had slipped in and captured the world without his notice. Across the street, the Capitol was lit up like a crown of gold-flecked stone. The traffic sounds were muted, the sidewalks empty. As he appeared at the top of the stairs, the rear door of a limousine opened to reveal a pair of emerald-stockinged legs.

As Wynn slipped in beside her, she said, "A word to the wise, Congressman. Diligence is indeed a noble concept." Valerie's outfit this night was an elegant muted gray. She leaned one shoulder against the black leather upholstery and allowed her hair to spill over her arm. "But Fridays do arrive, even in Washington."

"I noticed. The place upstairs was a tomb."

"Well, of course it was. Not to mention the fact that the Easter break begins next Wednesday. Come Tuesday afternoon, you'll find tumbleweeds blowing down the empty streets of Capitol Hill."

The driver pulled from the curb and called back, "The Watergate, Ms. Lawry?"

"That is correct, Gene. Thank you."

As she pressed the button to roll up the glass divider, Wynn started in, "Valerie, listen—"

"Just a moment." When smoked glass sealed them in, she slid closer and revealed a smile as fetching as her perfume. "I can't tell you how much I've been looking forward to seeing you again, Congressman."

But he would not be put off. "I don't want to go up with you."

Her lips were dark and full as vintage port, begging to be tasted. She mocked him with her smile. "Not that old thing again. I thought we had this settled."

"You don't understand."

"On the contrary, Wynn, dear. *You* are the newcomer here. I am the one experienced at Washington tactics." She had the hands of a pianist, fingers long and perfectly straight, with nails painted the same tone as her lips. She dragged one across the back of his wrist. "We'll be in and out of the Hutchings' flat in a flash, then off to someplace you'll love. You can drown your sorrows in a fine Merlot and regale me with tales from the Dismal Swamp."

"The Dismal is in North Carolina."

"The Everglades, then. Someplace full of wild beasties and woodsmoke and big dangerous men." She waved a hand at the built-in bar. "Can I pour you a drink?"

"No." There was nothing for it, save the truth. "You don't understand. You can't. Esther and I go back a very long way. She was my late wife's best friend."

Valerie did something with her legs, making a pretense of wrapping her skirt more tightly about her thighs, yet drawing herself closer still, almost curling up against him without touching more than the back of his hand. "You lost your wife two years ago, isn't that correct?"

"How did you know?"

"I told you at the reception, Wynn dear. It is my job to know." She used her free hand to sweep the hair from her forehead. "So Esther will be delighted to see you."

"Not a chance." Except for fleeing the car, he saw no way to avoid disclosing, "Esther was the one who told me Dianne was ill."

"I beg your pardon?"

"We had separated about six weeks earlier. Dianne hadn't told more than a handful of friends about her illness. I was locked into a court battle and an acquisition and running an understaffed company."

Not the image returned then, but the feeling. Of tension stretching him out on the corporate rack until every sinew and brain cell shrieked from intolerable strain. Of sleeping in breathless gasps, jerking awake to jumbled images of having forgotten something vital, or missing an unseen attack. Of never being rested or drawing a comfortable breath. Not ever again. "I returned home. We stayed together until the end. It seemed right. I haven't seen Esther since Dianne's funeral."

He lifted his eyes to find Valerie watching him, so full of sympathy he could have buried his head in the perfumed veil of her hair and wept for all the bad moves and worse motives.

She leaned forward and kissed him gently. No passion, no pressure. Soft as evening's wind. There and gone.

The car pulled up and stopped. Without waiting for the driver to come around, Valerie slid out, then leaned back in and held out her hand.

Wynn had no choice but to rise and follow her inside.

The upstairs corridor was lined with antiques and had little brass-and-crystal chandeliers attached to the high ceiling. The carpet was thick enough to absorb all sound save that of Wynn's own faltering heart. It was not merely that he dreaded seeing Esther again. This contact dredged up memories of a terrible time and hinged them to whatever hopeful might appear in the here and now.

The door was opened by an attractive young woman. Not in Valerie's class, neither in looks nor style. But good-looking just the same. Her skin held the translucent quality possessed by a very few blonds. No makeup. Silk T-shirt of midnight blue, matching linen slacks, and soft leather boots. Nothing Washington or tony about this woman. Perhaps a few years younger than Valerie, with a timeless poise all her own. "Can I help you?"

Valerie spoke for them. "We're here to see Esther Hutchings."

"She's busy right now." She stepped aside and led them into the parlor. They could hear angry voices in the distance. "Would you like to have a seat?"

Once more, Valerie said for them both, "Thank you, but we won't be staying long."

"That is most *certainly* the case." Esther Hutchings did not so much step through the swinging door as blaze into the room. She ignored Valerie entirely as she careened towards Wynn. "What on *earth* are you *doing* here?"

"Hello, Esther." As the rear door swung back in the opposite direction, Wynn caught sight of a vaguely familiar figure seated at the kitchen table.

"You are an utterly *appalling* man."

"I'll go if you want. I just thought it would be nice to . . ." Then he caught sight of the two figures in the back room. "Is that Carter Styles?"

"*Nice?* Did I truly hear you use that word?"

Carter rose from his chair, neither welcome nor warmth to his gaze. He stood in his stockinged feet, the newspaper dangling from one hand. The figure in the bed did not move.

Esther Hutchings closed the gap between them. "Of all the words that I might use to describe your actions, *nice* is certainly not among them. Appalling, self-centered, loathsome, greedy, false . . . Shall I go on?"

"I'll leave."

"Perhaps I should have told you this at Dianne's funeral. I wanted to. But I couldn't bring myself to do it." She took another fraction of a step closer, until he had no option but acknowledge the stretched features, the flaming gaze. "Dianne knew she was ill. But instead of going in for treatment, she ignored the warning signs until it was far too late. She knew how you loathed weakness. But you left her anyway. You spotted the frailty, and you fled. She might have needed more than you were willing to give. Isn't that right."

"No."

"You sacrificed everything on the altar of your own success. You murdered her in all but name."

Carter said quietly from the other room, "Esther."

"And if that weren't enough, now you've accepted a nomination the governor had *no* business making. But it was convenient, wasn't it. The fact that it desecrates my husband's good name means nothing to anybody."

"That's not true."

"Oh, spare me. And to find you here on our tiny patch of hallowed ground . . ." She inched forward. "You are the utter embodiment of evil in my eyes."

"Esther," Carter repeated. "Enough."

"Yes, dear," said the woman pushing through the kitchen door. Wynn recognized her then. Senator Kay Trilling. Perfect. The senator went on, "Do calm down. Graham can hear you. Not to mention our other guest."

Esther backed off a fraction and turned to Valerie. "Do I know you?"

"Valerie Lawry, Mrs. Hutchings. I merely wished to stop by and express my condolences. I admired your husband very much."

"I doubt the feeling was reciprocated." This from Trilling. When Esther turned her way, the senator added, "Ms. Lawry is one of our K Street friends."

Esther turned back, not to Valerie but to Wynn. "You would bring this hired gun into my house?"

Wynn found minor solace in retreating toward the door. "Goodbye, Esther. I'm sorry. For everything."

The door slammed behind them and echoed in his brain during the silent ride back downstairs. When the elevator deposited them in the lobby, Valerie said, "You look pale as a ghost." When he did not respond, she continued, "Listen, my dear. Esther Hutchings is bitter over the loss of her social roost. I am sorry she took it out on you. But there it is. What shall be remembered is that you kept your cool, you paid your respects, you did your duty."

He wondered how the flames had managed not to touch her. "I'm sorry. I really need to get back to my hotel. There's no way I'd be good company tonight."

"I'll let you off this one time," she said. "But only if you agree to do dinner with me tomorrow."

"I can't. I'm attending a conference in College Park and I don't know when I'll be done."

"Not that silly thing on debt relief. The issue is utterly passé."

"I said I'd go."

"Washington is like Hollywood on that score. 'Let's do lunch' is not an invitation but a polite form of farewell." When he did not respond, she pressed, "Sunday, then."

"Sure."

Valerie showed faint amusement over his shaken state. "You really must grow thicker skin if you are going to swim the Washington social waters." She motioned toward the car. "Can I at least offer you a lift?"

But Wynn was already moving away, searching for the nearest shadow dark enough to swallow him whole.

□ □ □ □

AFTER THE VISITORS DEPARTED, Jackie took a seat by the back wall. The air was sharp with the smell of scorched flesh. She'd had a lifetime's experience avoiding the aftershocks of anger and wanted nothing more than to be away.

But the room was no longer a dangerous place. The atmosphere, though still highly charged, was not unfriendly. Senator Trilling walked over and hugged Esther fiercely. The two women clung together for a long moment. Then the senator stepped back and spoke in a voice entirely different from the one she had used upon her arrival. "Are you all right, dear?"

"Nothing is all right." Broken and weary now. "Are you attending tomorrow's conference?"

"I can't. We're working flat out this weekend, finishing up last-minute details. I leave for Cairo on Thursday."

Carter Styles remained standing between the living room and the immobile figure in the bed. "Wynn Bryant is going to be in College Park."

That turned both women around. "What?"

"A pair of OEOB flunkeys put it to him Wednesday. Wanted him to go to Cairo, too. He accepted only for tomorrow."

The senator planted fists on both hips. "And precisely when were you planning on telling us?"

"Don't look at me like that," Carter replied, utterly unfazed. "You were the one who came in here with both guns blazing."

Kay Trilling glanced toward Jackie, showing the evening's first hint of uncertainty. Esther asked Carter, "Why didn't you mention this to me?"

"You already had enough on your plate. I had no idea Wynn was going to show up. Besides, right now you need to be focusing on tomorrow."

Kay Trilling turned back. "Tomorrow?"

Esther looked stricken by the coming confession. "We're moving Graham to a hospital in Fairfax. They want to do some new scans. If it turns out to be what they think, they'll operate immediately."

"Oh, Esther."

"Apparently he's not responding as he should. His deterioration suggests something other than a stroke. They don't hold out much hope, but it's better than seeing him locked inside the prison of his own body. You know how he would hate this."

Kay asked faintly, "What are his chances?"

Esther merely stared at the figure lying in the bed.

Carter spoke for them both. "She's doing the right thing, Kay."

Jackie watched as the senator walked to the bed, settled a hand upon the inert shoulder, and said, "I pray for you each and every day, Graham."

To Jackie's astonishment, Carter said, "Maybe you should give Ms. Havilland a chance, Kay."

The senator remained leaning over the bed. "Why should I?"

Carter gave a minute shrug. "Graham always said he'd take Esther's hunches over a full-on staff analysis any day." When the senator did not speak, he went on, "Just pray on it. I know that's what Graham would tell you."

Senator Trilling leaned closer to the head with the bright staring eyes. "Please get up and get well, Graham. I don't think I can do this without you."

"He's just resting up for the big push," Carter said, directing his words toward Esther, who had not moved from her place near the door. Carter folded his paper and reached for his shoes. "Just getting ready for the next battle on the floor."

The senator turned and walked back into the living room, where she glared at Jackie, then enfolded Esther into another embrace. "I'm so sorry."

"Don't be."

"These days everything I do seems either wrong or not enough." Trilling walked to the door and left without another word.

Carter approached Esther. "I'll see you at nine."

"Yes. All right."

He patted her arm, gave Jackie a swift nod, then let himself out. The room seemed to expand a fraction and take an easier breath. Esther sighed her way over to the sofa. "Please forgive us."

Jackie moved over to the neighboring settee. "There's nothing—"

"Graham was the first man I ever met who cared nothing for my money. Oh, he enjoyed it enough. But it had no hold over him. I was utterly fascinated by his indifference to wealth. I had spent a lifetime building barriers to keep out people who only pretended to care about me. Yet here was this man, dashing and fiery and full of ideas, who had no time for my airs or my reserve."

Jackie listened, knowing the words were not really meant for her at all. The older woman was simply trying to knit the fabric of her world back together. Esther continued to direct her gaze and her words toward the empty fireplace. "Graham refused to permit me to hide away. He could be positively brutal in his impatience. What he saw in me, why he forced me to open up, what he expected to find . . ." She turned so she could glance at the bed, seeing another time, another man. "I should have been more ready for this. I should have prepared myself better. Learned more. Become stronger."

Jackie waited long enough for the silence to press down on them both, then asked, "What do you want me to do?"

"There's a seminar at the University of Maryland tomorrow," Esther replied. "I was supposed to represent Graham. Now I'll have to be at the hospital. But somebody needs to go and observe the enemy's movements."

"You mean the congressman who was just here?"

"Wynn Bryant. Yes. A terrible man."

"I'll go," Jackie said. "It's no problem."

But the offer only left Esther more sorrowful. "I'm counting the hours and watching the sand fall. And I'm helpless to do anything that matters. Everything my husband fought for is threatening to unravel, unless I can find someone to champion his cause."

14

Saturday

WYNN AROSE LATE and took the day's paper and several files downstairs with him. He ordered a full breakfast to make up for the dinner he had not eaten the night before. The Willard's main dining room was a beaux arts masterpiece, the chamber's sweeping scope magnified by rich colors and gold leaf. People came and went, waiters bustled in hushed efficiency, daylight traced a silent timeline across the carpeted floor and linen-draped tables. He reread the Jubilee Amendment file but found it impossible to understand. The file assumed a background knowledge that he simply did not possess. When the lunch crowd finally began to trickle in, Wynn went by the front desk to request a car, then returned upstairs to call his sister. He got the Saturday switchboard operator at the governor's mansion, a recorded message on Sybel's cellphone, and no answer at all on their private number. He returned downstairs to find a new Lincoln and driver waiting by the front doors.

At his request, the driver took the Rock Creek Parkway, where Wynn was surrounded by a mint green world and the fragrances of springtime and rushing waters. Along both sides of the highway, dogwoods and tulip poplars offered cloud puffs of childlike peace. Wynn rolled down his window and set his face to the breeze, but found himself unable to shut out Esther's echoing tirade. His mind probed with the precision of a tongue moving across an aching tooth.

College Park was an aging middle-class town located out beyond the Goddard Space Center. The university itself was big and flat and sprawling, composed of redbrick buildings with white-pillared porticoes whose former gentility was sliding into urban seediness. As they drove through the university campus, Wynn used his cellphone again to try and raise his sister. Sybel was usually fastidious about remaining in touch. Wynn let the private upstairs phone ring at least a dozen times. Nothing. As they pulled up in front of the assembly building, Wynn called back to the main switchboard. The operator claimed to know nothing of Sybel's movements and said only that Governor Wells had left strict instructions not to be disturbed. Wynn rose from the limo with yet another unanswered question for his collection.

He climbed the stairs and entered a large outer chamber filled with people and coffee-break clatter. If the gathering found anything incorrect in his arriving six hours late, they did not show it. As soon as Wynn gave his name, he was surrounded. Eager faces and outstretched hands pressed in from all sides.

A beefy man in a wrinkled suit finally pushed his way forward. "Congressman Bryant, did I get that name right? We only heard yesterday you'd be coming. Couldn't believe it, to tell the truth. Reverend Dan Freedburg. Great to have you."

Wynn allowed the guy to pump his hand, then spotted a blond woman cruising in close behind the pastor. It was the young lady from Esther's living room. The wince gathered in his gut and rose slowly. But the woman did not speak. She merely stood there and watched.

"Really great you'd take the time to be here, especially your first week in office. But I guess we shouldn't have expected anything less from Graham's replacement. Only wish you had been elected earlier." The pastor grabbed Wynn's arm and turned back, saying to the crush, "Give us a little room, people. We'll all have a chance to speak to the congressman soon enough."

Wynn was distinctly aware of the blond woman trailing his movements. "Why earlier?"

"Because of his first stroke. The doctors warned him if he didn't slow down he'd be done for. We begged him to resign. But he wouldn't let the cause go. No surprise, I suppose. You know how Graham is."

"No," Wynn corrected. The blond woman was so close he could smell her, fresh soap and something natural. Lavender perhaps. "I don't."

That halted Freedburg. "Don't what?"

"I hardly know Graham Hutchings," Wynn said, determined to enter this without pretense of any kind. "And I know nothing about his cause."

The pastor did not look surprised so much as stricken. Wynn went on, "Two White House staffers asked me to come today. I'm here to listen and to learn. If you'll let me."

The gathering gave off a single unified sound, somewhere between a sigh and a lament. "Then you don't know anything," the pastor said slowly, "about the Jubilee Amendment?"

"The name, nothing more."

"So you're not here to address us."

"To be honest, I'd just as soon you not introduce me at all." The pastor looked so wearied by his words, Wynn repeated, "Like I said, I'm here because I'm interested in learning more."

"I'm sorry, Congressman. If you don't already know, I doubt seriously you can be brought up to speed fast enough to do us any good." He waved toward the main hall. "You're welcome to sit in, of course."

The pastor and most of the others trickled away, leaving Wynn standing by the entrance to the assembly room. People continued to drift by, giving him bitter looks. Only the blond woman remained close by. Despite the surroundings, Wynn found himself captivated by the young woman's gaze. The thought in his head was, Cop's eyes. Wide and absolutely alert. An expression that said no matter what he might do, no matter how deranged, she would not be surprised.

Wynn asked, "Esther told you to shadow me?"

The woman said merely, "That's right."

"Esther will be pleased to hear I've disappointed another crowd." He walked to an aisle seat midway back. The woman hesitated, then came over and seated herself beside him. Wynn offered his hand. "Wynn Bryant."

Small fingers with an almost masculine strength took hold swiftly, then released. "Jackie Havilland."

"You've known Esther long?"

Her gaze was steady and unyielding. "I'm not worth your worrying over, Congressman. And I hate small talk worse than anything."

"Take your seats, if you would, please, let's get restarted." The beefy pastor stood by the podium and waited for the din to subside, then continued, "I've just spoken with the hospital. Graham's operation is scheduled for seven this evening. I know a lot of you will want to be praying for him and Esther."

Wynn asked the Havilland woman, "Surgery?" But she waved him away like a buzzing pest.

The pastor went on, "Congressman Wynn Bryant, Graham's replacement, is here with us today. Raise your hand, please, Congressman. There he is. I'm sure some of you will want to go by and make him feel welcome." The announcement brought the pastor no pleasure. "You know we had hoped for Esther to be here with us this afternoon, to speak on her husband's behalf. But that's not going to be possible. So we've arranged to close with a recording from an earlier assembly, one a lot of us here won't soon forget." He craned and searched the back of the room, asked, "We ready yet?"

An unamplified voice called back, "Thirty seconds."

"Fine. Most of us consider Graham Hutchings a fallen hero, a martyr to the cause. He is also a dear friend. I'm sorry he's not here with us today, more sorry than I'd ever be able to express. But perhaps this video will help instill in us the fire we need to go on."

As the pastor stepped away from the podium and walked to an empty seat on the front row, Wynn leaned over and asked, "Any chance you can tell me what this Jubilee thing is about without biting my head off?"

There was nothing halfway about this woman, not even the way she studied him. "You don't know?"

"All I know," Wynn said, not wanting to risk anything but the truth, "is a lot of people want to see this thing go away. I've got a whole pile of questions and not a single answer."

"The Jubilee movement has been around for a couple of years," Jackie replied quietly, facing front. Giving him a profile of hard angles and blond-tinted skin. "It's a worldwide effort to reduce the debt carried by third-world nations. Over two dozen countries currently spend more on interest payments than they do for education and health care. American banks have fiercely resisted any attempt to write down these debts. Legislation has been enacted, but the appropriations have remained tied up in committee. The banking lobby has fought tooth and nail to kill these bills. The politicians have gone along with it, since they can point to the laws and claim they're doing something to help out. But without funding, the laws remain empty promises."

Wynn declared softly, "This doesn't make any sense."

"What doesn't?"

But the screen lit up again, and Graham Hutchings' face appeared. The lights dimmed, and Wynn asked his question to the shadows. Something wasn't right here. He was being struck from all sides—the governor, a senator, his own aides, White House flunkeys, the party chief, and for what? How much money could they be talking about here? A billion in debt relief? Okay, it was a lot, but less than what America spent on defense in a day. A billion or even twice that wasn't enough to generate this kind of heat.

The image that flashed on the screen was of a very different Graham Hutchings from the man Wynn had seen the night before. One not so much younger as *energized,* a world away from the living corpse trapped on the bed. "I am not going to mince words. I have come to the cause of financial reform from a completely different direction than most of you here. My intention has never been to serve the unwashed hordes of other nations. I am here to serve the people who elected me, and the nation I love and call my own. But it so happens that our aims coincide, yours and mine. You say we stand on a financial precipice. I agree. You speak of nations far beyond our shore. I speak of the here and the now. Our problem, ladies and gentlemen, is the same. Our foe is identical.

"Today, all ten of the largest U.S. banks receive more than half their profits from dubiously named 'investment banking' divisions. In truth, these divisions have nothing whatsoever to do with investments in the classical sense. They are paper traders. They deal in currencies, commodities, options, bundled mortgages, interest-rate spreads, corporate tax write-offs. Any number of such deviant aberrations of the banking industry's original purpose. The name given to this and a myriad of other high-risk actions is *derivative trading*.

"After the horrors of the 1929 Wall Street crash, our nation enacted laws to ensure that the level of risk taken by banks would be tightly controlled. But during my time in Washington, I have watched the banking industry and their sister organizations, the fund managers, use every trick in the book to subvert the will of the people and their elected officials. Through carefully worded amendments slipped into crucial pieces of legislation, the banking lobby has stripped away virtually the entire system of checks and balances set in place after the crash of twenty-nine."

Wynn cast a swift glance around him. The rapt audience came from every walk of life. There were numerous priests, pastors, and nuns. The hall itself was tawdry and as unimpressive in Washington terms as the people. He recalled the derisive comments of the White House lackeys and felt anger and agreement both.

"The worst risk takers of them all, ladies and gentlemen, are known as hedge funds. Hedge funds operate on very thin margins and take huge gambles, particularly within the currency markets. When they are successful, they make enormous profits. When they fail, the losses can be catastrophic. Why? Because the investors are not only liable for whatever amount they have invested in the fund. They are liable for *everything the fund loses*. There is *no limit* to their total exposure. Does that sound correct to you? Does that sound *sane*? Of course not. So up until a few years ago, hedge funds could not operate within the United States. Investors had to track them down in places such as the Bahamas or Bermuda or Liechtenstein or Singapore. But our banks watched these potential profits going elsewhere and had their lobbyists press Congress for another one of these little amendments. So now, lo and behold, not only are hedge funds operating within our borders, the largest of them are now owned by *our banks*. Only they don't call them hedge funds. Oh no. They are known as 'private equity funds,' and are operated within these investment banking divisions. As if that would make them safe. As if the risk is not still catastrophic.

"The dangers of such institutions are enormous. When Long Term Credit, a Wall Street hedge fund operated by two Nobel Prize winners, collapsed recently, nobody even knew how much outstanding debt they carried. Do you hear what I am saying? *Nobody knew.* And who was their largest investor? One of the country's biggest consumer banks. One of the cornerstones of our financial community had given a credit line to this group, and suddenly found itself facing a *mountain* of debt. How much? At the critical point, when the LTC meltdown was at its peak, it is said they faced *sixty billion dollars* in assumed liability. Enough to bring it crashing down. And that was just one hedge fund. Six of our top ten banks now operate hedge funds in-house. There are over fifty within our borders. Carrying how much risk? Who knows? Our federal reserve system certainly doesn't. Why? Because at this point the hedge fund industry and the derivatives trading industry are both *totally uncontrolled.*"

Wynn could see now why Hutchings had suffered his strokes. The man did not speak, he *raged*. He flailed his arms and he pounded the podium. He shouted his ire. The longer he spoke, the more furious he became. It was the performance of a man on the edge.

"Banks have utterly forgotten their creed to serve the clients entrusting them with their money. Banks are no longer there to serve the local community. Profits from such ventures are too small, too regulated. Banks are responsible first and foremost to their shareholders, most of whom could not care less about the banks' traditional role. So banks spend hundreds of millions of dollars, not just in America but all over the developed world, subverting the laws established after the first Great Depression. In the minds of many people far more knowledgeable than myself, it is only a matter of time before a second depression strikes.

"My premise, ladies and gentlemen, is simple. International hedge funds have become the demons of the globalization process. Those banks that have become mired in derivatives and hedged operations are time bombs waiting to explode. They threaten to demolish our entire economic well-being in the process. Globalization is good only so long as it *serves*. Globalization must *earn* its place in the world. How? By improving and stabilizing economies."

The speech was then interrupted by loud cheers and applause. It took Wynn a moment to realize the tumult was both recorded and live. Hutchings' response was interesting. He showed a great impatience as he waited through the interruption. The applause was not his intention here. He *burned* with the need to go on.

"But these so-called investment bankers don't *want* stability. Stability means balance and predictability, and this kills any chance for extreme profits. Hedge funds and derivatives traders all hold one point in common: *They feed on instability.* They want *chaos*. They *want* dramatic swings. And where they can, they will foster even greater swings. These so-called investment bankers act with utter disregard for the effects of their conduct on the small and the defenseless. It is a replay of the Roaring Twenties, now performed on a global scale. They are the barbarian hordes, threatening the empire with oblivion. They have to be reigned in. They *must* be tamed."

Wynn's final view of Hutchings was cut off by the people in front of him rising to their feet. As the lights rose over the assembly, Wynn caught sight of many faces staring into the now-blank screen with a tragic sense of lost hope and failed dreams. Yet they applauded still, shaming him with their sad fervor.

He turned to the woman beside him and asked, "What does all this have to do with third-world debt?"

But Jackie Havilland rose and left without a word or a backward glance. And the others applauded still.

15

Sunday

JACKIE'S SUNDAY MORNING began with a surprise all its very own. Kay Trilling called and asked if she wanted a ride to the hospital where Graham was recovering from surgery. Jackie's precoffee brain had difficulty wrapping itself around both the words and the woman's tone. Trilling did not sound friendly, but she certainly had lost her hostile edge. Jackie said, "Recovering?"

"Apparently Graham didn't have a stroke at all. The doctors are now calling it a subdural bleed. The important thing is he might recover. Graham is still with us. For the moment, that's enough."

"Where are you?"

"Outside in the hotel lot. Are you dressed?"

"Five minutes."

"I'll get you a coffee. How do you take it?"

"Black."

"I'm driving a gray Buick."

Jackie was down in three. Kay Trilling stepped from the car, handed over the cup, said in greeting, "I woke you up, didn't I."

"It's no problem." She peeled off the top, took the first welcome sip, and scouted the empty lot. "Where's your entourage?"

"You were expecting the senator to have a dark limo and a few Secret Service in tow?" Today Trilling was dressed in a pastel silk knit suit. She had the sleek look of a woman who battled daily against her age. "That just happens in the movies. In real life, senators and congressmen don't rank so high. Only presidents and cabinet members get such perks."

"Tell me about Graham."

"Apparently a subdural is a slow venous bleed in the membranes between the brain and the skull. A few weeks back, Esther found him laid out in the bathroom with a bump on his head. Everybody, including the doctors, assumed it was a second stroke. The scan showed nothing but the damage apparently from the first stroke, which can happen with these things."

Nothing could be done about the thrust of Trilling's jaw, the aggressive set of her shoulders, the way her hands wrestled the wheel, the force of her foot on the pedal. She drove with masculine impatience, holding to the inside lane, paying no attention to the speed limit. With the world hurtling past, Trilling went on, "The doctors say these subdurals keep drawing in other fluid once the actual bleeding stops. This forms a hematoma, and the thing just keeps getting bigger. What alerted them to a possible misdiagnosis was how Graham kept going downhill. This isn't common with strokes, but is with subdurals. So they drilled a hole in his skull, drained the fluid, and now we're waiting to see just how much he recovers."

Trilling waited until they were across the Potomac and heading onto the freeway to ask, "How did it go yesterday in College Park?"

Jackie gave her a slow look. No question from a woman this intense could be called casual. Nor had Jackie forgotten the hostility enveloping their last contact. "If you don't mind, I think I should wait and report to Esther."

"Loyalty. I like that in a person. So what did they do when Esther didn't show up?"

"They played a video of one of the congressman's earlier talks."

"Which one?"

"The perils of hedge funds and modern banking."

"I remember that. Landed him in a world of hot water. Graham never did learn how to mince words." A swift glance. "What did you think of it?"

Wrenching. No other word would do. Not just because of the passion in Hutchings' voice, or the fact that the topic was intimately close to her own studies. The assembly's response, their fervor and depth of passion, had made her ashamed of her own limited horizons.

The senator was still waiting for her response. Jackie asked, "Are you married?"

If the senator found the change of subject startling, she gave no sign. "Twenty-eight years next month. He's an insurance broker. And the reason I stay sane. One daughter, she's been a sophomore at

Stanford for four years. Majors in lost causes. Last year it was strip mining, this year it's ending the reign of some South American dictator, I forget which. What about you?"

"No."

Another glance, this one timed to a switch across lanes, a marginal lowering of their breakneck speed. The senator aimed for the off-ramp and asked, "A man?"

"Not for over a year."

"That bad?"

Worse than bad. A prince charming who grew into a nightmare demon. Shane was locked away now, caged like the beast he was. And still he terrified her. "That bad."

Trilling had the ability to be as spare with her expressions as her words. A single tight grimace, there and gone. "A lot of them out there. It horrifies me, all the risks my daughter doesn't see."

The journey took them through an endless suburban sprawl. From the freeway they took a stoplight-riddled asphalt ribbon to nowhere. Clusters of stores and condos reluctantly gave way to housing developments and a few trees fortunate enough to have missed the bulldozer's scouring. There was no order or center upon which the mind could rest easy, just haphazard bands of habitation through which they drove and drove and drove. A light mist began to fall, robbing the place of season as well as style.

The Fairfax County Hospital was just another building off just another road. Jackie waited while Kay Trilling made her way to the information desk, then followed her up to the third floor. The hallway outside Graham Hutchings' room was jammed with people of every race, walk, and status. Jackie searched the group but did not see Esther. She watched as Kay Trilling approached and was enveloped by arms and greetings. Jackie selected an empty wooden bench back from the fray, resuming the same spot she had occupied most of her life—on the outside looking in.

She sat and listened to the throng's attempt to be quiet. Watched the intensity of their expressions when Esther Hutchings exited the hospital room. Saw how they gathered tightly together, barely giving Esther room to reach over and hug the senator. Best buddies now. The argument of two nights ago apparently forgotten. Esther spoke in whispers, which were passed along. Jackie watched the crowd's tension ease a notch farther. One thing was definitely coming clear. These people were not an easy-living crowd. Many of their confessions would no doubt be as wrenching as her own. Yet they managed to confront the calamity of living with compassion and determination; Jackie wanted that for herself.

Esther had separated herself from most of the group and was deep in conversation with the senator. The women measured Jackie with grave gazes, then walked over together.

Esther seated herself and demanded, "How are you, dear?"

"I should be asking you that."

Esther bore the features of the emotionally drained. "Graham is better. We won't know how much better for another couple of days. But the surgery seems to have improved the circulation in his brain."

"I'm glad." The words were not enough. "I heard him speak yesterday."

"The evil banking empire address," the senator offered.

"I hated it whenever he gave that speech. He always looked ready to explode by the end of it. He used it quite a lot. Too often for his own good. How was the assembly?"

"You mean, how was Congressman Bryant?" Jackie watched Senator Trilling seat herself on Esther's other side, and addressed her directly. "You didn't just happen by my hotel and offer me a ride."

"I needed to know," Trilling replied, "what you wouldn't tell me."

"Congressman Bryant wasn't at all what I expected. He didn't seem to have any idea what he was doing there."

"He made no move for the limelight?" This from Trilling.

"He specifically refused to address the group. He didn't even want to be introduced. He chose a seat midway back."

Esther asked, "Did he say anything?"

"He asked me what the Jubilee movement was all about. When I told him, he said it didn't make sense."

"What didn't?"

"He wouldn't say."

The two older women exchanged worried glances. It was the senator who reluctantly said, "Maybe Sybel is right."

"I still don't trust him," Esther replied, too weary for rage. "The man is a menace to everything we stand for."

"Sybel doesn't think so." The admission brought Kay Trilling no comfort. "And we both trust her judgment above almost anyone's."

"I'm sorry," Jackie said. "Who is Sybel?"

"Wynn's sister," Esther said, her mind elsewhere. "Sybel Bryant Wells."

The name rang all sorts of bells. "The wife of Governor Wells?"

But the pair were already moving on to other concerns. "I hate how she's maneuvered us."

Trilling gave another of her swift smiles. "Like you maneuvered us over Ms. Havilland?"

"That was different."

"It always is."

"I suppose we'll need to send someone. Passing Sybel's message to her brother isn't something we can handle over the phone."

"Don't look at me," Trilling said. "It's one thing for Sybel to make these pronouncements, and another to get me publicly involved."

"How about Carter?"

"Not a chance. He's as busy as a one-armed paper hanger with a seven-year itch. He's personally reviewing all the material I'm taking to Cairo. Not to mention the fact that he loathes Wynn more than you do."

"I suppose," Esther said reluctantly, "I could ask Nabil to go for us."

"He'll do it," Trilling agreed. "But he's only met Wynn once, and that was in my office. We argued. Nabil is a formal sort of guy. You'll need to arrange an introduction."

Two pairs of eyes refocused upon Jackie.

Jackie raised a hand to halt Esther before she could begin. "First there's something I need cleared up."

Esther grew even more uncomfortable. "We could be here for days, trying to answer your questions."

"Just one point now. The rest can wait." She sought to remove the sting with a soft tone. "Why did you hire me?"

Even spoken as it was, the query drew a wince from the exhausted woman. Jackie resisted the urge to reach out, tell her to forget it, this didn't matter any more. She wasn't angry, not even now that she already knew the answer. She just needed to hear it said, have a level of honesty established on all sides.

"I had no idea," Esther said, "we would ever get to this point."

"I was a lure." Jackie spoke the words so Esther would not have to. "Just to see if they were still tracking you and the movement."

"Not anymore," Esther replied. "This is important work, and you are an important part of our team."

"But in the beginning," Jackie pressed as softly as she could. "I was tied like bait to the end of a pole."

"Done in utmost secrecy," Esther said, regret in her face, her tone, her stricken gaze. "Hoping you would never be noticed."

"But I was." Thinking aloud now. Fitting the fragments together. "They came after me and ransacked my apartment, which means they still consider you a threat."

"Us," Esther corrected. "Consider us a threat."

"So it wasn't just your husband they were worried about. Isn't that it? You needed to know whether they were worried about more than your Graham."

"They would never have come after someone so far removed from the Washington scene," Esther quietly agreed. "Not if this were just a battle over legislation we have less chance of enacting with every passing day."

"They're worried about us finding something out," Jackie said. "Which means time is important here. Important enough for them to show their hand when they learned I was sniffing around."

"She's good," Trilling murmured, not liking the taste of those words, but saying them just the same. "Very good indeed."

"There's something you need to know," Jackie said. She told them about the contact made upon stormy Intracoastal waters by a young man who had no idea how to handle this craft.

When she finished, the two women pondered briefly. Trilling said, "Boatman doesn't mean a thing to me. Or the description. Maybe it was one of Sybel's people."

"We can't worry about that now." Esther drew herself up and addressed Jackie directly. "We need to invite Wynn Bryant to Rome over the congressional spring recess. And we want you to go with him."

Jackie found the last segment impossible to grasp. So she focused on, "I don't have any problem with helping out. But it seems to me a U.S. congressman will have his own agenda. Which I imagine doesn't include a last-minute jaunt to Rome."

"Oh, Wynn is going," Trilling said. "Sybel has already arranged that. We just want to make it official."

16

Sunday

SUNDAY EVENING Wynn took a taxi from the Willard to Georgetown. The earlier misty rain had departed, so he had the driver drop him a few blocks from the restaurant where he was meeting Valerie. He walked the garish length of M Street, taking in the good-time crowds and the stores and the music that hammered out of every open door. The young and affluent swept by, all wearing the masks of people determined to believe almost anything, so long as it brought them what they wanted.

Midway down the restaurant's side street, Wynn slowed and called his sister for the fifth time that day. The switchboard operator not only recognized his voice but had grown to share a little of his concern. No, she did not know where the governor's wife was. No, the governor was still not available. No, she had not passed on his messages because the governor had neither called nor come in. Then, realizing she should not have admitted such a thing, the operator cut him off. Wynn continued down the lane, digesting just how much he had taken Sybel's open line of communication for granted.

The Ristorante Piccolo occupied a tiny Federal house lit with gas lanterns. Through lead-paned windows Wynn saw an intimate interior whose tables displayed sparkling crystal and napkins with stiff linen wings. The place offered all the charm that Georgetown claimed but seldom delivered.

Valerie was waiting for him at a table by the front window. She stood to greet him, revealing a thigh-length sheath of softly clinging beige. She kissed his cheek and said, "You like?"

"Very much."

"It doesn't rank high on the political power list. But the food is excellent and the rooms are small and intimate."

"Oh. You're talking about the restaurant."

She wrinkled her nose, her expression somewhere between a smile and an invitation. Once again, more softly this time, she asked, "You like?"

He still had his hand on the curve of her waist. "It's like holding a cloud."

"The material is called pashmina. A mixture of silk and cashmere." She took a pair of steps and a half-turn. Wynn thought she looked like a dancing fawn. "What would you like?"

Only then did he realize the waiter was watching and grinning hugely. "A minute to catch my breath."

When they were alone, she said across the table, "You looked so worried when you came in."

"I can't raise my sister. She's always available. Always."

"Sybel Bryant Wells. Quite a lady, by all accounts."

"I can't get over how much you know about me."

"You're a person of power, Congressman. Knowing who you are also includes knowing who can reach out and touch you. Friends, family close associates, allies, enemies. Ever since your nomination we've had our gophers at work, building your file." Valerie studied his face. "When you arrived, I thought you still might be bothered by the other night at the Hutchings' apartment."

"I am."

Valerie reached up and stroked a wayward hair from his forehead. "Poor little fellow. Still feeling a little singed?"

"More than a little."

"Then I'd say Esther Hutchings has received the fate she deserves." She changed the subject by opening her menu. "Shall I order for us?"

Wynn knew she was playing the mood, controlling the flow. Not minding in the least. "You are one impressive lady."

She matched the candle's glow with her own, a look broken off only by the waiter's reappearance. Wynn listened to her discuss the evening's choices and instruct the waiter as if he were one of her personal staff. When she turned back and saw his expression, she said merely, "What?"

"I was thinking," he replied, "I could do worse than put myself in your care."

That was enough to have her reaching across the table, taking one of his hands with both of hers. "A dream come true for every lobbyist the length and breadth of K Street."

The constant intermingling of business and intimacy was very jarring, very Washington. "Where would you take me if this was business?"

"It depends."

"On what?"

"Whether I wanted the world to know we were together." Her look was a subtle invitation, overlaying the words with a second unspoken message. "For the public meeting, I'd probably select La Citronelle. Ultradull outside, ultrasuede inside. A hundred and fifty a head plus wine. Top French chef. Waiters who love to play the unnamed source to the *Post*. Great place to leak secrets, let the chief whip know you've defected to the opposing team."

"And if it were a secret?"

"A private room at the Hay Adams. Or the Mayflower. A butler to usher you in, take your coat, guard the door. We'd sweep for bugs, then talk in whispers. And always assume that somehow the secret won't stay secret for very long."

"So what's a nice girl like you—"

She slid her hands away. "Stop. Please. Sarcasm doesn't become you."

"All right. Why Washington?"

"That's better. Honesty always, Wynn. There's almost none of it in our game. So let's have it between us."

"Okay. Fine."

"I love D.C. Always have. My father was chargé at the British embassy back in the early eighties. Leaving was temporary. I knew I'd come back and make it my home."

"Why?"

"Because it's so fresh. Vibrant and new and utterly alive. You don't know how rare that is in a capital. European capitals are so buried in history and tradition, any hint of freedom is utterly crushed. And Africa, what a dismal place. Asia is almost as bad, all those would-be potentates utterly terrified of change. Believe me, Washington is unique. This place reinvents itself every four years. Democracy in the electronic age. Give yourself a few months, you'll understand."

Over dessert Valerie asked him about the previous day's conference, and heard him out in the intent silence of a professional listener. Then she dismissed everything he said with, "They're typical of the well-intentioned losers who populate the wastelands out beyond the Beltway. Forget them, Wynn. They don't matter."

"Graham thought they did."

"I can see you were affected by his speech. I've heard it too. Passion is infectious, especially when it's genuine. And Graham Hutchings was certainly genuine in his opposition to the banking industry." She signaled the waiter for the bill. "Misguided but passionate."

He started to ask about the source of her knowledge, but she leaned over once more, this time to press a finger to his lips. "A request. Spoken with the wisdom of one who's been at this game a lot longer than you. Let's leave it there, all right? It was a mistake for me to bring it up at all."

"No it wasn't."

"I'll come by your office one day next week, lay it out for you in black and white."

"I look forward to that."

"Thank you, Wynn." She met the waiter and the bill with credit card outstretched, giving Wynn no chance to play the gallant. "Now it's your choice. We could take our coffee and a nightcap at Bijou Bijou, it's just up the street from here."

"Or?"

She rose from her chair and encircled herself with a matching shawl. When he joined her, she melted in close. "We could go for a walk."

"A walk sounds fine."

They left the restaurant and turned away from M Street's fluorescent bedlam. Valerie guided them down worn brick stairs and along the C&O Canal's towpath. They passed the waterfall alongside Thomas Jefferson Street, pausing to admire three couples in muslin and homespun maneuver a canal boat through the neighboring lock, then continued on in comfortable silence. Valerie led him up the next flight of stairs and into Dean & DeLuca, saying, "This is one of the reasons I love living in Georgetown."

A long line of fans marched down the high brick ceiling, dancing lazy circles over a brick-and-ceramic palace to fine cuisine. The air was spiced with rich fragrances and complacent chatter. Valerie led him past marble counters with smoked sausages stacked like logs, past the two hundred fresh cheeses displayed on reed mats, before releasing him with, "Why don't you go find us a nice wine for the dinner I'll make us next time." As she turned away she might have added, "Or later tonight," but he couldn't be sure.

Wynn made his way to the back of the shop, selected two bottles of Teledeschi's Pinot Noir, and met her at the front counter. She made a swift moue of approval and stroked his arm as he paid. The invitation was clear as fireworks across the sky.

But as they left the store, his phone rang. He shifted the wine to his other hand, pulled out the phone, checked the display, and said, "Sorry. It's Sybel."

But when he punched the button, it was Grant's voice that rang out, harsh and angry. "I sure hope I'm taking you away from a good time."

"What's the matter?"

"She's left me, that's what."

"Sybel's gone?"

"Didn't I just say that? I got back from a fund-raising jaunt down Miami way to nothing but an empty house. Her note doesn't say a thing except she's had enough. Wouldn't you think I deserved more than that?"

Wynn tried to disguise his rage with a casual tone. "You figure that pretty little aide was worth your marriage, Grant?"

"Now you listen up!" The governor was glad for the chance to vent a little of his own ire. "The only difference between you and me, buster, is you've got a whole lot less to lose!"

"Maybe you're right." Wynn forced himself to back off, knowing the outcome of any argument was futile and foreordained. "What do you want?"

"Go get her back."

He observed how Valerie stood by the wall, listening with a gossip's undisguised interest. "I'm not—"

"Sybel will hear you out. She always does."

"Not about this."

"Tell your sister, if she'll give us one more chance, I'll change."

Wynn bit back on his retort about lost causes and overlate transformations. Grant mistook his silence for agreement. "We can make it a trial run if she wants just through the next election and my campaign for the Senate. After that, if she still wants to leave me, I'll give her whatever she wants. The house, the boat, a good settlement. Anything."

The rage-sharpened edge returned. "But you tell her if she doesn't come back and see me through the next sixteen months, I'll destroy her like she's destroying me. I'll fight her for everything. You tell her that. She'll listen."

Wynn cut the connection, stood staring at streetlights splashing on the cobblestone way. He heard Valerie approach but could not risk turning his gaze and revealing what he felt.

In the soft tones of one who had been there, she said, "Washington timing. Positively dreadful. Has loathsome effects upon one's social life."

"Valerie—"

"Shah, now, wait and call me when you can hear yourself think." She leaned forward and kissed him lightly on the lips. Then she extracted the bag with the bottles from his hand, raised an arm to signal a passing taxi, kissed him a second time, and walked away. Valerie paused at the taxi's door to turn back and smile. Then she waved once and was gone. Ethereal as smoke.

17

Sunday

THE EGYPTIAN almost had to drag Jackie into the Willard Hotel. He left her standing beneath the huge central chandelier as he approached the reception desk. When he returned, he said, "The congressman is not here. We must wait."

"The guy has a suite here?" Jackie stumbled over her own feet as he led her to a sofa, the result of trying to look in six directions at once. "All the time?"

"I do not care for this." Nabil Saad's accent was much thicker now, from the strain of being pushed around a little too much. "One does not invite the cobra to sleep with the doves."

"So Wynn Bryant is really the enemy?"

"I hear what you hear, Miss Havilland."

"I thought we were going to be on a first-name basis."

"Yes. You are right. Jackie. Esther Hutchings has named him an enemy. Bryant's sister I have not seen since many years. You know Mrs. Wells?"

"Not a chance. Remember who you're talking with here."

"Of course. Forgive me. Tomorrow I fly to Cairo, where I will be forced to watch as Graham's life work evaporates." There were pale patches to either side of his nose and on his temples, brands of fatigue and strain. "I knew Wynn Bryant and his sister many years ago. I have not seen him since my childhood. This is not how I would wish to renew the acquaintance. Not here, and not in this manner, wondering whether the man who approaches is the friend we need or the enemy we dread. And not tonight."

"I don't think he's an enemy." Jackie tasted the air as Nabil slowly swiveled around to face her. Finding no wrongness to her observation. "He's totally ignorant of everything."

"Which means he still could be used by those who oppose us." Nabil fastened upon something beyond her and rose to his feet. "He is here."

The congressman entered with a phone attached to the side of his face. His gaze swept over Nabil without stopping, then fastened upon Jackie. He punched off the phone and walked over. "Mind telling me how you manage to show up at all the worst possible times?"

Jackie indicated the Egyptian. "I was asked to come and introduce someone."

But his gaze remained upon her. "First in Esther's living room, then in College Park. Now here. Your timing is exceptional."

Wynn wore what Jackie classed as rich man's casual attire. Suede jacket light enough for the balmy spring evening, gabardine slacks, shoes of woven leather so supple he could probably roll them like socks. She had a lifetime's experience fending off guys like this. "Nabil is a friend of Esther's."

"And that's supposed to mean something to me?" Wynn inspected Nabil. "We met in Kay Trilling's office."

"That is correct, Congressman."

"Does this have anything to do with my sister's vanishing act?"

Nabil cleared his throat, said formally, "I bring a message from Sybel."

"I should have known." Wynn crossed his arms. "So give."

"She asks you to join her in Rome."

"Not a chance in this world."

"She asks that you treat this as the birthday wish you did not agree to earlier."

Jackie watched as the bloom of pain she had seen back in Esther Hutchings' living room returned to his features. Wynn surprised her then, by directing the question to her and not Nabil. "Do you know enough to know what to ask this man?"

The words were strong, but not the gaze. He was more than wounded. He was frightened. "I might."

"Then ask the question for me, will you?" He turned back to the Egyptian. "Whether I go or not depends on how you answer her."

Jackie was unsettled to suddenly become an ally of this man Esther called their enemy. Before she could speak, however, Nabil inter-rupted, "Your sister is a good and brave woman, Congressman. Go to Sant'Egidio in Rome. Ask for Father Libretto. She asks that you see and decide for yourself. If you are with us, all will be explained. If not, you can depart and be safe in your unknowing."

"Does this have anything to do with the Jubilee thing?"

"Movement," Jackie corrected. "Jubilee movement."

"Whatever." To Nabil. "How does this third-world debt issue tie into what Graham was talking about in his speech, the banking crisis and hedge funds and all that?"

But the Egyptian was stalking off. "Come to Rome or do not come, that is all I was sent to say."

Wynn's voice rose enough to attract the attention of others in the lobby. "Why is it I've got people crawling all over me about this thing?"

"Your sister has made her request. Respect it or not, that is your choice." Nabil rammed through the revolving doors and was gone.

Wynn Bryant watched as the doors flapped ever slower, finally com-ing to a halt, empty and forlorn as his face. Jackie told him, "You should have added some names like Trastevere and Hayek to the mix. You might have really gotten him to dance."

He remained defeated by whatever he saw painted there on the empty doorway. "He looked familiar."

"His name is Nabil Saad." When that did not illicit a response, she added, "He says he knew you when you were kids."

The news deflated him even further. Wynn turned toward the back hall, carrying himself with the shuffling gait of one old and infirm. "Tell them I'll go."

"I'm supposed to tag along," she said, trying to hold the thrill from her voice. But Wynn just continued down the hall and out of sight. Leaving her to venture alone into whatever strange journeys tomorrow held.

Rome.

JACKIE WAITED to call Esther until she was safely back in her room at the Howard Johnson's. She found the freeway traffic rumbling be-yond her window a welcome reality-check after the glitz and polish of the Willard fantasyland. "How is your husband?"

Esther sounded happy, in the quiet way of the eternally spent. "When he woke up this afternoon, he held my hand. He tried to speak." Forcefully she drew herself away from the room down the hall. "What did Wynn tell Nabil?"

"He's going."

"I suppose that's to be expected. Do you have a passport?"

Excitement fizzed Jackie's blood until she was up and carrying the hotel phone around in tight little circles, unable to hold down the thrill or the words. "Preston made me get one. You know about Preston?"

"Your brother."

"We were always talking about going someplace far away. We took the occasional weekend trip, once even to the Bahamas. But I kept holding off on the bigger journeys until we had more time."

"You still miss him."

"Preston was the only real family I ever had." Saying it without pain. Almost. "So what do I do now that Wynn is going?"

"I'll have a staffer meet you at the airport tomorrow with your travel documents."

A shiver ran the entire length of her frame. Rome. "I mean, when I get there."

"Sybel said Wynn should contact her through the church of Sant'Egidio. It is in a place called—wait, I have the paper in my pocket. Piazza Trastevere. Do I need to spell that?"

"No."

Esther caught the change. "You have more questions."

"Thousands." But the woman sounded so tired, and the night's excitement was so great, all she wanted to ask at that moment was "How do I get for myself what you have with Graham?"

"That's not the question for this moment. You want to ask what I didn't fully answer earlier. About why you were hired."

Jackie took the phone over to the bed and sat down.

"After you left I did some very hard thinking. You were right to ask what you did. The trust between us needs to be based upon genuine honesty. Wouldn't you agree?"

Jackie slipped from the bed to the floor. Gathered her feet up beneath her. Leaned against the bed. "Yes."

Esther waited as the hospital intercom rattled out some message, then said, "I hired a private detective and instructed him to locate an employee of Hayek's with an ax to grind. Someone so embittered he or she would be more than happy to risk everything and search for what we could not find."

"You found Shane." The word was a dreg so bitter it caulked up her throat and left her spirit choking.

"We found you. And despite what Kay Trilling might think, I am convinced God's hand was upon this act."

The noose eased enough for Jackie to breathe and speak and turn the subject away. "I have to tell you, I don't think Wynn is an enemy. He's walking through this like a blind man."

Esther was silent through another pair of announcements. "Wynn Bryant will sacrifice anybody and anything on the altar of his own ambitions. His wife was sick for more than a year and he was too blind to see it. I was the one who held her hand at the doctor's, gave her a shoulder to cry on, then had to go and tell him . . ." She was interrupted by another voice over the intercom, or perhaps she just used it as an excuse to stop talking. When all was quiet once more, Esther merely said, "Watch him."

18

Monday

PAVEL HAYEK stood at his window and saw not his current domain but the suzerainties of his past and the one yet to come. His Orlando organization, though small compared to the sprawling Schwab campus farther north, had been featured in countless magazines, including the cover of *Architectural Digest*. The main building was a modern rendition of his family's former castle, a secret known only to himself. The architect had merely been given a photograph of what was now a museum and told to find a way to meld Hayek's Czech heritage with Wall Street. There were no turrets to this financial manor, nor lines of liveried servants to welcome his carriage at the start of each new day. But the sweeping grandeur had been well captured, and the sense of power.

In truth, he had never known the servants, but they lived for him still, branded in his mind by his mother's embittered ramblings.

The rumors were indeed true. Pavel Hayek was that rarest of creatures in the contemporary world, a prince. A blue blood. His lineage was linked through his mother's mother to the Romanovs, and through various other relatives to six reigning European monarchs. His fiefdom had stood east of Prague, an estate larger than Rhode Island. But his family had lost everything when the Nazis swallowed the Austro-Hungarian Empire's tattered remains.

Pavel had been born in the waning days of World War II, in what had formerly been the groundskeeper's cottage behind the palace stables. His family had managed to escape west in the frenetic period between the Nazis' defeat and the Russians' arrival. His earliest memory was of his mother standing in front of the gutted palace, shrieking invectives at the men who had bombed her world into antiquity. Then his father had

hustled them into a stolen truck laden with their few remaining posses-
sions and trainloads of shattered pride. Pavel had knelt on the seat beside his weeping mother, watching through the back portal as the moon
filled in the gaping wounds and made the palace whole once more.

They had landed in Paris with a generation of ragged nobility.
Pavel's father became an expert at using his tattered titles to mask the
fact that he was nothing more than a beggar with an attitude. When
their welcome wore out, they had shifted first to London and finally to
New York. There the last of his mother's jewelry had purchased a
neighborhood grocery in the Bronx.

From his shamed and embittered mother, Pavel inherited a desperate hunger for all he had never known, and mannerisms as empty as his
titles. From his father he learned the grim reality of poverty, and an unyielding determination to make it in this new world where money was
king.

Isolated by his dedicated arrogance, Pavel had grown ever more
confident that he was born to a ruler's mantle and a monarch's loneliness. He had excelled in school because it was the means to an end. Afterward he had accepted a job with Lehman Brothers for the same
reason. In the late eighties, when hedge funds began to grow in popular-
ity among the rich and mighty, Pavel went on his own. Fourteen years
and some good guesses and lucky breaks later, he was ready to breach
the final barrier, to finally arrive at his destiny.

The main building was crafted of glass and cream-colored stone. To
either side swept halfmoons of outbuildings—research to his left, legal
to his right—both fronted by Corinthian pillars of Brazilian marble. A
smaller rendition of the main building stood opposite Hayek's penthouse window, its three floors given over to sales and administration.
The internal pathways were of the same stone as the buildings, surrounding an oval plaza emblazoned with an immense *H* in polished
onyx. Semitropical flowers bloomed in carefully tended profusion. At
the ring's center stood a lake whose placid surface was marred by foun-
tains and the passage of six swans. When the occasional visitor arrived
from Wall Street and asked why he had moved so far south, Hayek always showed off this spread. In truth, however, he had left New York
because secrets were too hard to hide there, as he had learned from bitter experience. No, his Florida fiefdom was intended to do little more
than house his mercenaries and prepare in secret for the battle ahead.

This Monday, however, Hayek railed silently at the unseen flaw to his realm. The crystal clarity of his plans was blurred by ripples of uncontrolled risk. And from the most dreaded of sources.

Behind him there was a knock on the door. When he did not respond, the door opened and feet marked a measured tread to stand before his desk. Only one man was permitted entry day or night. Jim Burke knew his boss well enough to realize that whatever he carried, however urgent, it would wait until Hayek's musings were done. For an American, the man was not too poorly trained.

Finally Hayek turned from the window and his future. "Well?"

"Our man has just confirmed that Bank of America is going ahead as rumored."

Hayek slid into his seat. "He is certain?"

Burke remained standing because he had not been invited to sit. "He's already received his notice. His plane should be arriving in three hours. Apparently B. Of A. is canning their entire San Francisco trading staff and consolidating operations in Chicago and New York."

"Will the market absorb them without our intervention?"

"No way. I've checked. Wall Street is already shedding its own dead wood. Chicago is stagnant."

"So their traders should be panicking about now."

Burke showed momentary unease. He was paid to arrive with all the answers already in place. "I didn't ask anything specific. But it sounded that way to me."

"The twenty-five traders and support staff have been selected?"

"Ready to roll."

"Bring them in. Today. Remind them of their primary restriction."

"Total secrecy," Burke confirmed.

"More than that. They are a covert cadre. They must remain a tight-knit clan, isolated and apart. Any association whatsoever with the other traders and they will be instantly dismissed. All of them. Make sure they understand that." He pointed Burke into a chair opposite his desk, reached for his phone, and instructed his secretary, "Have Mr. Ready come up."

Burke watched him replace the receiver. "I don't trust Colin Ready. Not an inch."

"I am well aware of your feelings toward Mr. Ready."

"He's got access almost everywhere in our system. Not to mention the warped areas in his background. He's a hacker in corporate sheep's clothing."

Hayek inspected his number two. The man was really quite repulsive. Hair cut so short his scalp was visible, eyes as tight and manic as fiery pellets, clothes of unerringly bad taste. But highly intelligent. And extremely loyal. "You realize, of course, that our guests in gray are spies."

Burke showed surprise at Hayek's sudden change of direction. "Yes."

"Someone with the paranoid tendencies of our Brazilian investors," Hayek went on, "would not be content with mere muscle."

Burke's eyes widened. "You think Colin Ready is a mole?"

"You may look into that, but discreetly," Hayek replied. "And in the meantime, I am meeting with our Brazilians to complain about their gorillas. We can't have infiltrators rambling about, sticking their noses into everything. They must be identified and controlled. Otherwise they could destroy us."

COLIN SET DOWN HIS PHONE, took a deep breath, and muttered to the empty cubicle, "This could grow very bad very quickly."

He slipped into the jacket he kept on hand for visits to the royal chambers. He then checked his reflection in the *feng shui* mirror hanging from the back wall, the one Lisa had hated so much he had removed from his apartment and claimed he had thrown away. Overhead hung Lisa's final gift, a plaque reading "Destiny is reprogrammable, if seen from a higher perspective." The words mocked him as he headed upstairs.

Only Lisa had assuaged the soul-eating loneliness that wrenched him whenever he turned off his machines and entered loathesome reality. So long as she had remained alongside, the lonelies had never managed to strike. Now that she was forever gone, they never departed. Even the myth of her presence, and the one-sided futility of arguing with someone who had abandoned him for good, was better than staring the void straight in the face.

The number of gray-jacketed goons in the front reception area had multiplied like malignant spoor. The one who had slammed Colin into the upstairs window burned him with a look as he stepped into the elevator.

Once more Colin was shown directly into Hayek's inner sanctum. The Unabomber was there, today clothed from neck to ankles in shades of brown—shirt, tie, pants, belt—anchored at both ends by equally bizarre black, his eyeglasses almost as heavy as his shoes. Burke was definitely the group's most deviant relic from the twentieth century.

Hayek directed him to the chair beside Burke. "Curiosity is not always an excusable offense, Mr. Ready."

"Pardon me?"

Burke rapped out, "Stay away from the upstairs balcony."

"Oh. Yes, of course."

Hayek continued, "Now update us on this hunter."

"I'm sorry, who—"

Burke snapped at him again. "The Havilland female."

"She is hardly that. A huntress, I mean." His chair's angle was terrible. Colin could feel Burke's death rays drilling into the side of his skull. "This weekend she has done nothing more than cash a check, fly to Washington, and attend a conference in Maryland. To be frank, I regret bringing her to your attention at all. I thought she would be a stronger quarry."

"And yet she attended this conference in College Park."

"Well, yes. But I hardly see—"

"Perhaps you are not aware that Congressman Bryant was also in attendance?"

"I've not been instructed to follow the movements of, sorry, who did you say?"

"Bryant. Wynn Bryant." This from the Unabomber.

"What if I told you there was information," Hayek added, "that ties her closely to the congressman?"

Colin forced a laugh. "I would suggest it was a new hit for conspiracy theorists and paranoids everywhere."

"Then why is it," Hayek demanded, his accent etching the words with soft menace. "That Havilland is currently preparing to fly to Rome?"

"I beg your pardon?"

"With Bryant," Burke added.

Hayek said, "It seems your data is not as complete as you suggest."

Colin stared across the desk, at an utter loss for words. At this proximity it was easy to see why in earlier ages men worshipped their kings as gods. Hayek's power was that strong. "I don't understand."

"That much is perfectly clear."

"No, I mean, when she first appeared on-screen, and afterward when it became evident Esther Hutchings had hired her, I thought she might prove a genuine peril. A card-carrying menace, given your warning about any connection to Congressman Hutchings." He realized he was babbling, yet could not help himself. "But her findings have been paltry. I've uncovered nothing to indicate any sign of progress. I was certain Hutchings had brought her to Washington to criticize her lack of progress."

"And you were wrong," Hayek said. "Dangerously incorrect."

"Apparently so." Colin risked a single glance toward Burke. The man continued his unblinkingly hostile glare. "I am at an utter loss."

"That is unacceptable. I must know whether this woman is a growing tempest or merely a passing storm. There is nothing I despise more than the unknown risk." Hayek pointed him toward the door. "Go out there and determine precisely what is going on."

Colin bolted to his feet. "Right. Certainly. Of course."

"Answers." Hayek's bark chased him to the door. "All of them. Now."

19

Monday

JACKIE ENTERED DULLES AIRPORT as tormented as the day itself. A stiff wind had raised with the afternoon, gaining strength until the trees bowed submissive heads and shivered with the dread of knowing worse was still to come. Clouds gathered and powers wrestled along heaven's underbelly, the outcome revealed only to those who could read the script of lightning and lashing rain. She had spent her day fighting both highs and lows, and finding meager comfort in mall therapy.

First she had purchased some clothes and makeup, things she had not brought for a weekend in the big city. Then she spent two and a half hours luxuriating over what replacement computer to buy, before selecting a real prize—a superthin Sony with a 30 gig hard drive, optional CD burner, and 15 inch TFT screen. Not that she needed so much transportable power. She did it because she could, claiming Esther's paycheck as real and hers. Forcing herself to accept that she really was doing this. Living the life. Traveling to Rome.

Jackie had always recognized a good deal of her mother in herself. The bitter stink of undeserved woes constantly tempted her to view life with the lofty vision of one that disavows all connection. Perhaps that was why she had always fought Evelyn so hard, through the quiet stealth avoiding direct combat. She knew how easy it would be to assume life would never treat her any better, no matter how she tried, so not bother at all. It wasn't just life she quarreled with. It was herself.

Which was why, even as she walked through Dulles airport, part of her wanted to dismiss the entire journey as a lie.

"Ms. Havilland?"

She recognized the man who approached as Carter Styles, the overweight reader of newspapers. His piggy eyes were red with fatigue. His words grated like gravel tossed by a rusty shovel. "We've had a very bad night. Esther can't afford to give the press a moving target."

"Graham's worse?"

"No, actually the old man is better." He handed her a plastic envelope. "Flight, hotel, instructions." He turned to leave. "Have a good trip. Don't let Bryant out of your sight."

"Just a minute—"

"Lady, a minute is the one thing I don't have. Read the clippings and you'll understand." He scuttled away, soon lost in the bustling throngs.

Jackie opened the packet. On top was a newspaper article cut from the front page of that morning's *Orlando Sentinel*. The headline read "Former U.S. Congressman Linked To Illegal Arms Trade." Across the top was the curt handwritten note, "Will Call. Good Trip. E."

She threaded her way to the international check-in counter, reading as she stood in line. The article claimed to have uncovered documents linking Graham Hutchings to arms dealing with African despots— apparently the true source of what he had always claimed was his wife's wealth. The article went on to cite bank records revealing how Hutchings had acted as secret head of companies that transshipped weapons and skimmed profits. No mention was made of his stroke, only that he had recently resigned from Congress under a cloud.

"It is terrible, no?"

Jackie whirled about to confront a somber Nabil Saad. Today the Egyptian was attired in Ungaro mourner's garb, a midnight blue double-breasted suit with an indented pinstripe of identical thread. He cast a faint scent of Oriental spice, yet his features held the same haggard tension as Carter Styles'.

Jackie shook the paper at him. "Resigned under a cloud?"

"Esther warned you about this." The check-in line moved forward a notch. Nobody paid them any mind. Just two more hypertense Washington bureaucrats carrying their work into the friendly skies. Nabil shifted his carryall in order to reach for Jackie's case. "Allow me."

"I'm not interested in charm right now. I want answers."

"We have none." Lightning crackled and seared the Egyptian's features. Wind slammed rain upon the windows. "I am off to Egypt. Perhaps there we shall find answers. But not now. I have nothing now." He leaned closer, eyes so intent they lit recesses darkened by the tempest. "Here is a proper question for your journey. Why would the hedge funds manufacture such filth to bury a man already gone?"

Before she could respond, Nabil turned and departed. Which meant she asked the empty air, "How do you know it's a fund?"

WIND PUMMELED THE BUS as they left the main terminal for the departure concourse. People clung to the railings and peered anxiously out storm-buffeted windows. Thunder echoed louder than the departing planes.

The last person to enter before the doors closed was Wynn Bryant. The man looked like he had not slept for days. When he took the seat across from her, she waited until their eyes met, then asked, "You believe this weather?"

He was the only person on board who did not seem the least bit concerned. "We have almost two hours before takeoff. It should blow itself out by then."

Jackie moved to the seat beside him. "You know storms?"

"I live on the water. Weather-watching has become a part of my days."

She studied this man, the cleft chin, the deep-set eyes, the strong features. One step and ten years off movie-star looks. Which meant absolutely nothing except he had tools to hide his meanness down deep. If he wanted. If he had any to hide. "You have a boat?"

"Just a fourteen-foot Jon. Little freshwater swamp boat, nothing fancy."

"I sort of figured you for the chrome-plated yacht crowd."

"Can't take a yacht up a low-water canal after bass."

"The only thing I know about fishermen are the jackrabbit starts to tournaments. They're murder for windsurfers. We warn each other on a local website of every regional fishing competition. You get these wannabe tourney jerks buying flat-bottomed bass boats with twin two-hundred horsepower outboards. They dig trenches six feet deep and throw out killer bow waves. That is, if they don't hit a ripple and flip."

"You won't find me in that crowd. Twenty horse kicker, nothing more." He showed a little real interest. "You windsurf?"

"Intracoastal Waterway, mostly. Some wave jumping off the coast. I live for storms like this."

"My home is on Merritt Island."

"Then I've probably passed your place a hundred times." Wondering which of the waterside mansions was his.

The bus bounced and sighed and connected with the concourse. People surged forward. Wynn asked, "Buy you a coffee?"

Jackie reminded herself and him both, "You're supposed to be the enemy."

He hefted his leather satchel. "That's Esther talking. Isn't it time you made up your own mind?"

WYNN TOOK HER DOWN to the first-class lounge. These days, business-class lounges were merely leather-trimmed corrals. For a taste of the old style, the way air travel had been back before deregulation, there were only two choices—private jet or a first-class lounge. He found the day's first meager pleasure watching her take in the suede walls and inlaid furniture, the quietly hustling waiters, the soft hush of money at work. He waited until she had finished a slow sweep of the room to observe, "You're not a regular traveler."

"I've hardly been anywhere."

On an impulse so strange he did not bother to justify it even to himself, he said, "Let me have your ticket."

"What for?"

"I just want to check on your seat assignment."

"Oh. All right." But as she was about to hand it over, she said, "Could you lend me your credit card?"

The flat way she spoke matched the look in her eyes, leaving him certain this woman had crashed and burned her way out of life with the wrong man. He knew she was expecting either an argument or a lot of questions, so he simply reached for his wallet and slid out the plastic.

The simple gesture unnerved her. "I've just bought a new laptop computer. I need to set up an on-line account that's not under my own name. Someone suggested it as a way to check things without being watched."

"Fine."

"I'll pay you back."

"Don't worry about it."

He went to the front desk, handed over Jackie's ticket as well as his own, and swiftly explained what he wanted. Then he moved to one corner and used his cellphone to call Valerie's office.

Valerie came instantly on the line. Her voice revealed a tougher lady than the one he had dined with the previous evening. "Are you somewhere I can reach you in an hour?"

"I'm getting ready to board a flight for Rome."

"Just a minute." The silence was only momentary. "Sorry, I was in a conference. Did you say Rome?"

"That call I got last night. My sister has left her husband."

"Oh, Wynn."

"I found out she's taken off for Rome. I'm going over to see if I can help out. Probably futile, but she's all the family I have."

"I'm so sorry."

"Thanks."

"And I had such plans for the upcoming recess. Friends have offered me the use of their yacht, it's berthed in the Annapolis harbor." She spoke with the crisp gaiety of someone wanting to be intimate in a public place. "I was hoping you'd come along and crew."

"Maybe another time."

"Of course. I haven't been to Rome in ages."

He shook his head to the wall opposite. "This isn't a pleasure trip."

"Certainly not. Where will you be staying?"

He pulled out his own documents. "The Willard's concierge booked me into someplace called the Hassler."

"You've never been before?"

"First time."

"Some of the Hassler's guests have more money than sense, but the view is the best in Rome." Softening further. "Have as good a journey as you can, Wynn. I shall miss what we can't share."

JUST AS WYNN HAD PREDICTED, within the hour the storm had passed. The departing wind rumbled soft as a muffled bass drum against the concourse window, raising nervous glances from less experienced travelers. Jackie was not the least bit bothered. The wind was her very dearest friend. Perhaps that was why it had come now, in an hour that occasionally threatened to lift her from her seat and send her zinging around the first-class chamber. She needed something familiar and comforting just now.

Jackie was in the process of signing herself in as Wynn Bryant, new account holder with AOL, when he returned and dropped her ticket onto the keyboard. "I've had them upgrade you to first class."

"I can't possibly—"

"If we're going to be played like other people's puppets, we might as well do it with champagne." When she did not respond, he quietly added, "Please."

"All right." This was a come-on, no question. But one glance at Wynn's face was enough to know this guy would never press his case overhard. "Thank you."

Jackie watched him move to the next set of seats, plop down, pick up a magazine, and blindly leaf through the pages. As her computer continued the signing-in procedure, she found herself wondering about this strange lonely man who fed on other people's joy while feeling so little of his own.

Once on-line, she went straight to the internet address given her by the young man who was hopeless upon stormy waters. The website was a blank white screen with a heading that read simply *Trastevere*. Beneath the heading was only one large boldfaced word. *Go*. She slid her cursor over to rest on the word, and when she clicked, a message box appeared. She wrote out a brief note addressed to the Boatman. After a second, the message departed, and the single word reappeared. *Go*.

"Jackie, did you hear? They just called our flight."

"Coming." She tried to cut the connection, only to find the service frozen in download mode. "Hang on, I'm getting new upgrades. It'll just take a minute."

Wynn waited with weary resignation. As soon as the download was complete, Jackie slammed the computer shut, stowed it away, hefted her bags, and scampered.

She let herself be guided to the front of the cabin, where she took in the smiling flight attendant, the deference, the overwide seat, the silver tray of drinks, the space. Wynn sat there beside her, a tired smile on his face, saying nothing. He observed her with the glassy-eyed stare of a starving man watching another dine. The smile only touched his eyes once, when just after takeoff the plane did a serious dive-and-swoop, and Jackie could not help but laugh like a kid on a roller-coaster. Once they were through the turbulence, Wynn sank back inside himself, put the seat on full tilt, closed his eyes, and said, "Enjoy." End of tale.

Except for the fact that she was flying first-class across the ocean. Dining on roast tenderloin in a truffle sauce, fresh asparagus tips, chocolate mousse, all the silverware and linen she could hope for. Seventeen television channels, a stewardess there for whatever she might want, and up ahead lay Rome.

20

Tuesday

FOR WYNN, the drive from the airport into Rome passed in a golden blur. Normally he was more than willing to go along with Sybel on her do-good journeys, watch her back, feed the poor, let his remorse pour out with the heat. He could not say he had ever looked forward to these trips, but they did him good. He always returned with a sense of having cleaned out a multitude of wounds, albeit temporarily. Yet this voyage was different, of that he was certain. And the difference did not lie in the fact that Sybel had left Grant. His only hope was to rush in, do whatever was needed, and depart. Before he was hooked and dragged into whatever soul-wrenching maelstrom loomed just beyond the next turning.

Jackie spent the journey into town switching birdlike from one window to another. Wynn had never been to Rome before but could see nothing outside that would warrant such fascination. The city was just buildings and grime and noise. And traffic. Roman drivers did not steer, they hurtled with horns used as weapons of combat. Jackie seemed oblivious to all but the wonder of sunlight upon old stone. Wynn found himself vaguely jealous. "Did you get any rest on the plane?"

She spared him a single glance. "I'll never sleep again."

When they arrived at the Hassler, Wynn was completing his check-in before he realized Jackie was nowhere to be seen. He returned outside to find her staring over the steep-sided piazza fronting the hotel, out to where the rooftops of Rome gleamed from just another dawn. She watched the light and the day with shoulders hunched and hands folded across her chest, an awestruck penitent.

He had no time to indulge her veneration. "I have to go. The hotel car is taking me to the church where I hope I can find Sybel."

She turned reluctantly. "I can't believe I'm here."

"Stick around, why don't you. I've booked you into a room down the hall from mine. Enjoy the day. I'll be back as soon as I can."

"I really should come with you." But she did not move.

"Believe me, Jackie, there's nothing going on here except a brother looking for answers. Get some rest."

JACKIE TRAVERSED the hotel's public areas so fast she could almost hold her breath. Moving quickly was her best defense against the rich surroundings and these people who actually looked like they belonged. Upstairs, she showered and changed and spent a long moment staring out her window. The French-style doors opened onto a tiny balcony, not more than a foot deep and railed by ancient iron balustrades. The view looked straight onto the dome of the neighboring church, but off to the left there was a drop and then the whole of Rome, or so it seemed. She looked for just an instant, then forced herself to close the shutters. If she remained the bed would claim her, and that could not happen, not with Rome beckoning.

She walked and walked and walked. To merely look was a sacrilege. Jackie wanted to dine upon the day, devour everything she saw. Even the profane was bejeweled. She strolled the length of a grimy cobblestone street, where graffiti was scrawled upon palaces of ocher and age and stone. She stopped to admire a gated courtyard trapped in sunlight and medieval silence. Across the street and up two floors she spied a portico from which Juliet could have yearned for a Roman lover. From the handwrought railing hung plastic buckets filled with blooming daisies. Jackie felt an urgent need to pound on the nail-studded door and order the inhabitants to cultivate something extraordinary. An Italian lotus perhaps, or jasmine and lavender and plants for royal purple dye. Beyond the rooftops rose a hill crowned with trees and convocations of Roman doves. Higher still hung a painter's sky.

When her hunger became strong enough to resonate over her fatigue, she stopped at a streetside restaurant and ordered the lightest item on the menu. The Italian name was *caprese*, translated merely as a plate of tomatoes and mozzarella. What arrived deserved lines of verse. Tomato slices doused with oil so pungent it caught in her throat. Mozzarella balls little more than solidified milk wrapped in delicate skins.

A tiny espresso, a thimbleful of explosive flavor, then she was up and walking. It was lunchtime now, and she was surrounded by all the city's impossible contrasts—fumes and wood-roasted lamb, grime and spices, and five thousand years of flowers.

The sky grew steadily darker as she wound her way down toward the Tiber. Next to a bridge sheltered by poplars, an old man scraped ice off a block three feet thick. Back and forth his arm swept, shaving the ice with a metal grip, before ladling the snowball and fruit juice into a paper cup. He was surrounded by trees and laughing children and ribbons of green-tinted sunlight. The children's joy merely turned the man older still. Jackie bought an ice and let a tiny girl of perhaps six select the flavor and pay the old man from the money in Jackie's palm. She walked on to the sound of children singing a Roman farewell, her mouth drenched with the flavors of pineapple and perfect afternoons.

As she approached the Pantheon, a sudden deluge chased her off the cobblestones. She joined a thousand others under Hadrian's archway and relished an impromptu symphony of thunder and rain. She moved inside. The Pantheon dome was decorated with geometric designs that drew the eye ever higher up to the giant circular opening at its top. Through this central void fell a pillar of lightning-slashed rain. Down below, children danced about the watery border. Then the rain passed, and there came a single instant of metamorphosis, before the circle formed a pillar of light. The children danced on, transformed now into cherubs all. The crowded chamber halted to watch their flight.

WYNN SAT ALONE in the back of the hotel's limo, an oversize Alfa Romeo designed like a Mercedes with Italian flair. As the sunlight gradually gave way to approaching showers, he reflected on how much he already hated Rome.

He loathed its beauty and its deformities with equal fervor, and not merely because he had been forced to come. Hardly at all for that reason, in fact. He hated this city and this journey for the lie they made of his life. Money and success had not resolved his inner conflicts. Rather, they had enveloped him in an opiate dullness, distancing him from the wounds he still carried. He stared out the window as the limo pass over the Tiber, caring for nothing, wanting merely to be away. Anywhere was better than a place of such horrid truth.

The limo halted by a narrow cobblestone lane. The driver turned around. "Please sir, from here you must walk."

Wynn felt no great desire to enter whatever mission his sister had designed. "What is this place?"

"Piazza di San Callisto. Your church, it is down this street, but I cannot drive. Is permitted only at night."

"Sant'Egidio is there?"

"The movement, yes, but not the church. The church of Sant'Egidio is down farther, that way. But the movement is here now. Two years ago, maybe three, it came here to Trastevere. The first *eglise* was too small."

"You know about Sant'Egidio?"

"Everybody knows. All the city speaks of Sant'Egidio." He smiled with impossible humor. "There is a saying, Rome is a holy city for all but Romans. You understand? But for Romans who believe, there is Sant'Egidio. They feed the poor. They pray. They work for peace. You know the war in Rwanda? They help to stop. Algeria, same thing. Colombia, Bosnia, Congo, Sudan, so many places. Now Sant'Egidio's head priest, he is a bishop."

Wynn reached for the door. "Sounds like my sister's kind of place."

"Please?"

"Nothing."

"Sure, Vatican politics is big talk here in Rome. You know the Curia? They fight to keep Sant'Egidio priest out. Too many people not priests have power in Sant'Egidio. Too many not Catholics. But the Pope, he makes him bishop anyway." He pointed down the lane. "I wait here, yes?"

Rain began speckling the cobblestones, turning them slick as old glass. The lane opened into a grand piazza, anchored at one end by a truly monstrous church. If Sybel had been able to design her own church, it would have been this one. Not beautiful, as so many were in this city. But vast and old, pitted with hard use, and very busy. The piazza was lined on two sides by restaurants and shops, with a high fortress wall and the church along the others. Beggars and homeless people claimed the shaded fortress and the empty fountain as their own. They hunched and huddled against the gathering storm, but did not move. The church's tall iron gates were open and fronted by Gypsies selling flowers, pleading with toothless whines as he joined the chattering crowds and entered.

The interior was huge in the way of medieval halls, incredibly ornate, yet worn and faded. Even the ceiling's gold-leaf mosaics were smoky and muted. The place was packed with people of every race. And not for a service. Groups used side chapels for quietly intense meetings. They gathered along tables at the back. They sat and knelt and prayed. Wynn walked the right-hand aisle, feeling utterly the outsider. Their talk and their laughter all seemed directed at him, speaking in an unknown tongue of all the mysteries he could not hope to fathom.

"Can I help, please?"

He turned to face a dark-haired pixie of a woman. She was tiny, certainly under five feet, with a smile big enough for three of her. A small girl in a filthy oversize frock held one of her hands. "Welcome to Sant'Egidio. You are new?"

"Yes."

"Please to excuse the noise. We are building new rooms for meetings. Until they are done," she waved an apologetic hand over the din. "You see?"

"I'd like to speak with Father Libretto."

"The father is not here. I am Anna." She smiled beneath dark ringlets. "Please return tonight. For the *preghiere*. You understand? The night prayers."

"And Sybel Wells?"

"Who, please?"

"My sister. Is she here?"

"So sorry. The Father, he is busy with the poor. I do not think any Sybel is there, but perhaps." She made a gesture towards the back. "You wish to come?"

"Not a chance."

"*Va bene.*" Even at his refusal, she showed impossible cheer. "*Otto é mezzo.* Eight and one-half o'clock. Night prayers. You come back."

Wynn had no choice but to retreat, defeated by the welcome that was not his and probably never would be.

JACKIE RETURNED to the Hassler when a taxi was her only hope of moving another inch. She found a terse note from Wynn waiting for her: his sister was not found. He had to return to the church that night, but would she join him for an early dinner beforehand? She scrawled a yes at the bottom, left it for him, then almost fell asleep in the elevator on the way upstairs.

She woke three hours later, feeling more fatigued than she had upon lying down. Jackie ordered up coffee and spent a long time seated by her open window, staring at the people and the late afternoon vista. She studied a map and named what she could see—the Trinita Dei Monti church, the Piazza di Spagna, Via Condotti, the Spanish Steps. Trying to anchor herself through the process of identification, and make all this real.

She spent more time dressing than she had in years, almost convincing herself it was for the place and not for Wynn. Her outfit was a smoky buff weave of cotton and silk with collar and belt of nail-polish red. Open-toed shoes to match. She stood for a long moment staring at herself in the full-length mirror, wondering if she could afford to hope once again. Even a little. Yet knowing she had already left the power of choice far behind.

21

Tuesday

COLIN WAS ALERTED to someone's approach by a subtle shift in the backroom's atmosphere. The constant hum of techie chatter diminished to faint whisperings of fear. Doom, Colin knew, would not arrive upon boots of iron and lightning. Annihilation's tread would be softer than the breathless wait for thunderstorms. Like now. He wiped his work from the monitors and listened as the quiet expectation of dread moved along the central aisle.

"You're in. Good." Jim Burke actually wore a decent suit. A first. The Unabomber had traded in his polyester for linen pleats, but the railroad shoes were still intact. They had to weigh ten pounds apiece, their shine mirror-black, even the narrow shoestrings waxed. Amazing a man that skinny could even lift them.

And Burke was not alone. Another first. Burke had clearly learned that the solitary jungle beast moved more quietly and struck with less warning. Today, however, Burke was followed by a man of Colin's age, as slender as Burke but far better groomed. A tiger in training, raised on the streets of some well-styled metropolis. The newcomer wore a double-breasted suit in seven shades of gray and silver, black high-collared shirt, a silver lotus clasp in place of a tie, and titanium sunglasses. Colin sat up straighter. Burke slid into the cubicle's only other seat and declared, "I want to know what security arrangements you've put into our systems."

Colin watched the second man drag a chair over from a neighboring cubicle and slouch into it. Colin replied, "I'm not certain that's within proper bounds."

"You're questioning my authority?"

"Not yours, no." The newcomer's bug-eyed shades remained in place. Probably concerned about retina burn from the fluorescents.

"Never mind him," Burke snapped. "Tell me what's shielding us from outside attack."

In truth, most of Colin's responsibilities were basic null-level stuff. Chasing down the guy who called a hot-date service on company time, that sort of thing. For Colin, this meant merely designing a program that timed all overseas calls. Nine calls to Singapore and Tokyo of forty-five seconds each, no problem, the trader was checking with contacts on the state of other markets. But when the call lasted fifteen minutes and went to Manila, silent alarms were triggered. Kindergarten work. Yet when it saved the company a quarter of a million per annum, and nobody had thought of it before, the upper management tended to hand out kudos like candy.

Ditto for incoming traffic. Colin had lengthened the corporate access codes from four digits to nine and changed them quarterly. The traders grumbled and groused, until Colin pointed out that one phantom trader had been phoning in from Shilling Brothers' Wall Street offices, accessing the Hayek research department's morning market roundup. Then the senior traders adopted the security arrangements as their own and called Colin a prodigy. He could spend days talking such code and twaddle and give nothing away.

But as Colin lapsed into technobabble, the newcomer cut him off by telling Burke, "He's playing mind games. Handing us his own personal version of multidimensional trivia."

Two signals came out with the words. One, this guy knew his stuff. Two, he was definitely a trader. He had the deadhead voice of a dedicated adrenaline junkie. Colin inched straighter still. A serious adversary.

Burke showed enough of a smile to change the creases around his marble eyes. "So tell him."

The newcomer gave Colin a tight smirk. "People are being whipped into a paranoid frenzy by the specter of some rogues hitting us unawares."

"Excuse me," Colin said. Directing the words to both of them. "I seem to be missing something. This gentleman has joined the team?"

"As of today," Burke confirmed. "Brant Anker, meet our very own Colin Ready."

Brant Anker went on, "This new adversary might be the tip of an iceberg, one that could sink the company like the Titanic. Which means your passive surveillance is no longer sufficient." When Colin did not respond, Anker said more slowly, "Go out there and find out who is behind the rumors, and how they are planning to use the information."

"Systems infiltration," Colin interpreted. "Sorry. Not my bag."

Burke glared at him. "This could cost you your job."

"Better than prison, which is where your request could very well land me."

The two shared a quick communal smirk. Only then did Colin realize it was all a feint, a test. He should have been reassured, but something about the pair left him listening to steel fingernails scraping down a mile-long blackboard.

Burke said, "Tell us what you have in place to check out the Havilland woman."

"Her security authorization is weak. Low grade defenses. Single port of entry. Good data trail, no question of false identity. On-line data capture is set up to retrieve as soon as I come in."

"Details," the newcomer pressed. "Good data is in the details."

"About a month ago, Hayek mentioned a concern about a hunter going after in-house data. He said there could be a tie-in to accusations leveled by one Graham Hutchings, former U.S. Congressman and now active vegetable. I set up a hunter-sniffer in the form of a closed-access website. When we were struck, I automatically inserted a virus that grants me ongoing access in the worst way."

"Your design?"

"From the basement to the tower A/C. It zip-compresses all new files and ships them over every time she goes on-line."

"Tell me about her."

"A definite keeper." Colin tapped in the command, drew up the photo file he had downloaded early, and selected one of the lady on a sailboard. "Jackie Havilland. Orlando native. Twenties, single, great lines."

"So what do you call the virus?"

"The cookie monster. On account of it's a voracious feeder."

"Totally quantum. Plaudits, dude." A fractional pause, then, "So what was in your latest download?"

"Sorry," Colin was firm here, meeting Burke's glare head-on. "You want more, I need a direct okay from Mr. Hayek himself."

Again there was communication between the pair and on a frequency barred to Colin. Then the newcomer said, "This guy redefines clean."

Burke checked his watch. "I have to travel to Miami with Pavel." He glowered at Colin. "Let me see if I can put this in a code you comprehend. The balcony is off limits. You go upstairs again, you leave here in little pieces. Are we clear on this?"

"Absolutely."

Burke left without another word. The deadhead rose to follow. At the cubicle's entrance he turned, did a final scan, sniffed his disdain. "All these toys, you don't have idea one which prize is worth pursuing."

Once certain they were gone, Colin slumped back into his seat and stared at the ceiling. Too many questions, too many dangers. A conflict vector had been established. A menacing course of off-line events.

22

Tuesday

WYNN STOOD by the Hassler's rooftop bar and searched the evening sky, not for a sign so much as a way out. He had slept hard and woken unrefreshed. The air remained compressed by all that loomed up ahead. His chest fought for breath and room to maneuver. He was certain that Sybel had brought him here for a purpose. And equally certain that whatever the purpose might be, he was going to hate it.

The elevator doors opened, and Jackie stepped out. The failing light seemed to gather about her blond hair, encasing her in a brilliance not even the worst of his shadows could invade. "You look great."

"Thank you." But her gaze was already captured by the world beyond the balcony. The maître d' greeted her with ill-disguised admiration. The waiters graced her with the glazed look of smitten Romeos. She seemed utterly unaware of the commotion she caused. Jackie passed through tables and lingering gazes without taking her eyes from the view. "This is incredible."

"Yes." Hard as it was, Wynn could not help but accept a morsel from the day. Sunset painted the scene with strokes so gentle no imperfection could be found. But for Wynn, to look meant to see only his own tightly morose state, as though he viewed the golden world from a cage he had learned not to acknowledge. "Very nice."

Jackie took joy from everything—the menu, the meal, the very air. He observed her openly, knowing she was here yet elsewhere, too absorbed with the moment to be bothered by his gaze. Her skin seemed flawless, at least from the distance of casual acquaintance. Upon closer inspection, he could see a faint mist of freckles across the high-boned cheeks and ultrastraight nose. Tiny lines ran from her eyes, faintest indicators of her many secrets. Hers was a good face, with a gaze that saw all and expected nothing. Strength and goodness in a gentle form. Big wide-open green eyes, ready to accept whatever life gave with little more than a blink.

Jackie refused dessert, accepted coffee, silently toasted the lingering twilight, and focused upon him. "Can we talk?"

"If you like."

"Esther Hutchings is convinced you're working for the enemy."

"I don't know enough," Wynn replied, "to even know who that is."

She set down her cup, toyed with her spoon. Waited.

He recognized it as the only chance he might ever have to convince her. "Do you want the sugar-coated version, or the truth?"

"Hard and fast."

"Dianne, my wife, died from aggressive rheumatoid arthritis. It choked her to death. A terrible way to go. We'd been separated six weeks. She was preparing to file for divorce. Esther was her best friend. Dianne used to meet Esther once or twice a month, pour out all the details of our life together and describe just what a louse I was."

"Were you?"

"Oh yeah." He stopped while a waiter placed a candle on their table. Somewhere in the distance a church bell began to chime. The sound rose pure and courtly, shimmering in time to the candle's flame. "My business had become a parasitic animal, a worm I swallowed one day at a time. It grew in my mind and my heart and it poisoned them both. I started thinking the most absurd things were true. Like how everybody was out to get me, and the only way forward was to get them first. Or how love was just another word for being weak. Lies became my only reality."

"But you got rich."

He stared out to where the world below was now enveloped by flickering lights, earthly reflections of the stars overhead. "That's right. I did."

"So what happens now? I mean, here in Rome."

"You'll have to ask Sybel. All I can say for certain is she's brought me here for a reason."

"You don't know what?"

"No idea." Whatever conjecture he might have would only mock his lack of choices, the absence of personal mobility. "Mind if I ask you a question?"

"I suppose not."

"How did Esther link up with you?"

"My brother worked for the Hayek Group."

"The finance group that moved from New York down to Orlando, right? I remember reading about that."

The conversation's turn hardened her gaze and tone both. "The proper term is hedge fund."

"Sounds like you know about them."

"I was a graduate student at UF in international finance. My area of study was the currency markets. Usually referred to as foreign exchange, forex for short."

"Your brother does currency work for Hayek?"

"He did." There was something more to Jackie's wary tension than Esther Hutchings and any warning she might have passed on. Something so intensely personal it robbed the night of magic and flavor. Jackie sat across from him, awaiting his next question as she would a heavy blow.

Yet Wynn had no intention of inflicting further pain on anyone, if that were possible. "Can you tell me anything about Hayek?"

Her anxiety eased only a notch, as though disbelieving she would get off so easily. "Very secretive. A real powerhouse in the derivatives and forex trading worlds. The only time he's ever been quoted was in a *Journal* article on the rise of U.S. hedge funds. He said, and I quote, 'Every trader is probing, looking for the opponent's weak point. If you want to understand currency trading, study war. They are the same thing, only the blood on the trading floor remains unseen.' That's Hayek."

Wynn pushed his cup to one side. Leaned across the table. "I want you to do something for me. Pretend I'm telling you the truth. That I don't want ever to be your enemy. That I don't know a thing. And that I really do want to learn." He stopped then, giving her a chance to back off, move away, brush off the appeal. Instead she simply gave him that wide-open look. Measuring. Cautious. Full-on alert. "Okay. Who is Hayek and how does he tie into all this?"

"You'll have to ask Esther."

"You know precisely how far that would get me."

Further guarded inspection, then, "All I have to go on are my own conjectures."

He moved back out of her space. "That's fine."

"There is a growing sentiment among many economists and pundits that our banking system is on the verge of a very real crisis. Hedge funds like Hayek are what you might call the worst of the worst. A malignant vein pumping poison though the system."

She seemed to recognize his interest as genuine, for she revealed a hint of new energy, or perhaps one long submerged. "Hedge funds deal in any number of markets, but they specialize in foreign exchange and related derivatives. The problem with forex derivatives is precisely what appeals to these funds. No super-regulator. There is no body with the power to control the movement of funds. And so forex funds can get away with things that would have them screaming bloody murder in the world's stock exchanges or standard banking markets. Like collusion, where insiders profit from the trading of supposedly secret information. Or operating on tiny margins, thus opening themselves and their investors to huge risks. They regularly assume market positions that anybody in their right mind would consider truly insane. In short, they whip exchange rates around just as much as they can."

Wynn was not the least disturbed by just how little he understood. If it was important, he could ask more later. For the moment, it was enough to watch her reveal this utterly new side of herself. "So why isn't a watchdog agency established?"

"Two reasons. First, because globalization means an increasingly porous economy. We live and breathe from exports and imports. People worry that any forex restriction would choke off the flow of goods."

"Would it?"

"No." She came back definite and hard. "This is all smoke and mirrors manufactured by lobbyists for the banking industry. The fact is, curbs on wild forex fluctuations would be *good* for business. But that brings up the other problem, which is, any regulating body would have to be international to be effective."

"I think I see."

"Sure you do. Any time people start talking about reining in the market's excesses, the banks and their hired guns wave the red flag of international government. They start talking about American sovereignty, and financial meddling, and all the other buzz words that send Joe Q. Public into high-altitude orbit." She stared unseeing at the night. "There used to be three carefully designated markets for currency exchange—cash, forwards, and futures. But those precisely drawn lines have been erased by the derivatives market. If currency futures have

seen explosive growth, derivatives have gone off like a nuclear detona-
tor. It's an utterly unregulated market, and that is exactly how the
banks want it to stay. They pay the K Street lobbyists huge bucks just to
make sure no little surprise regulation is slipped into some bill. Regulation would slow things down and restrict new financial maneuvers. So
for the moment at least, the best way to describe derivatives is, Anything goes."

But Wynn's mind was snagged by the term, "K Street."

"That's where the most powerful lobbyists dwell. Using that address is like planting a flag." Her pace continued to accelerate, her mind
clicking into a long-disused gear. The words became clipped and precise
and trimmed to perfection. "Derivatives traders have poured unbelievable amounts into the pockets of Washington lobbyists, paying them to
keep things free and easy. These funds make more money on trades than
on holding. They often buy only because they think they can swiftly re-
sell, tacking on their percentage as they do so. This tactic is called flip-
ping, or washing. On a hectic day of derivatives trading, where the
backroom lags three or four hours behind the traders, the floor may
close without anyone knowing the fund's actual position. They could be
holding ten billion dollars in high risk D-mark futures they thought
they had balanced against something else, only to discover that another
trader sold their safety net ninety minutes earlier. They simply mark it
down as what will be the next day's first sale. To them it's only paper.
The fact that the existence of a medium-size bank, one that's been
around for a hundred years, might be destroyed because of this super-
fast washing, means nothing. To them it's only paper."

"Sorry, I'm playing catch-up here. Why do the traders care about
Washington politics?"

"They care because the lack of regulation is how they make their
money. Today's currency market is based on a ludicrous system of easy
credit. Imagine the oldest, most stable company in the world going into
a bank and saying, hey, I want to borrow ten billion dollars with nothing down. No collateral, no margin, just my good name. They'd escort
him straight to the loony bin. Yet the funds do this in currency derivatives every day of the week. It's standard practice.

"The answer is to regulate the currency market just like all the others. This was the basis of my master's thesis. All other markets require a
margin up front and a clearing of all debts before the end of that business day. Simple. That way, the winners pay the losers every single

night. They immediately know the status of everyone's business. If someone is in trouble, at least the risk is restricted to one bad apple and not a total collapse of the banking system."

"But that's not the case?"

She looked at him, but he was not sure she actually recognized who he was. "Ever hear of Nick Leeson?"

"No."

"He brought down one of the oldest banks in the world, Barings. Single-handedly. He traded over his limits on the Singapore and Tokyo exchanges. How? Because no system is in place to detect any fund's end-of-day position."

He noted with admiration, "Your voice has changed."

She halted in the process of reaching for her glass. "What?"

"The way you talk. It's changed. You're all charged up."

She left her glass where it was. "I think we're done here."

"I'm sorry I said anything."

But she was already rising to her feet. "We should be going."

"Jackie—"

"We need to see about your sister, isn't that what you said? Ask for the bill."

JACKIE WAS GRATEFUL for the driver's cheerful chatter. She needed time to sort through the confusion. The day had obviously been too potent, a draft more stimulating than her system could handle. That was the only excuse for the closeness she had felt over dinner. And, if truth be known, still felt now.

Even the streetlights seemed different here in Rome, turning old stone into theater backdrops, making artwork from shadows. As they crossed a bridge strung across mystic dusk, the hotel driver talked of how the Trastevere area had formerly housed Rome's working poor. Now it was a place of nightlife and romance, he said, then leered until Wynn reminded him they were going to Sant'Egidio. But it was Wynn's demeanor more than his words that finally silenced the young man.

They left the car and followed a cobblestone alley to a night-washed piazza. Anywhere but Rome, the church she faced would have been preserved, vacuum packed, and turned into a museum. Here it merely anchored another square, this one without the attractions of a working fountain or Bellini statue. The church's exterior was unadorned brick, a manifestation of poorer past centuries. The interior was a mosaic of battered grandeur. In this visual banquet of a city, it offered nothing extraordinary. Tourists did not come. Which was a good thing, Jackie decided. There would be no room for them.

Jackie found the evening service remarkably moving, despite its simplicity. The church was meant to hold perhaps seven hundred people, but tonight contained well over a thousand. Black, Asian, Hispanic, Roman, Scandinavian blonds and the stylish backpackers of America— they all were present here. The Bible reading and the brief sermon were done in three languages. The prayers were sung chants, and translated on leaflets scattered among the benches. There was no priest in attendance. People from the assembly came up to lead various segments of the service, then resumed their seats. All in an orderly yet casual fashion.

She knew Wynn was bitterly unhappy at being here. She also knew she had the capacity to help him. It was hard, so very hard. But the night was too beautiful to do otherwise. She turned and waited for him to glance her way, then she smiled. Not with her mouth. With her heart. Showed him a glimpse of the joy she had found in this day. Though it left her naked and far too frightened for this public place, though she had to swiftly turn away, though her mind shrilled a lifetime of warning. Still she was glad she had done it. And gladder still when she sensed him relax a trifle. The night held that much power.

After the service, Wynn stood by a side alcove and seemed uncertain what to do, until a smiling young woman no taller than a child approached. He showed no pleasure at her appearance. "Father Libretto isn't here?"

"He came and he left again. He sends you greetings." She smiled at Jackie. "Hello, I am Anna."

"Jackie."

"Your first time at Sant'Egidio?"

"Very first."

"You are most welcome." Back to Wynn. "He has left you a message. Perhaps you wish to come with me?"

"I'll take it here."

"The message, it is confidential."

"Here is fine."

"*Bene.*" She tucked her hands into her shapeless sweater. "Your sister has already left."

"She's gone back home?"

Anna smiled. "In a sense. Yes."

The air whooshed out of him, as though the candles and the incense and this small quiet woman had combined to deliver a vicious blow. "You can't be serious."

"The priest says, your sister gives to you the excuse to travel. Now you have two choices. Follow her, or return to safety and blindness." She withdrew one hand long enough to pass over a slip of paper. "But to go forward means great risk. You understand?"

23

Tuesday

THEY LEFT THE CHURCH, crossed the piazza, and caught a taxi back to the hotel. The streetlights painted Wynn's face into lines as bleak and hard as night-cut stone. Jackie leaned against the taxi door and studied what even in despondency was a very handsome man. Darkly chiseled features, eyes like the melancholy clouds of pending gales. A man who would age well. But she had long since learned that good looks were not such great shakes. "Your sister's not in Rome any more?"

"No."

"Do you know where to find her?"

Slowly, he raised and lowered his head. Not a nod so much as an admission of nightmares still to come. Jackie said, "You don't mind me saying, you take an amazing amount of trouble for your sister."

The taxi drummed across the Tiber and joined the flow about yet more ruins out of time. Spotlights drilled the tableau into black and silver etchings, frozen there against the backdrop of night. Wynn remained blind to it all. "My parents died when I was five and we went to live with relatives. They were a miserable lot. Do you know Lakeland?"

"Sure. Out on the other side of Orlando."

"Back then it was nothing but orange groves and hot rods and beer joints. The Vitalis crowd at its worst. My dad's family owned a packing plant. Dad was the only one of them who ever made it out, the only one to finish high school, much less go to college. He was everything they despised—a professor at a university, smart, married to a Yankee from New Hampshire who was a teacher herself. They mocked our accents, they mocked our parents."

Jackie pressed herself more tightly against the taxi's opposite door.

The guy was too close to the bone just then, the reasons to care all too obvious.

Wynn gave no notice to her movements. "The day Sybel turned eighteen, she forced the family lawyer to hand over our inheritance. Much as my dad's folks didn't like having us around, they still fought tooth and nail to keep us. So Sybel went to court and officially adopted me. There wasn't much in the way of money. Back then no life insurance company would cover my folks, since they lived in Egypt. What there had been in the way of savings was pretty much drained away. But enough was left to get us settled in Gainesville. She started school, and then she met Grant."

Everything he said fueled her hopeless attraction, no matter what she thought or wanted to have happen. "Have you ever wondered if maybe life makes a random selection, chooses a person and just pegs them to the dart board of that particular time? Let everybody throw sharp pointy objects your way."

He grew very still. "No."

"Don't mind me. I'm a font of useless ideas." She forced herself to turn around and stare out her window, drawn by the loud drumming of tires upon cobblestones and the sight of the Coliseum up ahead. "And look where they got me."

WHEN THEY LEFT THE TAXI, Wynn watched as the doorman tipped his hat to Jackie. She entered the lobby before him, with shoulders squared and chin held rigidly high. The chandeliers illuminated an internal struggle, which finally gave in to the confession, "This day has held so much I don't even know what to say."

"My thoughts exactly, but for entirely different reasons." He did what she least expected, which was to take her hand and bow. Not drawing it completely to his lips. But doing as he had seen others do, giving her all the respect he could muster. Then explaining why. "The only nice thing about my entire journey is having you here."

She softened then. For the first time, he saw beneath her bulletproof shell and glimpsed another woman entirely. "I can't even remember the last time a man said something that sweet to me. Thank you, Wynn."

"Do you know, that's the first time you have ever spoken my name."

She parted her lips, uncertain, torn. A shaky breath, then, "You," she said, for his ears alone, "are a very dangerous man."

"Only to myself."

She turned and crossed the lobby, the light caught and held by her hair. She nodded her thanks to the bellhop, who used a white-gloved hand to hold the elevator door for her. She pressed the button for her floor. Only then did she look up. Catch his eye. And whisper his name yet again.

Wynn SCARCELY HAD TIME to step over to the concierge desk and make his travel requests before a too-familiar voice behind him said, "I can scarcely believe my eyes."

Hearing those dulcet English tones in this place, at this time, raised the hairs on the back of his neck. Like the mockingbird's song heard at midnight. Lovely, perhaps, but in such a place the sound became a warning. He turned to Valerie nonetheless, with as much surprise as he could muster. "What on earth are you doing here?"

"Hoping to see you, of course." Anger shone in eyes flecked with an improper season, autumn perhaps, or the facile passion of easier times. "I scurry about like a madwoman, putting my affairs in order, racing against the clock. A mad dash to the airport, barely making the last flight out. Arrive shattered, scarcely aware of where I am. Expecting to find you in misery and panic, searching high and low for your sister. Instead, what do I discover?"

But Valerie did not look shattered. She looked as if she had just stepped off a yacht. Sleek and lovely and alert as ever. Wynn said, "I've found Sybel. At least, I know where she is."

A vehement shake of her head, hair spilling about in lovely disorder. "Don't you dare try to tell me that was your sister I saw you giving the little bow and scrape upon farewell."

"No."

"I saw that woman at Esther Hutchings' apartment, remember? I was there with you. Right at your side."

"Esther sent her here."

Valerie caught herself in midbreath. "I beg your pardon?"

"Esther thinks I'm working for the enemy. She sent Jackie Havilland to spy on me."

She glanced about, then reached over and took his arm. "Come, dear Wynn. We are entertaining the staff."

Valerie led him back into the bar, a darker alcove off the main salon. She wore gray slacks of Shantung silk and a matching blouse with four seed pearls for buttons. A gray silk jacket hung from the back of a chair by the corner table. "What will you have?"

"Nothing, thanks."

She waved the bartender away. "And just precisely what enemy might this be?"

"I have no idea." When she looked at him askance, he added, "To be honest, I don't think Esther knows either. Not for certain."

"Esther Hutchings belongs in the bed beside her husband." Valerie swept her hair back, using both hands to smooth the auburn flow. She eyed him in a coquettish fashion. "You're certain this was all that was at work back there in the lobby?"

"Absolutely."

"Well Jackie, is that what you said her name was? She seemed a very nice young lady, but operating utterly out of her league."

Wynn knew she was waiting and expecting him to agree, to close the distance and speak words of invitation. Yet her magic, however potent, was not working. Though she belonged to this moneyed world, though he had always thought this was the class of woman he sought, still his mind remained captured by the day and by the silent word spoken from the recesses of a departing elevator. "I have to leave tomorrow."

She crossed her arms. "That is not funny."

"Sybel is no longer in Rome."

"So just where, pray tell, has your errant sister strayed now?"

He found himself not wanting to tell her. An utterly illogical response, but strong enough to keep him from speaking. The sound of approaching footsteps came as a welcome interruption. The late-night concierge took great pride in announcing, "I have managed to book you on the first flight to Cairo tomorrow morning."

Valerie repeated, "Cairo?"

"Excellent," Wynn said, though it was anything but. "Thank you."

"It leaves at six forty-five, I'm afraid."

Which gave him the perfect excuse to rise and say, "I'm so very sorry, Valerie."

She remained where she was. "You can't be serious."

He chose to misunderstand. "I'm still jet-lagged from the trip here. I've got to get some rest." He reached down, took both her hands in his, squeezed hard. "Enjoy Rome for me. Will you at least do that?"

He followed the concierge back across the lobby, traded a tip for his booking confirmation, and waved back to where Valerie still sat. He entered the elevator and punched his button, sighing as the doors closed. He felt a sibilant hush of confirmation, bubbles rising from his gut to the mental recesses where logic held no sway.

When he entered his room, he walked to the telephone and asked to be connected with Jackie.

She answered with the guarded alertness of having been half-expecting this call. "Yes?"

He knew what she both anticipated and dreaded. Which was why he spoke as briskly as he did. "Something's come up. We have to talk. Now."

To her credit, she did not play coy or feign sleepiness. "I'm in 601."

He copied out his travel details, walked down the hall, and waited without knocking for Jackie to open the door. The face beneath her tousled hair showed wary caution. So he started in while still standing in the corridor. "You remember the woman who came with me to Esther's that evening?"

"The lobbyist."

"Her name is Valerie Lawry. She's here."

"In Rome?"

"Downstairs. Right now."

Jackie pulled open the door, revealing an oversize Orlando Magics T-shirt tucked into jeans. Bare feet. An athlete's taut, balanced stance. Still cautious, but willing to accept him at face value. "Come in."

He took the seat by the open French doors, feeling mocked by laughter rising from the plaza and steps below. "My sister has gone to Cairo. Bringing me to Rome was just a ploy to get me started. She's wanted me to travel down there since before I was elected to Congress. Why, I can't say. But I'm pretty certain it has something to do with a conference I heard about at the White House. You know the one?"

Jackie lowered herself to the edge of the bed. "Kay Trilling is going. And Nabil, the Egyptian who invited you here."

"I want you to find somebody who will track Valerie. Find out where she goes. Who she reports to." He handed over a sheet of paper. "Travel details and my hotel in Cairo, according to the woman at Sant'Egidio. Talk to somebody at the church. Maybe they can help you find a PI. The bottom number is my credit card. Charge everything."

Hair the color of winter wheat spilled across her face, hiding every-thing but her voice. "I can do that."

Suddenly the distance between them did not seem so great. An arm's reach across the expanse, a single step, and he would be seated there beside her. Jackie sensed the sudden change as well, for she looked up, revealing a woman who had come to expect little of life. And men. But not refusing him. Just waiting.

At that moment, however, Wynn desired nothing more than to ele-vate himself in her eyes. "I'm not the enemy, Jackie."

"No," she said softly. "I don't think you are."

He watched her waiting still, but perhaps hoping he was more than just another guy. Or maybe it was just him. So when he rose to his feet, it was to aim toward the door. "I guess I better do a few hours of jet-lag coma."

She followed him over, asked, "What is happening here?"

He shook his head, not at her question, but rather at how easy it had been to leave the woman downstairs. The one who belonged, who invited. And how hard to depart from the one who offered nothing but a mirror of his own sad state. "I'm getting tired of being played like a puppet. More than that, I can't say."

24

Tuesday

PAVEL HAYEK was not a traveler. He preferred to sit in his castle and command the world to come and bend the proper knee. But this journey to Miami was unavoidable. People with the kind of money he was after expected him to appear, if not at their doorstep, then at least at a suitable middle ground. As the Biltmore's presidential suite was already booked, he was ensconced in the Coconut Grove Ritz-Carlton's penthouse, as far from the tawdry glitz of South Beach as he could manage. Beyond his window, evening graced the Intracoastal basin with a quilt of subtle greens and golds and blues. The doors to his private balcony were open, admitting the sweet-scented breeze and a vague discord from streets far below. Hayek breathed in the myth of a gentle season and tried to keep his anger from showing. "I had expected to have Duclos himself here to speak with me."

"Monsieur le Chairman sends his sincerest regrets. He was unavoidably detained." The woman was a product of generations of French overbreeding, no doubt a graduate of one of their top echelon schools—INSEAD or the Ecole Nationale or somewhere equally pompous. She was not utterly without charms but her hair was overly foppish, her clothes far too modern, and her perfume just hideous. "He has asked me to obtain the further information required to reach our decision."

Hayek waved an irritated hand, motioning for Burke to respond. This really was too much. Duclos was either not going to invest, or he was expecting further concessions. This young woman was sent as an excuse for Duclos to avoid making a decision. And of course she was too full of herself to understand. The French were detestable creatures to do business with. Not for the first time Hayek regretted contacting them.

His search for coconspirators had been meticulous. From Switzerland had come NBS, runner-up to Credit Suisse for years. Nine months earlier, the bank had begun leaking institutional investors. Eleven billion dollars had flowed in the wrong direction in as many months, enough to have the senior directors quaking. The staid Swiss conservatism had been chucked, replaced by a frantic search for anything that would put them back in good stead with the money crowd. Hayek's proposal was clutched in a two-fisted panic.

Hanyo Bank of Yokohama was the world's seventh largest, with two hundred and twelve billion dollars in assets. Forty-seven forex and derivative traders worked in New York, out of a total U.S. staff of two hundred. Five years earlier their New York operations generated over one-third of the bank's total profits. This year they lost a cool billion and a half. From kings of the hill to lords of the dung heap. Desperate times. They had been Hayek's easiest sell.

The Frenchwoman used her gold pen to check another item off her list, then inquired, "When, exactly, will your plan be put into play?"

Really, this was too much. "Duclos knows perfectly well that I can't say."

"But my superiors demand—"

"Our goal is to wait for a moment when the market is at a euphoric high, then hit it with catastrophic news. News that we control. Which Duclos is already aware of."

It was a lie, of course. But there was no need to tell these people or anyone else precisely what he had planned. Anyone who knew his true design was instantly an uncontrolled risk.

She then asked the logical follow-on, which was, "How do you control such events?"

It was Burke who answered. "By having the catastrophic news already in-house."

"This is news of your government, yes?"

"News that the controllers are desperate to keep under wraps," Hayek lied. Not even Burke knew the truth. Which was as it should be. "News that will wipe twenty percent from the markets within hours of its release."

"When this news is amplified by the market's current volatility,"

Burke added, "we should have a genuine stampede on our hands. We go in fast, we strike hard, we win while the market is still reeling."

"So when—"

Hayek rose to his feet. This meeting was over. "The minimum input is two billion dollars," he said.

She accepted the dismissal with stiff grace. "I will report to my superiors and come back—"

"No. Play or don't, it's your choice. If you're in, transfer the money. Finish."

When Burke had shown the woman out, Hayek told his number two, "Hire someone good. Use the Liechtenstein bank for cover. Put tags on her and Duclos both."

"You don't think he's coming in?"

"Whether he is or not, we have to assume the information will be passed on or used." Neither of which he could afford. If their plans were successful, there would be an enquiry. The SEC and Fed would like nothing better than to hit him with a charge of collusion. Which was why no one knew the whole picture—not even Burke, and certainly not Duclos. Still, it was best to be safe. "Despicable people, the French."

Burke shuffled papers and tried to make his query sound casual. "What about the Brazilians?"

"I am meeting them tonight." Hayek noted the underlying tension in his own voice. "That is another group quite beyond belief. Those gray-jacketed security oafs endanger everything."

"I still don't see why you sent them to search the Havilland place." Burke hesitated, then added, "Unless you meant for them to fail."

That was the trouble with hiring intelligent people, Hayek reflected. They might just surmise the underlying enigma. He countered with, "Not to mention roughing up my security technician in front of the entire trading floor. Such brutality might work where they come from. But it accomplishes nothing here."

"The Brazilians won't agree to pull out their security."

Not yet, Hayek silently amended. "They're multiplying like lethal spoors. We really must find a way to contain them."

"What did you have in mind?"

Hayek was tempted to tell him. Which was genuinely remarkable. He never gave his secrets away to anyone. It was the clearest indication yet of the strain he felt. So many years to arrive at this point, so much riding on each step, each motion, each and every word. The answer to Burke's question was the same as to them all: find a solution that would turn the liability into his advantage.

He said simply, "Call for my car, will you."

Burke did so, then helped him on with his coat. "I still don't have the goods on Colin Ready."

"No doubt you'll find them, if they are there to be found." Lemmings, Hayek thought as he watched Burke spring for the door. A fraternity of highly intelligent, gilded lemmings. That's all these traders are. They are a breed driven by rumors, he thought, nodding to his aide's farewell. They prance about like princes, they bray like stallions, but at the first hint of peril they show their true nature. As the world would soon see.

THAT EVENING Hayek dined in solitary splendor at Norman's, not an altogether foul restaurant in Coral Gables. But neither the meal nor the Spanish colonial surroundings held his attention. He found himself given over to another place and different meals, ones shared with his mother at Manhattan's Russian Tea Room. It had been his mother's favorite place, the red velvet and brass and padded linen tablecloths all vaguely reminiscent of the grandeur she had once known. One of the waiters of Pavel's youth had been a minor Hungarian noble, someone his mother would most likely have scorned in another era. Even so, she would always sit at one of his tables. They would say little to one another, and speak only French, the social tongue of the central European aristocracy. And never, ever would they mention the lost realm. There was no need. A subtle shift of one eyebrow, a lingering sigh, a languorous glance at the restaurant's pedestrian crowd. It was enough. The waiter always called her Principessa and referred to the young Hayek as Monsieur le Comte. In return she had always used the most powerful of his vague connections, just the one word—Romanov. Upon departure, as she offered him a gloved hand, he would give the stiff half-bow of royalty, and she would bestow upon him a second title— that of Cousin. He was long gone now, as was Hayek's own mother. But the memories made for pleasant company. His mother would no doubt approve mightily of his present strategy.

Afterward he proceeded to the Jackie Gleason Theater of the Performing Arts, known locally as the TOPA. Tonight the full Kirov Ballet was dancing Stravinsky, providing the only reason Hayek had agreed to this journey at all. The director's box had cost him a twenty-thousand dollar donation. Hayek sat in solitary detachment and watched the dancers take leaps of which even Nijinsky might have approved.

Before the intermezzo applause had died down, a dark-suited young woman appeared at his elbow. "Would you follow me, Mr. Hayek?"

"Everything has been arranged?"

"Just as you requested. This way, please."

And indeed it was, a remarkable feat in this most variable of towns. The upper floor had a small open mezzanine, guarded now by yet another official. Hayek had ignored the Brazilian banker's insistence on meeting in their downtown offices, knowing the disadvantage would be too great. Controlling the turf was half the battle won. The young woman opened the door for him, accepted the tip with grave thanks, and shut the door firmly behind him.

"My dear Pavel, this is marvelous. Really." The Brazilian was portly and wore a saint's wreath of white hair. He waved his cigar to the balcony, the spring night, the champagne in the beaded silver bucket. "How you find these islands of privacy in the midst of this glorious city is utterly beyond me."

"There is nothing glorious about Miami," Hayek replied loftily. "Nothing whatsoever."

"But it is your closest metropolis, not to mention a place of Latin flavors. Even the crime is served with salsa." The banker beckoned at a shadow hulking by the balcony railing. Another man stepped from the night and entered the light splashing through the doors behind them. "A new associate of our group, and a new potential investor for you."

Hayek accepted the absence of name with a sharp nod. The man gave the same back. His face was all angles and danger, his eyes Siberian ice. Hayek shifted to Russian and said, "Will you take champagne?"

The man showed an instant's ire at being caught out so swiftly. The Brazilian banker poured laughter like oil over the disjointed moment. "Pavel, Pavel, you are too piercing for us. Of course, pour us some champagne, and let us speak of how you will make us all rich."

Hayek stripped the foil and the wire netting and popped the cork. Russian mafia money buying Brazilian banks, then aiming at an American hedge fund. A world gone truly insane, ripe for its own destruction. "You are already rich."

"As are you, my dear sir. As are you. But a little less rich than before your Ecuador fiasco." The Brazilian cut him a scalpel-sharp look, there and gone so swiftly Hayek could pretend to have missed it. The banker accepted the first glass, as was his due. "But there is always more power to be gained, is there not. More power and bigger toys." He sipped from his glass, nodded approval. "My youngest mistress does so dearly love her helicopter."

Hayek gave the second glass to the Russian, raised his own, and said, "If you retract your gray-suited dogs, we might just succeed. Given the present circumstances, we risk yet another disaster."

The dark eyes congealed. "We had nothing to do with the girl's demise in Washington. As I have repeatedly told you."

"Washington is history. There have been more incidents, as you well know. Those dolts of yours create havoc wherever they go. Only one of them manages to speak anything resembling English. They endanger everything."

"Pavel, Pavel, I shall speak frankly. You have the habit of treating other people's money as your own. We shall therefore have people in place to ensure you follow our agreed-upon policy."

Hayek bristled. "Nobody regulates me."

"Ah, but that is precisely what we shall do, if you want our money." The voice turned soothing. "I have spoken personally with their chief. They shall obey you to the letter from now on."

Hayek pretended to accept the inevitable with bad grace, and groused, "If there is one more problem, one more failure of any kind, they're out."

"Yes. Very well. To that I agree." He moved the cigar to the hand holding his champagne so that he could pat Hayek's shoulder. "You should be pleased with the gift, Pavel, not complaining like an old woman. These are highly trained specialists. If they have failed, it is because they are not used to, how shall I say it, handling such minor matters. Their connections cover the globe and are there for you to command."

Hayek hid his satisfaction with a gambler's skill. "You just make sure they learn to follow orders."

"Of course, my dear Pavel. Of course." The smile returned. "Now let us enjoy this excellent champagne while you explain to my new associate why he should help to finance your little project. What was that remarkable name you gave it?"

Hayek took a long breath, and replied evenly, "Tsunami."

□ □ □ □

HAYEK'S CELLPHONE chimed just as he was ushering his guests back indoors. Burke sounded as frantic as Hayek had ever heard.

Hayek felt a sudden rush of rage at the report, so great he could only manage, "I will call you back in two minutes."

"But—"

"Two minutes." He slapped the phone shut, wheeled about, and strode to the balcony's railing.

Not even the night could mask Miami's rough edges. South of TOPA rose a ghastly high-rise parking garage, leering at him like a face with rotting teeth. Beyond that, crowds streamed along Lincoln Avenue, a pedestrian mall filled with nightclubs and shops. Hayek grimaced at the sound of Latin rap exploding from a car trolling Collins Avenue below him. Those who found Miami enticing drew their points of comparisons from more barbaric lands, of that he had no doubt. He forced himself to take a slow breath, to relax in stages, to think.

Hayek knew what others did not. There was one path to holding dominion over might and wealth. Just one. He was not referring to what satisfied most people, what passed for achievement. No. To attain the pinnacle, the rarefied heights for which Hayek had been born, there was only one narrow trajectory. There must be a tightening down of all energy, every shred of emotion and force and desire, until all life's impetus was aimed at the one goal. A hunger so great it redefined the very breath of his body. A motive so strong every action and personal contact must help achieve the goal or be counted as dross to be scattered and forgotten. Aspirations must be honed to such a level that they became fiercer than the sharpest blade, cutting through all of life, carving away everything but the essential kernel. Nothing counted except the goal. Nothing. All else was simply the debris others lived for, what they lied and claimed was enough.

Then he realized that the night had already presented him with the answer. Hayek tossed a laugh to the garish scene and punched in Burke's number. Hayek informed him, "Our opposition must be pounded and ground and milled to the fineness of Caribbean sand."

"A tough thing to do," Burke replied, "considering who they are."

"Not if the work is done for us and cannot be traced back." Hayek then outlined his plan.

Burke's reply was instantaneous. "They'll fail."

"Then they seal their own fate." He cut the connection but remained at the balcony's railing until he had fully repressed the flush of triumph.

Only then did Hayek return inside. He followed the waiting usher back to the director's box, utterly content with how events were developing. The Brazilian's men would botch at least one of these new jobs. Of course they would. The resulting chaos was the perfect weapon to free him from their menacing presence. Hayek was under no illusions as to why the gray-suited dolts had been sent. They were not there to guard the Brazilian's money. They were there to remind him of what would happen were he to fail. A constant reminder, and a means by which Hayek's mind would be kept from searching out the Brazilian's *other* mole. The one who would send word back so the Brazilian could mimic Hayek's actions, and win double.

Hayek slid into his seat just as the curtain was rising. He tried to check his program, but the light was too dim. Then the orchestra played the first faint strains, and Hayek smiled his satisfaction. Stravinsky's *Firebird Suite*. His mother's favorite piece. Even the Russians danced to his tune this night, signifying to all the world that the phoenix was about to rise.

25

Wednesday

WHEN JACKIE ARRIVED downstairs the next morning, a trio of impossibly elegant women were doing coffee in the Hassler lounge. Several groups of businessmen watched her passage like lazy predators. The doorman gave her the sort of good morning that came with a five hundred dollar room, and ushered her into the sunlight. She crossed the cobblestone plaza and sought breakfast and a dose of reality in a corner café. Even if by some fluke she was ever granted the money and the ease, she would never become a Hassler type of gal. Her view of reality had come at too high a price to ever put her nose that far in the air.

Twice during the taxi ride to Sant'Egidio she glanced behind her, but the only things tracking her progress were sunlight and pigeons. The church was empty save for an old couple polishing the pews and four women kneeling before a side altar. The air smelled of dust and cold incense. Jackie pursued the sound of quiet chatter to a hallway leading off between two chapels. At the end, four Gypsy children sat sentinel outside a closed door. As soon as they spotted her, they rose and adopted the tragic whining cadence of professional beggars. Jackie did as she had seen the locals do the previous evening, touching their heads and outstretched palms, wishing she had an accompanying blessing to offer as well.

Her knock was answered by a musical protest in Italian. Jackie opened the door and inquired, "Was that a hello or get lost?"

"Jackie, hello, please forgive me." When Anna rose from the chair behind the desk, she grew shorter. "I thought it was the children. Some days . . . Come in, please. No, no, *va via!*" This to the children crowding in behind her. "Shut the door, quickly now. Good. Sit, sit. Will you have coffee?"

"No thanks."

"Please take something. It will delight the children no end to have me assign them something to do."

"All right."

"A *spremuta*, perhaps? Orange juice?"

"Anything."

"Excellent." The children greeted her reappearance by jostling for position. There was an argument over who was to go, settled only by Anna handing lire to the middle one and shutting the door once more. "Forgive them. They are starved for more than food and a bath." She returned to her desk. "Mr. Bryant has departed safely?"

"As far as I know." Jackie waited until the small woman was seated to say, "We need to hire a detective."

Anna inspected her for a somber moment. "This request. It has to do with your visit here in Rome?"

"Yes."

"Then the enemy has tracked you here?"

"Wynn thinks so."

Anna cocked her head to one side. "Do I wish to know more, Ms. Havilland?"

"Probably not."

"*Bene.*" Anna rose from the chair and gave what was perhaps her first false smile. "Please wait here."

The children returned soon after Anna's departure, proudly bearing a tray with a frothy glass. Jackie sipped the juice and enjoyed their company. The room suited them perfectly, unadorned save for the cross behind the desk and the furniture worn to bare bones. Once the children accepted that she neither understood them nor would give them money, they made a game of one-way conversation. Jackie responded with smiles, delighting in their dark-eyed frivolity.

When Anna returned, she let the children remain clustered about Jackie, as though seeking a witness, however flimsy. "Sadly I cannot help."

The flat turndown was unexpected. "Do you have any idea where I could go?"

"Perhaps one thought. Do you travel with a computer?"

"Yes."

"You know our website?"

Jackie thought of the blank screen and the unanswered message. "I'm not sure."

"Not the official Sant'Egidio address. I mean the other." Anna waited, examining her closely.

"Trastevere?"

"Ah. Excellent." This time the smile was very real. "That was the gift of one of our young members. An American like yourself. The work was done by a friend of hers. But that is unimportant now."

"I'm not sure I understand."

"Oh yes, of course, the single word can be most confusing. The one choice, to go or not." Anna raised Jackie with a gesture, and led her toward the door. "Make your request again there. Our friends can hear and remain hidden. Most important."

"Why is that?"

The long stone hallway turned Anna's words into a litany, the children into a cluster of filthy acolytes at her heels. "This other young woman worked in your Library of Congress. She was a dear friend. She loved life, Ms. Havilland. She loved God. And now she is gone."

The final word drifted up and away as they reentered the church. Jackie recalled an earlier conversation and wondered where Nabil was at that moment. "She was killed!"

"The police claim she died by her own choice. Leaping from a building. During a protest she helped organize. Please, you will return tonight and tell me what you have discovered?"

"Yes, all right."

"Where are you staying, may I ask?"

"The Hassler."

"A lovely hotel." Anna offered a parting smile. "Go with God, Ms. Havilland. And take great care."

BY THE TIME Jackie returned to her hotel and e-mailed her request, she was ready for lunch. She returned to the tiny coffee shop crammed between the intersection of two streets, across the cobblestone piazza from the Spanish Steps. The two old gentlemen seated by the doorway greeted her with the solemn nods of men who had learned the Italian etiquette of charm early and well. She felt the eyes of the young men tending bar even before she passed through the doorway, but in this time and place she did not mind. She ordered another *spremuta* and looked over the sandwiches arrayed in disciplined ranks beneath the glass. The older bar owner left his place by the cash register and shooed off the young man making famished eyes at her. He scooped up a spoonful of cream cheese and fresh herbs, spoke with the fluid arrogance of the native Roman, and gestured for her to smell. She did so, inhaling all the fragrances of a fresh-cut field. He grinned at her response, and pointed her to an outside table. Again the old men nodded and welcomed her with murmured flirtations. She sat and sipped her orange juice until the café owner appeared and set down the plate with an impossible flourish. The entire café watched as she tasted. Toasted black-olive *ciabatta* with fresh tomatoes, cream cheese, and prosciutto. Roman sun, a host of men watching her eat. All the world eager to see her smile. It was very hard not to be blinded by the day.

After lunch she returned to her room to check the electronic message board. She logged onto the Trastevere site, stared at the enigmatic command, then hit the key for Go. The screen instantly revealed the query, *Incoming direct coded signal. Will you accept? Go/NoGo.*

She studied the message as she would an alien life-form. There was no reference to anything she understood. But she hit the key for Go.

The message board dissolved, then filtered back again. This time there was the query, *Payment?*

She typed out, *Who are you?* Hit 'send'. The message slip folded itself into smoke and evanesced. The reply was swift in coming: *You made a request for assistance in tracking an individual from Rome. I am a detective and a friend of a small lady known for strong prayers.*

Jackie stared at the screen long enough to realize this was all the response she would ever receive. So when the incoming slip returned with the payment query repeated, she typed in Wynn's credit card number and a query of her own, *How can I know this is confidential?*

All Trastevere messages are automatically anonymized.

"What choice do I have," she asked the empty room. *When will you have the requested info?*

Soon.

This is urgent. How can I contact you?

But the screen remained blank.

□   □   □   □

JACKIE DECIDED IT was necessary to call Esther, despite the hour in Washington. "I know it's too early."

"It's fine. Really. I was just leaving for the hospital. Graham is coming home."

"That's wonderful news."

"He spoke my name yesterday." She sounded close to singing. "What do you need?"

"I just wanted to pass on what's happened." She related the events, or at least some of them. She spoke only of the church and Wynn's departure and Valerie's arrival and Anna's warning. Leaving out the images that floated about as she spoke. Saying nothing of their dinner, their talk, their leave-taking in the lobby. Or the way she had felt as Wynn left her room the night before, the sudden desire to walk down the hall, speak his name again, holding him as she did. The first time in over two years she had felt anything more than warning.

Esther must have heard the slight tremor that escaped, and understood. For her voice flattened when she said, "Wynn Bryant is a handsome, dangerous man."

Jackie swallowed. It was so hard to speak up on behalf of any male. "I don't think he's the enemy, Esther."

"No? You've spent, what, two days in his company and you know him that well?"

"People change. They learn, they grow. Not often. But it happens."

She waited for the bitter retort, but to her surprise all the older woman did was sigh the one word. "Cairo."

"Should I have gone with him?"

"No. I suppose you might as well follow your instincts. Let me know what the detective says. And remember what that woman told you. Be careful."

26

Wednesday

I F YOU HAVE THE security right, you can do just about anything and do it safely. My task this morning is to be an enabler, and to help you protect your data and maintain the integrity of your sources."

Colin was two-thirds through his standard monthly spiel to the corporate fresh meat. All but three of the newly hired were finding it hard to stay awake. Which was very good, since he had designed the little talk to bore them senseless. It was his very own introductory course in corporate drivel. After this half hour, they'd do a moondance in feathers and warpaint in Hayek's front office before ever seeking Colin out again.

"The next step in data service is authentication, which is your way of ensuring the system that you are who you say you are." He walked around the room handing out plastic blanks like unfinished credit cards. "These are your very own scratch-and-sniffs. Scratch the silver line there, then memorize your ID number. Don't write it down. Don't forget it. There is a five hundred dollar penalty for losing your number, and a five hundred dollar reward for finding someone else's. You will receive a new one every quarter."

In his early days, Colin had found the nine-digit numbers scrawled in every imaginable place. He had used the rewards to finance the down payment on a new car. Since then people had wised up. "Access control is the other side of the coin. The Hayek Group uses a program known as Resource Access Control Facilitator, or RAC/F. This is a standard roll-base enabler and monitors all departments on an independent system. You will be permitted entry only to your designated portions of the mainframe's data bank. Those sections you will find outlined on pages six and seven of your personalized folder." Only one of them bothered to look. "If you require anything outside those areas, you will need to speak to someone with dedicated access."

The final pair of eyes glazed over. Total oblivion had set in. Proof that Dilbert clones were not born, but molded. "Today's final point deals with data confidentiality, which is the system's way of ensuring anything you write or, for you traders, any deal you make, remains hidden from all except those with . . ."

His pager was set for silent alarm and vibrated against his belt. He glanced down and saw it was a call from Eric on the trading-room floor. Anything from the floor during office hours was to be treated as critically urgent. Colin looked out over the room. Not a single face showed any awareness that he had even stopped talking. He was momentarily tempted to just walk out in mid-sentence, see how long they would remain caught in soporific stasis. "To finish up, our internal corporate data system must be treated as a secure world. Our electronic premises must have each and every one of you acting as vigilant guards at all times. Any questions? All right then. Welcome to the Hayek Group."

Colin flew down the outer corridor. If it was a true emergency, seconds might mean millions. He slipped into the back of the trading room and waited to be noticed. Dealers raced and shouted their way through a normally frantic day. Eric caught his eye, lifted one finger, used it as an arrow to plant Colin where he was. Eric juggled two telephones as he went back to punching numbers into his board. Then he called over to his senior trader, "I've got a broker on the line from London. Looks like we might have an arbitrage opening up here."

That caught everyone's attention in the spot trade section. The word meant different things to different kinds of traders. For currency hounds, an arbitrage was basically a gap between one group's offer and another active bid. With e-trading, arbitrages grew smaller and flashed out quicker. But canny traders still found them. And grabbed them with iron teeth of greed.

Alex, the senior spot trader, scooted his chair out far enough to see the trio of aisles that made up his world. "Who's the shop?"

"Won't say," Eric replied. "But Rawls is the broker. A troll might be at work here."

This meant Eric was probably up against a minor Swiss player who was keeping his sale confidential by acting through a currency broker. It had taken Colin months to understand both the lingo and the action. The study had become a hobby, something tied to his e-world but beyond it, another linked universe that amplified the high. The "shop" was either a bank or fund active in currency trading. These days there were two classes of shops operating out of Switzerland. The gnomes were the top-league traders, biggest of the big. Credit Suisse alone handled over six hundred billion in assets. Contests with gnomes usually turned into scalding experiences. It was critical when trying to play an arbitrage to make sure a gnome was not involved.

Trolls were something different. Trolls were would-be gnomes. they operated in regional Swiss banks and pretended to a knowledge they often did not have. A true gnome would not allow a troll to open his car door, much less have access to a gnome-type lead. Which meant occasionally trolls would open arbitrage pockets big enough to hold a truckful of profit. Eric handled dollar-euro, and the euro had been on a wild and woolly ride since its introduction. Instability like this bred occasional chances for big profit. And bigger losses.

"They've put up a bid for eighty million dollars at fifty." Eric spoke in hushed tones, even though his phone mikes were muted.

"What's the market say?"

"Stable at thirty points higher."

Thirty points was a spread of one-third of a cent, a huge difference for a relatively calm day. The senior trader rose to his feet. Alex quietly addressed his cadre, who waited poised at the cliff's edge, every one of them ready to leap. "Call one friend each. See if there's something out there we don't know about." The traders scattered.

Eric said, "I've found a bid on-line for fifty at ten higher." This meant he already had a buyer for fifty million of the anonymous seller's eighty million, at ten points above the offered price. After commission it represented a marginal profit, less than a quarter-million dollars, but not bad for a sixty-second play.

"Buy eighty, sell fifty," the senior man ordered. "And put your broker on the horn."

Eric routed one of his phones through the speaker above his central screen. He shut off his mute button and said, "I buy your eighty at one-fifty."

"Sold at one-fifty," intoned the dull voice over the speaker. "You in the market for more?"

All brokers spoke like they were coming off a ten-week drunk, the effects of living on the knife's edge of spot trading. One-fifty was a reference to the final cent and points, or hundredths of a cent. The rest of the exchange rate was not mentioned unless the shifts came in violent increments. Then the rates were not spoken but screamed. Colin had seen it happen twice, and both times the trading floor had become a battle zone.

Eric was already flashing the sell order on his keyboard. He covered his phone mike. "Bought and sold."

"Right." The senior trader rose up and hissed to his team, "What have you got?"

He received a chorus of head shakes. One woman muttered, "According to Lehman, dollar-euro is holding stable."

Alex dropped back into the saddle. Said to Eric, "Tell the guy we're in for more."

"How much?"

"Go for a quarter. See what he says."

Eric tried vainly to hold to his calm. But the bug eyes gave him away. A quarter billion dollars was twice his limit and the biggest trade he had ever made. His voice was slightly strangled as he uncovered his mike and said, "Back to you with second query."

"Go."

"What's your posit for more dollar-euro?"

"Give me a size."

A nervous glance at Alex, who nodded sharply. Go. "Two hundred and fifty either way."

A fractional pause, then, "This is an authorized trade?"

An authorized trade meant the query was backed by an actual right to deal. "Affirmative."

"Hold one."

The senior trader raised his hand like a conductor ready to lead the band into frantic song. The broker came back, "Two hundred fifty at one-fifty-sixty."

Either-way trade offers included both buy and sell prices. One-fifty-sixty meant the unnamed source was willing to either sell euros at eighty-one and fifty hundredths U.S. cents, or buy at ten hundredths higher. This buy-sell difference also included the broker's minuscule cut.

The senior trader's upraised hand pumped violently. Nineteen traders went into hyperdrive. The first response came from across the aisle at, "Buy fifty at one-seventy!"

Another, "Seventy at one-sixty-nine!"

The senior trader's arm pumped harder. Over the speaker the broker demanded, "Are we trading or am I walking?"

Eric uncovered his mike but could not keep the tremble from either his voice or his hand. "Hold one."

"I don't hold for nobody, boyo. Especially not some schmuck trading out of his league. You drop this, you don't ever call me again."

A voice from across the room shouted, "Sixty-five at one-sixty-one!"

The senior trader snapped, "Buy it all."

Eric's voice raised an octave as he shouted, "Buy two-fifty at one-fifty!"

"Done and good-bye." The broker cut the connection.

The senior trader shouted, "We're still holding twenty-five. Find me *anything* over one-fifty!"

"Twenty-five at one-fifty-six!"

Eric stabbed his screen and managed, "Euro-dollar's going south. The market's gapping down!"

The senior trader walked over to clap Eric on the shoulder. "Add fifty to your limit and a half-bill to your bonus." He said more loudly, "Way to go, team!" Then he headed toward Colin.

Colin said in greeting, "Eric buzzed me."

"I asked him to." Up close Alex had the stretched-mask face of a trauma victim and a voice to match. He pointed to the balcony. "You see the new guys?"

"I do now." The glassed-in parapet was alive with activity. Upstairs traders went through a normal trading day. Only they were cut off by a glass wall and gave scant indication they were aware of anything down below.

"Can you tap in and find out what's going on?"

"No. They're using a secure line."

"Independent of the group's computers?"

"Independent of everything."

The senior trader looked very worried. "This is a bad idea, putting them up there. Traders deal in rumors, and I'm stamping out a dozen at a time. Half my guys have feelers out for new jobs. They can't work in a place where they're getting secondhand reports."

"You don't know that."

"I don't know anything. Hayek's just getting back from Miami, the Unabomber's not available, and I've got twenty new faces standing on top of my head. And I don't know why." The senior trader's attention was caught by arm-waving from one of his cadre. Alex was a man who lived in twenty-second bursts. Colin's time was up. "You hear anything, you let me know, right?"

"Absolutely." Colin watched him move away, grateful for this public connection. Alex had not met him today to ask about the new scene overhead. He wanted to show all the members of his eighty-by-eighty world that Colin was one of the good guys. His place was swiftly taken by Eric. Colin told him, "You did good out there."

"Today, maybe." Eric's high was gone, the fizz now flat. "You know what they say about the higher you climb."

"Yeah," Colin replied. "The more money you put in your pocket."

"If that's so, how come I'm the one always in debt?" Eric headed back to his desk.

Colin searched the upstairs glass cage for the deadhead in Armani, but all the faces were fleeting blurs backlit by a hundred monitors. Colin turned from all the unanswered questions and headed back to his safe little hole.

But he was halted at his cubicle's entrance by the sight of a well-dressed foe perched on the edge of his seat. The usurper's ivory linen jacket was pulled up his arms to reveal a gold Rolex. Super-dude shades sat on top of his spiky waxed hair. Colin could not believe his eyes. *Nobody* entered someone else's cubicle without permission. It was one of the backroom's unbreakable codes. "What are you *doing?*"

The guy knew he had gone too far. He tried for cool, but the jerky way he snapped about, then flashed back to kill the screens convicted him. "Easy there. Just hanging around, playing the odd game."

But Colin was no longer listening. He seldom felt rage, even less often acted upon it. But to find this man seated in *his* space working on *his* system pushed him way beyond redline.

"Chill, dude. It's all part of a day's play. I mean, it's not like you've got anything worth hiding, am I right?"

A weapon. Colin found nothing to hand except the ficus tree guarding the cubicle opposite his. He raced over and hefted it, bucket and all.

"Hey!" A voice from inside cried, "You can't—"

But Colin was already hurtling back across the narrow aisle, gathering what speed he could. He hefted the tree, bucket first, aiming straight for the deadhead's slack-jawed face.

It was a lousy shot. The guy ducked in time, and Colin managed only to graze the top of his head. But it was enough to dislodge the bug-eyed shades and dump a ton of dirt down the back of the guy's shirt.

"*Help!*" The guy was down on all fours now, or at least threes, with one hand wrapped over his head. "This idiot's gone berserk!"

"You miserable cretin!" Colin flipped the empty bucket to one side, gripped the tree by its branches, and whipped the roots down on the guy's back and shoulders. Leaving filthy stripes across the guy's jacket. Feeling the shades crunch under his foot. "You ever come in here again I'll *kill* you."

The worst blow came not from Colin at all, but rather from the guy catapulting out of the cubicle still blinded by the hand covering his head, and ramming straight into the opposite wall. He went down hard, which gave Colin time to get in another two swipes across his back and one solid kick to the ribs. The guy shrilled a noise too high for human vocal cords and fled, leaving a trail of dirt and leaves in his wake.

Chest heaving, Colin stood staring down the corridor. Then he realized he was not alone. He turned to find the aisle behind him jammed with round-eyed spectators.

Somebody said, "Plaudits, dude."

"Yeah, way to rage, Colin."

"Was that one of the new guys?"

Colin nodded, then said to his colleague from across the aisle. "Sorry about the tree. I'll buy you another."

The young woman was an Indian who rarely said more than hello. Surree somebody. "My mother gave me that thing. I've always hated it."

The neighbor to his left asked, "Need a hand cleaning up?"

"Sure, thanks." But when he reentered his cubicle, he ignored the dirt and leaves and burrowed under his desk. Searching. "Anybody see him come in, or how long he was here alone?"

"No."

There it was. Duct-taped to the back of his server. Wired in and out between his dedicated lines. A second ghost feed. A tracer. Colin pried it free, reattached the wires as they should have been, and slid out.

The sight froze all motion. "Is that what I think it is?"

Someone else asked, "Why would anybody want to bug their own security guy's system?"

Colin rose to his feet, brushing futilely at the dirt. "I've got to see Alex."

COLIN'S CUBICLE HUMMED with a power all its own. He had maneuvered for an ergonomic chair like the senior traders, nylon strung tight as a pro's racket, balancing every part of his body and offering flow-through ventilation. His desk held six monitors, two more than the average trader, and his were all twenty-one inch Fujitsu LCDs. State of the art, five thousand dollars a pop. Not to mention his two independent servers. Six dedicated lines, three in, three out. It was the nerd's equivalent of strapping into the saddle of an F-16. Clicking in, blasting off. Locked and loaded.

The gabardine menace's invasion left Colin seriously assaulted.

He sat as Alex led in five other senior traders, a third of those managing the Hayek floor. All of them were tense and impatient over being dragged away from the end of trading. He watched them do a quick sweep of his gear. A couple of them whistled appreciatively.

Alex instructed, "Show them what you found."

Colin handed him the coupling, explained, "It's a high-speed drone, flashing a duplicate signal of every incoming and outgoing message I send over the wires. A wiretap for computer transmissions."

"Now show him the others."

Another trader barked, "He found more?"

"Two on the trading floor's outgoing feeder lines," Alex confirmed.

They handled the bugs with cold fury. Colin did not know them well. Senior traders occupied a universe all their own. They were blooded gunslingers with countless notches in their belts, carrying life and death and corporate profit in both fists. Over twenty-eight billion dollars in daily limits were represented here. A total personal net worth of forty, maybe fifty million dollars. But as they inspected the bugs, Colin saw just five men and one woman in rumpled sweat-smeared clothes, strung out from another day in the electronic trenches.

The lone woman was a recent import from New York. "This is a normal part of the Florida game plan?"

"Not on my turf." Alex bore two white spots over the bones beside each eye. "I've done some checking. Any of you catch the guy this morning wearing a rose bush in his hair?"

"Hard to miss," the woman replied.

"Nice touch, by the way," the senior bonds trader offered Colin. "Your work?"

"It was a ficus tree," Colin replied. "But yes, thanks."

"Whatever." Alex's hands trembled slightly, perhaps from anger, perhaps mere tremors from too many days balanced on the razor's edge. "His name is Brant Anker. Formerly of San Francisco. B of A. Number two Forex spots desk. He was shed when they closed the SF trading ops. Him and a hundred and sixty others."

The news silenced the room. The bond trader demanded, "So how many landed here?"

"Far as I can tell," Alex replied, "something like two dozen."

"You mind telling me why Hayek would graft on an independent Forex arm?"

"Only two reasons that I can come up with, both of them bad. One, he's going to let me and my team go."

"That's a no-brainer." This from the head of their derivatives arm. "You're outperforming the entire floor."

"I've got no time for the Unabomber. Maybe Hayek wants somebody who's more of a team player." Alex's eyes were bleak. Ancient fatigue gripped his face and pulled it back until the edges rippled with the strain.

"So what's the other option?"

"He's setting them up to move a big parcel of new money."

"Using restricted data?"

"That's my worst-case."

The woman's face was lined by an overdose of reality. "Looks like it's time to dust off the old résumé."

"I don't buy in." This from the head of the corporate desk. "Why plant these guys right under our nose if they're using confidential info? Why not stick them where we'd never know? Hayek's got no reason not to put another arm in Luxembourg, hide it from all but the elves."

"This afternoon Hayek came in from Miami, stayed maybe five minutes, and took off again." Alex went on, "My thinking is, tomorrow morning we hit Hayek all together. The module, the Gucci warrior sneaking around, the goons in gray, the new traders dancing on our heads, the lack of answers, everything."

The new woman rose wearily to her feet. "Here I was thinking my kids would get to know a world of schools without guns and chain-link fences and guard dogs. I should have known it was too good to last."

"An hour before the opening bell," Alex told the group. To Colin, "You with us?"

27

Wednesday

WYNN'S FLIGHT FROM Rome to Cairo took less than three hours. Everything about the airport and the highway into town was newer than his memories. Yet even when the new gave way to the old, when street corners became filled with men in djellabas smoking and talking, when the horns blared and the potholes bounced his taxi, still he remained untouched. Which was very good.

Sybel had booked them into the Inter-Continental, one of the new downtown hotels. The balcony of his ninth-floor suite held sweeping views of Cairo and the Nile. Traffic flowed along the Corniche, the road fronting the riverbank. The Nile flickered green and cool. As he stood on his balcony and watched the river cruisers, the first recollection struck. It came neither with sight nor sound, but smell. Wynn tasted a fragrance of river water, woodsmoke, spices, and diesel fumes. In the distance, beyond the Nile and the dusty day, he thought he heard a boy's laughter. It was enough to press him back inside.

Wynn swept the curtains shut, closing out the hated place. He stretched out on the bed but did not sleep. He had dozed the entire flight down, and now was trapped in his own wakeful lair. He was still awake when the muezzin called the faithful to late-morning prayers. The cry rose from everywhere, including Wynn's own mind.

Their houseboy, Ali, had taught him to mimic the muezzin's call and the intonations, then laughed delightedly when his piping voice had imitated the long-drawn-out syllables. Wynn had practiced with Ali for days. His debut performance had been at his parents' weekly Saturday dinner, a gathering for as many as thirty guests. On those nights the table stretched through the parlor's double doors and extended onto the apartment balcony. Wynn had stood there and done his chant and made many of the guests laugh. All of them applauded afterward, all save his parents.

The next day his father had shown him a book, the most beautiful book Wynn had ever seen. Each page was illustrated with designs of gold and violet and blue. "This is the most valuable thing I own," his father told him. "Your mother gave it to me for our first anniversary in Cairo. We keep it in the ebony box your mother has ordered you never to touch. It is more than three hundred years old."

Wynn's finger had reached out to trace a line midway down the right-hand page, one set aside from the other writing by thin gold lines. The writing itself was gold as well, and shone ruddy and yellow in the daylight.

"This entire book was written by hand. This first line, what you now touch, is the same for each chapter, or *Sura*. It is part of the muezzin's prayer, what you chanted. You see how this last word is drawn out long, just like the muezzin's call? The scribe writes this prayer, and then draws this word so very long, you see? Why? Because this is the word *Allah*. Just as the muezzin draws out the word until his mind is focused, the scribe does this as a prayer. He asks help to clear his mind. He is about to copy a chapter of what for him is the holy book. His mind must be clear and silent and thinking of nothing save Allah."

Wynn's own voice had piped up then. "But we are Christian and this is Muslim. And when I learned the chant it made Ali laugh."

"Ali is not a believer. That is his choice. We believe in the Lord Jesus. That is our choice. For the man who wrote this, for the muezzin who calls out to Allah, this is a vital part of his life. I would like all the world to know the message of Christ's salvation. But to those who do not, still I can offer respect. Jesus calls us to love everyone. How better to begin than through respect?" When Wynn did not respond, his father had continued, "So when you next sing the muezzin's prayer, I want you to do it with a heart full of respect. For the muezzin, and for all believers everywhere."

Now Wynn tossed back the rumpled covers and padded to the bathroom. Angry at having lost himself in what was so far gone.

He remembered all right. He remembered everything.

WHEN WYNN RETURNED from the bathroom, he knew his sister was there. He was alerted to her presence by the shifting of the wind, a faint trailing edge of scent. All his senses were heightened by the threat of approaching memories. He stepped onto the balcony and found her watching as heat and dust gathered with the daylight. Late spring was the season of *khamsin*, the desert winds that could blow so strong they stripped clothes and skin from bone. But today was mild for Egypt, balmy and almost pleasant. Even the cacophony of traffic noise rising from below held a contented air.

Wynn said, "This conference is so important you'd bend heaven and earth to get me here?"

She turned reluctantly from the riverside scene. "I wanted you to come before Grant offered you the position. Remember?"

"I never expected such subterfuge from you. My mistake."

"You were the one who said you'd give me anything I wanted. You never asked my reasons before."

Sybel's dark hair was silhouetted against the shimmering light. She seemed to belong here, even with her vibrant features smudged by fatigue and strain. Her hair was tied back as tight as ever, with a few tendrils slicked down over her forehead. Her eyes remained brilliant and deep and always caring. Wynn said, "So you got me here. How about telling me what you really want."

"My sweet sad Wynnie. Do you remember the name I had for you here?"

"Answer the question, Sybel."

"Pooh. My dearest little Pooh-bear." Her eyes gripped him tightly. "Do you remember anything at all of that time?"

"I was five when we left."

"You had just turned six, and who is avoiding the question now?"

"No. I don't remember."

"You can't, or you won't?" When he did not respond, she went on, "I want you to be happy."

"So you bring me back to the place that wrecked my life?"

"Sometimes the only way to discover a wrong turn is to go back to the beginning and look closely. Is that so much to ask?"

"You know how much I hate this place."

"You don't hate Cairo. You hate how life was taken out of your hands here." When he tried to leave the balcony, she gripped him hard and wrenched him back to the railing. "Ever since Dianne died and you sold your company you've been absolutely miserable."

"It takes time—"

"Not this much. Not for you. You're down because all the things you've managed to hide from yourself have finally caught up with you. And the only way you're ever going to rise from this tragic pyre is to face those things and *deal* with them."

He hid behind sarcasm. "So this Jubilee thing and the conference, all this has nothing to do with why I'm here?"

She released his arm then. A gesture of defeat. Wynn started to go inside but stopped at the balcony door to say, "Grant and his pals really don't want this to happen."

"Grant isn't here." Her voice was flat and dry as the desert air. "The conference doesn't start until this evening. Will you at least go around with me before then and see some of the old places?"

SYBEL STARTED HIM off slowly, ordering the driver to take them on a meandering tour. She passed him little bits of information, too excited to do her job well. They began by driving past the apartment house in Zamalik where they had lived, then ambling by the Gazirah Sporting Club where Sybel claimed they had spent countless afternoons. They drove across the Kubri al Tahrir bridge and through Tahrir Square, then down the lengths of Kasr El Nil and Shiek Ashah Streets. The streets were packed with shoppers and dozens of stores selling shoes and jewelry, since even the most conservative women could show off feet and ankles, neck and wrist. Then they took a slow drive past the Royal Automobile Club, where they always came for Sunday lunch. Wynn sat and listened to her recount how he had loved to watch them roll back the restaurant's retractable roof, and how their parents let him have all the ice cream he wanted. His mouth shaped the words, vanilla or strawberry or chocolate, only one flavor made each week and done fresh that morning. But he remained quiet.

They halted before the Gamaliya, where Hussein, the grandson of Muhammed, was buried. The Fatimid Mosque and the surrounding Hussein Plaza were fronted by shops catering to pilgrims who came from all over North Africa. As they alighted she pointed out a *sibeel*, a fountain alcove carved into a former palace wall, where the poor could stop to drink and wash themselves. Overhead were carved the Arabic words "And Allah gave them a pure water to drink." Sybel claimed their mother had often brought them to the neighboring coffee shop.

Today the corner table was occupied by three women in bangled bedouin garb, drinking mint tea and smoking the *shisha*, or hubble-bubble. The windless lane alongside their table was packed with people and smoke and memories.

Together they walked the alleys of El Fustad, built in the eleventh century by the first Muslim rulers as the center of *Qahira*, the name from which later English rulers derived Cairo. Wynn passed grit-encrusted buildings whose ornate stonework rose like geometric lace. He spotted the *iwan*, recessed alcoves where people could sit and rest, gifts to pilgrims from those who formerly owned the buildings, now often as not filled with stalls selling leather, amber, brass, or inlaid boxes. He raised his gaze and spotted arabesque shutters and doors and wished there were some way to shut his mind to the torrent of images.

Sybel strolled him through the antiques market, passing on other bits of memories. Wynn listened grudgingly, for he heard not his sister but rather his mother's voice. This was his mother's love, shopping the alleys, arguing with the Egyptian and Syrian and Persian and Sephardic shopkeepers, learning the city's lore. They passed through the Serah, the jewelry area, then crossed the Gauhar El Kata Street where the original Fatamid Gates still stood. Beyond El Mouez El Din, the Street of Scales, they entered the pungent rainbow world of the spice market. Wynn waited while Sybel haggled over a jar of saffron, gold and rich as sun-laced oil. He remembered his mother doing the very same thing, and recalled how he had loved the way the tiniest touch of the spice would color everything—the rice, the floor, the woodwork, his clothes and hands. Sybel kept glancing his way, waiting for him to speak, to admit that he remembered and was there with her. But it took all the strength he had just to stand and find a breath of air.

They returned to the car and drove to the Misr Al Qadimah, the old Christian quarter. The memories came faster now, unbidden, unwelcome.

The car halted before a wall. Just a wall. The city possessed millions of them. But something about this place drew him up short.

"Mother loved to come here," Sybel prompted. When he said nothing, she reached over, squeezed his hand, said, "Let's go see why."

Sandstone walls the color of desert turned the corner with them and began to close in, tighter and tighter, until the lanes grew so narrow they were ever in the shade. The air was tainted by dust and heat and the deposits of horse-drawn carts. The only life Wynn saw was an old woman in black, sunken into her doorway until she seemed only partially drawn from the shadows.

Sybel halted before a door from another era, when stout oak was bonded by great leaves of metal to repel barbarians and swords and metal-tipped staves. Overhead protruded a *mashrabiya*, the harem balcony whose wooden slats were woven too tightly to permit passers-by any glimpse within. The muezzin's cry rose then, at home in this harsh and empty realm.

Beyond the portal, a garden bloomed. Impossible colors. Hundreds of flowers, their beauty almost obscene after the dry arid nothingness without. "We're in the forecourt of St. Mark's church, one of the oldest in Cairo. Momma loved it here," she said. "Do you remember any of this?"

"Nothing," he lied.

"She brought me when I was very good. And you, once or twice. Usually you waited out in the plaza with Daddy. For me these visits were more than a reward. It was Momma's way of welcoming me into the secrets she would only share with another adult." They descended stairs made slick by centuries of feet, left their shoes at a second, grander set of doors, and entered the cool chamber. "This place spoke to her of faith's primitive beginnings."

Benches ringed the grand hall, as tall as it was long and beamed by smoke-blackened planks thick as five men. The reed mats were soft and gave gently beneath his feet. The art was so ancient as to appear alien, done by another race of souls entirely. A supplicant chanted over prayer beads. A trio of women sat at the far wall and chatted softly with a black-robed priest. Four couples prayed in a side alcove, one wearing the white shawl of coming marriage.

"Momma called this a comforting place, yet one that offers no false hopes." Sybel's voice was soft enough to rise swiftly and be enveloped by the incense and the centuries of echoes. "The first time we came here, I will never forget, a woman entered wearing a black, tassled prayer shawl. I watched her kneel where we are standing now, crawl toward the altar, then prostrate herself. She covered her head and lay as one dead. Momma pointed out to me how her feet were blackened and callused, her heels and ankles tattooed in a tribal pattern. All the stories hidden beneath that black shawl, all the sorrows in those immobile feet.

She just lay there, using her prayer mantle as a shroud, giving herself over to the grief of hopeless prayer. Asking not for answers. Only peace. Immeasurable, beyond understanding. Peace now and forever."

Wynn turned and walked back into the sunlight. He slipped on his shoes, crossed the garden, passed through the outer portal, and walked back down the cobblestone lane. Cairo was filled with the crumbling relics of many empires. Four thousand years of invaders had left many prizes and exacted heavy tolls. Hyssops, Romans, Vandals, Ottomans . . . The list was endless. Their legacies were everywhere, from the fading glory found upon almost every street, to the stoic tragedy on virtually every face. Wynn stopped by the car and waited for Sybel to join him. Leaning against just another wall.

She rounded the corner with shoulders hunched, her expression lost behind sunglasses. Just the tightly compressed lips were visible. Wynn pushed himself from the wall and demanded, "What possible good did you expect to come from all this?"

"What possible good are you accomplishing now? What joy have I deprived you of by bringing you here?" The words sprayed like hot pellets. "Wynn, we *need* you. Graham's illness has left a gaping void at the heart of our cause."

"So I'm expected—"

"No. Not at all. *Nothing* is expected. Nobody would dream of *expecting* you to do anything except *exactly* what pleases you at the moment."

He surveyed Sybel's stance, hands cocked on her hips like dual triggers, chin jutting as she readied herself for whatever objection he levied. "Nobody can tell you anything, can they. You know what's best, and no matter what anybody else thinks, you're going to push and prod until they do what you say they should be doing."

She flushed the color of taut fury. "For years people have been pressing Congress and other governments to do something about third-world debt. So they pass laws, then let the forces ruling the financial trade come in and strip away everything but the words. Most politicians don't care about what's happening in another country. Those foreigners can't vote. If it's so important to the banking lobby to keep milking this third-world cow, fine. Then Graham comes along. He's on fire over another scandal within the financial world. Same war, different battle. Graham is desperate for allies. We meet, I put him in contact with Sant'Egidio. Graham fits right in. He's not after glory. He's not after the next fun thing. He wants to serve his people and his God. He views this battle as having a divine purpose—"

"All right, Sybel. I get the picture."

"You shut up and *listen*. Graham claims it was Father Libretto who suggested a way to make our two causes one. Father Libretto says all he did was listen and let Graham hear God speak. All I know is, suddenly there is a link. Something so totally enticing Graham can take this new idea of his to friends in Congress. They sat up and said, yes, here is something that just might work. So Father Libretto and his movement brought in allies from other countries. Very quiet, just laying the groundwork. But the idea caught fire. It turns out there are a *lot* of people very worried about the dragon of international finance."

"So you bring me to Egypt, thinking I'll find something that rocks my boat enough to make me take on Graham's work. Is that it?" He watched his dark and distorted reflection in the lenses of Sybel's sunglasses. "Only you didn't figure Grant into the equation, did you. How he'd find the leverage to turn this to his advantage."

"I don't know what I thought, only what I hoped." She waved to someone behind him. "Here comes Nabil and his father."

The Egyptian was groomed as always, every hair in place, suit immaculate, no sign of feeling the heat. Wynn stared at the old man leaning on Nabil's arm but felt no flicker of recognition. For the old man it was an entirely different story. He left the safety of his son's arm and tottered forward, leaking Arabic and tears. First to Sybel, kissing her hand, then both cheeks, switching to English, saying merely, "So good. So good."

"You are looking fine, Uncle."

"Yes. On this day, of course. Fine." He then moved to Wynn, bowed and salaamed with the regal gestures of one long denied this moment. "My heart soars. The son stands and casts the father's shadow."

Nabil spoke. "Abu, this is Congressman Wynn—"

"I am not knowing this man? From so high I am knowing him." He lowered a trembling hand to the ground. "Your father was a great man. A friend to all Egypt, your father. And now you are here."

Wynn endured the words and the embrace, relieved when Sybel glanced at her watch and said, "We need to be going."

They set their pace to match the old man's, rounded the far corner, then waited for a funeral to pass. Wynn watched as men bunched about the coffin, jostling in ill-mannered grief for the chance to help carry the body. The women paraded more sedately behind, a long flowing line of black and gray, piercing the heat with their wails. Wynn followed them through high peaked gates, and only then did he understand. But the old man had him in an iron grip, Sybel was at his other side, and they were already moving forward. Into the city of the dead.

They walked the dusty lane and through the gates with the Islamic quarter-moon on one side, a Coptic cross on the other. It had to come, he knew. He was here and this was Egypt. It had to come. Wynn felt Sybel cast darting glances his way, knew she was trying to gauge how close he was to the edge. So he asked the old man, as casually as he could, "My parents' funeral was like the one we just saw?"

"Oh no, sir. Nothing like. Bigger. A funeral for royals. But not together. First your mother. Then your father nine days later."

Sybel tried to interrupt, "We don't need—"

"We're here," Wynn cut her off. "Let him speak."

"Your mother went fast. Very fast. Three days in the hospital, then gone. The day you leave for America, that night she goes. And why to stay? Her children are safe, she can leave. Your father, he sleeps for eight days, he wakes, he asks for his wife. He hears. He asks for his children. He hears this, then he sleeps again. And does not wake any more." The arms raised theatrically. "The crowds, sir. Twice they come, for wife and husband both. Miles and miles of people. All the old city was shut down."

"Thank you." It was all a vast exaggeration, of course, an old man's gift of a memory born out of respect and not reality. "I am most grateful."

IT WAS NOT Wynn who was affected by the visit to his parents' tomb, but Sybel. He stood before the dusty waist-high structure, already tilted by roots growing from two sheltering olive trees, and felt nothing. There were names, but in Arabic, and two crosses, one upon each door. He stood with Nabil and the old man as Sybel knelt in the dust. All the way back to the car and during the drive to the American University, her shoulders trembled under the impact of suppressed sobs.

They used the university's back entrance, on the Kasr El Dobra. As soon as they entered the administrative building, Sybel excused herself and vanished. Nabil led them down a long hall and out into a side square. Before them powered a domed Ottoman villa whose second floor was flanked by the broadest *mashrabiya* Wynn had ever seen. The old man wheezed himself down into a leaf-strewn chair. The sounds of traffic rose from beyond the cover of trees and high stone fencing. Wynn moved closer to where Nabil stood and said, "Tell me what I see."

The Egyptian nodded toward the residence with its striped facade of white-and-black marble. "This was the university's original building, a palace built in the 1870s for one of Sultan Ismail's ministers. The man was apparently very busy with things other than affairs of state, for he soon moved the ministry out to make room for his expanding harem. Forty years later it was purchased by Dr. Watson, a Presbyterian missionary."

Vague recollections of flying paper airplanes out an upstairs window came and went. "Where was my father's office?"

"On the second floor, there on the corner. Your mother's was around the back, overlooking the inner courtyard."

"You knew me?"

Nabil looked at him for the first time. "I do not expect you to remember, Congressman. I was ten years older, and a nobody. Just the son of the college gatekeeper. You were the son of the great Doctors Bryant."

"My parents helped you gain a place at the college?"

"First at the English school, then here. Your parents were known for their habit of enriching everyone they met. This was the name they made for themselves, why you are made so welcome here today. Your mother, she was known by the staff as the *Saleh*, the one who offers comfort."

"And my father?"

"Upon my return from America this week, my father asked what I thought of you. I said, you are your father, only asleep." Nabil's gaze was flat and oblique as rain-washed obsidian. "Your father was the most awake man I have ever met."

Another wave of exhaustion struck Wynn, and suddenly he was no longer able to accept more memories, his or anyone else's. "Our hotel is that way?"

"Two blocks over, by the river."

"Tell Sybel I've gone back to get some sleep. It's either that or fall on my face at the conference."

□   □   □   □

WYNN AWOKE TO utter dark and the softest tapping. He crossed the room, and opened the door to admit both light and his sister. "What time is it?"

"Almost midnight."

"You let me sleep through the conference?"

"Does it matter?" Sybel swept past him, turning on the overhead light as she did. She opened the balcony doors, filling the room with noise from the street below. "I came by earlier. You might as well have been in a coma. I thought it best to let you rest up for tomorrow."

"Just a minute." He stepped into the bathroom, washed his face, and tucked his shirttails into his wrinkled trousers. He reentered the room to find Sybel seated behind his desk. That had always signaled a serious confrontation, preparing the ground, setting up her defenses behind the safety of a desk or table or something. Her back to the wall, her words carefully prepared.

Strangely enough, his traditional responses did not kick in. Wynn walked over, seated himself directly before her, and waited.

"There is a second conference," Sybel began. "A secret one. It takes place tomorrow in the Baramous Monastery at Wadi Natrum." She waited, steeled for all the reasons he might have for not going.

"This was why you brought me, wasn't it."

"The conference that started here tonight is on third-world debt. Important, but ultimately its most vital function is to act as a cover for tomorrow's gathering."

"People coming here are under threat of attack?"

"This idea of Graham's has galvanized a lot of interest. But international financial reform is a dangerous topic these days."

He repeated the words. Spaced them out. As though saying them more slowly would help him understand. "International financial reform."

"The only way financial reform will work is if a majority of nations act together. Up to now, this has been the political out. If America got serious about financial regulations, the big money would simply go somewhere else. Graham found a way of making this matter to everybody. Rich and poor nations alike."

"That sounds impossible." The instant he spoke, he regretted the words. So before she could erupt, he said, "All right."

"You'll go?"

"I've come this far. I might as well."

"But you won't *commit*." Bitter. Still looking for an argument.

Normally that needling aggressive tone was enough to have him ranting. Their pitched battles were the stuff of legends. But not this night. Wynn leaned his arms upon the desk, closing the gap, entering her space. Asked softly, "Tell me what you remember."

"What?"

"You knew an entirely different world here than me. You were, what, eleven when we arrived?"

"Twelve. You'd just had your first birthday." She worked that over, the mental gears shifting reluctantly. "It had such an impact on me, coming here. I hardly spoke at all that first year. And never smiled. The *sofragi* thought I was partly mute. You remember that word?"

"The servants," Wynn recalled, words rising from dim recesses. "*Khadema* and *Dahdah*, I remember those too."

"Dahdah was your nanny. She adored you. Everybody doted on you, the son our parents never thought they'd have." It disarmed her, this unexpected change, his sudden willingness to speak of their shared beginnings. Her mind was locked now on her own internal vista. "I remember how shocked I was by the ugliness of everything. The buildings were just thrown up, many didn't even have plaster, just raw bricks with straw hanging from the mortar. And of course the traffic was so frightening. Father was busy with . . . everything. Mother took me under her wing. Never pressing, just bringing me along. Letting me sit in her classroom or her office, talking if I wanted to speak, letting me be silent when I wanted. Which was most of the time."

"So what happened to change things for you?"

She looked at him then, really looked. And smiled for the first time since their arrival. "Om Kalthoum."

He searched his memory. "She was a singer, right?"

"They called her *Qal-Kab Al Sharq*. The Planet of the East. Life was very hard back then, not just for the poor. There was so little of anything, rationing and lines everywhere. Mother and I used to spend hours preparing lists of things for people to bring from the States— toothpaste, Kleenex, medicines. Our second Christmas someone brought over a canned ham. I remember Daddy made Momma let him open it; she was crying so hard he was afraid she'd cut herself."

She stopped then. Staring out beyond him. Softly he reminded her, "The singer."

"She gave a concert every Thursday night. The entire city stopped. There was no traffic. No people. Cairo was completely dead. People who didn't have radios gathered with family or friends." The smile was still there. "One of Daddy's students was Nasser's youngest daughter, Mona. She heard that I liked the music and gave us two tickets. They were like fairy dust, those tickets. Impossible to find. I remember how Momma spent hours getting ready, dressing me and then making me sit without moving while she got herself ready. And the servants were all racing about, beside themselves with excitement. Not that we would be sitting with Nasser's family. That meant nothing. That we would be in the box closest to the stage and Om Kalthoum."

"I don't get it," Wynn said. "You grew to like it here because of a concert?"

"Of course not." Sybel was a striking woman in a knife-edged way. Intensity ran through her as naturally as blood. "That was the first time I began to see the beauty of this place. I learned that to be happy here, I had to look beyond all the grit and the grime and the sadness. To see the wonder of these people, their resilience in the face of crushing hardships. To accept that life here was hard and often dangerous, but still could be very precious, full of joy and beauty. Daddy always called Egypt the land of thyme. It was a quote from Plato. 'Just as bees make honey from thyme, the strongest and driest of herbs, so do the wise profit from the most difficult of experiences.' "

He sat across from this woman whom he had never understood, the rock of his early years. He wondered if it would have been possible to have grown up more like her, had he been older when they came, or known his parents longer. The threat that he might have failed to meet her standards left him so hollow the night breeze off the balcony wafted straight through him. "I don't remember any of that."

"No." She rose to her feet, scarcely looking his way as she crossed the room. As though she finally recognized just how little there was to her brother. "We leave for Wadi Natrum at dawn."

28

Thursday

THREE COBBLESTONE LANES descended away from the Hassler and the Spanish Steps, and at the juncture of two stood Jackie's café. Thursday morning it was full of light and old men enjoying the springtime freshness. They murmured greetings as she entered, and eyed her appreciatively. The young waiter was already busy preparing her cappuccino. He remained standing there, polishing the bar's gleaming surface, calling the day *bella*. Finally she opened her *Herald Tribune* in defense, and the waiter retreated.

There were no other English speakers in the café at that hour, so when the voice came from behind it was more startling than the hand on her arm. "Don't turn around, Ms. Havilland."

She watched a second hand slip about her other side and set a file upon the counter. Instantly she flattened down her paper, covering the folder. "Who—"

"You wanted information." The voice whispered an uncertain tenor. "Now you have it. Good-bye."

All Jackie saw of him was the back of a brilliantined head, a jacket, then nothing. She reached beneath her newspaper and drew out an old-fashioned cardboard folder of forest green. She unwound the string catch and flipped through the documents. She felt another hand then, this one imagined but still capable of gripping her throat and squeezing fiercely.

She glanced around. The café was now filled with Roman statues, men well trained in the art of seeing nothing untoward. Even if she had spoken their tongue, she knew they would not have told her a thing. Jackie scanned the pages again, struggling to fit the answers around the tumult of questions and mysteries.

She flung down a bill, bundled up the folder and paper both, and hurried back into the hotel. Back in her room, she first tried to call Cairo. But what telephone lines there might have been did not open for her. She checked her watch. Three o'clock in the morning, Washington time. Even so, she had to wake Esther Hutchings. But the phone rang and rang.

Jackie booted up her computer, waited impatiently for the internet connection, went straight to the Trastevere site. This time the screen was not blank. As soon as she came on-line, the message shone *Incoming direct coded signal. Will you accept? Go/NoGo.*

Go.

A message drifted out of the white nothingness. *Did your requested data arrive?*

She hammered the keys instead of screaming out loud. WHO ARE YOU?

She watched the message fade, wondering how long she would have to sit and wait this time. Days, she decided, if need be. But the response was as swift as it was strange. No words. Just a cartoon figure of a gondolier paddling a boat.

Jackie watched as over and over the clumsy stick figure came to the brink of falling overboard. And whispered, "Boatman."

She typed back, *I need more. Can you help?*

Every time we connect, it puts us both at risk.

I was told this site was safe.

Lesson one: Nothing is totally secure. Witness this conversation. I tapped into the detective's request for funds. Others might have done the same. Contact me only in dire emergency.

Like now, she wanted to write, but could not.

When she did not respond, another message appeared. *Have you come across the code name Tsunami?*

Negative, she replied.

Then you are looking in the wrong place. A momentary fade-out, then the final words bloomed like a poisonous monochrome rose.

Welcome to the war zone.

WHEN THE CAIRO phone lines remained blocked, Jackie wrote a fax to Wynn, left it at the front desk, then exited the hotel. Across from the Monti church rose a waist-high concrete balustrade carved in

Roman arches and curves. She leaned over the barrier and stared down at all the carefree people thronging the Spanish Steps and the Via Condotti. She was utterly alone among lovers exchanging wet kisses and musical endearments. Jackie wished their ardor did not mock her so, or speak of a man she did not know well enough to miss as she did. She felt separated by a lifetime's distance from all the easy laughter. She raised her face to the sky and whispered the single word "Hayek."

The detective's evidence was utterly clear. Valerie Lawry had departed the previous morning at seven-twelve local time from Aeroporto Roma-Fiumicino, a half hour after Wynn's Cairo flight. She had traveled via private jet leased to Bank Royale, Liechtenstein. The file contained a photocopy of the flight plan. Nonstop trans-Atlantic, destination Orlando. There Lawry had checked into the airport Hyatt. She had placed one call. A copy of the hotel bill showed the call had been to the Hayek Group's organization.

The data on Hayek himself had been interesting, informative, and old hat. Preston had regaled her with these details and many more. Everyone who had ever worked for the group knew the stories. The prince, the King. The menace.

Jackie raised her eyes to the rooftops. There was no longer any choice. With weary resignation she accepted the inevitable. She would contact the man she had vowed never to see again.

She traced her way back along the cobblestones with a deliberate tread. Spacing out her steps in time to her plotting. It made the future more endurable. First she would see if the hotel operator had managed to connect with Cairo. Then she would book her flight home. Then try Esther Hutchings again. Then check the internet site to ensure that the notoriously fickle federal prison system still held Shane. Wishing there were some way around the move, knowing she had no alternative.

In the moment of dread and indecision, they struck.

Two faceless moped drivers. They appeared in noisy comedy, the most innocuous of Roman sights. Their vehicles were a parody of transport, with narrow wheels and motors that produced more smoke and noise than power. Jackie noticed them only because they came at her together, one from each of streets fronting her café.

She stopped in midstride. Part of her brain realized they were aimed straight for her. Yet she was unable to move. Making the perfect target.

A blow sliced her left shoulder, then a third moped raced by from behind. She spotted the batons held by the other two just as she felt the pain. The third moped driver's baton came up red and dripping over his head. She knew it was her own blood, knew also in an instant of impacted time that razors were imbedded in the wood. She heard a scream just as she fell to the stones, and heard the whizzing swoop of blows aimed too high, and the roar of motors passing to either side. Jackie could not tell if the scream was her own. But the noise unlocked her fully. That and the pain.

By the time the mopeds slowed and turned, Jackie was up and moving. She took one step toward the hotel, then halted. The plaza seemed freeze-framed as one moped spun around to block the hotel entrance. The driver swiped the air with his baton, the threat enough to throw every person in the plaza up against the closest wall, or into the nearest doorway. All but Jackie.

She raced for the café. Two old men with gaping eyes and toothless mouths bounded like adolescents for the doorway. Her hyperactive senses formed an auditory radar, warning her of another attack racing up from behind. She took a flying leap for the doorway.

The blow meant for her head caught her calf instead, and sent her spinning into the outside tables. Which was not altogether bad, because she slammed one of the metal-topped tables around in front of her, shielding herself from the other moped's oncoming assault. The baton whanged and the razor zinged across the table's battered surface. Jackie crouched tightly behind the metal barrier and took a breath. Another. Breathing in not air but fury.

When she heard the mopeds whine through a tight circle, she leaped to her feet and offered them a scream of her own. Knowing it was her voice, yet hearing the cry of some more primitive woman. She hefted the nearest metal chair and took a hard two-fisted aim.

The nearest moped was already committed and racing toward her. The driver was much burlier than the normal teenage moped driver, which granted her a larger, more solid target. Jackie met the baton head on, heard it snap before her chair connected with a padded elbow. It was not her best strike, but she intended to improve on the second go.

Still shrieking one continuous note, she ignored the second baton entirely. She took furious aim straight for the man's helmet and struck with a crack heard on all seven of Rome's hills, or so it seemed at the time. Jackie felt the clout in the soles of her feet. The man went careening off the back of the bike. A solid triple. Jackie wheeled about, searching for the third man, wanting to try for a home run.

The square was empty save for two red-soaked batons, one groaning man, an idling moped, and a host of gaping onlookers. Then she heard the racing engine. Not a moped. A car. And knew it was not over yet.

As usual, the hotel limo was parked just around the bend, between the hotel entrance and the church. The same young man who had driven her and Wynn gawked from behind the wheel. Only when Jackie raced across the piazza did she feel the slice in her leg. It slowed her down, but not overmuch. She flung open the back door and vaulted inside. "Drive!"

"Signora, your leg, the blood—"

Through the open door Jackie heard the squeal of rubber and the roar of a hyperstressed engine. "They're coming! *Drive!*"

Now the young man heard it as well. He put the car into gear and gingerly pulled away. Habit kept him in gentle tourist mode.

That lasted only until the car entered the cobblestone square. It slowed long enough to fling open a door and gather up the moped driver, who was already shouting and pointing toward Jackie and the car.

She reached over, slammed her door shut, and screamed, "*DRIVE!*"

The limo driver floored it just as the approaching car took aim. Jackie flung herself against the opposite side as they were hammered by a silver-gray blur.

The limo driver fishtailed about and took off down the nearest lane. The attackers followed so close Jackie could make out their mustaches bouncing around inside.

Perhaps the young driver had always lived for this moment. Or perhaps it was a latent Italian gene, waiting for the chance to break loose. Whatever the reason, the polite chauffeur was gone. In his place sat Mario Andretti. "*Dové?*"

Jackie bounced around the back seat like a lone pea in a tightly padded can. Leaving bloody stains wherever she hit. "What?"

"*Dové!* Where?"

Only one place came to mind. "Sant'Egidio!"

Having a destination only added fuel to the flame. The driver met an oncoming split in the road by feinting left then flying right. He took the corner too tightly and met the stone angle with an abrasive whine and a shouted curse. He oversteered and whacked the opposing wall. He then avoided by a hair a car that appeared from an invisible intersection. He dove down the increasingly steep incline with a shout of his own.

People shrieked on all sides, jumping with lightning reflexes into doorways and windowsills. Shopping bags flashed across the windshield. Horns blared. Sidewalk tables and chairs leaped into the air at their passage. Barrages of fruit from an overturned stand spilled across the windshield. Sirens. Searing flashes of sheer terror.

They entered the Via Tritoni in a four-wheel skid, slipped under the nose of an incoming bus and threaded through a red light, following a narrow track that was not there. Jackie risked a backward glance. "They're gone."

Instantly the driver slowed, pulled into a sudden alcove, and drove sedately around a cobblestone bend. There he halted behind a tinkling fountain, lowered his window, and listened. Nodding once, he rose from the car, and searched in all directions. Nodding a second time, he walked to the fountain and dipped his handkerchief in the water. He returned to the car and handed it over the seat to Jackie. Only then did she realize the backseat was smeared with her blood. As were both side windows, floorboards, roof, door handles, and the rear shelf. Jackie touched her shoulder with one hand, her calf with the other. Suddenly both burned with sticky fire.

"The hospital, miss?"

"Sant'Egidio," she weakly repeated. "Hurry."

THE GYPSY SELLING roses in the church doorway would not give up her position, not even when Jackie left a bloody handprint where she leaned against the wall. But the Gypsy's cries brought Anna from within. The young woman's every movement showed that Jackie was not the first to arrive wounded. She led Jackie around to the side entrance to avoid tracking blood inside the sanctuary, then settled soiled towels about Jackie's chair and called to others for hot water, hand rags, scissors, and a bottle.

"Here, drink this."

"What is it?"

"Grappa. So you don't faint."

Anna watched as Jackie tasted the fiery liquid and coughed, then winced at how the cough pulled at her wound. "Don't sip. Drink like medicine. Big swallow. Good."

"That's strong."

"Yes. But now you are not so pale like the linen. Can you move up your arms, up like this, over your head?"

"I don't think so."

"No matter. We will cut off your T-shirt. Lean forward." Anna helped Jackie do so. As she snipped she asked, "Who did this?"

Before Jackie could respond, the hall rang with other voices. Two other women rushed in, one carrying a black bag. There was a swift torrent of Italian, then Anna asked, "Was it a gang?"

"I don't . . . Ow!" The doctor's probing fingers retreated. She held a bloody finger up in front of Jackie's face. The message was clear. Don't move. Jackie gasped as the fingers resumed their probing of her shoulder, and said, "Three men on mopeds."

This was also translated. Anna said, "They used clubs with knives, yes?"

"Or razors. Something sharp."

"Yes, this is the gang's favorite new toy. Every night the hospitals greet their victims."

Jackie held the T-shirt to her front, aware of how many legs and shoes were crowding about her. Strangers all. "You think we could cram a few more people in here?"

Anna strung together a verbal push, and the room quickly emptied. Jackie lifted a blood-stained shoe and told the doctor, "They also hit my leg." Sounds of protest lifted her head in time to see the driver being shoved towards the door. "Let him stay a moment, please."

When calm was restored and the door closed, Jackie said to the driver, "I can't thank you enough."

"It is no problem, *signora*." He grinned broadly. "We make a good chase, yes? Like the movies."

She watched the doctor begin to cut away her trouser leg. "My things are all at the hotel. I'd really rather not go back there."

Anna understood immediately. "They may still be after you?"

"I think so."

There followed a swift exchange between the driver and Anna. Then she said, "Someone will return with the driver and check you out. We will keep you here. How long do you stay?"

"I'd like to leave tomorrow for America, if I can."

Another discussion, this one including the doctor. The driver pulled a cellphone from his pocket and dialed. Anna told her, "Your cuts are not too deep. The driver thinks the hotel will not give out your name. The Hassler would not like to say a guest was attacked on their doorstep, you understand?"

"Yes." She felt two pinpricks, local anesthetics for her leg and shoulder. Then the queasy tugging of thread being sewn.

The driver pocketed his phone and reported, "Is no problem."

Jackie said to the driver, "I'm so sorry about your car."

The driver's smile was tainted by the sight of the doctor's work. "Was not my car, *signora*. And the hotel is very rich."

Anna said, "I fear our chambers will be not so nice."

Jackie leaned forward and shut her eyes to the pile of bloody gauze. "If they're safe, it will be just fine."

29

Thursday

THE NEXT MORNING the traders presented Colin with a bottle of champagne and a tiny bejeweled tree. Eric gave a little speech that started, "On behalf of King Elvis and all his loyal subjects—"

"Don't let him hear you say that," Colin warned. "You'll meet the street long before your time."

"You going to let me do this or not?" Up and down the aisles, traders moved in to be a part of the fun. "Okay. In recognition of your part in ridding us of the menace, we hereby bestow upon you these tokens of our undying gratitude."

Colin made no move to accept. The tree was as high as his hand, gold plated, and had tiny crystal leaves at the end of each branch. "Who is rid of what?"

This only made the traders grin harder. Eric replied, "Take a look upstairs."

Colin was anything but pleased to see the balcony absolutely empty. "That's not possible."

"All thanks to you and the bugs you found." Eric shoved the tree and bottle into Colin's hands. "Enjoy."

Colin was still giving the balcony his bleakest inspection when Alex moved up beside him. "You're not fooled by this either."

"Hayek wouldn't fire them all just because one guy stepped over the line," Colin agreed.

"Which means they've been buried somewhere." Alex surveyed the traders prepping themselves for the battle ahead. "There are days," he said softly, "so intense, I walk out and can't believe it's the same sun shining as when I went in. Ice ages should have passed. Civilizations risen and fallen. Eons melt and flow and still I'm in here, fighting the market."

Colin studied the spots market chief. At this proximity it was easier to see the permanent stains of commercial war, the wounds to face and gaze and spirit. "This thing really has you worried."

"If he's planning to feed the new group data we can't access, we might as well hang up our guns and go farm sheep." Alex circled one finger overhead, gathering up his troops. "Let's go see if we can discover the battle plan."

THEY CROWDED INTO the elevator together, the five senior traders who could be pulled off the floor, and Colin. He was squashed up next to the hard barrel belly of the derivatives chief, a red-cheeked man who stank of some prehistoric aftershave. The ride was silent. But when the doors opened, the trader planted a meaty paw on Colin's shoulder and told him, "Nice work finding those listening devices, kiddo. Definitely one for the late night tales."

Hayek himself was out in the front office to greet them. A first. As was the solicitous apology for disturbing their week. "Such a nuisance to discover a new member of the team has proven so unreliable. Please, gentlemen, ladies, accept my sincerest regrets for such a disastrous intrusion."

Hayek gave them an open-armed escort, leading and guiding both. Colin spotted the attractive Washington lobbyist in the waiting room and wondered if she had somehow been involved.

The senior traders entered Hayek's office like infidels passing through cathedral doors. They shuffled a bit and they craned and searched and cleared their throats, and wished themselves back down in the fray. Most came up only when there was a major offering, their presentation carefully orchestrated. There was no script here. No precedent, no deal. Only the sullen rage of people who knew they had been wronged.

Hayek directed them through his office and into the conference area. To their amazement, the table was decked out with gourmet fast food. Spode china. Crystal goblets for the soft drinks. Blinis. Silver palavers for the smoked salmon and the French air-dried *saucisson*. A cheese board on a traditional reed mat, six different selections. Iced caviar. Baskets of fresh-baked bread. Two waiters in solemn white livery. Hayek showed eager concern as they made their selections, taking nothing for himself until all were served. Gradually he eased them away from the purpose of their meeting with kingly grace, until all but Alex were chatting and eating heartily. The more they talked, the quieter Hayek grew. He ate almost nothing.

Without preamble, Hayek launched into his spiel. "I made a grave error, bringing the new group in as I did. The fact is, we are in the process of receiving new investment capital. A significant portion comes from a source who insists their funds be kept separate. I have done my best to explain that this makes no sense, that we all trade using the same information. It may actually hurt them in the long run not to have access to the full power of our floor. But they have insisted. And quite frankly, the size of their investment is such that we cannot refuse. So I attempted to move this new group in first, intending to explain things once we had sorted out the situation. I now recognize this to have been a grave error. I apologize. I have therefore moved the entire team into the Capital Markets section of First Florida Bank."

It was the longest speech Colin had ever heard the man make. The accent was clearer now, the tone barrel-rich and commanding. "As for the insertion of the electronic monitoring devices, I am utterly baffled. It was a grave error. The person responsible has been punished."

Only when Hayek fell silent did they realize this was all they were going to get. Alex searched the faces of his compatriots and realized no one else was going to ask the obvious. "How much new money?"

"Four billion is to be directed into the First Florida Fund."

There was a low whistle, an intake of breath. Four billion would not bring the new fund anywhere near the top ranks, but it was enough to carry weight. Four billion would establish First Florida as a player. But before the dismay could take hold, Hayek added, by way of an aside, "And an additional eleven billion into the Hayek ordinary fund."

The traders turned jubilant. Eleven billion was enough to make waves on Wall Street. Many of these senior guys had followed Hayek south against their own better judgment, hoping for a coup such as this. Eleven billion in new ready cash would have them talking as far away as Tokyo. It was a clean hit for the home team. Eleven billion meant a huge upsurge in fresh trades. And increased bonuses all around.

Only Alex remained unfazed by the news. He cast the others a furious glance for forcing him into the limelight alone. "Any particular reason why we get all this money now?"

"We have been courting these funds for almost a year. The timing is theirs. We can only be glad the sources have chosen us above all the competition, and must do our best to offer them a solid return." To their surprise, Hayek actually smiled. "I like a man who thinks of the downside even when things look positive. I have been forced to send Mr. Burke over to manage the new fund. I need a new top man, my personal link to the markets. Are you interested?"

Alex blinked. "Thank you, Mr. Hayek. But my place is on the floor."

"Very well." Hayek rose to his feet. "Thank you for your time. I shall not keep you from your work."

Obediently they began filing out. Hayek added, "Remain behind if you will, Mr. Ready."

When the room had emptied, Hayek asked, "Anything more on our huntress and her companions?"

"Nothing, sir. It's like they've disappeared."

"Very well. Keep me posted."

The Washington lobbyist was still there when Colin departed. He paid her scant notice, as Alex waited for him by the elevator. The other traders were gone. When the elevator doors slid them into isolation, Alex asked, "What did the King say to you?"

"There's a local woman hired by a troublemaker up in Washington. Hayek's had me trace her. She's a nonstarter, believe me."

Alex chewed on his upper lip, muttered, "He didn't give us enough."

"Just because they're moved off-site doesn't mean the threat is gone," Colin agreed.

"The man's not perfect, much as he'd like us to believe otherwise. Did you ever hear about what happened in Ecuador?"

Colin glanced at him. These were confidences of a new order. "Rumors only. Something about how he almost lost his silk shirt, then went on a rampage."

"I've heard enough to be fairly certain the rumors are all true. It happened just before Hayek made the move south." Alex stabbed at the elevator controls, the machine not moving at a trader's speed. "Wonder what he's calling the new group."

"How about the Elvis Fund," Colin suggested, then worried he had gone too far.

Alex gave him the tight rictus grin of a man ready for battle. "You're okay, kid. Ever wanted to give the floor a shot?"

"Not a chance in all the whole wide world," Colin replied solemnly. "Thanks just the same."

Alex was already moving before the doors slid open. "And smart to boot."

BURKE WAITED UNTIL the last of the traders and the techie had left before emerging from the alcove behind the conference area, where Hayek had a private bathroom and dressing area. Burke stepped into the open, still uncertain why he had not simply been invited to join the others. Hayek stood by the window behind his desk, staring out at the fountain and the glimmering afternoon. Hayek asked, "You heard?"

"Yes."

"Do you think the trader who spoke, what was his name. Did he believe me?"

"Probably not. It was Alex. Senior spot trader." Burke remained standing beside the chair. "You offered him my job."

Hayek remained silent.

"Am I out?" The mere possibility was a pain that threatened to twist his guts into a Pythagorean knot. Hayek had raged at Brant Anker for inserting the module but had not fired him. And had said nothing to Burke. Yet. "I had no idea Anker would—"

"Did I ever tell you what happened to my former aide?"

He swallowed. "No."

"It was after Ecuador." Hayek turned around then, revealing the stress lines racing out from his eyes and mouth. The rage. "Certainly you've heard the rumors swirling about downstairs."

Burke found himself comparing this to Hayek's earlier tirade. This was definitely real. The other now seemed mere theatrics. But why? "I try not to listen."

"Ah, but you should. The only way to profit from past mistakes is to study and dissect and study further. Ecuador was a mistake. A grave one. Undoubtedly the worst of my career. But I have studied and I have learned."

Hayek began to pace back and forth in front of the window, trapped by bars of unyielding sunlight and harsher memories. "The Ecuadorian setting was perfect for a huge financial coup—official corruption, a massive banking crisis, El Nino–driven crop failure, falling commodity prices. Inflation stood at thirty-two percent a month and rising. The Ecuadorian currency, the sucre, stood poised on the precipice. Working through confidential intermediaries based in the Cook Islands, I bought sucres with both fists. I then went short on almost the entire Ecuadorian stock market. I bought sell options for every Ecuadorian raw material. I prepared to push the currency and the country over the edge.

"Then the gray ghosts at Treasury caught wind of my plans. I have tried without success to discover the source of the leak, to no avail. At first I assumed it was their brother spooks at Langley who uncovered my plot. But evidence kept cropping up. Signs that the information was less than complete. If it had been Langley, I would not be here today. The case would have been too perfect. I would have been stripped clean and defeated."

Hayek turned to him then. Beneath the silver-white brows his eyes were beyond black, fire blazing hot in a molasses pit. "No. Some blasted social charity outfit, a measly group of grubby do-gooders, *they* were the ones who managed to pierce my intricate veil. Their evidence was not enough to destroy, merely wound. Sant'Egidio was the most likely source of my woes, but I have never managed to prove this. Have you ever heard of the group?"

Relief swept through Burke in a flood surge so strong he could have wept. This was not about him at all. Hayek would not have revealed such incriminating evidence to somebody on the way out. Burke slumped into a chair because he had to. "No."

"An international chain of pests and meddlers of the first order. They are the reason why burning at the stake should never have been banned. Someone flew down and told the president of Ecuador what I had planned. The president came up with a response no one had anticipated. Overnight they froze exchange rates at below what I had paid, dumped the sucre, and adopted the U.S. dollar as the official Ecuadorian currency." Hayek paused long enough to give Burke a thin-lipped grimace. But it was doubtful he saw his aide at all. "Needless to say, I was enraged. I took the logical move, which was to finance a coup. And the coup succeeded marvelously. Three days later, a ragtag band of left-leaning Indians and the military was in power—a crippling concoction if I had ever seen one."

He resumed his taut pacing. "But those muddling idiots in Foggy

Bottom would not leave it alone. Under pressure from Washington, the coup leaders backed down, and power was handed over to Vice President Noboa. Overnight, the dollar transfer was back on.

"But my own trauma did not end there. I then received a visitor, some nameless gray specter from the Treasury Department. Someone utterly removed from my lobbyists and power politics and the influence I have garnered over elected officials. This Washington apparition looked down at me in the most humiliating manner, spoke around his mouthful of Ivy League marbles, and said they would not be going after me. The U.S. financial markets were already nervous after the Long-Term Credit debacle. So I was simply going to swallow my sucres and never exercise my options. All eight hundred million dollars worth. Amazingly, this spook actually had the correct figure, despite my best attempts to hide my actions. The American government made a paper write-off of this amount from Ecuador's outstanding sucre debt. Which meant I had effectively financed the country's transfer to a dollar economy."

Hayek stared out the window and said in a tone dulled by old fury, "I learned my lesson well. I removed myself from the porous Street, where information is bandied about by everyone from the bus drivers to the corner newsboy. But I did not move so far away as to raise warning flags with the SEC. I began paying careful attention to the do-gooders and their interference. I established a new electronic security system. And I replaced my entire senior team. I doubt seriously they had anything to do with my failure, most of them probably had no idea what had happened. Only four people even knew what I had planned. But I fired them anyway, as a warning to all future employees that failure of any kind was not to be tolerated."

"I won't fail you."

"Esther Hutchings is involved with the Sant'Egidio band. So is the new congressman's sister. Which makes the risk of their meddling absolutely unacceptable."

"What do you want me to do?"

"Proceed with the next phase. Meet the bankers this weekend."

Burke had to smile. Forcing a bank's board to meet on Easter weekend would establish the perfect atmosphere for what they had in mind. "And the funds?"

"The first installment will be transferred on Tuesday."

Burke hesitated, decided he had to say, "I don't like how the senior traders have made Colin Ready their pet techie. It only means his reach has been broadened even further."

"Don't give me mere chatter," Hayek snapped. "It is time for proof."

"I could put Anker back on him." Then Burke waited. When Hayek did not object, Burke knew with utter certainty that Hayek in truth had not objected to Anker's tactics. Only his failure. "And if it's Colin?"

"Proof," Hayek insisted. "Hard and fast. And spread your net further in case you're wrong."

This time Burke did not move. "What do I do if Colin Ready is spying for the Brazilians?"

Hayek did not like being trapped. "Must I really spell out every detail for you?"

"No." Burke headed for the door, vastly satisfied. "Absolutely not."

VALERIE LAWRY SAT in Hayek's outer office and pretended to fume. Thus far she had been kept waiting precisely two hours and twenty-three minutes. No one kept her waiting two hours and a half. Not even the President of the United States, when twice she had attended conferences in the Oval Office. And to have it be Hayek, a man known for his eccentricities and his swagger, was doubly galling. Not to mention the fact that she had just risen from seven hours of ragged sleep, after two transatlantic flights in thirty-six hours. Even so, she didn't want to leave, or even complain. In truth, she was far too shaken for much real anger.

People were coming and going from Hayek's office in a constant stream. Initially the great double doors had opened to reveal a genuine shouting match inside. Valerie had never heard Hayek raise his voice before, or show any emotion stronger than scorn. Then the doors had expelled a waxy-headed young man in Rodeo Drive garb, looking utterly crushed as Hayek blistered the silk wallpaper. Even Hayek's secretary was frightened.

Then Hayek had emerged, but not for her. A line of sullen traders had entered Hayek's office. Among them was the slender techie who had sat in on her last bout with Hayek, a man who appeared frightened of his own shadow. Strange that he would be there among the heavy hitters. Valerie made a mental note to find out who he was. But not today, when the atmosphere stank of gunpowder and dread.

She would not be there at all, except for the fact that Hayek was her first real client. Not of the K Street firm where she slaved and struggled. Her own. Almost six months earlier, Hayek's android, Burke, had sought her out at the close of an international banking forum and explained that they were looking for a private rep. Her firm was the chief lobbyist for the American Investment Managers, or AIM, so there was certainly the potential for a conflict-of-interest claim. But these things happened all the time within lobbyist circles. They were far less organized or monitored than, say, the lawyers. Which was why Valerie had hung tough, obtained her secret dream, then signed.

Valerie had fought tooth and nail for a contract clause that stated if she reached the six-month mark, she would be kept on for an additional five years. Which meant a solid base with which to go indie and start her own firm. Next week marked the six-month window. Which made this meeting crucial.

"Ms. Lawry?" The secretary gave Valerie a pasty smile. "Mr. Hayek will see you now."

She rose to her feet, took a moment to straighten her jacket and smooth the lines of her skirt. But her mind refused to throw off the jet-lag clumsiness. Valerie decided she would hear him out, then claim fatigue. Which was both understandable and the truth. She would not be pressed into making any decision until she had rested.

Even so, her ankles wobbled on her high heels as she entered Hayek's office. He waved her into the seat opposite his desk. "How are you this morning, Ms. Lawry?"

"Tired. I have just gotten back—"

"From Rome. Yes. Rome." Hayek wore his most infuriating smirk, his dark eyes glittering and mesmerizing. The man's authority was what had struck her the first time they had met, and it affected her still. He was far from handsome, with his eagle's beak of a nose, eyebrows like silver-gray shrubbery, hair Brylcreemed to his skull, and lips both sensuous and cruel. The jaw of a prizefighter, cheekbones of an Indian chief. But his demeanor was so awesome the physical attributes were secondary, if noticed at all. He rested calm and omnipotent, surrounded by a storm of his own making. Sucking whatever he required from those about him, giving nothing back. She was merely another pawn for him to put into play. There was only one way to give the situation any dignity at all. And that was to use him just as cynically, playing this situation to accomplish her own agenda. Lawry and Associates. Offices on K Street, three blocks from the White House. A name known to everybody in the business of power.

Hayek asked, "How was your journey?"

In truth, it had been as grand an experience as any intercontinental flight could be. Hayek's new private plane was the largest Gulfstream made, equipped with deerskin seats, a six-screen entertainment center, butler, bath, and a double bed whose silk sheets smelled of lavender and rosewater. "Long."

Hayek asked, "Will you have coffee?"

"Thank you, but I've had two and a half hours to drink your coffee."

"Indeed so." Hayek leaned back in his chair, swiveled so as to stare out the back window. "You saw the congressman in Rome, did you not?"

"Of course I did. Since that was why you sent me over."

"And then you did what?"

"Came straight back. Oh, I took time for one decent meal. Would you like to know what I ate?"

"That won't be necessary." Hayek remained absorbed in whatever he saw mired in sunlight. Forcing her to watch his silhouette. The window's glare scratched at her eyeballs. "Tell me, if you would, what you thought of our congressman."

"The same as before. Utterly lost at sea. It was a wasted journey."

"Was it indeed." Hayek mused to the world beyond his window, "Then I must assume you are not aware that you have been traced?"

"Traced?"

"Correct. From Rome. To here."

"Here?" Hating the way she sounded. But her astonishment was too great to hide.

He turned around to face her now. The eyes were as harsh and brilliant as she had ever seen, the voice soft as a snake's hiss. "Correct again. You see, Ms. Lawry, there was indeed a purpose behind having you wait. I needed to have this confirmed. And steps taken in response."

"But . . ." She fought against the mental bedlam. "How did you know?"

"We almost didn't. They apparently managed to hire themselves an extremely capable team."

"No, I mean how did you *know?*"

"Because we've been tailing you." Hayek showed no unease whatsoever. "What do you think?"

She started to object, but there was no future in that. "I can't believe Wynn would be capable of such a thing."

"Perhaps it was not the congressman at all."

"You can't mean that woman." She searched her mind, squeezed out the name, "Havilland."

Hayek merely raised one eyebrow and lifted the corner of his mouth. But the contempt was as clear as a slap to her face. "There are others beyond them. We can no longer ignore this risk."

She wanted to ask, risk to *what*? But she knew Hayek would not answer. She also knew she needed further strength to match the man's mastery. "You must forgive me. I must have a brief rest. We can meet later, if you wish—"

"About your contract."

She halted midway to the doors. "Yes?"

"I have no problem with continuing our arrangement," Hayek said. "But only if you remain in your present position."

Valerie did her best not to gape. She had shared her secret ambition with no one. She was being struck by too many surprises, and from too many unexpected directions. "But were I to go independent, I would be able to concentrate more fully upon your needs."

"On this point we must disagree," Hayek replied. "It is far more important that I be able to mask my activities within the framework of your functioning for AIM as a whole."

Defeat and victory mingled like ashes in her mouth. "Very well. I accept your terms."

"My secretary has an amendment to your contract awaiting your signature." Hayek turned back to his window. "Good day, Ms. Lawry."

The casual dismissal galled so that Valerie demanded, "What will you do about this risk?"

Hayek focused once again upon whatever lay beyond his window. "It is already done."

30

Thursday

WHEN THE MUEZZIN woke him to the gray light of another predawn, Wynn entered the suite's sitting room to find breakfast already waiting. He poured a cup of coffee and moved to the balcony, where Sybel sat with her legs propped upon the balcony railing, her Bible open in her lap. Her hair was unbound, a ripe black field stroked by the dry morning wind. He sipped his coffee and recalled other mornings, back when they shared a tiny room in a house void of love and welcome both. Sybel had sat then as she did now, hunched over the open Book, clutching at the words with a fierce ardor that shone on her face.

He knew she was aware of him, so when the muezzin grew silent he said what he had often thought, but never spoken before. "The only part of the whole religion thing that I could ever stand was mornings like this."

She flicked the hair from her face as she lifted her gaze, but said nothing. Just watched and waited.

"I hated everything to do with Christianity. It's what took us to Cairo. It robbed us of Mom and Dad."

"It defined them." Another swipe at her hair. "It defines me."

"Is that why you did this?" He knew his tone was hard, but couldn't help that. All he could do was pull over a chair and sit down. Show her that he really wanted an answer. "Why you pulled me away from the life I've made for myself?"

Sybel started to say, What life is that. He could read the words in her eyes, see them form, watch her open her mouth to speak. But she bit back the retort and said instead, "Wynn, listen to me. The only difference between a person who just exists and a person who lives is the vision of what lies ahead. Beyond tomorrow, beyond measured time. It's not having a *cause*. People give themselves to causes all the time and still grow bitter or bored, or just empty themselves out in the endless battles of life. Causes don't give you hope. Causes don't give you a future." She hefted the Book, held it between them. "I do what I do because I feel called by the One whom I love and to whom I have given my life. He gives me hope, even when there is none. Even when all is lost, still will I love Him. Because in the end, when time is gone and all is over, I know God will prevail."

Wynn shook his head in such a wide sweep he took in the wafting curtains at one end and the tin-shaded river at the other. "I just don't get it."

She rose, wearing the same defeated expression he had seen a thousand mornings before. "We'd better be going."

KAY TRILLING STOOD in the lobby, watching Wynn's approach with undisguised hostility. "This can't possibly be a good idea."

"He's coming, Kay."

Sybel's hard resolve was too much even for the senator. Kay stalked through the glass doors and over to where Nabil stood beside a gleaming new Mercedes. She said something angry enough to shake her entire body. The Egyptian replied with a noncommittal shrug. Sybel sighed, a tight sound.

Nabil drove them across the river and through the southern reaches of Giza. Kay Trilling sat beside Nabil. Sybel was in the back seat with Wynn. Both women were frozen into immobile stubbornness. The predawn light illuminated snarled traffic and pedestrian hordes. From within the safety of the Mercedes' back seat, Wynn observed all manner of dress, representing a society in explosive transition. Fundamentalist women wore black tents that hid all but their eyes. The merely conservative made do with gray *chadors* and brightly colored ankle-length dresses. The nonreligious wore just about anything, particularly the young. Teenage girls in T-shirts and tight suede jeans wore even tighter expressions of fear and defiance. The fundamentalist papers daily offered remedies for their behavior—whippings, brandings, the shaving of heads.

Once upon the desert highway, Nabil drove with reckless Egyptian verve, using the horn as much as the wheel and both more than the brake pedal. All about them, traffic rumbled and blared and flew. Wynn focused upon the view outside his window and did his best to ignore Nabil's weaving and bobbing at eighty miles per hour. They passed clusters of half-finished apartment buildings in pale Nile brick that pushed back the verdant green of irrigated farmlands. Forests of date palms rose a hundred feet and more. Hawks hung high overhead, their wings fluttering ruddy gold in the sunrise. In the distance, the Giza pyramids rose from the morning mist, floating and shimmering like mystic islands.

Then the desert struck, and the green disappeared. The asphalt ribbon and the dusty billboards and the flashy new cars were mocked by the emptiness that stretched to either side. Kay snuffled her discontent and buried herself in the papers spread across her lap. Sybel kept her attention focused upon her side window. Nabil remained locked upon the challenge of Egyptian traffic. The car's silence was as complete as a noose.

By the time they turned off the highway onto the road for Wadi Natrum, the sunlight was so fierce it was impossible to see any horizon. Brilliant sand weaved and melted into hazy hostility with the sky. They drove another hour and entered the valley approaching the wadi, or oasis. The cavern walls held none of the smooth-flowing grace of ancient waterways. Here tides of fierce winds had etched away the softer earth, leaving strange rounded shapes and alien markings in a hundred shades, all of them yellow. They descended deeper into the valley, where the rising wind no longer touched them, only the heat and the light.

Gradually the cavern walls lessened and they rejoined the flat blanched desert. Soon after they entered the village of Natrum. They were slowed to the pace of the donkey cart up ahead. An Egyptian passed on his bicycle, wide-splayed feet pedaling furiously and leather sandals flapping like castanets. His daughter perched on the handlebars, all bright eyes and soft blue shawl. The buildings were baked to colorless unity, even the signs painted mostly with dust. The sky held no color, the earth no shade. Wynn sat in his air-conditioned car, insulated from the world, yet sweating from the furnace raging beyond his window.

They drove a further hour beyond the village, along a road so sand-blanketed only the occasional sign suggested there was any path at all. One moment there was nothing but heat and a track turned white by reflected light, the next, a wall appeared to their right.

Nabil said quietly, "We are here."

The wall surrounding the monastery was a mile to a side, high and stained a muted ocher by the dust of centuries. The broad wooden gates and the shutters around the sentry post were faded yellow with time and heat. So very much of both.

Within the outer wall, the desert was not vanquished, merely softened. Low buildings fronted carefully tended gardens of cactus and palm and hardy plants. The tallest dovecotes Wynn had ever seen rose like guard towers and marched two abreast along the outer wall. They drove on to where a second wall rose, higher than the first. Two modern buildings flanked the wall, fronted by a dusty courtyard filled with cars and people in severe modern dress.

Wynn rose from the car and watched as Kay Trilling marched resolutely over and began greeting the gathered throng. He looked across the car to where Sybel squinted into the sun and wind. "What should I do?"

"I wish I knew what to tell you."

"That's it? You bring me out here and that's all you've got to say?"

"Kay has come here to convince the representatives of nineteen different national governments that we remain committed to making this happen. That without Graham at the helm, we can still make it work." She did not sound as though she believed it herself.

Wynn spotted a familiar figure in a black cassock. "Is that Father Libretto?"

"I told you. Sant'Egidio is the group that helped organize this meeting."

"So they're in charge."

"No, Wynn." Explaining adult things to an exasperating child. "This is a council of equals. Sant'Egidio has played the role of messenger."

He realized that Nabil still stood by his door, watching with the stone features of a human sphinx. "You've got something to say?"

"This is important work, Congressman." The Egyptian hesitated, then added, "Your father would call this the kind of work that makes God smile."

The words struck Wynn like a fist to his heart. He waited until the Egyptian had walked over to join the others, then said to Sybel, "What about Grant's threat to destroy me if I don't do what they want? And don't tell me he hasn't got the goods because he does. Line and verse. He could send us both to prison, and I could lose everything."

"What if I took care of Grant?"

He understood instantly what she was saying. "You'd do that? Go back to him?"

"I haven't left him yet. But you heard Nabil. This work is vital."

"Tell me why." When Sybel responded by glancing over to where the crowd was moving inside the conference hall, Wynn pressed, "Two minutes. You can spare me that much."

"Eighteen funds are now larger than all but six national economies. Two are larger than Italy's GDP. Of America's top ten banks, eight derive more than half their total profits from derivatives and currency transactions. Their power to make or break economic recoveries and governments is a constant threat. They not only make profit from instability, they *want it to continue*. They respected no nation, no law, nothing except profit. National sovereignty and control of finances is at risk."

As though to emphasize her words, the wind chose that moment to attack. A giant's fistful of grit was flung into Wynn's face. The dreaded *khamsin* dominated that time of year, a blistering breath from the southern deserts that blew so hard and long it deposited tons of ocher and gold high up in the Alps, two thousand miles to the north.

Sybel tightened down her face to where not even the wind could penetrate. "During the first economic boom of the twentieth century, the robber barons had to be reined in through governmental control and their monopolies broken. Now there's a different threat, one that knows no borders. To harness the globalized power, global laws are needed. Hutchings' plan was to levy a very small tax on every international currency transaction, one-tenth of one percent. Not enough to harm any business making currency purchases for normal trade in goods and services, but enough to slow the tidal surges of speculation. Funds generated from this tax wouldn't go to any country's treasury. Instead, a world body would be formed. Perhaps a revamped World Bank, perhaps something entirely new. They'd use these funds to pay off all outstanding debts of the developing nations, starting with the poorest first."

She stopped and waited. Wynn knew she sought what he was unwilling to give, a commitment as total as her own. "I'll think about it."

Sybel whirled about. "Sure. You do that."

"You can't expect me—"

"I've already told you, Wynn. I don't *expect* anything."

□   □   □   □

WYNN SAT IN the corner of the conference hall by the exit. He sought to concentrate on Kay Trilling's address, but felt barred from understanding as well as admission. Sybel sat far enough away for him to observe her tragic resignation. He had years of experience disappointing Sybel, yet the act never came easy. When she took the coffee break as an excuse to leave the building, he followed her. As they crossed the parking area, Wynn half expected to be told to disappear. He took her silence as the only welcome he deserved, and followed her towards the monastery's fortresslike walls.

Wynn slipped through the narrow gate behind Sybel and entered an interior square. The wind was muted here, kept at bay by the thick high walls. Eucalyptus trees perfumed the air. Together they crossed the square and started down a broad lane, shaded by a wooden lattice woven in geometric design. They passed several monks in their long black robes and strange embroidered caps. Most did not appear to notice them at all.

They turned a corner and found themselves at the entrance to a chapel. Wynn followed her example, slipped off his shoes, and stepped inside. The church was composed of three interconnected rooms, with perhaps two dozen penitents scattered throughout. There were no seats, of course. But the reed mats were cool against his feet and gave way to thick Persian carpets up by the altars. Sybel approached the front, stood there a moment, then abruptly spun about and departed.

Wynn found her standing outside, slipping on her shoes and blinking against the transition from interior cool to desert light. He asked, "Are you all right?"

Before Sybel could respond, a robed figure stepped up and said, "You are wishing to see my home, yes?"

Sybel seemed genuinely relieved at the invitation. "Very much."

The monk's beard fell in gray waves upon his chest. He offered his hand to Wynn, but only a smile to Sybel. The man's fingers were cool and hard as the surrounding stone. "I am Father Binyamin. Where you are from, please?"

"America."

"America. How nice. Please, you are Christian?"

Sybel answered for herself alone. "Yes."

"You are welcome." He gestured to the right. "I will show you our heart, our church. This way, come please."

Sybel asked the monk as they walked, "That was not a church where we were?"

"Oh yes, is chapel. We have seven. Where we are, this is outer court. All you see here is new. Seventeenth-century church, sixteenth-century walls."

"And that is new?"

"Here, yes. Very new." He stepped into an alcove, pushed open a heavy door, and beckoned Sybel to enter. Sybel hesitated, which the monk found humorous. "Is safe," the monk assured her. "All is safe within these walls."

She ducked down and entered the passage, far thicker than it was broad. Wynn bent over, took the three steps, straightened and gasped aloud.

"Is surprise, yes? Of course, of course, Baramous Monastery is a place of many surprises. Many mysteries. Please, you come."

The inner courtyard was ringed by walls so high Wynn felt as if he were standing inside a sky-domed cavern. The lane they walked was soft as golden flour, and broad enough for a line of poinciana trees to stand attendance down the middle, their red flowers bursting flames of color. Along one wall stretched a series of ancient doors. A sudden burst of wind hummed low and sullen overhead, hurtling great yellow spumes above the ramparts. The monk accepted the returning storm with a tiny shrug. "Do not worry, please. Our home has lived through many, many khamsin."

As they walked, he explained, "To our left are cells for monks who come out. You understand? Like me. We see the visitors, we work with poor, we farm, we teach. Farther on are cells for those who do not come out. There is a word, yes?"

"Hermits," Sybel supplied.

"Hermits, yes, of course. Before, they live in caves. Now, we make caves for them here." He pointed to the open chambers lining the right-hand wall. "Here we make lime for the walls. Olive press. Grape press. Grain room. Kitchen. Wells. All this is the middle court. Ninth century, some eleventh. Mostly ninth. Here another chapel, no, we do not enter here. This way, please."

He led them down six crumbling steps and into another deep-set alcove. He halted before a door of barred iron and parched wood, searched his robes, and extracted a ring of keys. The door was almost a foot thick but swung open with silent ease. They stepped into another world, one of impossible age.

"Saint Anthony was world's first monk. His monastery was in Western Desert. He passes to heaven in 325. His student was Saint Baramous. He and others come here in 310. They build this home."

Wynn stood before a limestone monolith. There were no windows on the ground level, and those higher up were mere cross-shaped slits. High overhead ran a wooden drawbridge.

"Saint Baramous is man of peace in time of war. Barbarians come here many times, attacking oasis villages of Wadi Natrum." He pointed to the left. "This is northeast corner of monastery. This wall and this house, all fourth century. There you see our caves for hermits."

Along the outer wall's rim were crudely carved openings. They looked indeed like entrances to caves, set far apart and utterly isolated. The wind moaned overhead but did not enter. Here the world's storms were not welcome. Here was only light and heat and silence beyond time.

The monk escorted them away from the hermit caves, toward a flight of stairs carved up the outer wall, steep and curved and slippery with age. "Careful here, please. Very careful."

Sybel cast Wynn a glance full of questions, then turned and followed the monk. Wynn used both hands to search the decayed surface for holds. They followed a narrow path around the corner of the wall, until the drawbridge came into view. There they halted once more.

When the monk realized they were no longer following, he turned and laughed delightedly. "You think this bridge stands for sixteen centuries, waiting for pretty English lady and gentleman to come and fall down?"

"We're American."

"American, English, is making no difference to bridge. Please to come."

When she turned and looked at him a second time, Wynn said, "Your call."

Sybel followed the monk. The planks were warped so that Wynn could see the sandy lane far below. One railing was gone entirely. The other shivered in what wind found its way over the parapet. He chose his steps carefully and did not breathe until he reached the other side.

The monk welcomed them with benevolent humor. "When barbarians come, they are not liking bridge either. The monks pull it into long hall here, you see? They close this door, then they wait. There is well for water, there is meal for bread. One time they wait seven years."

He led them down the narrow hall, dark save for light filtering through cross-shaped windows. His keys rattled again as he unlocked another door. "Here is the church of Saint Baramous. Our heart, our home. Please, you are welcome."

A faint breath of wind followed them inside, as the monk walked to the nave and returned with a lighted candle. The flame weaved and beckoned, causing wall frescoes made faint by eons to come alive and bid them silent welcome. Seventeen centuries of incense perfumed the air.

The monk carried the candle back to stand before Sybel. His smile danced with the flames. "Here in the heart of our home, we may speak the truth, yes? I think you carry sadness with you."

If she found the comment strange, Sybel made no sign. Perhaps she shivered, perhaps it was a nod. The monk seemed satisfied, for he said, "Also I think you carry a servant's heart. The eternal lesson is hard to remember sometimes for servants. So I remind you. You can save only one person. Who is that, please?"

"Myself," she whispered, the trembling visible now.

"Yes, is very true. We pray for others. We serve with joy. We trust in the One who can save all else. And we hold fast to His gift." He ushered them from the chapel. "Peace. Peace now. Peace always."

Sybel's words rippled like wind scattering dust over the parapet. "This lesson is beyond me."

As the monk relocked the chapel, he said, "No, Miss. No. You do not understand. So many servants, they learn only to work, to struggle. But this peace, you do not earn. Is *gift*. To receive, you must only do as desert teaches. Be still. Trust. Wait."

The wind had quieted while they were inside. The sky was once again an utterly unblemished blue. They clambered along the narrow seam and descended the steps at a very slow pace. The monk smiled at Sybel, made the sign of the cross, and said, "We hunger, we thirst for the realm beyond words. This is your destiny, to drink at the eternal well."

"I—"

"Mrs. Wells? Congressman?" A wide-eyed Nabil Saad came around the corner, leading a group of four monks. He cast astounded eyes at Father Benyamin, at the central monolith, at them. "How do you come to be here?"

"He wanted to show us."

"No one is allowed here. No one. In all my years of visiting this place, never have I been invited." He greeted the monk with a deep bow and words half chanted. The monk replied with a brief murmur and another sign of the cross. The monks behind Nabil smiled and chattered among themselves.

As the monk turned to go, Nabil fell in beside Wynn and said softly, "Father Benyamin is a very famous teacher. He has been named head of this monastery, the youngest ever. Did he say anything?"

"Not a single word to me." Wynn pointed with his chin to where the monk continued his soft conversation with Sybel.

"He spoke with your sister? About what?"

Before Wynn could respond, however, the entourage came to a halt as one of the hermit doors creaked open. A man of impossible years hobbled out, blinking in the light. And smiling. He waved one claw in the air, calling to them with the rusty sound of a crow taking flight. One of the younger monks rushed forward and helped him down the stairs. The man scarcely saw him. He used the young man as a crutch, but kept his eyes focused upon the group. Even the monastery's new abbot appeared poleaxed by the hermit's sudden appearance.

The man was scarcely higher than a gnome, shriveled and dried as desiccated fruit. He stopped before Wynn and spoke words that set all the monks to chattering. Nabil stammered, "The father is inviting you to visit his cell."

Wynn would have paid good money to do nothing of the sort. "Is this normal?"

"Please, sir, he is doing you great honor. The men in these cells, they are legends." The monks behind Nabil chirruped a musical mystery. "I beg you, do as he asks."

Impatiently the old man plucked at Wynn's shirt. His touch was feather-light, soft as death. Even so, Wynn found himself drawn forward. He glanced behind him, a swift cast that swept up several images—Sybel weeping now as Father Benyamin leaned over and spoke in delicate tones, the other monks watching with the wonder of men seeing the sun set at noon, Nabil following a few paces behind him.

"Father Marak is known throughout all Egypt," Nabil continued.

"Seven years ago he fell very ill. He was then the abbot of Bishoy, another monastery not far from here. For days he lay as one dead. He was given the final sacrament. Then he recovered. No one could explain it. Father Marak resigned as abbot, saying he would spend whatever days he had left praying here for a fallen world."

The desert cell was beyond austere. And small. There was scarcely room for Wynn to stand up straight. The ceiling sloped downward and formed a tight little alcove around a single window, ten inches to a side. Wynn could reach out and touch all four crumbling stone walls, but did not, for fear of making the space smaller still. A tallow cross was burned into the ceiling. A wooden cross hung upon the eastern wall. A bed of leather straps was tucked under the window overhang. Two blankets. A wooden bookstand stood at shoulder height, pointed so that the reader could look out the square window and inspect a forsaken world. An icon hung on the eastern wall, so old the face was no longer visible. Wynn could not even say if he stared at the picture of a man or woman. It did not matter. After his years in this cell, the old monk no doubt saw it in his dreams.

The monk shuffled in closer beside him. His odor was like that of dry earth, strong but parched. Wynn looked over his head to where Nabil stood in the doorway. "Should I offer him money?"

"Oh no, it would be a great insult. If you wish, there is an offering urn by the front gate."

"Fine. Can we go back . . ." He was halted by the monk suddenly touching his arm and speaking. The monk's voice sounded like the reluctant opening of a rusty gate.

Nabil's eyes widened further still.

When Nabil did not translate, the old man turned, inspected Nabil's face, and cackled. He offered Wynn a claw of benediction, then ushered him out.

Wynn stepped back into the desert heat, heard the cell door close behind him with a permanent thunk, and listened to the monk cackling from within. "What did he say?"

Nabil's eyes rested upon the closed cell door. "That you will do great deeds," he replied numbly. "If only you can come to remember your own name."

31

Thursday

B Y THE TIME the conference ended and the gathering dispersed, the afternoon was crowned in amber heat. Wynn stood by the car, partially sheltered by the surrounding palms, and watched as a gardener passed along a nearby row of young plants. He splashed a cupful upon each in turn, carrying the water in an urn on his back. Sparrows followed in panicked droves, drinking before the earth could suck the surface dry and filling the air with the thunder of tiny wings. Almost all the diplomats had already departed, leaving the place increasingly empty and isolated. Still there was no sign of Kay Trilling, Sybel, or Nabil.

Wynn felt tormented by an emptiness so vast he could not take it in, much less name it. Even the rising wind carried messages, if only Wynn had the wisdom to understand. Even the dove's murmur, and the flickering script of tree shadow upon sand. All mysteries there to be unlocked, if only he were a better man.

All the borders that had safely defined his carefully constructed world had been stripped away. Instead of standing on his veranda, watching another slow, sultry Florida afternoon spread gold on the western bay, he was trapped in a place of angry wind and fathomless desert reaches. Wynn was impatient to return to safety, even if it meant an air-conditioned hotel cage and the grinding din of a third-world city. Anywhere else was better than facing the yellow-tinted mirrors of sand and heat.

"There you are." Kay Trilling walked over. Sybel followed a few steps behind, shadowed by Nabil. Perhaps it was a trick of the light, but the two women seemed to share one expression, gaunt and tight and robbed of any satisfaction. "We're ready."

For once Kay appeared too weary to spear him with hostility. Wynn watched as Nabil reluctantly disengaged himself from Sybel's side, and he knew Nabil had still been trying to find out what the monk had told her.

Wynn said to his sister, "You know what I hate most about this place? How they've managed to make a single day seem a hundred years long."

They drove down the long central lane, past the monks bent over in timeless labor, through the gates, and out into the desert. Wynn leaned forward and asked Nabil, "I still don't understand how those monks knew enough to talk to us like that. Did somebody ask you about us earlier?"

"The monks do not ask such questions of anyone save the supplicant."

"They must have heard about the conference," Wynn said, struggling to make the day's experiences fit into the comforting box of his world. "And just assumed who we were."

"Mr. Bryant." Nabil's voice held a hint of quiet humor. "The monk who spoke with you has not been out of his cell for years."

"At least, that's what the monks told you."

"Why would they lie?"

"There has to be some explanation."

"Of course, Mr. Bryant." Nabil smiled at the sun-drenched road. Neither Sybel nor Kay Trilling gave any indication that they even heard the exchange. "Of course."

A half hour into the return journey, the winds picked up. Dust and pellets attacked the car, acrid and hissing. The dust tainted Wynn's nose and mouth and eyes, even with all the windows tightly closed. Nabil slowed and pressed on through the swirling clouds, driving now by feel.

The dunes unfurled like great spinning flags, which slammed into the car. The wind buffeted and shook, then departed. All became calm once more, the sky utterly empty.

Then over the sound of the motor Wynn heard the growl. A desert beast was rising from its lair, hungry and mordant. Nabil gunned the motor. The car took the next pothole like a ski jump.

When the senator complained, Nabil replied, "Either we reach the main highway before it hits, or we pull over and sit out the storm."

"How long will it last?"

"Sometimes hours, sometimes days."

Trilling did not complain again.

They hammered through the village with their horn blaring a constant frantic note, scattering chickens and donkey carts and snarling dogs. Children pointed and danced, laughing at the outsiders who feared the desert beast.

Just beyond the village, the *khamsin* attacked with vehemence. As they descended into the valley, the cavern walls with their wind-etched shapes became as indistinct as waves at night. Pellets and sand rattled the car. Overhead poured a dismal stream, laced with dark tongues of ocher and brown.

Where the road began rising into the storm, the attackers struck.

Bullets slapped down the right side of the fender and the hood, then erupted against the windshield and right side window. Wynn was showered with glass. Sand and dust streamed through the shattered windshield. Nabil spun the car over hard to the left, or perhaps he fell that way and pulled the wheel with his body. They tumbled off the road at full speed, braked not by Nabil but by scraping along the canyon. Then the wall opened and they shot into darkness, slamming into the cave's opposite wall. Wynn was catapulted over the seat in front of him, landing atop Nabil.

Before he had managed to unwind, the car was pounded from behind with blasts of automatic fire rattling across the trunk, shattering the rear windshield. Kay screamed. But it was another sound that froze his blood, the sound of a woman gasping and choking. Drowning in a sea of dust and wind.

Wynn pushed himself back down, pounded open his door, and fell to the sand. He pried open Nabil's door and shouted, "Get out!"

Feebly the Egyptian tried to obey. His left arm and hand were streaming blood. Wynn wriggled forward, gripped Nabil with both hands, and pulled hard.

The Egyptian spilled down onto him just as the next spray of bullets spattered overhead, showering them with rocks and sparks and whanging noise. Kay screamed again and piled out by his feet, crawling with the adrenaline panic of one who had not been injured, or at least not badly. From Sybel there was no sound except a frantic search for air.

Wynn crawled through the door and up across the seat. "Oh, no, no, Sybel, please."

She sat against the far door, watching him with the wide-eyed expression of a terrified little girl. Her front was splotched and stained almost black in the poor light. The same color pooled about the seat.

As gently as he could, Wynn pulled her across the seat and out of the car. He took her weight in his arms as she spilled helplessly onto the sand. Her eyes never left his, not even when the next shower of metal hail rang about them, chipping stones and sand and sending Kay into another screaming fit. She had pulled Nabil back into a narrow alcove, a cave within a cave, scarcely large enough for them to fit with legs drawn up tight against their chests. There was blood on the sand in front of them, but not much. Kay's only injury appeared to be a gash across her forehead and the frantic dread in her eyes.

Wynn half-pushed, half-carried Sybel into a neighboring alcove, its wind-carved surface smooth and cool. Sybel rested in the position he placed her. He did not want to let her go, not even when another round of gunfire pelted the car and the opposite wall. But a single glance at the blood drenching him, all of it hers, left Wynn in no doubt that to stay would doom her as surely as another bullet.

Wynn crawled past Kay and Nabil, then crouched by the rear left wheel, and searched the empty space beyond the cave. It did not matter that there was neither sense nor hope to his actions. He raised his head a fraction and saw the pinpoint flashes of light from an alcove on the road's opposite side. He crouched, ready for the rush he knew would be his doom.

"Wynn!" Kay's shriek seemed joined to the demented wind. "*No!*"

Then he heard a different roar, and realized a single threat of hope had just entered the storm-blasted canyon.

As soon as the great square shape appeared in the shadows, Wynn was up and sprinting. When the truck rumbled past, he raced up alongside, jumped up on the running board, and flung open the passenger door.

The driver was caught in the act of laughing and speaking to his mate, who sprawled in the cubbyhole behind the two seats. They both froze and gaped at Wynn, who stretched out one hand far enough to see the blood coating his fingers, his shirt, his body. He felt the stickiness on his face as well, when he opened his mouth and screamed so loud he felt the muscles of his throat tearing loose, *"STOP! NOW!"*

Whether or not the driver understood the words, or whether he thought Wynn pointed a bloodied weapon into his face, he rammed on the brakes with both feet. The second driver tumbled out of his perch and down upon Wynn. Together they fell out of the truck and onto the ground. The terrified Egyptian raced off screaming, losing himself in the desert and the wind, headed pell-mell in the direction of Wadi Natrum and safety.

Before the truck had shuddered to a full halt, Kay Trilling was already moving, her arms locked around the badly limping Nabil. Wynn raced back to the cave, the truck blocking him from the attackers. His mind was filled with images of them appearing at any moment, splattering him with close-range fire. He hefted Sybel and raced back. Kay stood half in, half out of the truck, waving him forward and shouting words he could not hear.

Together they managed to pull Sybel inside the cab. Wynn slammed the door and shrieked, *"Drive!"* But the truck was already moving.

Wynn looked around to see Kay staring with dread at the bloody mess of Sybel's chest. Nabil was sprawled in the rear cubbyhole, eyes shut, taking shallow breaths. Wynn attacked him with an elbow. "Don't you pass out on me! Don't you *dare!*"

Nabil groaned and opened his eyes. Wynn shouted, "Tell him where to go!"

Nabil moaned the words, received a distraught and trembly response from the driver, then collapsed.

As they joined the main desert highway, the wind keened a new note. Which was strange, since they were jammed inside the cab of a battered produce truck, the windows shut tight against the swirling maelstrom and the engine racing. Wynn could not even hear Sybel's gasping, though he knew she was making sounds because he could see the frantic search of her eyes and feel her lungs struggling within his sheltering arms. He did not need to urge the driver on. The truck bounced and rattled at a frantic speed. The driver either looked in horror at them or held his chin inches above the wheel and squinted through the yellow fog, swerving to avoid slower-moving vehicles only at the last minute.

Even so, Wynn heard the change to the wind's shrieking melody. A new note, higher than the rest, not a keening of grief so much as one of separation. Higher and higher it sang, as Sybel's struggles grew weaker and her eyes glazed. Finally her clutching hands released him. Higher still it climbed, far beyond the range of mortal ears, until only his heart heard the tone. His poor, shattered heart.

32

Friday

A S SOON AS THEY arrived at the hospital, even before she had her head seen to, Kay Trilling called the American embassy. Within minutes the ambassador's staff had slipped into well-oiled gear. A seemingly countless number of earnest young men and women appeared like magic, as well as three Egyptians drawn from the embassy's security office. From that moment, Wynn was not left alone for an instant, not even when he noticed the truck driver still standing in the corner and watching the scene with frightened village eyes. Wynn asked the American now attached to his side, "Do you speak enough Arabic to thank him properly for the ride and his help?"

In response, the young man addressed the driver with fluent ease. Immediately the driver began pouring forth his story, raising his voice every time a policeman happened by. Clearly he was terrified at being drawn into a tragedy not of his making.

Wynn had to lean against the wall to wedge his hand into his pocket and pry his wallet loose. It was not so much that he was tired as every action required furious concentration and strength of will. His hands shook violently as he peeled open the sticky billfold. Then he found that he could not make the bills come apart. So he extended the entire wad. "Here."

The driver's avarice overcame his aversion to touching a hand caked with someone else's life, or taking bills drenched with calamity. The driver used both hands to accept the money, then lifted the payment to his forehead as he murmured a formal thanks, not realizing he smudged his brow with Sybel's blood.

The young man from the embassy watched it all with round amazed eyes. "Congressman, if you'll excuse me, I think you're going into shock."

"You're wrong there." Steadying himself on the wall, Wynn made his way down the hall and sank onto a bench. "I took that corner about three hours ago."

Kay Trilling was seated farther along the same uncomfortable bench, talking with another embassy official. She waited as Wynn eased himself down, then reached over and took his hand. "You need to let the doctor give you something."

"I'm not hurt."

"Wynn," she said, her voice softened by sorrow. "Honey, let the doctor give you a pill."

She signaled a passing nurse, and within moments he was given water and a couple of pills. Not long after, the world receded somewhat, cushioned behind a foul-tasting fog.

From within his chemical cocoon he observed the approach of another American, this one senior enough to draw both the junior officials and the security detail to attention. The new man identified himself as the chief of the embassy's American Citizen Services Section, responsible for dealing with all problems between visitors and the local government. He apologized that the ambassador was in Alexandria attending a ministerial conference. He inspected Wynn's blood-drenched form and spoke faster. By his mere presence he forced the process along. Soon they found themselves being ushered downstairs, through a few yards of stinging wind, and into the comfort of an embassy limousine.

The chief aide filled the limo with mindless chatter, telling them that the Egyptian embassy was the biggest in the world, with thirty-nine federal government agencies. Egypt was America's largest recipient of foreign aid after Israel, which guaranteed their current problem would be looked after well. They would spend the night in the new ambassador's residence, which stood within the embassy compound. Kay interrupted his attempt to seal out the tragedy by repeating what she had already told several more junior staffers, that Nabil Saad was one of her own aides, on secondment from the World Bank. Instantly the man used his cellphone, speaking in tones too hushed for Wynn to catch. Wynn regretted the absence of the man's droning lecture. Anything was better than being forced to hear the howling storm.

The next morning the wind still bit fiercely as Wynn crossed the embassy compound and took the elevator to the ambassador's suite on the main building's twelfth floor. He stood by the outer office window, staring at a city without edges. This stormy Cairo lacked the softness of glistening fog or rain-drenched clouds. Instead, the world was harshly indistinct. Even the river flowed feverish and yellow.

The ambassador's secretary was busy on the phone, arguing relentlessly in the quiet way of one experienced with Arabic etiquette. She hung up finally and said, "The National Security and Investigation Office is handling this matter. It appears they will let you go this afternoon. You will need to make a formal statement, and for that you'll have to go to the Gamal, that's the tall building on Tahrir Square. The square is—"

"I know the square and I know the Gamal."

"Ease up, Wynn."

He turned to see Kay seated in the corner, giving him a look of quiet reproach. He had not even known she was in the room.

"I'm sorry, Congressman. But it appears unlikely the Egyptian authorities will release your sister's body until after the inquest. On that point they remain adamant."

He gritted his teeth and nodded. Once. He was not yet ready to speak about that. "I want to go to the hospital and see Nabil."

"Sir, the storm is raging. Not to mention the fact that the police still haven't apprehended your attackers."

"That was not a request."

Kay walked over to offer support. "Surely you have security detail who could accompany us."

"Yes, but—"

"I want to go alone, Kay."

She inspected his face, then accepted his decision with a single nod. "Tell Nabil I'll be by later. I'm working to have him flown back to the U.S. for treatment. I spoke with the ambassador last night. It's not simply a matter of hospital care. There is too great a risk the state security will try and pin the matter on him, as an Egyptian and a Copt. I don't want to risk his being interrogated after I'm gone. Tell him I'll be by as soon as the matter is taken care of. The ambassador has tasked it out to his best men."

Wynn left the embassy compound in the ambassador's bulletproof limo, accompanied by three sharp-eyed men bearing automatic weapons. They drove to the new Kasr Elani Teaching Hospital on the banks of the Nile. Wynn emerged from the limo, turned his back to the river, cupped his hands about his eyes, and stared across the street. He was surrounded by a dead wind, a breath of hatred and hopelessness.

"Sir?"

Wynn remained where he was. He recognized that building opposite the new hospital. The battered entrance was branded into his bones. "That's the old hospital, isn't it?"

"Sir, please come inside."

Wynn swiveled about. "I asked you a question."

"Yes, sir, that is the old hospital. But your driver is here. We know, sir. We checked."

"He is not my driver. He is my friend and colleague."

Angrily the officer by the door waved him forward. "Please come away from the exposed street *now*, sir."

They flanked him and refused to permit anyone to share the elevator. Upstairs there was a moment's angry confrontation before Wynn pulled rank and insisted on seeing Nabil alone. Two men inspected the room before permitting him to enter.

Nabil was awake and watching him. Wynn passed on Kay's message while standing by the door. Wanting it over and done with. Nabil clearly understood, for he said nothing until Wynn was seated beside the bed. Then he asked, "Your sister, she is gone?"

Wynn glanced down at his hands and their invisible stain.

"What you did, sir, that was the bravest deed I have ever seen."

"Call me Wynn." He leaned back, flooded by all that was past. Perhaps it was the smell and the noise and the metal bed and the same gray despair seeping from the walls. Or perhaps it was because of his own helpless fatigue. He knew Nabil was watching him. Wynn had no strength to hold back the deluge. "I remember watching my parents die."

Nabil shifted slightly, his body held by strappings and tubes. But it was enough of a motion to show he was totally awake.

"When we came into the hospital room, my father was rolled over on his side. His eyes were open. But he didn't see me at all."

Outside the room a metal trolley rattled noisily down the hall, the wheels banging and squeaking like the chuckles of cold death. "Then they took us downstairs, but the nurses spotted us kids and tried to keep us from going down the corridor. But I heard Mom screaming. I pushed through them and ran. I came through the door. Mom was lying there with her hair plastered down and her face purple and her mouth was open so wide."

Strange that he could sit there and speak calmly. As though his physical body felt nothing, his nerves already numb, his emotions suffocated. "I ran away. Somebody tried to stop me, but I got away. Only things got worse. I ran downstairs looking for a way out, but instead I wound up in a children's ward. Two kids to a bed, sometimes three, their heads at either end and their feet touching in the middle. Relatives camped on reed mats between the beds, fanning away the flies, holding hands, whimpering with the kids. The place was full of stink and noise. All the kids had these big dark eyes, and I knew they knew. They'd never get better, never get out."

"Cairo was not a good place to be hospitalized," Nabil agreed. "It still isn't."

"I freaked. Totally, utterly wigged out. Then suddenly Sybel was there. She hugged me fierce enough to break the spell, then pulled me outside. She brought me back to America and cared for me ever since."

Nabil watched and waited, offering no false comfort, no empty words. Just a man listening to another come to grips with the impossible.

"The family learned never to talk to me about Egypt, or Mom and Dad, not ever. I would scream at them, shout anything that came into my head. Sybel was my only constant." Wynn forced himself to meet Nabil's gaze. "Do you remember anything about that time?"

"I am about the same age as your sister. I remember everything. My father spent his every waking day down the hall, your parents' unofficial mourner."

"Did they ever figure out what made my parents sick?"

"They think poison. Egypt was going through an agricultural upheaval, trying to move from medieval farming methods to modern, all in one giant leap. Some farmers never could understand pesticides. They were given jugs that should have been poured into barrels of water. But water was precious, so they sprinkled it full strength onto the closest rows. Then they complained that those plants grew sickly, and never used the pesticides again. But still the farmers took those poisoned plants to market." Nabil might have shrugged, or maybe just winced. "You see?"

The futility of compounded loss threatened to swallow Wynn whole. His only lifeline dangled madly out of reach. Wynn raised his eyes. "I need to know what else the monk of Wadi Natrum told Sybel."

"She did not say."

"You were talking with her when you left the building. I saw you."

"I stayed with her, yes. I asked several times. But she would not speak of it."

"She didn't say anything?"

"I am sorry, Wynn. I would tell you if I knew."

It was the first time Nabil had ever used his name. Even in the depths of his remorse, Wynn recognized the moment and took note. It gave him the courage to ask, "And what the hermit said to me, did you understand that?"

Though the features were smudged deep as bruises, still his eyes remained alert, dark, penetrating. "Your father and mother were missionaries as well as teachers. This you know."

"Yes."

"For the government and most people, they were here only to teach at the university. Their mission work remained secret. Speaking of Christ to Copts, that was one thing. We were persecuted from time to time, but not too much here in Cairo. Not then. But preaching to a Muslim, that was a crime. It still is. At that time, a foreigner who converted a Muslim could be put to death. A Muslim who prayed to Jesus, the same. Your parents ran secret home churches for believers among the Muslims. Very secret. My father, he was one of their messengers. The churches, they grew and grew. This was why your parents did not leave when Nasser declared that all Americans were enemies and must leave the country. They stayed for their secret flocks. Nowadays, every time I come home, I meet some of these people. The churches are tended by others now, but still they grow. A forest rising from seeds your parents planted."

Wynn sat and waited for more. Staring at the floor by his feet, wishing he had listened better, spoken with his sister differently, learned enough to be whole now. When he looked up, Nabil was asleep.

Defeated and empty, he rose and left the room.

By MIDAFTERNOON, when Kay and Wynn had both given their statements to the security officer at the Gamal and returned to the am-

bassador's suite, the wind had stopped. The office windows were encrusted with a patina of grit, filtering the light a sickly beige. The suite
was empty save for Wynn and Kay. The chargé was off somewhere and
the ambassador's secretary was arranging Wynn's travel documents,
everybody busy and scurrying for the congressman and senator. Kay
had spoken twice with the ambassador, assuring him that he should
remain at the ministerial meeting, and that she would pass on his condolences to Congressman Bryant. Wynn's two suitcases stood by the
desk, waiting for the limo to take him to the airport. Kay was taking
a flight the next day, hoping to personally shepherd Nabil out of
danger.

A young aide appeared, possibly one of those at the hospital the
previous evening, Wynn could not be sure. He had not taken any more
of the tablets, but now and then he drifted away, as though his body
was producing its own chemical veil. The young man explained that
they had to put out a press release, and it would be taking the official
police line, which was that the attack had been the work of local funda-
mentalists. Wynn observed how the filtered light cast the man's features
a sickly tan, as if he had emerged from some dismal netherworld to ex-
pel more bad news.

When they were alone once more, Kay offered, "You don't look too
good. Are you sure you're up for the flight?"

The flight was not the problem. He would take his pills and sack
away the hours. He forced himself to form the tumbling thoughts. "I've
got to do something, Kay. I can't just let this pass, like it doesn't matter,
like Sybel never stood for anything."

"You saved our lives back there. That should do for a start."

He looked down at the floor between his feet. There was no need to
say what they both knew.

Kay eased herself farther into the sofa. She extended her legs, massaged one knee, and said, "I was born and raised in Oakland. The city's
basically a poor stepsister to San Francisco. Always undergoing one re-
vitalization project or another, but nothing ever works. It's got the naval
yards and Berkeley and everything the rich San Francisco folks just refer
to as East Bay. All the poor, tired working jerks who have to live on the
other side of the bridge and spend their mornings and evenings stuck in
the worst traffic you ever saw. My dad was a surgeon, which meant I
was raised in Oakland Hills, nice house with a pretty view out over the
bay. But when I go back, I like to spend time down in the low-rent ar-

eas. There's a church down there I've been visiting for years. Keeps me in touch with the little people. You know what I mean?"

"I know." Giving her what she wanted, which was a signal he heard her at all.

"I was elected to the state legislature right in the middle of the savings and loan debacle. Entered the Senate just as we were sweeping up the last of that mess. I watched as banks began gradually growing ever larger, claiming that size was necessary in order to compete. Only large financial institutions, they argued, could withstand the difficulties that had closed down most of our S and Ls, or allow them to compete on an international scale. Let's be perfectly honest here. I had every reason to want to believe them. They were financing my campaigns in a big way, especially when I got myself appointed to a couple of key committees. But these little people down in that Oakland church, I tell you, it was hard to shut out what I was hearing and seeing on a Sunday morning. Like I was getting hammered by a message at my most vulnerable moment. Otherwise I'd have just turned away. Something every politician learns to do. Every *successful* politician, that is, who aims on getting reelected. The key to success in Washington is, choose your battles wisely."

A veiled beam from the window cast Kay's features into translucent depths. The bandage across her forehead gleamed with a color beyond white. Wynn clutched at her words and the moment with desperation.

"What those people down there in the valley showed me was the slow and steady demise of the local branch bank. So gradual it would be very easy to ignore the trend. But over time a lot of those branches were closing down. Traditionally, our local banks were there to *serve the community*. They maintained branches in lower income areas because their bank served as an anchor to the local businesses and tradespeople. Only now these branches were disappearing. Why? Because these huge mega-banks don't care overmuch about the local community. They exist to serve their shareholders. And these small branches did not turn sufficient profit. The result was, the low-rent branches were shutting down, and their places taken by what I call the financial tapeworms. Credit unions, check-cashing offices, pawn shops, car equity loan offices, storefronts offering second mortgages. All of these have one thing in common; they live by usury. These newcomers, these *sharks*, charge higher interest rates than the credit card companies. They care nothing for who they consume. They destroy families. They destroy communities. And they exist because the banks are retreating, leaving a vacuum for these demons to fill."

The outer door opened, and noise filtered in from outside. Wynn leaned in tight, not wanting anybody or anything to interfere.

Kay did the same, coming in close enough for him to see amber flecks in what he had previously thought were utterly dark eyes. "That's when I met Graham. I started attending a Bible study on Capitol Hill. He was there. You learn pretty fast not to talk shop at one of these things. People get very prickly at the idea of being hit while their guard is down. I had to hunt him out."

The figure hovering just beyond Wynn's peripheral vision said, "Excuse me, Congressman."

"Be right with you."

"But sir, your—"

Wynn raised a single threatening finger. "Back off." To Kay, "Go on."

"Maybe it was just how I caught Graham, walking away from the group, telling him I'd heard he was involved in financial reform. But he refused to talk with me about it that day. It was like he could look inside me and see all the convoluted motives, all the internal conflicts of interest. You know what I mean?"

Wynn gave her a tight nod of understanding. He knew.

"So he tells me, and remember now, he's talking to somebody on the appropriations committee, a senior senator with significant clout. Somebody who can really wind his clock, for good or bad. But what he says to me is, Your doubt is written all over your face and there's nothing I can say that will convince you."

"He said that?"

"He did indeed. He goes on, If this is your cross, the Lord will have to be the one to tell you. Not me. Then he just turned and walked away."

The aide was almost dancing with nerves. "Congressman, please. Sir, the limo's waiting and the police escort is downstairs and your flight to Washington leaves in just over an hour."

Kay rose to her feet, waited for Wynn to stand, then hugged him fiercely. When she finally released him, she smiled and said, "Hard to argue with that, isn't it?"

33

Friday

FRIDAY EVENING WASHINGTON time, early Saturday morning Roman time, Jackie limped past the Dulles Airport customs barrier. Instantly she was enveloped by a jubilant Good Friday din. The religious among the waiting throng stood out like shiny new pennies. Young boys tugged futilely at the collars of their first suits and chased pink-frocked girls in patent leather shoes. Parents holding ribbon-bedecked flowers hugged and welcomed family with tears and words in two dozen different tongues. Jackie pushed her trolley with her ears still ringing from the bells that had awakened her that same morning in Rome. Thousands and thousands of bells, tolling continuously from the moment she woke until the taxi took her to the airport. She had slept her way across the Atlantic, dreaming of music that was a welcome for many but only a farewell for her.

Jackie's previous morning had been spent in slumber and solitude. She had risen just after noon and felt the pain returning, but decided not to take another pill. Her room had been lost down some Trastevere alley, high enough to transform the street noise into a continuous clatter rising from a stone forest. The chamber was dingy and old, the walls yellow and cracked. The shutter would not open. Downstairs the church ran a soup kitchen, and the smells finally enticed her to endure the agony of dressing. Every motion had brought new throbs from her shoulder. She had descended the four flights by gripping the stair rail and timing each step to her breaths.

She took her place in the *menza* line with the poor and the homeless. Her shoulder and leg throbbed constantly, bowing her slightly, adding a shuffling gait to her walk. There were hundreds of people and she heard a rainbow of tongues. Volunteers brought food to the tables.

Jackie spooned up pasta and broth, then ate every scrap of her roast chicken with peas. When she looked around, no one met her eyes. Even so, she felt a comfortable bond with this place and these people. Her pain might be better hidden, but she understood.

"Jackie, welcome." Anna smiled to all the table as she touched Jackie's good shoulder. "Everything hurts, yes? But while you slept the doctor came, she says all is fine."

"This is some operation."

"Sant'Egidio started here with this kitchen. Now we are all the world over. We study the Word of God, we pray for peace, we feed the poor, we speak for all who have no voice."

"What about the conference in Washington, and the one now in Cairo?"

"Many conferences." Anna found cheer in the words. "All are the same. We feed the poor and we pray for peace."

After lunch, Jackie used her credit card and the phone in a neighboring café to call Esther. The older woman was suitably horrified by news of her moped attackers, and reluctantly agreed to try to pass on the warning to Wynn. Afterward Jackie found herself unwilling to return to her room and the slats of light and the imprisoning bed. Instead she walked to the church piazza. She moved slowly, favoring her wounded side. She sat on the waist-high bench shelf running along the piazza's western wall, joined there by dozens of other homeless and lost. The shadows and the church bells were the only clock they needed, counting out just another empty day.

After a time she stretched out on the stone bench and dozed until shadows draped the square in coming dusk. Upon awakening she crossed to a neighboring alley market and bought an olive *ciabatta*, cheese, grapes, and bottled water. As she was finishing her meal, the church bells pealed their nightly invitation. She found herself joining the throngs approaching the church, her internal protests the meagerest of whines.

Anna stood just inside the doorway, smiling a welcome. "You are feeling better?"

"Not really."

"Ah." The smile gentled but did not fade. "Perhaps you are not just speaking of your outside wounds, yes?" Anna matched her own pace to Jackie's shuffling gait. "Perhaps the question is not what you face, but what you choose to face *alone*. You understand?"

"Maybe."

"Of course, life is possible without God. So many desperate people, they survive with nothing but themselves. But hope? Who can stand alone and still know this?"

Her smile was so infectious, Jackie found the response came easily. "I'm missing the connection here."

Anna smiled her down the aisle. "You see? Already you know where you belong."

Still more people kept pressing in behind her. Jackie spotted a pew near the front. The Bible reading started, each passage translated twice. An Arab woman sat to one side of her, a bulky man in a tight suit to the other. The singing began, a chant beyond time and space, one almost too soothing for her own good. The choir stood to her left, a few young people who chanted one line and then were echoed by the packed congregation. The responses were great wellsprings of music, free verses of gentle might. Jackie picked up the leaflet with the English words but was afraid to read them. The music alone was already too much.

Suddenly she was crying. She did not know why, or even for whom. There was no space for reason, scarcely any for breath.

A hand reached over and patted her shoulder. Roughly she shook her head. The hand retreated, then returned, but only to drop a tissue into her lap. Apparently tears were not new here, nor the desire for solitude in the midst of many. She had heard of tears that held a cleansing, a gladness. And always discounted such words as bitter fable.

Jackie straightened and used the tissue to wipe her face. She never cried. It was a luxury she could not afford. Which was why these easy tears frightened her so. She sought strength from the incense-laden air, rose, and headed for the door. For a moment she wished she had never heard of Rome.

JACKIE SEARCHED the overhead signs for the bus to Reagan National Airport and tried to ignore her throbbing wounds. The prospect of seeing Shane again kept her moving forward, glancing at her watch, calculating how much time she had before her connecting flight to Orlando. Which was why she did not see Esther until the woman stepped forward and said, "Let me have that, dear, and sit yourself down."

Jackie did not want to meet the woman's gaze. There was no place here for yet more tears, be they from weariness or pain or what lay ahead. She buried her head in Esther's shoulder and gripped as hard as her wounded shoulder permitted.

"Are you exhausted?"

"Tired, yes. Sleepy, no. All I've done for two days now is doze." She let the older woman ease her down into the wheelchair held by Carter Styles. She smiled at the carrot-headed man. "I really don't need this."

"Indulge me." Esther took hold of her trolley and led them over to a relatively quiet corner, where she lowered herself into a seat. "Can we see to one other matter before we take you home?"

"The answer is yes, but I'm headed for Orlando." She checked the concourse clock. "I've got just over three hours to make it to National. Everything leaving from here was full."

"You're not going anywhere. You can't."

"I have no choice, Esther."

It was Carter who asked, "Hayek?"

"I might have a lead," Jackie confirmed.

Esther rubbed hard at the lines compressed into her own forehead. Carter slipped into the seat beside Esther and leaned forward until his belly rested upon his thighs. "We've got some good news and some bad news."

"I'm starved for the good."

"Tell me. Okay. First, Graham is better. Not great, not even good. But back among the living."

"Probably as good as he'll ever get," Esther added.

"Don't say that. Don't even think it." Carter took hold of the older woman's hand and said to Jackie, "And we instituted legal action against the newspaper, the one that ran the story about Graham. Our lawyer's done some background research. Turns out the paper has a new minority shareholder. Some foreign bank."

"Let me guess," Jackie said. "Banque Royale of Liechtenstein."

"Right first time."

"They owned the plane that took Valerie Lawry down to see Hayek."

Esther said, "You might as well tell her the rest."

Carter took time to shape the words. "The Congressman and Senator Trilling were ambushed coming back from what we thought was a secret conference outside Cairo. They're both okay, but Congressman Bryant's sister was killed. And our friend Nabil was wounded."

"They're calling Wynn's flight," Esther said, using first the seat, then the back, and finally Carter's shoulder to push herself upright. "You can tell her the rest on the way."

WHEN THEY STARTED back across the concourse, Jackie found she could not abide being seated in that wheelchair. No matter how nice it felt to rely on the strength of others, her skin crawled at how people carefully avoided looking down at her. She had spent a lifetime depending on no one but herself. "I'll walk."

Carter merely helped her up, then rolled the chair aside and matched his stride to her own. Esther continued to push her trolley. But when they came within sight of the international arrivals gate, Carter said, "Let's stop right here."

"What is it?"

"Cameras at ten o'clock. I don't believe it. Look who's pushing through to greet the Congressman."

Jackie spotted the familiar face. "Is that Governor Wells?"

Carter offered, "There was a White House meeting of southern governors yesterday."

"He couldn't possibly be using this as a photo op," Esther said. "He wouldn't dare."

Wynn emerged through the sliding doors like a man stumbling from his own tomb. Eyes wide but seeing nothing, he lurched forward on unsteady legs. When the first camera flashed, Wynn's entire body recoiled.

Grant Wells stepped forward and hugged Wynn. In a flash of assimilation, Wynn took in the entire tableau. Instead of pushing himself away, however, he gripped Grant harder. But not in sorrow. His features stretched so taut the blood was squeezed out, turning his face into a feral mask. His lips drew back fully from his teeth, so that he appeared ready to bite Grant's head off.

Jackie saw Grant's muscles contract and realized the governor was trying to break away. Wynn held him fiercely in place and kept whispering into his ear, twisting slightly so that Grant's head shielded his own from the cameras. The side of Grant's face came into view. The governor looked ill. He heaved harder, a convulsive jerk, and broke free. Wynn ducked his head and shoved through the crowd. The governor stared after him, still cringing.

Jackie walked over so that she fell into step beside him. "Slow down a little. I can't move that fast."

Wynn looked as if he had aged fifty years. "They got you too?"

"Back and leg. I tried to call and warn you." When he continued to barrel through the throng, she said, "I have information you need to hear."

A reporter appeared at Wynn's other side. "Congressman, could we please have a statement about—"

"Not now. Call my office."

"Our embassy in Cairo claims it was the work of terrorists—"

"I said, not now." Then he saw Esther and Carter. He found enough strength to snarl, "Don't either of you come near me."

Esther began, "I just wanted to say how sorry—"

"Save it." To Jackie, "Come on."

She took the trolley from Carter and tried to match Wynn's pace, though his elongated steps stretched her leg until the wound shrieked. "I've got to catch a flight from National."

"I'll drop you off." Wynn hurtled through the doors, not bothering to check for oncoming traffic, ignoring the indignant horn and squeal of brakes. He aimed for the line of limos like a man on a mission. Once there he talked a language they clearly understood, because one driver leaped forward. When Wynn pointed back at Jackie, the driver raced over to take her trolley.

When she slipped inside, however, the anger and the energy were gone, and she found instead a man who shrank away from her and the surrounding world. "I'm so sorry, Wynn."

He waited until the driver had slid behind the wheel to say, "National Airport, then the Willard. And close the divider."

Only when the glass panel had slid into place did he speak directly to her. "Tell me what I'm supposed to do."

His grief was enough to draw her close. She settled one arm behind him, took his hand, sat there. Let him absorb the fact that she was with him. In the here and now. Gradually the tension seeped away, until he was able to slide down and place his head upon her shoulder. Nestle in. Like he belonged. "I'm so tired."

She stroked the fine dark head. "I know."

They sat thus, not speaking, through the long ride until the first National sign swept overhead. Jackie pushed at his chest, a gentle nudge, and said, "I have news."

Reluctantly he moved away, rubbed his face, and listened as she sped through the detective's report, the message from the Boatman, the attack. She then went back to her earlier discussion with Esther, and concluded, "Everything is still pointing at Hayek having an agenda and a timetable. That's the only reason I can think why he'd attack us. It's not about some amendment. Something else is at work here."

Wynn still had not spoken when the driver asked over the intercom, "Excuse me, which airline?"

"United."

"Then we've arrived."

They pulled to the curb and halted. Wynn gripped her hand. "Stay here."

"I can't."

"I need you, Jackie." The entreaty cost him dearly. "Please."

Gently she released her hand from his. "Later maybe." She moved for the door, fleeing temptation. "Right now I've got to catch this flight to Orlando."

He craned over, asked through the open door, "What's so critical about right now?"

She reached back in and touched his face. Gave him a sad, sad smile. "Tomorrow is visiting day."

34

Saturday

SATURDAY MORNING Jim Burke had one of the company limos take him downtown. The car smelled faintly of cleanser, stale ashes, and other people's sweat. Burke stared out the windows at soporific downtown Orlando, the world caught in another ritual feast.

Yesterday and again that morning he had met with Hayek over the debacles in Rome and Egypt. Hayek had shown genuine pleasure over how wrong things had gone. His only sign of frustration had come not over the attacks themselves, but rather over their inability to track down the Brazilian banker. Burke tried not to give it all much thought. The potential deviations were too great. He would follow orders and expect all to be made clear soon enough. With Hayek, it was simply the way.

First Florida was one of the state's oldest banks, and its Orlando headquarters looked the part. The squat stone behemoth took up almost an entire block, a cross between the Treasury Building and a demented mausoleum. Burke climbed yard-wide stairs and gave his name to the security man guarding mammoth brass doors.

Burke despised the board members on sight, pinstriped losers hiding their nervousness behind golf course laughter. They clutched to the premise that since he had come to their offices, he was the one being welcomed into the club.

"Jim Burke, do I have that right? Bob Carlton, President of First Florida. Can't tell you what a pleasure it is, yessir. A real pleasure."

Burke accepted the handshake. "Right."

"When my secretary said you sounded American, I thought to myself, this is too good to be true." He was all teeth and rosy cheeks and tight, worried eyes. "I mean, it's all well and good to have the

Banque Royale of Liechtenstein buy us out—did I say that right? But communication between people who know their own turf is easier. Makes for less chance of a false start here."

Robert Carlton the Fifth was the great-great-grandson of First Florida's founder, and as far removed from the first Carlton as modern Orlando was from the pioneer settlement of the midnineteenth century. Carlton the original glared down from an ornately framed portrait on the wall, obviously enraged over what his progeny had done with his creation.

"What say we get to business." Bob Carlton beamed his other board members into their seats, keeping the head of the table for himself, holding out the chair to his right for Burke. "I think you'll find this comfortable, James. Or should I call you Jim?"

"Mr. Burke will do just fine." He took a seat in the center of the table, switching the top position from the head to his own chair. "I'm afraid I don't have much time."

"No problem. Harry, swing on over here by me, why don't you. That's great." He slumped ponderously into his chair. "What say we get you up to speed on all our operations and—"

"That won't be necessary." Burke shoved away the bank's embossed leather portfolio. He pulled an envelope from his jacket pocket, set it on the table, and sent it shooting towards the bank's CEO. "This is for you."

Robert Carlton the Fifth stared at the envelope as he would a snake. "Mind telling me what's going on here?"

"Everything in there should be self-explanatory." Burke settled back and waited.

The silver-haired gentleman did his best to glare down the table, but there was too much fear in his eyes. "We had an agreement. There would be no radical changes."

"Just read the letter, Mr. Carlton." When the chairman's trembling fingers finally managed to tear open the envelope, Burke turned and said to the others, "Your new owner intends to leave the board as is and raise salaries by twenty percent. The only change we wish to make at this time is an increase in Interbank trading operations. We also want a place made available on the board for your Vice President of Capital Markets."

Carlton looked up. "Capital Markets?"

The board secretary offered, "Thorson Fines, sir."

"I know perfectly well what the man's name is. Now look here, Mr. Burke. This really won't do."

"It is not a request."

"We've kept that department only to service the needs of several of our larger customers. Our Capital Markets operation is minuscule."

"That is about to change."

"With what?" Carlton bore the look of a man whose world had been grabbed and shaken for the first time in a very long while. "You can't expect us to take money that's been entrusted to us because of our conservative lending and investment policies—"

"Which have consistently lost you money." Burke had had enough. "Thorson Fines is now a member of your board. You will be receiving an inflow of new investment capital. This meeting is over."

"THORSON FINES?" Burke waited in the doorway until the man hung up the phone. "Jim Burke. Appreciate your coming in on a holiday like this."

"You're the rep from Liechtenstein?" Thorson rose reluctantly to his feet. "I'm surprised they sent an American."

"The merchant bank has just one customer. Its owner." And a brass plaque on the front wall of a fine old building. Burke shut the door behind him, walked over, sat down without bothering to offer his hand. This was a man with months of hostile frustration to talk away. "For all intents and purposes, your new boss is an American."

Thorson Fines mulled that over as he lowered himself back behind the desk. His expression showed he had decided it didn't matter much. This, Burke knew, was a man looking for the exit. Thorson said, "So who's the mystery man?"

"First let's see," Burke replied, "if you're part of the team or not."

"You're here to size me up?"

"Oh, we've got all the information we need about you and your operation, Mr. Fines."

"There isn't any operation."

"We realize that."

"I'm like the pet monkey they pull out to show potential new investors. Any time I go to them with an idea, they freak."

"All this," Burke soothed, "is about to change."

Thorson was like most of the senior traders Burke had ever met, utterly refashioned by his trade. He could once have been fat or smooth or tall or a jock. Now he had been crammed into the hot press of the trading floor. His face was expressionless, the gaze scalded by the suppressed fire of the floor at full cry. "I've been making enquiries. For other jobs."

"We know."

"You think you can change my mind?"

"Absolutely."

"All right." He crossed his arms. "So talk."

"You have just been made the newest member of the First Florida board of directors."

The news brought a grim smile. "Bet that made old Carlton dance a jig."

"What Carlton thinks is no longer important. We acquired this bank for one reason and one reason only."

Thorson's eyes widened marginally. "Me?"

"Of course not. First Florida's Interbank connection. But it would be excellent if we could have you as well."

Currency trades operated in a two-tier system, much like stocks. Currency markets in Chicago, New York, London, Zurich, Tokyo, and Singapore operated as centers for most transactions. Until recently, small and medium-size trades—anything up to a hundred million dollars—went through brokers tied to one or more of these exchanges. But electronic trading was fragmenting the system. Increasingly even smaller currency swaps could take place on-line and direct. Brokers stayed in business for two reasons: the confidentiality they offered, and the information they brokered along with their trades.

Just as with stocks, however, a second tier operated high above this one. In the lofty spheres of big-fund secrecy, major currency swaps called blocks went through the Interbank Exchange without ever touching the street. Once the deal was done, the electronic tape showed a crossed order for some massive amount, anywhere up to five billion dollars a pop. The exchanges had no choice but to take note of the new currency position and recognize themselves for the small fry they were.

The Interbank market was the most exclusive of the currency exchanges. Entry was restricted to the top fifty U.S. banks, the biggest

Wall Street mutual funds, and the huge brokers heavily involved in currencies. The list was very tightly restricted, and for good reason. On the Interbank Exchange, all transactions were *one hundred percent leveraged*. There was no money down. Credit lines ran among all players, with no collateral required. Every player had settlement limits. Any transaction was ticketed against the limit. But the limits had nothing to do with solvency and everything to do with reputation.

Hedge funds were kept strictly outside the Interbank Exchange. Which meant Hayek had to post margins, or put down hard cash as a percentage of each transaction. It also meant every currency trade was held up to the public eye, or had to pass through brokers who were notorious for selling information to their best clients. Not only that, but the more conservative Interbank players refused to deal with hedge funds at all. In Forex vernacular, the Interbanks would not do Hayek's name.

Thorson's mind scanned the new data at a trader's speed—lightning fast. "You're fronting for an American fund?"

"That is correct."

"Which one?"

"Are you with us or not, Mr. Fines?"

"Oh, I'm definitely willing to give this one a chance."

"Then the answer is the Hayek Group."

The news blew him back a fraction. "Can he get away with it?"

"We're working on that. But for the moment, this information needs to remain confidential."

In strict accordance with the law, hedge funds could not own a bank. But the same law also outlawed banks from owning hedge funds. The banks hated this part. So they had spent millions lobbying to have the law's teeth pulled. Now six of America's top ten banks either owned sizable portions of hedge funds or operated their own in-house. Derivatives and foreign exchange transactions were classed by American accounting law as *contingent liabilities*. This meant that the banks did not need to show these holdings, or these risks, on their official balance sheets. Which meant they did not have to set aside reserves to cover any portion of these contracts. It was the first time since the Depression that banks had found a way around one of their most hated federal laws, the cash margin requirement.

Thorson nodded once, accepting the new world order. "So what now?"

"Talk to your guys. Tell them they're going to be flooded with new capital. And the new owners know everything there is to know about incentive payments."

"Nice little bo'," Fines agreed. *Bo'* was trading vernacular for everything above and beyond actual salary. "Why not just park the fund in your Liechtenstein bank?"

Burke simply waited, letting the guy work that one out for himself.

"You don't want your new asset management team sitting on the other side of the world." Eyebrows raised a notch. "I guess that means we're talking serious money."

"Tell your team they're going to make a fortune off this."

"There's a catch," Thorson said. "There has to be."

"Hayek is known for his secrecy. It's one reason why he's been on top for so long. It's not enough for your traders to do well. They have to do it quietly."

"Anybody who talks gets the street. I can handle that. And so can they." A quarter-second pause. "How much new capital are we talking here?"

"Four hundred million dollars will be transferred to your Capital Markets account on Tuesday. Another four hundred Wednesday." Burke pulled a second envelope from his jacket. "Account instructions and confirmation of your new position. And new salary."

Thorson's hands trembled more than those of his chairman's, but for different reasons. The sheet Fines held declared him to be a rich man. "You're bringing in your own senior trader?"

"That's right. His name is Brant Anker. Top quality. Formerly with B of A."

"We don't have the staff in place to handle another eight hundred million in trades."

"You do now."

Thorson glanced up from the sheet. "Or the space."

"They'll just have to cram in. For now."

"How many people are you bringing in?"

"Twenty-five to start. We're doubling your staff, effective to-morrow."

"So the eight hundred million—"

"Is just a start. We want you to begin establishing Hayek as a pre-ferred customer. Open a credit line for Interbank exchanges. Start as high as you can without creating a backlash. Say half a big one."

Fines could no longer hide his astonishment. "Half a billion is twice my current ops."

"This is just a start. If Hayek wants to move beyond this level, call me day or night." He set his card on the desk. "My private number is on the back." Burke rose, glad to see the man rising with him. The two were moving in tandem now. "The new staff will be here Tuesday."

35

Saturday

THE FEDERAL MEDIUM-SECURITY prison farm was just as Jackie had always pictured it. The visitors' parking was surrounded by pines and fronted the Beeline Expressway. The air was very quiet, the heat cloying. What in Orlando had been just another muggy spring morning was now compacted tight with dread. Jackie fumbled with the bottle of pain pills, spilling two into her shaking hands and another three onto the sidewalk. She stood there a long moment, then slid the pills back into the bottle.

She joined the line of dejected mothers and lovers trudging through security. Jackie could not help but look up as she passed beneath the first line of chain link and razor wire. The unblemished sky did not so much beckon as mock her every step, saying in those blue-blue depths that she was as imprisoned as anyone inside. She handed her driver's license to the gatehouse security guard, endured the pat-down, and almost vomited as she spoke Shane's name.

She took a seat beside two heavy-set women smoking and talking in Spanish. Jackie leaned her head against the coarse brick wall and fought for control.

At the beginning of their relationship, Shane had been all polish and allure and chiseled good looks. He was a master at enticement. Shane could fool anybody for a couple of hours. Which was how she had been won over, that and the fact that her brother had introduced them. Shane had started off easy, keeping their meetings brief enough for him to hide his deeper nature, until she was well and truly trapped. Then he had revealed his other side. The menace. The terror.

Over the course of their eight months together, he had driven away all her friends. He'd throw fury fits when she attempted to go anywhere without him. Steadily he had peeled away all protection she might find in others, even throwing Preston out of his apartment one night. The only person he had welcomed or felt comfortable around was Jackie's mother. Which should have been all the warning she needed. But by the time their kinship was revealed, Jackie was already snared.

Gradually she had been stripped by his acid tongue and pent-up venom, reduced to a trembling mass too spineless to leave. Before that, she had never understood how a woman could become trapped by a man known to be dangerous. Now, she ached for them all. Toward the end she had become unsure of her own identity, uncertain of whether there was enough of herself left to leave for.

In truth, Shane had never intended to marry her. Early on he had used marriage as another lure. But only when she began to nurse Preston, and he sensed she had found a way back to a life without him, did he pressure her. In the end Jackie had left him, not for herself, but for Preston. No one should be forced to die alone—that was the litany she kept repeating to herself as she escaped late one night, her brother bundled into the back seat, everything she owned packed into two suitcases in the trunk. She took an apartment under a false name, paying cash out of Preston's dwindling reserves, and kept what was left under his sweat-stained mattress. She lived out those terror-filled days with a stun gun charged and armed at her side, breathing easy only when she learned that Shane had problems all his own. The news had been good for a few final laughs before her brother left her all alone.

"Jackie Havilland?"

"That's me."

The guard was black and huge. "This way."

But she had trouble rising. The air was gone from where she sat, and strength as well. The two ladies beside her turned and smiled with the bitter memory of their own such times. Jackie used both hands and clawed her way up. Once standing, nausea rose in a violent wave. She rested her head against the wall.

The guard rumbled, "Lady, nobody is pushing you down this path."

She rolled around and winced as her shoulder wound came into contact with the wall. "It's high time I killed these old ghosts."

One of the women grinned up at her, a gold incisor sparkling in the sunlight. "You might feel like a train wreck going in. But you clean his clock good, you'll come out floating on air."

When the guard was certain she could make it, he turned and led her across the path to the lockdown. Jackie focused on his broad back so as not to see where she was going. The guard moved lightly as a dancing bear, the keys marking time. "We don't usually restrain folks here. But you say the word, I'll put a shackle on the man."

Jackie said nothing. The guard grunted his acceptance and pushed through the door into a long hall of concrete and industrial gray. He pointed her toward an empty table. "I'm stationed right over there where I can watch the whole thing. You hear what I'm saying?"

The room was sixty feet long and forty wide, yet held less than a dozen groups clustered around tables set far apart from one another. Jackie sat and remembered how Preston had excitedly prepped her for that first meeting with Shane. A genuine showstopper was how Preston had described him, the guy most likely to become the next senior trader among Hayek's currency team. That was before Shane had been caught double-dipping.

On tense market days, currency trades flipped as fast as ten to twelve times an hour. Shane had bounced certain trades through a Jamaican bank, flipped them once for himself, then reinserted them back into the day's flow. All went smooth as silk until one day the market had gone against him in a very bad way. Shane had tanked, come up so dry he had been forced to dip further. And further still. Which was why he had been caught out.

Hayek had stripped away everything Shane possessed—the cars, the bonds, the pension fund, the house. Everything. Then Shane had taken the fall for felonious embezzling and been sentenced to twelve years. As far as Jackie was concerned, the verdict had been a very bright spot in an otherwise dismal time.

"Jackie?"

She was not ready. No matter how much she had prepped herself, she was not prepared. Shane slipped into the seat opposite her. "I don't believe this."

She swallowed and forced the gorge out of her throat. Swallowed again.

"You came. You really . . ." He looked the same, rapier sharp and virile. Fourteen months of prison had paled his skin and thinned his hair. But his looks were still arresting. "I wrote you three times after I saw the light."

"I got the first." She found her voice with strangled effort. "Tore it to shreds."

"Don't blame you." The real difference was in his eyes. "You're looking good. Great, in fact."

"Save it." Having him this close left her wishing she could scrub off her own hide. Strip away everything he had ruined with his touch. "I'm here because I want to go after Hayek."

Shane froze just as his denim-clad elbows touched the table. "What?"

"You heard me. Hayek is hurting friends of mine. I want some leverage. Somebody with access."

For the first time, Shane showed a hint of the other side. She saw the familiar tightening around his eyes, the skin drawn back by the rage he kept so well hidden. Then it vanished. There and gone in less than a breath. But it was enough to transport her back to the terror hours, caught and trapped and hopeless.

Shane glanced about the room. Whispered, "Hayek."

She pulled herself back from the verge of screaming wrath. Locked it down with an effort that had her trembling from knees to voice. "I need an insider with confidential access."

Shane seemed to be speaking to somebody else. "I don't know if I should get involved in this."

"You're already involved."

Shane nodded slowly, the savage side utterly gone, a strange soft light back in his eyes. "You're right. I can't do this for myself. But I can for you. I owe you, don't I."

She forced herself to sit there, her hands clenched below the table, her jaw so tight her teeth felt cemented together.

"There were two of us working the scam. I needed a partner to move the funds unseen." He lowered his voice. "Guy by the name of Eric Driscoll."

"Another trader?"

"He was then. I never ratted on him. I claimed I did it all on my own. Far as I know, Eric's still there, climbing the ladder, pulling down the big bucks." He smiled thinly. "Man with a lot to lose. You tell him I said that."

"Right." She slung her purse over her shoulder, winced as it hit her wound.

"You okay?"

"Fine."

"You've toughened up, Jackie. It looks good on you." As she started to rise, he reached for her hand.

Jackie jerked back so hard she slammed into the wall behind her. Then cried aloud as the pain shot through her shoulder.

Instantly the guard was moving toward them. "What's going on?"

"Nothing, sir. Everything's cool, right, Jackie?"

"I'm out of here."

"Wait, please. Just a minute."

She was halted by the seemingly genuine plea, the look, the way he held himself, one hand open and outstretched. The handsome knave turned beggar.

"You think a lot in here. There's nothing else to do but think. About how I got addicted early on to the trade and the floor." He rushed through the words, as though he had spent months waiting for this chance to tell her, "The adrenaline drug killed everything good I had in me, I know that now. I lived on ashes and anger. Whenever I let myself be around normal people leading normal lives, I could actually feel the cancer growing inside me. Probably why I hated them so much."

Jackie released the loathing with the words. "You put yourself in here. Nobody else. And it isn't half the punishment you deserve."

"You're right. I know you're right."

"What is this, your latest charm offensive?"

"No. Just a guy who's come to see how important it is to tell you how sorry I am. For everything." He backed away from any further confrontation. "Hoping maybe saying the words will help me forgive myself."

Jackie fought a losing battle for control as the guard led her back outside. In a prison-hard voice, the guard told her, "Tough to watch a man hide his evil behind a mask of God."

Jackie swiped hard at her face. She'd shed more tears in the past three days than in twice as many years. She felt eroded by weakness she could not fathom. "Excuse me?"

The guard moved with the light-footed grace of much hidden

muscle. "A lot of them take to the religion kick in here." He pushed open the gate for her, stepped aside, and added, "I don't have no trouble with it. Anything that keeps them docile is fine with me. But it don't mean a thing on the outside, not till the day they step through those big main doors. Not a thing. You just remember that."

36

Saturday

AT FIVE O'CLOCK THAT afternoon, Wynn was seated in his office dealing with the attack's aftermath. An agent manning his front room stepped inside to say, "Senator Trilling is on line two." Addressing not Wynn but the two senior agents across from him.

It was the pretext Wynn had been looking for. "You gentlemen will have to excuse me."

"Just a few more questions, sir."

"You've been repeating yourselves for almost an hour."

"We need to have a word with the senator."

"Fine. Call her." Then he just sat there holding the phone, watching them finally get the message and leave. As soon as his door closed, he punched the button. "Kay?"

"Was that a Fibbie who answered your phone?"

"Them and Secret Service both. They've been crawling all over me for hours."

"Guess it's to be expected. My turn next, now that I'm back. Nabil was on my flight, laid out on a stretcher across three seats. He's resting at Georgetown Hospital. Happy to be out of that one, let me tell you." The voice honeyed. "I won't ask how you are because I think I already know."

"They got Jackie, Kay."

"Yeah, Esther told me. At least she managed to land a punch. First one so far. Looks like I was wrong about her." A pause. "As well."

"The Fibbies want to put a security detail on me."

"It's your call, Wynn. They can't force you."

"Are you taking one?"

"I can't afford the risk. Just more loose ends, people I don't know talking into mikes and phones to people I can't see."

"I don't want one either."

"I'll take care of it, then."

"Kay, I need something to do." When the senator did not respond, he went on, "Please. This is vital."

"You know St. John's Church?"

"I can find it."

"Episcopal church on Lafayette Square, across from the White House. The parish house was the British Minister's residence back in the bad old days. We're meeting there tomorrow."

"When?"

"Nine o'clock. Right after the evening Easter service."

"I'll be there."

37

Sunday

SUNDAY AFTERNOON, Hayek came out of his back door and walked down the length of his paddock. He carried his cellphone with him, in case his secretary finally located the Brazilian banker. Obviously the man knew of the catastrophes in Rome and Egypt and had gone into hiding. But Hayek's secretary would track him down. It was only a matter of time.

His staff knew not to show themselves when he was home at weekends. His gray stood saddled and stomping in impatient readiness. Hayek had never bothered to name the horse. To do so would imply an attachment. Hayek swung into the saddle and took the sawdust trail along the paddock and into the forest. Through the trees he caught brief glimpses of the manor's peach-colored stone. Anywhere else on earth the estate would have been wildly garish, but in central Florida, where even Disney's castle looked appealing, it simply belonged. The house was far too large for him, especially now that he was between wives. But the lie of permanence needed to be convincing and stated very visibly.

Hayek employed eleven staff to keep the place and his ninety-seven acres in perfect order. And it meant nothing. He was merely passing through. The transfer to Orlando was a feint, nothing more.

His true residence was to be in Liechtenstein. He was already in negotiations to buy a breeding and racing estate currently owned by the Shah of Oman. Liechtenstein was a place that understood the power of money. It had thirty thousand inhabitants and six hundred and twenty banks. The country's ruler was a distant cousin who had personally designed the country's new motto: "A Clean Tax Haven." The country was too small and too dependent on its neighbors to publicly defy

Europe's dictates for financial disclosure. So the legal system had been designed to bury any case in years of bureaucratic muddling. When European prosecutors had found half a billion dollars belonging to the former Nigerian dictator stashed in a Liechtenstein bank, it had taken the court system three years just to set a trial date. The judge who was finally assigned the case was also a banker. Hayek knew he was going to be very happy calling such a place home.

The trail wound up a gentle slope, the wind and the whispering pines his only company. Which was as it should be. Triumph was not found in the right mate but rather in needing none. Hayek pushed through the forest and emerged on a hillside's verdant slope. Ocala possessed a few rolling hills, a genuine luxury on the Florida peninsula and one of the reasons why Hayek had selected this particular estate. Another reason was the grass. The region around Ocala was the only area outside Kentucky where bluegrass grew without fertilizers or other contaminants. Bluegrass was known to be the finest natural diet for young horses. An estate with pastures of natural bluegrass could cost five times more than one not holding the proper nutrient level. Some of the world's finest yearlings were now gamboling about the paddocks Hayek rented to his less fortunate neighbors. For now, the gray would do him just fine.

As he set a leisurely pace along the hillside, his phone chirruped. He pulled it out, took a long moment to review his strategy, then answered with a clipped, "Yes."

"Your call to Brazil is now ready, sir."

"Put him through."

The phone clicked, the line hissed, and the São Paolo banker cried, "Pavel, where on earth have you been, I've been looking everywhere—"

"Your so-called security have done it again." Not raising his voice. "They leave today."

"Pavel, Pavel, I thought we had reached an understanding on this matter."

"We did. They were tested. They failed. They leave. What part of this do you not understand?"

The Brazilian's tone hardened perceptibly. "You sent them into an impossible situation."

"You were the one who told me their previous tasks were too insignificant, and that I should use their vast range of connections. Frighten them off, I said. Not create international incidents."

"Do not make me retract our funds, Pavel."

"We are nine days from doubling your investment. Your ham-fisted oafs threaten everything. Not just your money but everyone else's is at stake here. They have to go."

A big sigh. "I am sorry, Pavel. You will do this without us."

"So be it." Pleased with the cool bluff, the calm lie. "I have enough to carry on. It would have been easier with you, but if not, it can't be helped."

Even the wind held its breath at the enormity of his gamble. Hayek raised one finger and wiped a trail of sweat from his temple.

Then the gray flicked one ear, its first sign of life since the conversation had begun. Instantly the spell was broken. The banker announced, "I will speak with my associates."

"Do whatever you wish," Pavel said coolly, wanting to shout, to exult to the brilliant sky. "But your men are no longer welcome."

The banker replied by cutting their connection. Hayek cradled the phone to his hammering chest and forced himself to breathe easy. Then he nudged his gray back down the slope. Burke would have an open field now to identify and eliminate the trading floor spy. Then the pieces of his strategy would fit seamlessly together.

Afterward they would not see the scheming and the worry. Only the success. That was how it was in his world. Years of detail, seconds of action. But he would win. And his name would live forever.

38

Sunday

LISTENING TO EASTER bells chiming in the sunny distance only added to Jackie's bitterly boring day. She sat in a 7-Eleven parking lot, her Camaro shaded by a very smelly dumpster. Across the street stood the gated entrance to an enclave of expensive town houses. It was the sort of place she and Preston had joked about one day moving into, with the floodlit tennis courts and the Olympic-size pool and the beautiful people offering one another comfortable little hellos.

The previous night Jackie had used her coded access from the detective agency to pull a data search on Eric Driscoll. She was relieved to discover through his credit rating that Eric still listed himself as employed by the Hayek Group. His address was two blocks beyond the gatehouse, a prime condo that backed onto the golf course. Eric carried a big mortgage and another hefty credit line for his Porsche Cabriolet. Not to mention a swath of overdrafts. It was the financial picture of just another trader living on the edge. The search had taken her all of thirty minutes.

Afterward she had checked the Trastevere site before signing off. There was a message waiting for her, one requesting direct access. She had agreed, then watched the unsteady gondolier appear and vanish before the communication drifted into focus, *Heard about the attack. You all right?*

Fine. No, not fine. But functioning.

Have you learned anything about Tsunami?

Not yet.

Then you're asking the wrong questions.

What can you tell me?

If I knew anything, do you think I'd be bothering you? Be careful. Hurry.

Jackie pushed herself from the car, walked away from the shade and the odors, and did a few stretching exercises. Her wounds were feeling much better, despite a restless night filled with bitter memories. In the distance the bells rang and rang. Not like Rome, but appealing just the same. She watched the cars driving by, families with somewhere to go, places where they belonged, and people they could trust to be there when their world was threatened. She knew it was just a fable of her own making, but that did not mean it shouldn't be true.

The ringing cellphone was a welcome interruption. As was hearing Wynn's voice on the other end. "Where are you?"

"My office. Reading through Graham's files. Wishing I knew more. What about you?"

"Parked beside a garbage dumpster, wishing I had someplace better to go."

"You do. Here."

The invitation warmed her. "I'd like to come up. Really. But I can't. I've got to track down this lead."

"Jackie—"

"Don't press me, Wynn. Please. Not now. After yesterday, I might give in."

"What happened yesterday?"

"I want to tell you," she said, then had to stop. She was that surprised. The desire as strong and easy as yesterday's unexplained tears.

"But?"

"But I want to do it when we're together. Does that make sense?"

"More than that. It gives me something to look forward to."

The warmth spread, melting barriers she had carried so long she wasn't even aware of them any more. Not until they began to open. "I never thanked you for Rome."

"I wasn't the one who sent you."

"In a way, you were. But I meant the flight and the hotel and the dinner. And the company."

Wynn seemed to take forever to draw in the next breath. "I woke up this morning feeling like if I didn't find a place and a time to be weak, to set down all the things I'm carrying, I was going to shatter into dust. Does that sound crazy?"

"No." In the distance, the bells continued their gentle ringing. "It sounds like you're pulling words from my own mind."

□   □   □   □

WYNN WENT TO the evening service. According to the brochure he picked up on his way inside, St. John's Church dated from the era of rebuilding that followed the War of 1812, as did the White House and the Capitol. Despite its impressive size, it was a homey place of comforting closeness, the balcony a curved operatic design of brass-railed waves. The central dome was unadorned, the ancient pews flanked by waist-high gates. As the capacity crowd launched into the first song, Kay Trilling slipped into the pew alongside him. She gave Wynn a tight little smile, neither welcoming nor hostile. The bandage on her forehead gleamed white against her skin. "You okay?"

He looked back down to the hymnal in his hands and shook his head. No. Kay reached over and supported the hymnal with him, skin touching skin, and began to sing in a deep mellow alto. Saying nothing more directly, but the message there just the same.

Before the Eucharist, when the pastor invited them to offer one another the sign of peace, Kay was there waiting for him. She gripped his shoulders and said, "Sybel is not here, Wynn. And if you've come looking for her, you're just trading one wrong path for another."

"All these years she dragged me along, kicking and screaming," he said bitterly. "I don't know who to ask for answers now. Or even what to ask."

"You want to understand?" Kay remained so tightly focused the surrounding tumult might as well not have been there. "Start with this. It's something my grandmother told me when I was six years old. 'There ain't no inheritance plan in heaven. God don't accept no joint savings program.' My grandmomma was an uneducated woman who took in laundry to pay my daddy's way through school. But she was smart in the ways of the Lord."

Kay hugged him then. Hard. Then she drew back far enough to let him see the tiny flecks of lighter color in those strong, hard eyes. "You know the best place to do your searching and your asking? Down on your knees. That's what my grandmomma would tell you. I can hear her saying those very words."

AFTER THE SERVICE, Kay allowed the crowds to envelope her. She spoke with warmth to all, responded swiftly to concerns about her health, then with the gentle diplomacy of vast experience she removed herself and returned to Wynn. "Ready?"

He fell into step beside her. "I don't want just to observe, Kay. I want to help. Give me something concrete to do."

She led him around the corner and down H Street, the illuminated White House rising beyond the fences and the lawns. She was quiet long enough for Wynn to become convinced she was preparing to shut him out again. But when she spoke, it was to say, "What we're missing here is the critical edge, something that will press the issue home to the U.S. voters. My constituents don't care unless the problem is related to one thing and one thing only, their jobs. If New York slipped into the Atlantic and every Wall Street banker drowned, outside of a few financiers nobody in my district would blink an eye. The success of the Jubilee Amendment comes down to connecting the dots, from the globalized world's financial future to a mechanic in Hometown USA. We must make the average voter want deep down in his gut for Wall Street to suck air."

At the gated entrance to the church parish house, Wynn drew her to a halt. "Did you even hear what I said?"

"Sure I did. And I just answered you, but I guess you weren't listening." The warm churchwoman was lost now beneath rock-hard resolve. "Wynn, this isn't about you. Or me. It's about linking into a new global watchdog strategy with maybe two dozen other nations. You want to help? Fine. I'm glad. But don't whine about it, man. You're a United States Congressman, remember? Start acting like one. Get in there and dig for yourself."

THE REASON BEHIND Kay's show of bad temper was revealed as soon as the meeting came to order. This was a Washington sort of conference, tense people in a hurry even on their days off. Perhaps three dozen people in all were present. Esther was seated across the room from Wynn. Carter sat next to her. Both gave him the flat gaze of the undecided.

There was a whispered confab at the front of the room before Kay ended it by rising and saying, "We all know one another, or should by now. So let's cut to the quick. The first thing I have to say is how sorry I am about Wynn's loss. One that is shared by many of us who called Sybel their friend." The weight of all those sympathetic yet measuring gazes left Wynn burning with shame. Not over his presence now, but rather his absence before.

Kay went on, "The only thing I have to report from Cairo is that the majority of nations represented are ready to go ahead. Which means that we've got to push the Jubilee Amendment through on schedule."

Even with his lack of political experience, Wynn could sense the worry in the room. "Since Graham isn't around to carry us through the House," Kay continued, "I propose to introduce the amendment in the Senate."

"They'll hammer you like a bent nail," someone predicted.

"Maybe so. But somebody has got to pick up the torch and run with it."

"Do you have the votes in the Senate?"

"Not yet. But I've got a lot of favors I can call—"

Wynn was standing before the thought rose to full consciousness. "I'll introduce it on the House side."

Kay turned, as surprised as the others. "Wynn, you don't know what you're saying."

"Whoever introduces the amendment is going to be recognized as the point man on this, right? Which means their career in politics is toast." He shrugged, pretending to an offhand manner he hoped would mask his suddenly thundering heart. "I'm just playing caretaker here. Which means I've got the least to lose."

Everyone in the room tensely gauged him. To Wynn's utter astonishment, it was Carter who spoke up. Eyes on his new boss, he said, "We're sitting on a clearer number of votes in the House. Especially if we move ahead as scheduled."

Kay's frown formed an arrowhead of creases across her forehead. "Thank you for your very kind proposal, Wynn. Would you excuse us while we discuss this?"

39

Monday

WYNN WAITED UNTIL midmorning to call Jackie again. She answered with a terse, "What."

"Maybe I should call back."

"Wynn?"

"Yes. What's wrong?"

"I've been sitting out here for almost two hours. My shoulder hurts. It's hot. It's muggy. I didn't sleep well and now I'm trapped inside a car that's twelve years old and smells like a dirty sock."

"Sitting where?"

"You don't want to know."

"Yes I do."

"I have to track down a lead. And it has to be done outside the office."

"Hayek?"

"Who else. This guy is probably sunning himself on the upper deck of one of those cruise liners, sipping his drink, eyeing the girls, having himself a grand old time."

"You think you can get one of Hayek's own men to talk with you?"

"I told you, Wynn. Don't ask. Where are you?"

He decided it was definitely not the time to bring up his suite at the Willard. The heavy silk drapes pulled back from the sunlit windows, the utter quiet of downtown Washington on Easter Monday, the breakfast tray pushed to one side. He glanced at the folder at his side and said, "Working. I've got a meeting with Kay Trilling this afternoon. I've been going through Graham's old files."

"And?"

"And nothing. Most of it I'll probably never understand. He spent years on this. I've got days. The currency trading issue is just impossible."

"Slice it into bite-size chunks. There's bound to be somebody who can help on that. What about the guy in your office, the one who looks like a boiled turnip."

"Carter Styles. As far as he's concerned, the jury's still out on me."

"Then find a point of agreement and make him come around." A different Jackie this morning. Terse and sharp as the Washington crowd. No room for play. "What you need to focus on is the fact that giant funds like Hayek's are sharks patrolling the financial seas. They seek out weaknesses and then they attack. Over the past seven or eight years, what was once a disturbing issue has become an ongoing international crisis."

"I wish you'd come up here and work with me on this."

He might as well not have spoken. "The monster hedge funds have grown both in size and number. We're talking hundreds of billions of dollars worldwide now. And remember what I said about this in Rome? Hedge funds operate on margins. Which means they do business on a huge multiple of their actual assets. Because they're so enormous, they're now able to transform controllable problems or minor economic swings into major catastrophes. Fund managers claim they're simply profiting from globalization and the natural outcome of opening markets. But this is just not true. They *make* problems. They identify a potential weakness and they throw all their weight at it, creating calamity."

The longer Jackie spoke, the faster the words came. "And it's not just the currency markets they seek to destabilize. In the Asian meltdown of the late nineties, when they began bombing down the currencies, they also threw billions at the local stock markets. They sold short hundreds of locally owned companies. They pushed and pushed until five regional economies crashed. The intention was to make the swing as drastic as possible."

Then she went silent. Wynn waited a moment, then asked, "Jackie?"

"Hang on a second." An instant's pause, then, "I have to go."

"Will you call me?"

"Yes. Okay. I can't say when. Oh, and Wynn."

"Yes?"

There was the sound of a car door opening and shutting behind her.

"Did your sister ever mention a contact she had, somebody called the Boatman?"

"Sybel never spoke much about her work." He could not hide the bitterness. Or the remorse. "I never gave her a chance."

"Esther thought he might be somebody working for her. Listen, when you see them, ask if they've ever heard about something called Tsunami."

"That's Japanese for tidal wave, right?"

"It may mean something to Hayek." She was on the move now. "Bye."

"Be careful, okay?" But she was already gone.

JACKIE SLIPPED the phone into her fanny pack and zipped it shut. She watched as Eric Driscoll's Porsche pulled past the guardhouse and rumbled down the otherwise quiet lane. Jackie wore wraparound shades and her brightest spandex outfit with a matching sky blue bandana. Clamped to her ears was a radio Walkman with the sound cut off. Most of the security at these places were concerned only with vehicular traffic and keeping out the riffraff. Jackie gave the gatekeeper a casual wave as she jogged past. The guard didn't even lift his gaze from the television on the counter. Just another local lady out for her morning run.

She sped up as she saw the garage door closing behind the Porsche. The compound was silent. The grass was the color of careful grooming. Each town home was slightly different—a skybox sort of attic alcove on one, smoked glass overlooking the central lake on the next. Eric Driscoll's place had a tiled driveway and crown molding around the recessed front door. Jackie jogged straight up, puffed out a single nervous breath, and rang the bell.

As soon as he opened the door, she gave him a tight smile and the words, "Hi there, Eric. Shane told me to stop by, give you his best."

The guy wasn't at all what she had expected. He did not look a bit like Shane. In fact, he resembled Preston so much that she ached to watch the terror grip his features. "Who are you?"

"My name's Jackie."

"I'm sorry, I don't—"

"Look. We're going to talk. The question is, do you want to do it out here where people might see?"

Before he could recover, she pushed past him and into his house. Taking control. It was how this was going to have to play. In and out so fast he was left gasping from the blows, with no chance to either recover or duck. "Nice place."

His weekend tan did not begin to erase the telltale signs of his profession. Dark smudges were still there under his eyes, the layer of excess flab about his middle. Eric Driscoll was strung out from being three days away from his last adrenaline hit, as well as suddenly very scared. "You have to get out of here."

"I will. Don't worry. Soon as you and I have a little chat." She walked to the dining alcove, selected a seat. The place was neat as only a full-time maid could make it. "Are we alone, Eric?"

"I'm calling the cops."

"Sure. Fine. While you're at it, go ahead and tell them how you helped Shane with the scam. Or better still, call Hayek." She reached into her fanny pack, pulled out the phone. Gripped it hard to keep her hand from shaking. "If you prefer, I could do it for you."

"What do you want?"

"I want you to come over here and sit down."

Up close the similarity was even more telling. Eric was just another little kid playing the macho game. Through Shane and Preston she had come to know well the civilized savagery of most trading room floors. Some were different, sure. Schwab had a reputation for fair treatment both of minorities and women. But other floors celebrated their macho rivalry like tribal lore. "Where are you from, Eric?"

"I still don't get—"

"I asked you a question."

"Boston."

"What part?"

"South."

A Southie. Boston's notorious gangland. Figured. Good traders were often utter failures at mainstream life. Hard fighters willing to do whatever it took for another notch on the gun belt. "But you got out. And that means you're smart. I'm glad. I was hoping you'd be smart." She gave him a closer inspection. "You know, I think we met once. A party or something. My brother used to work on the floor. Preston Havilland. You remember Preston?"

"H-He's dead."

"That's right. He is." And to sit beside this man-boy who resembled her brother had her dying from a thousand cuts. "Here's the thing, Eric. I need information. Inside data."

"On Hayek? You've got to be kidding me."

"You know I'm not. We're sitting here. I'm talking. You're listening. And I know all about you and Shane." She let the terror do its work, then continued, "Hayek is planning something."

"I don't know anything about that side of the ops."

"But you do know something. Right? I mean, anything that big can't be a total secret."

"Sure, I've seen the guys around. But they're totally cut off. They've gone."

"Gone where?"

"I don't know."

"Yes you do. Tell me."

"Word is, Hayek's bought a bank. Not directly. Through a dummy corporation overseas."

"Which bank?"

"First Florida. He's parked his guys over there, is what I hear."

"I want to know what's coming down."

"I can't—"

"And fast." She rose to her feet. "You've got until Wednesday. Do it, or I'll personally have a talk with Hayek."

She walked to the door, glanced back, saw him collapse at the table, head in his hands. "One more thing. We're hearing the word *Tsunami* being passed around. See what you can find out about it."

40

Monday

WYNN STOOD OUTSIDE the entrance to the Hutchings' Watergate apartment, staring at the door and dreading what he might find inside. He did not need to have them explain the reasons why he should not be given the job. They were all painted upon the doorpost in front of him.

Upstairs the elegant corridor echoed with the litany of all his weaknesses and failures. He forced himself to push the doorbell.

Esther opened the door with a gaze as hard and flat as the previous evening. "Come in."

Graham's wheelchair was pushed close to the fireplace. The former congressman was a flaccid shell, unable to bring his head upright, the skin on his face folded and creased. His mouth was frozen into an overbite. His left hand was curled into a half-fist and shook uncontrollably. But his eyes tracked Wynn across the room and watched him settle into the sofa opposite Kay and beside Carter Styles. Two more sets of flat-eyed expressions greeted him there. Wynn did not even bother to speak.

Kay waited for Esther to return to her seat beside Graham before saying, "We're going to give you a chance. But there are conditions."

Wynn reached for the arm of his chair and grappled for a hold on the news. "Anything."

"Anything pretty much sums it up," Kay affirmed. "There's no way we're going to be able to bring you up to speed in time."

"I realize that." He found it necessary to wipe the burning sting from his eyes. The relief was that strong. "I won't let you down."

"We'll see. Carter and I are going to be feeding you the tune and the steps both. You're our puppet. First time we pull your string and you don't perform, it's over."

"Yes. Fine."

At a glance from Kay, Carter reached into the briefcase beside the sofa and pulled out a typed page. He slid the sheet over in front of Wynn. "Read and sign."

The words swam before his eyes. On his official letterhead was an undated resignation. His own.

"You are going to be our point man in name only. You will take the heat, but I and my team will hold the reins. You have to live with that, Wynn. There isn't any other way for this thing to fly." Kay pointed at the page. "This is both insurance and our way out, if anything goes wrong. And believe me, if I have to use it, I won't hesitate. Not for an instant."

Wynn took the pen Carter was offering him and signed his name. "Smart."

He watched Carter inspect the signature, then slip the paper back into his case. Esther's expression clearly said she had been hoping he would refuse.

"Tomorrow night we're pulling a page right from the lobbyists' own game book," Kay said. If she felt any pleasure or regret over Wynn's capitulation, she did not show it. "One of their favorite ploys is to hit Congress at a downtime, stack the floor with their supporters, and pass amendments to vital legislation. That's exactly what we've got planned, only in reverse."

"What do I do?"

"Carter will walk you through it tomorrow." Kay looked around the room and said, "Looks like we're good to go."

When she started to rise, Wynn halted her with, "Does the name Tsunami mean anything to you?"

The tableau froze. It was Carter who demanded, "Where did you hear that?"

"Jackie has an internet contact she knows only as the Boatman. He mentioned it to her."

"She told me about that mystery guy. I thought perhaps it was one of Sybel's people." Worry tightened Esther's face and voice both. "We've got to get her out of there."

"Not a chance," Wynn said. "I've begged her to come help out around here. She's following up on something down in Orlando. She won't say what, only that it has to do with Hayek, and that she's got to do it herself."

"Jackie has proven herself to be a pretty solid lady," Kay offered.

Wynn demanded, "What's going on here?"

"We lost a key person over this name, far as we can tell," Carter said. "A researcher at the Library of Congress. But we haven't been able to find out a single thing more."

"A wonderful young woman," Kay added. "A friend."

"She was tracking down Hayek and came across a reference to Tsunami. Next thing we know, the lady was thrown off the roof of a downtown hotel."

"The police claim it was a suicide," Kay said.

"We know exactly what it was," Esther replied. "And it wasn't just one victim, it was two. That was the night Graham had his second stroke, or whatever it was. Right after we received the news about our young friend."

Kay glanced at her watch. "I've got to go."

Graham Hutchings gave what Wynn thought was a moan of pain. The others went on full alert but showed no alarm. Esther leaned in close to the wheelchair and asked softly, "What is it, dear?"

Graham made a feeble motion with his right hand. Esther clearly understood, for she said, "Just a minute."

She slipped a pen into his fingers, held it until he had gripped it firmly, then lifted the pad into place on the wheelchair's arm and put the pen down on the page. With her other hand she reached into her pocket, drew out a handkerchief, and wiped a line of spittle from his chin.

Graham took a very long time to form the letters, each one requiring dogged effort. He signified completion by dropping the pen. Esther examined the sheet, blinked, then asked stonily, "Who do you want me to give this to?"

The hand lifted a fraction, far enough to point toward Wynn.

Reluctantly, Esther tore the sheet free, but handed it to Kay instead. The senator stared at the page a long moment, then handed it to Carter. The aide humphed a humorless laugh, then handed the sheet to Wynn.

On it was scrawled a single word. *Friend.*

41

Tuesday

WYNN'S OFFICE STARTED off in low gear after the holiday, but by midmorning the staff was cranking. Everyone stopped to express sympathy over Sybel's demise and gauge his response. They sought the day's tone from his own reaction. When he showed that all he wanted was to get on with business, they switched to high speed. Simple as that. Like the lady had never been.

His secretary and Carter's number two handled the press. Same as always. Carter stopped by twice, but only to prep him on upcoming meetings, two leftovers from Graham's calendar. Wynn kept waiting for Carter to begin the Jubilee briefing. But the day just ticked along with C-Span marking time in the background. Late morning he forced himself to call his niece. As soon as Wynn came on the line she began to sob. Wynn sat and listened as long as he could, knowing she was crying for them both. He confirmed what Grant had already told her, that it could be weeks before the body was released. She took it very hard.

Jackie called soon after he had set down the phone. "I've got some information for you."

"Tell me something first. Who exactly is this Boatman?"

"I wish I knew. You won't believe how we met."

Wynn listened to her tale with mounting incredulity. "He just happened to float by in the middle of a nor'easter?"

"The one and only time we ever connected. In person, I mean. He's been in touch by e-mail."

"I spoke with Sybel's aide this morning. She's never heard of any Boatman, and she checked Sybel's e-mail address book while I waited. Nothing."

"That doesn't mean anything. He could have made up the name while we were out there on the river."

"Did it ever occur to you that he might be setting you up?"

"For what? They've trashed my house once already, remember? They know where I live."

"What's the matter, Jackie?"

"I didn't sleep well. And I don't like myself very much this morning."

"Just be careful, okay?"

"I've already heard that from Esther. Listen, I called because I've got some news. My contact down here says Hayek has bought himself a bank by the name of First Florida. Ring a bell?"

"I used to do business with them. This is from the Boatman?"

"No. Somebody else. And Esther's already grilled me and I'm not saying anything more, okay?"

There was a knock, and Carter stuck his head around the door. Wynn waved him in, said, "I'm worried about you, Jackie."

"I'm okay, I tell you. What you need to know is I did some checking this morning. First Florida was sold to Banque Royale of Liechtenstein."

"I've heard that name."

"Sure you have. They owned the plane that carted Valerie Lawry back and forth to Rome."

He scribbled the words, turned them around for Carter to read, received a shrug in reply. "What do you want me to do with this?"

"I wish I knew. I'm hoping to have something more for you tomorrow. And don't worry."

Carter waited for him to hang up before saying, "There's this guy at the Fed. Hutchings danced the Washington two-step with him but they never could connect. Graham was undecided whether he could trust the man. Especially as he stayed surrounded by people who wanted to drink our blood. But the guy kept insisting in private that he was a secret ally."

Wynn was already up and moving. "So now we can trust him?"

"No, we're just running out of options."

The day had warmed into a welcome embrace. The taxi dropped them off in front of the Federal Reserve Bank, an imposing structure off Constitution Avenue in Foggy Bottom. Carter gave their names to the uniformed guard, pulled him over to a quiet corner, and said, "The global banking system is a mess. And the situation is growing worse, not better. Central banks are becoming pawns of the hedge fund and investment banking communities. Our own country's regulation of the national financial institutions has not been this lax since the late 1920s. Back then, the flashpoint was every bank's ability to print their own money. Today we're back in a similar situation, only the paper isn't called money any more. It's called derivative certificates and currency options. But the effect is the same. Once again banks have found a way to extend risk beyond what is prudent."

The marble-lined lobby was segmented by pillars and stairs and mock balconies. Clustered beneath the three-story ceiling were other dark-suited knots of serious faces and important murmurs. Everybody carried a briefcase, everyone expected to be noticed. A young man wearing the plastic badges of entry around his neck approached the guard, who pointed in their direction. Wynn demanded, "What do you want me to do here?"

"Just pretend like you're talking straight into Hayek's ear."

The staffer said, "Congressman Bryant?"

"Just a minute." He turned his back to the young man. "Go on."

"These guys always travel in packs, it's their way of sharing any possible blame. The one we're interested in probably won't say a word. His name is Gerald Bowers, and he makes me look pretty. Say whatever you think might make Hayek the most nervous. You know our situation. If this guy's on our side we need to find out now."

"CONGRESSMAN, WE ARE indeed grateful that you would take the time to bring these matters to our attention." The spokesman was handsome in the way of manicured pandering. Another was rail-thin and heavily jowled. The third man was short and bald and had the complexion of a wizened toad. Other than that, they were identical. All three were in their sixties, all spoke with the nasal twang of inbred Ivy League snobs, all eyed Wynn with polite condescension. "We also regret very much the recent demise of your sister at the hands of Islamic terrorists."

"They weren't terrorists."

"That's not what the FBI is stating," interjected the slender man.

Carter leaned forward, asked in an over-soft voice, "And just how would you be knowing that?"

The spokesman harrumphed his way back into control. "As I was saying, we are obliged to take note of your assertions. But I must also tell you that they are utterly without merit."

"The fact that First Florida has been acquired by a Liechtenstein bank fronting for the Hayek Group doesn't concern you?"

"We are well aware of the Banque Royale's recent acquisition. And we have made an official request to the Liechtenstein authorities for a full list of shareholders."

Carter snorted. "Which you will definitely be receiving. In about fifteen years."

The spokesman gave Carter the fish eye before proceeding. "As to these other matters, I am certain even in your bereaved state that you can well understand how unfounded these allegations of yours are."

Wynn caught Carter's signal, rose to his feet, and let a little of his heat show. "Hayek and his group are responsible for the death of my sister. He is a menace."

"He is a respected member of the hedge fund community," interjected the spokesman.

"Same thing," Carter said.

"Have your people ask him about the code name Tsunami," Wynn said, turning for the door. "And do it fast."

WYNN STOOD BEFORE the unlit fireplace in his suite and read off his note cards, "Currency traders are champagne-swilling speculators who treat the world's financial markets like their own personal casino. These international gamblers produce nothing and help nobody. Their days are filled with maneuvers that endanger the lives and jobs of normal working people." He stopped. "How's that?"

"Be better if you could get the shimmy out of your voice." Carter sat on the edge of the sofa, briefcase open beside him and notepad on the table in front of him. "But not bad."

"I look nervous?"

"Like a rabbit staring down the barrel of a gun." Carter glanced at his watch. "We have to go."

Wynn reached for his coat. "I still feel like I ought to give them something with more meat to it."

"If they want stats, have them talk to me. Every chance you get, hand the press a thirty-second soundbite. Anything more and you give them the power to edit you down." Carter reached the door, gave Wynn's suite a final glance. "Kay is going to have something to say about your present abode."

Walking along the long hall and twice more in the elevator, Wynn had to stifle the sudden onslaught of panic. The Willard's brass-framed mirrors reflected a man on the verge of serious meltdown. Carter met his eye just as the doors pulled back but said nothing. Too much was on the line for empty solace.

They were midway across the lobby when Carter murmured, "Well, just lookee here."

The toadlike man from the meeting at the Federal Reserve was making his way toward them. Beside him walked a man in a red-and-blue-checked jacket and navy polyester pants. Despite the seventies golf attire, the second man carried himself with arrogant ease. Behind the pair walked the senior FBI agent who had wrecked Wynn's Saturday. The squat man with the reptilian complexion said, "Gerald Bowers, Congressman. Far as the world is concerned, this is a no-hard-feelings little confab. Smooth the waters with the freshman in Hutchings' seat after today's set-to. Catch my meaning?"

"Yes."

"This is Reed Brink, Vice President of the SEC and Chairman of the Arthur Brink Brokerage Company. Out of Saint Louis. A good man to have on your side. Agent Welker you already know." Bowers planted himself within probing distance. "We're here to tell you that we know the hedge fund community, Congressman. And as far as we're concerned, they are the enemy. They're a cancer that must be destroyed before it wrecks our entire financial establishment."

The man barely made it up to the middle of Wynn's chest, and smelled of hair oil, cigars, and the drink he had just had in the bar. "You guys came all the way over here to teach us the alphabet?"

"You look like a smart man, Congressman. Word is, you held your own when you went up against Jackson Taylor's group. That's good. We need us some fighters down in the front line trenches."

"I'm still not clear on one thing. Just exactly why are we having this meeting?"

"Because once you unleash your firestorm tonight, officially we are going to be standing with the opposition."

"I would never have suspected anything else."

"Officially, I said. But we'd like to see things otherwise. Even so, we can't box with shadows. Get us something real and we'll do our best to help you take them down."

"Explain one thing, please. Why is it I'm all of a sudden supposed to trust you?"

Bowers bristled. "If you were half as sharp as they say, Reed here and the agent are all the bona fides I should need."

"Right. A man I don't know and an agent who spent four hours in my face. Great references, Mr. Bowers."

The agent stepped forward. "Tsunami is a name we haven't had on our radar screens for some time, Congressman. Last time it popped up, the young lady who told us about it got very dead."

Carter edged his way into the huddle. "What did she tell you?"

The agent held his focus on Wynn. "Little more than we have from you so far. A supposed connection to Hayek. Nothing more."

Bowers repeatedly smoothed his tie, the nervous gesture of a man ready to bolt. "This has already taken too long. All you need to know is, if you come up with some real ammunition, we're on your side. Otherwise, we'll be just two more faces watching you from behind the enemy's cannon."

THE TAXI DROPPED them off at the member's entrance to the Capitol. Wynn wanted to stop and catch a final breath of free air, but Carter grabbed him by the arm and pulled him forward. "Waiting won't do anything but spotlight all the things that might go wrong."

The stairways and corridors passed like a marble-lined maze. "I couldn't find my way around this place with a map and a guide dog."

"Remind me to give you the five-cent tour. That is, if we ever have time."

"You think things are going to get busier?"

Carter smirked. "You're about to redefine the term, upwardly mobile."

Kay Trilling was waiting at the front doors, Esther one step behind. "How's our man tonight?"

Carter answered for him. "Raring to go."

"He looks a little green around the gills to me. You nervous?"

"Absolutely terrified."

"Probably a healthy attitude." She withdrew a sheet of paper from her navy jacket. "Graham wrote you out another missive."

Wynn read the shakily printed letters. *Pray.*

"Man has a way with words, doesn't he?" Kay patted his lapel. "We'll be up there in the balcony doing just that."

THREE OTHER MEMBERS of the House of Representatives stood to shake Wynn's hand and thank him for his assistance. Carter and Kay were upstairs and seated by the time he reached his own desk. The chamber was not particularly large; he had addressed the final meeting of his employees and shareholders in a ballroom twice this size. The desks were scarred, the carpets scuffed, the odors mostly of dust and beeswax. But the pressure of history and brilliance and power squeezed his chest until Wynn was panting with the exertion of having made it this far.

To his right, a man was droning into a microphone. He wore no jacket. The top three buttons of his vest were undone. His tie dangled at half mast. He read from a tome of typed sheets with the bored voice of one who had been at it for a very long time. The Speaker's chair was taken by a man Wynn did not recognize. None of the other front desks were occupied. The stenographer appeared almost asleep behind his machine.

Gradually the chamber filled, both the desks about Wynn and the balconies overhead. Without warning, the orator at the lectern turned and said, "Mr. Speaker, I relinquish my place to our newest representative from the great state of Florida, the distinguished Wynn Bryant."

"Congressman Bryant, do you wish to address the House?"

It took him three tries to rise. "Yes, Mr. Speaker."

"You have the floor."

The orator patted his back in passing. "Way to go, son. Way to go."

Wynn fumbled in his pockets, came up with the sheet of paper he had prepared, and flattened it on the lectern. Four breaths later, he realized he had pulled out Graham's message by mistake. He stared at the single word, illuminated now by the chandelier overhead and by his own churning dread.

"Congressman Bryant?"

"Just a minute." With an eerie sense of calm, he pulled out the proper page and said as instructed, "Mr. Speaker, I move for the inclusion into H.R. 451, the current appropriations bill, an amendment entitled . . ."

"Yes, Congressman?"

Wynn looked up at the balcony and saw Esther seated beside a very worried Kay. The name on the page suddenly seemed incomplete. "Entitled the Hutchings Amendment."

The speaker shifted through the pages before him. "You are renaming what I have here before me as the Jubilee Amendment?"

"I am. Graham Hutchings dedicated his life to seeing this matter addressed." Esther watched him with a look of stunned disbelief. Kay Trilling, however, crossed her arms and leaned back in her seat. She gave him a single nod. "It seems the least we can do is honor him in this way."

"Very well. I have before me a motion to amend H.R. 451 with the Hutchings Amendment. Do I have a second?"

A voice from the chamber intoned, "Seconded and move for a voice vote, Mr. Speaker."

"Seconded."

"Very well. All in favor of the inclusion of the Hutchings Amendment, say aye." Wynn added his voice to those others from the chamber. "All opposed?" When no one spoke, the Speaker rapped his gavel. "The ayes carry. Congressman, do you have further business before the House?"

"Yes, Mr. Speaker." Following the script to the letter now. "I move to vote on appropriations bill H.R. 451."

"Seconded."

"So moved and seconded. All in favor? All opposed?" Another bang of the gavel. "The ayes carry it. As the companion legislation has already moved out of the Senate, H.R. 451 will next be considered by the Conference Committee."

"Mr. Speaker," Wynn continued, "I move to recess."

"So moved."

"Seconded."

"All in favor? Very well. The House is recessed until ten o'clock tomorrow morning."

Wynn accepted a few more handshakes on his way out the rear doors. He noted a few solemn thanks, then heard the man who had relinquished the lectern tell his neighbor that it was a historic event. The congresswoman beside him shook her head, eyed Wynn with unmasked pity, and said, "Now the blood will flow."

42

Tuesday

ERIC DRISCOLL SAT behind the wheel of his Porsche and worked to unfreeze his mind. He had followed the traders from First Florida's downtown headquarters to the Kissimmee strip. The town had not so much grown as mutated, grafting on one hideous segment after another until the main drag became a twenty-mile-long neon netherworld. Eric sat in the parking lot of a bar sporting a fifty-foot-high sign that promised honky-tonk heaven. The lot was full of pickups, mud-spattered SUVs, and customized vans. His Porsche stood out as boldly as the Lexus and Ferrari and two Mercs the traders had parked in the handicapped zone. He watched the last of them careen into the club as the bouncer greeted them and held the door. They had claimed this place as their own and paid to ensure they were well protected. Eric swallowed hard and worried over past and future mistakes, just inches away from real nausea.

Reluctantly he left the safety of his car and hurried across the parking lot. It was raining slightly, a warm, sticky mist that felt like the world was sweating with him.

The doorman gave him a brief look, then jerked his chin toward the collection of gleaming metal parked alongside. "You with them?"

"Y-yes, I guess . . ."

"You better move your machine over where I can keep an eye on it."

"No." If he got back in the car, he wouldn't be able to resist the urge to flee. "I won't be long."

The bouncer shrugged massive shoulders. "Your wheels, man."

The music struck with fists of acid rock. A trio of ladies danced the central aisle, while another pair concentrated on the poles rising from the circular stage to his right. The boys from First Florida were clustered in two booths to one side of the circular stage, waving bills and drinks at the women. Two of them rode the padded hammock separating the booths. Eric tried to saunter over and slip into the booth, but failed. One trader spotted his move, hooked an elbow into his neighbor, and instantly Eric confronted a phalanx of hostile faces.

"I'm a spot man on Hayek's floor," he shouted.

One of the traders, the guy Colin had attacked with the bush, used the partition as a saddle and slid down beside Eric. Up close the man looked bloodless. "So?"

"So I want a switch. The world's getting stale over there. Word is, you're the guys in the know. The hot data's all coming your way."

The trader rolled his cigar in the ashtray and exchanged silent communication with his pals. One passed a quick hand signal, too fast or too alien for Eric to catch. The trader asked, "How'd you know where to find us?"

"I followed you guys. Figured it was best to chat where others wouldn't see."

The trader raised up and whistled once. Loud.

Instantly a man bigger than the doorman was by the booth. "You rang?"

The trader pointed a thumb in Eric's direction. "This slimeball is bothering us. You know how much we dislike being bothered."

"Hey, wait, I came all the way out here—" But a hand gripped Eric's jacket and plucked him away.

The trader was already climbing back onto his padded saddle, flicking lint from his jacket. "Bye bye, slimeball."

Eric made the mistake then. Worse than his foulest trade. Worse than having gotten involved with Shane Turner. But the entire club was watching this gorilla drag him across the floor, guys pointing with their beers and laughing at the joker in suit and tie being hauled away. So he took a swing.

The bouncer didn't even flinch when Eric's fist struck the stone-hard muscles covering his ribs. He just veered slightly. Not far, a couple of feet. But he also accelerated his forward motion, until Eric connected head-first with the nearest pillar.

Stars erupted, a skyrocket explosion of pain and light. Eric wanted to black out, but he couldn't even do that. So he was still alert enough to hear the laughter and the jeers as an entire bar bid him a fond farewell.

The world was canted slightly to his left now, as the bouncer dragged him toward the exit. The bouncer slammed through the door and dumped him in the puddle beyond the awning. "Don't ever come back."

COLIN SAT IN HIS car two rows back from the entrance, his wipers clearing the mist. He watched as Eric raised himself from the oily water. He saw the doorman's mouth move but did not open his window to hear what was said. Colin doubted whether Eric heard the bouncer either as he blundered toward his Porsche. His suit was streaked, his forehead bleeding. Eric touched the rising welt and winced. It seemed to wake him up slightly, for he managed to find his keys and unlock the car. He slipped out of his jacket, used it to smear the greasy water from his face, then tossed it on the pavement. Ditto for the ruined tie. He touched the welt another time, then his rapidly swelling lip.

Colin watched the Porsche fire up and rumble from the parking lot. Softly he asked the night and the rain, "Who are you doing this for, and what have they got on you?"

43

Wednesday

WEDNESDAY MORNING JACKIE showered and dressed and drove to Eric's development. This time she simply parked on the street and walked by the gatehouse. The subterfuge was over. If security wanted to question her and call ahead, that was their problem. But no one said a thing. She followed the street to where the town houses bordered the golf course. A central lake in front, acres of green beyond. The place sparkled.

The morning dimmed the instant she saw Eric's face. "What happened to you?"

"Take a wild guess." He backed away from her and the day ahead, took another look at the mirror over his sideboard, and dabbed his eye with ice wrapped inside a towel. His left eyebrow was gouged with a bloody furrow, his eye was black, his bruised cheek so swollen he could have been holding a pear in his mouth. "I've been at it for an hour. The swelling hasn't gone down and the color's gotten worse. What am I supposed to say to the guys?"

"Who hit you, Eric?"

"Don't go dumb on me, okay? Come in here."

She stayed where she was. "We can talk right where we are."

"It's safe, Jackie. That's your name, right?" He stepped back into view. "I'm not the one doing the whacking around here. And we are definitely alone."

Reluctantly she moved into the house, letting the door close behind her. Tasted the air.

"Come on through, will you? I've got to get to the office." Eric waited until she had followed him through the entrance, then swept a hand over the cash piled on his dining room table. "Fifty-three thousand dollars. Free and clear. Take it and get out of my life."

"I can't—"

His voice rose a full two octaves. "Get a good look at my face, will you? This is what it's cost me so far, having you show up out of nowhere and shove me into the twilight zone." He pushed the money toward her. "I've been stashing this away for Shane. I knew sooner or later he'd be coming through that door, telling me it was payback time."

"This was for Shane?"

"You don't listen so good. This is *yours*. Shane's got what, another two years before he's up for parole. I'll scrounge up another bundle for him."

"I need that information, Eric."

"Don't you get it? Those guys are going to wipe me out!"

Jackie found herself at a loss. Causing such havoc and pain was not part of her game plan. But the need for information compressed her heart into a space half its size. "What if Shane agrees to never get on your case?"

"What?"

"I have to have answers, Eric. What if Shane will agree to let you keep the money and never bother you again. Not ever." She could scarcely believe she was saying the words. "Say he writes out a letter and I get it notarized, that you had nothing to do with it, and as far as he knows, you're a perfectly honest employee?"

Eric gaped. "He'd do that?"

"If he did, you could keep the money and maybe even get a decent night's sleep."

He fumbled his way into a chair. Touched his eyebrow, winced, probed the side of his eye. Mused aloud, "None of these guys will talk to me. That's how I got winged, trying the front door approach. They must've been warned."

She tried to hold her attention exclusively on Eric and ignore the screaming in her brain over what she had just set herself up to do. "You're talking about the traders at First Florida?"

"Who else?" Eric was still walking through potential strategies. "Hayek has gotten a truckload of new money from someplace."

"How much?"

"We're talking an entire new fund. Four big ones, maybe more."

"Four billion dollars in new trading capital?"

He looked at her then. "What you said, it's for real? Shane will cut me free?"

"I'll go see him today." Every word was a nail driven into her bones. "So Hayek set up these new traders to manage a new capital fund of four billion dollars. And this could be the Tsunami project?"

"I don't know exactly how large the thing is or what it's called. But it's got to be pretty huge. First he set them up as a new in-house trading division, but that went down the tubes. Whether he then bought the bank to house them is anybody's guess."

"I'm not following you."

"What I'm saying is, these guys are totally cut off. There's no way I'll get them to come clean." He thought a moment longer. "What if I could get you the access code to one of their computers?"

"You can do that?"

"I don't know. Maybe. But that would be it, okay? Nothing more. You'd have to find somebody to make the tap and interpret the data." He used both hands to swipe away mounting terror. "If I try this and get caught, I'm fried."

"Find me a computer access code for one of the Tsunami group and we're done," Jackie confirmed. "When can you get it?"

"No idea. Call me in two days. No, call me soon as you've talked to Shane. We'll meet, you'll show me the paper. Signed, sealed, notarized. I want to know this is for real before I commit."

44

Wednesday

L A TARBOUCHE, THE LEBANESE restaurant on K Street, had been the client's choice, not Valerie's. The place had the sort of suede and chrome pretentiousness that appealed mightily to people eating on someone else's ticket. Across from her sat the chief of the American Investment Managers, or AIM, the trade association that represented investment banks and portfolio managers and hedge funds.

He smiled as the waiter set down his plate of salmon *tagin*. In the restaurant's meager lighting the lobster sauce looked yellowish green. There were six of them together in the quietest alcove the restaurant had to offer. Valerie sat beside one of the firm's four partners, and her direct boss. Three other associates were also present, so the partner could bill AIM for their lunch hour. Valerie was there because the AIM chief had specifically requested her presence.

He used his fork to point at Valerie's own salad and said, "That rabbit food's not going to take you very far."

"I don't have much appetite today, I'm afraid."

"You will." The AIM chief wasn't bad as lackeys went, fairly polished and able to mouth almost anything with sincerity. But he had the annoying habit of claiming his superiors' comments as his own original thoughts. "I've been watching you operate, Ms. Lawry. You're our kind of people. Sharp, hard-hitting, take no prisoners. I want you to head up our account."

The senior partner dropped his fork. "Don't you think that's something we should discuss—"

"I've talked it over with my people, and that's how it's going to be." As though the decision had been his to make. "Far as we're concerned, it's a done deal."

Valerie wished she could be pleased. But she remained locked upon the morning's bizarre beginnings. As she had left her Georgetown home, Jim Burke had called and demanded they meet him in a Rock Creek Parkway rest area. He had tersely spelled out directions and cut the connection.

Valerie made the drive in dark despair, knowing Burke had been sent to deliver the killing blow. She had let the Hutchings Amendment slip by her. They wanted her head on a chopping block somewhere private. She spent the drive searching frantically for some defense and coming up blank.

But when she pulled in behind the airport limo, Burke emerged only to hand her a cellphone and point toward the private overlook. With the morning traffic thundering behind her, Valerie lifted the receiver and waited for Hayek to attack.

Instead, the man had sounded almost jovial. "You must forgive this rather unorthodox means of communication, Ms. Lawry. But matters are coming to a head just now, and I wish to be utterly certain that our conversation is neither overheard nor recorded. This will be our last chat until things have settled down. I would be grateful for your assessment of events."

He gut told her a carefully worded PR exercise was not required here. "Things," she replied, "do not look good."

"Please explain."

"We've been blindsided. The appropriations bill was passed with the Jubilee Amendment attached, and this morning I've heard they plan to push the bill through Conference Committee at a record pace. Which means the time we have available to act is cut to a minimum."

"Then fight harder."

"We will, I assure you. We can pressure—"

"I want you to do more than pressure. I want you to create absolute havoc."

Valerie hesitated. "Havoc comes at a very high price in Washington."

"Spend it."

"Just a minute. Please. You have to understand, we're talking about people who shape national agendas. To make this a highly public issue will require bringing in the type of consultants who work on presidential races and shape national party politics. These people are not selling us their time. They're selling *access*. Which they can use only so often.

This means the price they charge is astronomical, far beyond anything we could logically bill our clients."

"I will handle that. You will be hearing from the AIM representative today, just to make things official."

"It would be wiser to hold off on a full frontal attack until the bill returns to the House and Senate floors for the final vote."

"Impossible." Hard and definite. "Timing is critical. I want national attention, I want battle, I want upheaval. And I want it now."

"Nothing at this point can be guaranteed. No matter how much money you throw at it."

She might as well not have spoken at all. "Whatever it takes, Ms. Lawry. Aim for havoc. I assume you do not require me to spell that out for you."

VALERIE'S BOSS WAS nothing if not smooth in the clinch. "Well, certainly, Ms. Lawry is one of our most prized associates, and we're delighted to see her appreciated by our top clients."

As the waiter stepped in to refill their glasses, Valerie smiled coldly at her boss. His gaze flicked her way and held. Message received. Associate was no longer sufficient. She wanted her own partner's chair.

"We're also extremely concerned about the amendment the House attached last night to the appropriations bill," the AIM chief went on. "Of course you're aware of this."

Valerie allowed the partner to stutter a moment before supplying, "We are."

"I asked for this meeting to tell you that we want you to defeat it now."

Valerie pushed her salad to one side, leaned forward, and took control. "It's not that simple."

"We're paying you to make it simple."

"The Conference Committee is stacked against us. There are a number of waverers, but not enough for us to be certain we can turn the tide."

"So you'll have to work a little harder. That's how you justify your outrageous fees, coming through in moments like this. I want you to kill this thing while it's still in committee. Under no circumstances is this amendment to make it back to the floors for a final vote."

□ □ □ □

A SINGLE BUILDING took up the entire eighteen-hundred block of K Street. The central atrium was eleven stories high and home to a semi-tropical forest and a stainless steel waterfall. The floor was tiled in a mosaic of marble and granite, the elevators at opposite corners guarded by dual security desks. The upstairs office suites came in two flavors, rich and opulent for the partners, cheap and tacky for everyone else. K Street rents were among the highest in Washington, and associates clustered in cubicles the size of padded cages. Natural light was something associates rarely glimpsed. The furniture was cubed and coldly modern, the atmosphere charged with desperate ambition, the infighting vicious.

Valerie's sudden elevation to chief lobbyist on the AIM account meant her entry into the conference room was met with hostile envy. She fed on it as she would a carnal feast. "We are about to enter lockdown mode. Everything else on your desks is to be scrapped. We are going to attack, and we are going to do so tomorrow."

While the shock registered, she bisected the chalkboard behind her with a line and continued, "We have to grimly salute the opposition. They have managed to place the amendment in an appropriations bill the President considers crucial and that contains perks for almost every district. Our only hope is to eliminate this one amendment while the bill is still in committee. But we are not into stealth tactics here. I fear the committee itself has been stacked against us. We must therefore create so much heat around this specific amendment with *all* the Senate and *all* the House that the committee members are forced to change direction."

Someone along the table said the obvious. "This is going to cost them a bomb."

"Bomb is the proper term," Valerie agreed. "They are paying us for nuclear assault, and that is precisely what we are going to deliver."

45

Wednesday

JACKIE SAT OUTSIDE the prison gates, studying them as she would the doors of death itself. The prison parking lot was surrounded by a high stand of loblolly pine, shielding the Beeline Expressway drivers from all but a fleeting glimpse of chain link and glinting razor wire. Jackie listened to the whispered wail of her own heart. Start the motor, back out of the lot, take the entrance ramp in either direction. Put some solid distance between herself and the most idiotic thought that had ever entered her brain.

Why she had made such a preposterous offer to Eric she could not begin to say. Every ounce of logic told her there was still time, she could go back and heft that sack of cash and name it her very own far-away fund. But despite her finest arguments and the rising cry of her own heart, she started toward the gate and the line of visitors passing through security.

The same guard was there doing escort duty. "Figured you for somebody who'd said all her good-byes."

"So did I."

He moved ahead of her down the path. His belt creaked in time to his steps, and his keys and baton jangled like alarms of coming flames. "You see it all in this game. People can get stuck on just about anything, they try hard enough." He pushed open the metal door leading to the front hall. "Start seeing pain as just another part of their day, instead of a wake-up call to make tracks. You hear what I'm saying?"

This time Shane was already waiting for her. Which made leaving the guard's safety and walking over all the more difficult. She covered the distance to the table as if she were scaling a ninety-degree incline. He waited for her to sit down to say, "I've been hoping you'd come back. There's so much more I wanted—"

"Eric Driscoll has fifty-three thousand dollars he's been stowing away for when you get out of prison. The only way he'll help me is if you forget the money and agree to let him go." It wasn't even close to the smoothness she needed. But the bile in her throat caught all the right words and stripped them down to a slurred rush. She fumbled in her purse, drew out the envelope, forced her fingers to pull free the single page and flatten it on the table between them. "I want you to sign this."

He read the few sentences, stating unequivocally that Eric Driscoll had nothing whatsoever to do with Shane's embezzlement, and anything stated to the contrary was merely a lie. She could run it by the office afterward and have a friend supply the notary stamp—a small crime compared to what she was doing to herself right now.

Shane kept his head down long enough for Jackie to begin fearing one of the old explosions, when the rage spewed like acid. She reached into her purse and pulled out the pen, wishing it were something far more substantial. A machete, maybe. Or an Uzi.

But when Shane spoke, it was in a cautious manner that was not his own and never had been. "He's right, you know. I didn't turn him in because I wanted somebody there to pave my way back to easy street."

He raised his gaze then. And revealed no rage. Resignation, maybe. Bitter regret. A trace of longing. But all he said was, "Can I use that?"

Numb fingers dropped the pen on the table. Not wanting to make the slightest contact with this man. "I don't understand you."

"I'm not surprised." He scrawled his name along the page's bottom. Penned in his social security number. "Not much in my past for you to hang this on."

She grabbed the paper away, folded it, and jammed it inside the envelope. She had to fight off the urge to leap up and away. "Why are you doing this?"

His eyes had always been his best feature, that and his ability to lie with grace. "It wasn't for you. Not just, anyway."

Jackie used both hands to rise. All her strength was captured by the words boiling up inside. The words she couldn't choke off, no matter how much she tried. When they emerged, it was the sound of a strangled intruder who gasped, "I accept your apology."

She turned and fled, moving so fast she had to wait for the guard to catch up and unlatch the barrier. Which gave her time to glance back. Shane was still seated at the table, staring down at his folded hands.

46

Wednesday

THE MORNING WAS so gray even the Capitol's garden was
muted, the flowers only slightly more tinted than the surrounding
granite. All the trees wore minty adornments. The air tasted of diesel
and conflict and coming rain.

Outside the Dirksen Senate Office Building's largest committee room,
Wynn found Father Libretto in tight-knit conversation with Kay Trilling
and Carter Styles. As soon as he spotted Wynn, the priest disengaged
from the others and approached with hand outstretched. "Congressman
Bryant, forgive me for interrupting your morning."

"You're not interrupting, and the name is Wynn."

"Wynn." The priest spoke his name like a gift he had himself received. "I cannot tell you how sorry I am about Sybel. How are you?"

"Struggling."

The priest scarcely moved, yet gave the impression of bowing with
his entire body. Up and down, a slow rocking that took him a distance
of scarcely an inch in either direction. A movement of spirit and mind,
not of flesh. "Sometimes God can only capture our attention when we
have been stripped down to our very bones. People spend so much time
asking, how did this happen, and why to me? I have no answer for
them, except to ask another question. It is the role of priests sometimes,
not to give answers but to show how to seek through tears. How to
search out what is there, yet remains hidden. Even when it is painful,
yes, even when the emptiness eats at you like an abyss."

Wynn licked his lips. Knew the others were watching, measuring
him. "What question should I be asking, then."

"Oh, I think you already know. You are a very intelligent man, very
perceptive. You know the words. Having me say them will not make

finding the answer any easier." Father Libretto patted Wynn's shoulder, the benediction of a caring friend. He lowered his arm and dropped a card into Wynn's coat pocket. "My role is that of servant and messenger to all drawn into service. You may call on me at any time."

Kay stepped forward but continued to watch the priest's departing back. "I've always been comforted by the extreme promises of faith. The healing of wounds seen and unseen. Eternal salvation. Love and peace even here, in a town run by blind ambition." She looked at him then, her gaze guarded. "It all boils down to one thing. Are you still searching for the chance to tell your sister what a fool you've been? Or are you finally at the point where you want to speak the words to someone else?"

Wynn swallowed around a suddenly dry throat. It cost him, but he kept a lock on her gaze.

Even so, Kay took his silence as defeat and turned away. "See how simple it is?"

THE COMMITTEE CHAMBER was very imposing, very Roman. The royal purple carpet was bordered with silver-gray laurels, as were the drapes. The ceilings were forty feet high and tiled with indirect lighting. The walls, curved into a pointed oval, were lined by mahogany columns and fronted by curved rows of desks. Kay took the committee chairman's seat, flanked by flags and the oil portrait of a long-dead power broker. The place had the burned-powder scent of previous battles.

Carter indicated Wynn's seat by standing behind it. Kay rapped for attention, then began a drone that she could keep up all day. Only seven of the fourteen seats were taken. The rest of the room was empty, save for a scattering of aides.

Wynn motioned Carter forward and asked, "What am I doing here?"

Carter's voice was pitched for Wynn's ears alone. "This is an omnibus appropriations bill. Ten thousand pages. The president considers it a take-it or leave-it bill, which means every congressman, every senator, and every lobbyist was out to make attachments. We hope we've been able to slip this in without raising too much of a stink."

"What do you want me to do now?"

"Sit tight. This won't last long. The Conference Committee has an equal number of senators and congressmen, and their job is to iron out the differences between the House and Senate versions of this bill. Once we've constructed the final version, the two chambers will vote on it again. Staffers have been gathering for a couple of weeks now, defining all the areas where there's no real conflict. That's taken care of sixty, maybe even seventy percent of the issues. Tomorrow the committee members will begin hammering out the divisive points."

While Carter was speaking, Kay banged her gavel to adjourn the meeting. She rose from her seat, shook a few hands, then aimed for Wynn. He braced himself for another onslaught of unanswered challenges, but all she said was, "Is it true you're living at the Willard?"

"That's right."

"A suite?"

"For the moment."

"Do us all a favor. Move. You want to stay in a hotel, go someplace that won't make such a splash on the six o'clock news."

"It's my money, Kay."

"There's nothing the press would love more than a photo of you getting out of a limo at the Willard with a pretty girl on your arm. I can see the caption now. Fat cat Wynn Bryant, so out of touch with his district he thinks a thousand dollar suite is real life."

"You really think it'll come to that?"

She gave him a look of brittle experience. "Try the Four Seasons. Nothing but a brick wall to shoot. Could be anyplace."

As SOON AS Wynn entered his office, his secretary announced, "The governor's office is on line two."

"Right on time," Carter said.

"You knew about this?"

"He caught me before the committee hearing. Yelled at me for a couple of minutes since you weren't in range. I figured there was no need to worry you in advance." When Wynn showed no interest in picking up the phone, he went on, "Sooner or later you're going to have to let him sing his tune."

The governor's assistant, whom Wynn had known for more than ten years, treated him like an utter stranger. Or a pariah. "Hold for the governor."

But when Grant came on the line, there was none of the screaming

Wynn dreaded. The man's voice was barely above a whisper. "Do you have any idea the kind of storm you've raised for yourself?"

"Just doing my job, Grant."

"Your job. What about our agreement?"

"What about your responsibilities to my sister?"

He hit a high note then. "You leave Sybel out of this!"

"Afraid I can't do that. Which you know as well as I do."

"Go on up to Washington, I said. Have yourself a high old time. Sign a few bills, get your picture taken with the powers that be, meet some fine big-city ladies. Vote down one piece of legislation. Keep your nose clean until I got myself elected to the top club in the world. Was that so much to ask?"

"Yes, Grant. It was."

"Well, this here's your demolition notice. They're coming after you. And when they're done, we'll be hard pressed to find a greasy stain."

"Who's behind this, Hayek?"

"That name happens to belong to one of my top supporters. You can't possibly be implying he'd be mixed up in anything as nasty as what's going to happen to you."

Wynn countered, "You don't have any trouble being the spokesman for the same group that murdered your wife?"

Another hard breath, then the phone slammed down.

"That wasn't too bad," Carter observed from his place by the door. "I don't see any singed hair."

Wynn swiveled his chair around to face the window. Through the sunlit curtain he could just make out the stone wall across the courtyard. Trapped in a cage of his own making.

Carter said, "They've got something on you, don't they."

47

Thursday

JIM BURKE SPRAWLED in the corner of his patio Jacuzzi, a drink the color of a tropical depression at his elbow. He felt as lifeless as the pictures he had seen in the development's brochure—the couple seated just exactly where he was, strong-limbed and empty-headed, giving each other these full-tooth smiles. As if being here was the answer to every problem they'd ever had. He sipped from his glass, grimaced, and pushed it away. Since coming in with Hayek, these were the first free days he had taken while the trading floor was open. He absolutely loathed it. The world was spinning, the markets were flying, and he was trapped in a concrete square that made its own bubbles.

When his phone rang, Burke checked his watch. Right on time. He punched the button and said, "Burke."

"Thorson here." The man sounded suitably wired for somebody who had been taken from the cellar and launched into multibillion dollar orbit. "The senior trader's had a phone-in order. Hayek's group wants to buy another three-fifty worth of dollar-yen. That puts them a hundred million over the current Interbank limit."

"Let me check with headquarters and get back to you." Burke hung up the phone, leaned back, and imagined all the action he was missing. He felt the absence in his gut, a hunger that burned so bad he'd willingly swallow acid just to give it a physical name.

The Central Markets department of First Florida was in absolute chaos. This he knew from Brant Anker. Burke closed his eyes and saw it like he was there, standing in the corner, feeding off the frenzy. Thirty-seven traders operating in a space maxed out at twenty. Everybody sweating and screaming and moving money in great heaping piles. He understood why Hayek had ordered him to lie low and monitor activities from a distance. Thorson needed time to get used to his posi-tion as board member and top man. During this start-up phase, their In-terbank line would be nudged up in three hundred million dollar increments. Enough to be noticed, but not enough to cause alarm. Not when they were literally awash with money. A billion had been injected so far. Double that in forty-eight hours. Another billion the next day. Then the big hit. Five billion more.

Burke decided he had waited long enough. He called Thorson back. "That's a go on the three-fifty in yen."

"Right." Thorson was too experienced a trader to let much of his ebullience show. But it was there just the same. "I've had six calls from the Interbank crowd so far this morning. More than I'd usually have in a month. People asking what's going on. I'm giving it to them straight, just like you said. At least so far as the money is concerned. Nothing about the new owner."

"Good."

"When they hear we've lined up Brazilian money, the envy starts pouring down the line." Thorson sounded tightly jubilant. "Had three offers so far this morning to raise the size of our Interbank lines."

"Take whatever they offer. Tell your senior trader to use it all."

"Hang on a second." The trader paused, then came back with, "The bank's very own personal pachyderm has just entered the room. He looks hot."

That would be Robert Carlton the Fifth. "I guess you better put him on."

There was the shuffling of a phone being passed, then the fruity voice of history demanding, "Is this Burke?"

"It is."

"I want to know what you're going to do about these security peo-ple you have camped in my front lobby!"

"It's a temporary measure," Burke said, not caring whether the man believed him. "Just until we get the Capital Markets sectioned off."

"One of them refused to let me pass until I showed him my driver's license! Those dolts are frightening off my best customers!"

"Your best customers," Burke replied calmly, "are the ones cur-rently pumping fresh blood into your bank. I don't suppose you've heard they just placed another half-billion with your foreign exchange department this very morning."

"I want them out of here!"

"Look. Your Capital Markets division is now dealing in highly confidential information. And they're making your bank a ton of money. We need to ensure no one from the outside gains access."

Carlton took a couple of heavy breaths, then crashed down the receiver.

Burke raised his glass to the sunlight and the unfolding of Hayek's strategy.

48

Thursday

THE HEAD OF THE Senate Appropriations Committee was not large, yet he rolled from side to side as though his limited physical bulk were weighted with political muscle. Trailing behind was his chief of staff, which in itself was an indication of the importance the senator gave this meeting. He dropped into his chair and motioned his visitors toward the seats opposite him. "You've got ten minutes."

"Appreciate the time, John." The lawyer at Valerie's side was a desiccated veteran of Washington power brokering. Polk Hindlestiff had sat on three presidential cabinets, lawyered two heads of state through courtroom crises, and advised more high-level campaigns than even he could recall. "I mean that."

"The request coming from your office is the only reason we're here at all." Staring at Valerie as he said it. Letting her know just how far down the totem pole she sat.

To punctuate the ticking clock, his secretary poked her head through the door and said, "You are expected at Treasury in a half hour, Senator."

"Don't I just know it." Ire coated his features like a layer of putty. "All right. Let's hear what's so all-fired important I've had to rearrange my afternoon."

Hindlestiff settled back, his job done for the moment. Having him make this and four other appointments had cost Valerie sixty-five thousand dollars. But it was the only way to meet privately with the heads of both parties and the top committee chairmen, all in one day. Not to mention the fact that merely by hiring such a heavy hitter, Valerie Lawry was declaring this a major league issue.

"Thank you very much for seeing us, Senator. The matter I bring before you today is one of vital importance."

"It always is."

"Hear her out, John," the lawyer murmured.

"Last night the House forwarded the omnibus appropriations bill to the Conference Committee."

"It's about time."

"Yes, sir. But the problem is, they also inserted a last-minute rider that will add immensely to the corporate tax burden and undermine our national sovereignty."

"Remarkable feat to manage, shooting those two birds with one stone." But the senator was listening now. He was a conservative of the old school and nothing pushed his buttons harder than taxation and threats to America's regal status. As Valerie well knew.

She outlined the basics of the Hutchings Amendment, then concluded, "What makes this amendment so alarming is that parallel measures are being put forward by other governments. We need to act swiftly if we are going to keep these maniacs from giving control of our financial institutions to other nations. This is a killer issue, Senator. If this gets out of committee it is going to cost your party seats in the next election."

IT WAS THE first conference Valerie had ever chaired within her company's boardroom. Just standing and surveying the people awaiting her green light was a rush that left her almost panting. "I assume everyone knows each other."

There were a few wary nods across the table. The two assembled crews were more accustomed to battling than cooperating. Conservatives to her left, liberals to her right. Four administrations were represented, five presidential races fought with these people in key positions. Her own crew clustered at the table's far end, agog at the power and history on display. "As you know, one of the problems we face is that support for the amendment comes from both sides of the aisle. Unfortunately, several players have also threatened to turn renegade if their parties take a contrary stand. So on this particular occasion we are expecting you ladies and gentlemen to bury the hatchet and work together."

The first two chairs, one to either side, were occupied by people known in Valerie's circle as policy wonks. Retired lawmakers, now prestigious talking heads. To them she said, "You will use every connection you have to address this issue in public. Explain in the soberest possible terms how this proposal robs America of its heritage."

"A threatening precedent," the liberal intoned.

"Precedent, schmecedent," the conservative barked. "They're aiming to nuke our banking industry."

"Enough," Valerie said. The next two opposing chairs were taken by outside campaign experts. These were her gutter fighters, authorities on designing negative campaigns. "You gentlemen don't have much time. We need to see this amendment become a threat to Middle America."

"Down and dirty," the liberal agreed. "Show how this will kill people in Colorado Springs."

The conservative bristled. The Colorado flatlands were among his most prized territories. "We can have something ready for release by tomorrow. Maybe a photo of an ox goring people through the streets of Boston."

"Just so long as it's in time for the six o'clock news." Valerie nodded to the next pair, think-tank personalities with national followings from both sides of the arena. "We need editorials and air time explaining why this will be bad for the American economy, how it's going to cost jobs. We need to make this something more than just an arcane argument about Wall Street. This has got to be turned into something that hits farmers. Makes things harder for small businesses. Threatens workers' abilities to obtain full benefits."

"I got you." The conservative was male and white and pompous. "Five percent of the population understands what the currency market is about, one percent cares. But everybody understands tax increases. Everybody understands interest rate hikes."

The liberal was black and female and a porcupine who found offense in a sneeze. "Thank you oh so much for such a clear explanation of the painfully obvious."

"All of you have just one task here," Valerie continued. "Make it impossible for them to slip this one by. Go out there and frighten people to death."

49

Thursday

KAY TRILLING OPENED the Hutchings' apartment door that night with the news, "It's started. AIM's chief hired gun has spent the afternoon declaring our amendment a free-fire zone. I shudder to think what kind of chits they called in to arrange meetings with the heads of both parties, the appropriations chiefs of both houses, and the senior party whips, all in one afternoon."

Wynn followed her inside, nodded to Carter, and returned what he assumed was a wave from Graham parked by the fireplace. Then Esther called to him from the adjoining room. When he walked over, she handed him the phone and said, "Talk some sense to her, please."

Wynn took a good look at Esther, but saw nothing save weary tension. No anger, no bitter resentment of his presence. He lifted the phone and said, "Who is this?"

"Who do you think?" Jackie was armed for serious battle. "Look, I know this isn't much to somebody living in a Merritt Island mansion. But this place is all I have. Do you hear what I'm saying? I'm not letting a worm like Hayek push me out of my own house!"

"I don't blame you."

"Wynn," Esther complained.

"You don't?"

"No. And I don't have a mansion."

"This is not what you need to be telling her," Esther complained.

"If you feel like you've got to stay, then do it. Just be careful, okay?"

"This is getting to you too, isn't it."

"In a very big way."

Esther huffed, "You're as bad as Graham."

"I take that," Wynn said, "as the greatest compliment I've heard in a very long while."

Jackie said, "Are you all right?"

"As long as I'm moving. When I slow down I sort of worry about choking on the dust. You?"

"Hanging in there."

"I talked to a priest this morning. Father Libretto worked with my sister."

"He was the guy you tried to connect with at Sant'Egidio."

"That's right. This afternoon I called and asked him to have one of his people check on you. Just give you a friend there in the vicinity. I hope that's okay." When he received only silence in return, Wynn asked, "When are you coming up?"

"Soon as I corner this lead I'm chasing."

The words had to be said, regardless of how close Esther was standing. "I miss you, Jackie. And I think about you a lot."

A different woman emerged from the other end of the line. "I wish I could be sure you're more than just another sad ballad in the making."

"That's not why I'm here, Jackie."

In reply, Jackie hung up the phone so quietly he heard nothing until the line clicked dead.

Esther was there waiting for him. "I owe you an apology."

"You don't owe me anything." He rubbed at his face, seeking to erase the fatigue and the rush of memories. Succeeding at neither. "Every word you spoke in Dianne's final days was the unvarnished truth."

Esther moved a step closer, wanting to be sure who it was she inspected. "Do you think people ever really change?"

"Probably not alone, and maybe not of my own will. But yes. I do think change can happen."

Esther closed the space between them. Slipped her arm through his own. And as together they walked back into the other room, she said softly, "Friend."

AS SOON AS she hung up the phone, Jackie fired up her computer, as much to escape from what she had just said to Wynn as to make the daily check. The day had scalded her so badly, she now feared another burn from anything and everything, including the evening breeze. She was almost disappointed to arrive at the Trastevere site and find another request for a direct link. And angered by the cryptic message: *Anything?*

Jackie typed back, *If there was, why should I tell you? Seeing as how you haven't given me a thing but bad dreams.*

The screen showed nothing for a long time, and then the empty message frame reappeared. Jackie was tempted to log off, give him a little of his own medicine. But she couldn't bring herself to do it. *I might be able to obtain an access code to one of the Tsunami Group computers.*

This time the reply was instantaneous. *If you do, don't use it. They catch you and your life won't be worth last year's computer virus.*

Great news. *What are you saying?*

It will be time for us to meet. Again. Any idea when you might take delivery?

None. Eric had been mired in anguish when she appeared with Shane's letter. Too worried about what was coming now to find any comfort in his possible deliverance.

Same time tomorrow, then.

Wait. Determined to get something more from this guy than cryptic threats. Ready to demand and threaten if necessary. *You're bound to know something. Tell me about Tsunami.*

He seemed to have already resigned himself to the necessity, for the response came without delay. *Signs point toward a carefully orchestrated attack on American currency and financial system.*

"Wow." *By Hayek?*

But the guy was already gone.

THE OMEN, though vague, was too important to sit on. Jackie called Esther, repeated the information, then endured further warnings and worries. But as she was hanging up, a thought touched the recesses of her weary mind. Not a concept so much as a recollection. Jackie remembered an elderly professor she had admired at Gainesville telling tales to heighten the power of his lessons. Speaking as one who had lived through similar events, making dry theories come vividly to life. But she could not remember more than the image of the professor standing before the class, speaking in calm tones that resounded through her brain again now.

She left her apartment, went downstairs, turned on the garage lights, and began rummaging through the boxes stacked against the back wall. Her textbooks from Gainesville were naturally on the bottom. By the time she had found the box and peeled off the tape, she was sneezing from the dust. Memories and familiar aches assaulted her as she searched.

Then she heard the footsteps.

She rose to her feet and held her breath. The gravel drive scrunched beneath a light, swift tread. Her heartbeat rammed into overdrive as she dropped the book in her hands and stumbled over the open boxes. She fumbled along the side wall, clanking through rusty gardener's tools and coming up with a hoe. Jackie took a two-handed clench and fought down terror.

A voice called through the open door, "Ms. Havilland?"

"Who wants to know?"

"My name is Reverend Healey. May I come in?"

"Who sent you?"

A bespectacled man whose graying hair did not match his unlined features emerged into the light. "Does the name Father Libretto mean anything to you?"

She dropped the weapon. Found it necessary to grip the wall for support. "Yes."

"Are you all right?"

"You scared me."

He took another step inside. "Father Libretto was contacted by someone in Washington named Wynn Bryant. He said you might be in danger." He took in the pile of books, the discarded hoe, her shaking form. "It looks like they were right."

Jackie leaned against the wall. "I'm not leaving my home."

"I can understand that." He walked forward, offered her a card. "But if you need anything, feel free to call. My church is about a half mile from here."

She could not bring the words into focus. "You're not a priest?"

"Lutheran. Sant'Egidio is an ecumenical movement. It is open to all believers. The head of the German group is also a Lutheran and a friend of mine. Which is one reason they have as many problems as they do with the bishops in Rome."

"Thanks for stopping by." She waved an arm over the pile of textbooks. "I'm a little busy right now."

"Yes, so I see." As he turned to leave, he said, "Do you belong to a local church?"

She had to laugh. "No."

"You'd be welcome to join us. The company of believers is a vital part of the walk." He stepped into the darkness. "That and knowing when to ask for help."

50

Friday

BURKE MET THORSON Fines in the First Florida parking lot, where the wind blew a constant sullen breath. Fines wore the expression of one with grievances against everything he saw. "Meeting out here isn't going to preserve your masquerade. The chairman's done some checking. He's found out you answer to Hayek."

"This was bound to happen." So long as information about the bank's new owner was not verified from Liechtenstein, the Fed had no official basis upon which to act. And Hayek needed only one more week. "Now tell me the real problem."

"Your man Anker is spending too much time away from the market to be any good as a senior trader."

Burke gripped the steering wheel and twisted it back and forth. The leather squeaked and shuddered. Just as Colin Ready should be doing. "I'll have a word with him."

"He's stashed a pair of geeks in the back room. They've brought in a mountain of electronic gear. He slips out every chance he gets to watch them play with their toys. This is no way to run an overcrowded trading room that's drowning in cash."

But Colin Ready continued to elude them, Burke wanted to shout. The man had firewalls on his firewalls. Time was running out, and Hayek refused to snuff him out unless they brought in hard evidence. Which they did not have. No wonder Anker was obsessing.

Thorson wasn't finished. "This overcrowding is the pits. We got some new desks, but the traders are still falling all over each other. There aren't enough screens or phones or lines for orders, nothing."

"It won't be for much longer."

"That's not good enough."

Burke examined the other man. His features bore a strange mixture of flush and white splotches, the tension clearly moving toward the cracking point. "It's a different world," Burke observed. "Handling three billion and change."

"I need answers," Thorson snapped. "Not theory."

So did he and Anker. That morning, Hayek had summoned Burke out to the manor and explained what he had planned. Burke had sat and listened as the pieces fell into place, then spoke the only word that had come to mind. Brilliant. It was a meager expression of the awe he felt, but for the moment it had to do. And the need to discover the Brazilian investors' mole was now beyond critical.

"Answers," Burke agreed. "We're moving the entire team out."

"When?"

"They'll be gone Monday, just as soon as the current line of transactions has cleared."

Fines was not expecting such a response. Which was no surprise, given how his former bosses had blocked his every move. He still had a lot of arguing left inside him. "Where to?"

"An upstairs room at the Hayek Group."

"I thought you said we were supposed to stay totally separate."

"They will. Believe me. This place is completely sealed off."

"What about our trading positions?"

"For the rest of today, I want your team to switch everything to dollars. Do it as quietly as you can. Talk to your new guys. They'll have a list of confidential brokers who value the business enough not to spread the word around."

Thorson spoke very carefully. "You want me to put all this money into going long on dollars."

"Every dime."

He did a swift calculation. "Working at current margins, we could do, say, thirty billion in dollar derivatives."

"Fine."

"But the dollar's already overvalued."

"Hayek has decided it is going to rise."

"And you want me to do it quietly."

"If you can, place the entire amount without your name ever being known by the market," Burke agreed. "And while you're at it, clear out your Interbank lines."

"But I've been spending every minute I can spare talking up our operation and extending our Interbank credit limits."

Burke smiled. "Trust me."

"You're taking away my cash?"

His cash. The man was definitely hooked. "Just the opposite. Monday you'll be getting more."

"How much?"

Burke wished he could savor this moment and gloat over the power at hand. "Five billion dollars."

Thorson Fines blanched. "If you take away those guys, I won't have the manpower to handle that much fresh money."

"You will," Burke replied, "if you invest the entire amount through the Interbank."

Fines chewed on that. The Interbank was designed specifically to handle huge bundles of cash, and on the quiet. Bank to bank. Confidential, discreet, never touching the trading room floors. "All right. I'm listening."

"The funds you currently hold are to be managed by the group moving into the Hayek trading room. But they will remain on your books and be traded under your bank's name. Tell that to your men. Their bonus situation remains the same. As does yours."

"And the new funds?"

"Clear the Interbank accounts. Try to open as many new lines as possible. We're looking for maximum leverage. We need the lines in place by Tuesday at the latest."

"The Forex convention is this weekend," Thorson pointed out.

"It would be best if you and your team skipped this year." The annual foreign exchange convention was a clannish gathering of senior traders and those marked as up-and-comers. "Just to make sure nothing gets out."

Burke could actually see the man's mind racing through this new input. Coming up with the assessment at trading-floor speed. "You've got access to confidential data, don't you. You're going to use the Interbank lines to leverage the five big ones into a hundred, and make a killing on one huge bet."

The man was almost too smart. "Be ready to move when you get the word."

□   □   □   □

HAYEK WAITED UNTIL the afternoon sun was roasting holes in his Persian carpets to summon the senior traders. He watched a pair of hummingbirds beat tiny thunder as they drank from the highest point of the central fountain. Events were unfolding at a pace so precise he felt able to halt the birds' wings and peer at them between beats.

Hayek made appropriate noises as he ushered the traders into the conference area and offered beverages. He pretended not to notice the week's strain, the old sweat, the market's aging effect on their features. Hayek settled himself into his chair at the head of the table and inquired, "How is the market?"

Alex, the senior spot trader, waited until the others had made their reports to say, "The dollar's on the rise. We've done all the checking we can. Somebody's buying big numbers. We've been holding back, trying to find the reason."

Hayek nodded slowly, as though the information was both valued and new. "I want us to clear our holdings and go heavy into the dollar."

There was a long silence. A unified expelling of breath as the adrenaline took hold. The derivatives man finally said, "Sell *all* our holdings?"

"Do it smoothly," Hayek replied. "No panic. Run this on through Monday and Tuesday. But strip away everything that holds us to anything other than a long-dollar position."

Alex was the only trader to voice what should have been the obvious. "In other words, you want us to *follow* the market."

"In this instance, I feel it is a justifiable move."

"No chance the market's first step was taken by our little brothers over at First Florida, is there?"

"A justifiable concern. But not the case, I assure you." Hayek smiled false approval and hastened on, "By necessity, you will need to miss the Forex convention this weekend. We can't afford for word of our actions to get out. In order to make up for this, I have rented a private Caribbean island for you and your guests the week after next. All expenses paid."

One of the traders asked, "You're telling us we're looking at an active bull market?"

Another trader asserted, "The dollar's already at record highs, right across the board."

"Which means we can catch the market off guard." Hayek knew he had to sell them if they were to sell the others. "Call the brokers you know will pass the word on. Tell them you've caught wind of something big."

"So we use our mouths to talk the market up even higher." Once again, it was Alex who caught the drift. "Then next week we're going to sell off."

Hayek rose to his feet very slowly, giving himself time to hide his sudden rage. He met the group with yet another smile. "Be ready to move fast. On my command."

51

Friday

THE FRIDAY COMMITTEE meeting was very well attended. Almost all the seats around the rotunda were taken, as well as most of the visitors' chairs. C-Span had positioned a live-feed camera at the back. The questions went more sharply, the exchanges faster.

As Wynn departed that afternoon, he spotted Valerie speaking with one of the committee members. The senator from Oklahoma apparently did not mind in the least being corralled by a striking lobbyist in heels and form-fitted dark suit.

Carter moved up alongside Wynn. "We need to get back to the office. You've got a live television broadcast coming up."

"This won't take but a moment." When the senator moved away, Wynn stepped up alongside Valerie. "I wish I could say I'm disappointed. Or even surprised."

Valerie used the hand not holding her briefcase to sweep the hair off her shoulders. "Good afternoon, Congressman. Could I take a moment to inform you of the incredibly vital dangers of the Hutchings Amendment?"

Wynn replied softly, "Honesty."

"What about it?"

"That's what you promised me. Our dinner together in Georgetown, remember? You said there wasn't enough of it in this town."

"Fine, you want honesty? No problem." She managed to make glacial look sexy. "I'm going to make you scream with public agony. Shriek in CNBC-captured distress. Pain and no gain. That's how this is going to play out."

Carter moved up alongside him, watching her high-heeled departure.

"Lobbyists make you feel like a penny waiting for change. That's their specialty."

Wynn knew that hers was not an idle threat. "Is it too late to change my mind, take a graceful bow, and ride into the sunset?"

"Come on." Carter steered him around. "We've got other guns to load."

THAT EVENING, WYNN was walking through the main lobby of Georgetown Hospital when the squat little Fed executive and the FBI agent caught up with him. "If I didn't know better, I'd say you guys were stalking me."

"Our agent observed you enter Mr. Saad's room and called it in," Welker told him.

"I didn't see any agent upstairs."

"Then he's doing his job, Congressman."

Bowers drew Wynn out of the flow. "You've left the Willard?"

"Moved into a room at the M Street Marriott."

"Smart, very smart. Give them less of a target. How's your friend?"

"They're going to let Nabil go home tomorrow." Wynn crossed his arms. "This is not a social call, so let's hear the bad news."

"We've been getting messages for two days now," the agent told him. "Evidence slipped through the mail slot, under doorways, left in cryptic code on our website. About how you've been involved in some serious business. Felonious activities in the form of insider trading, using your sister as a front. Enough to warrant a full investigation and a possible freezing of all your assets."

Wynn nodded slowly. Trying to figure out what he felt. Deciding the shock would strike soon enough. "Are you here to arrest me?"

"No, Congressman. We're not." Gerald Bowers was not just ugly. He was a pusher. He shoved with his words and his gestures, punching the air between them, getting in close enough for Wynn to catch the stale odor of cigars. "Last time we met, you questioned our bona fides. So we're laying it out plain as we know how. We're not going to do a thing with this."

"Which doesn't mean the press can't attack you," the agent warned.

"They might, but we won't." Bowers leveled a stubby finger at

Wynn's nose. "Here's the deal. We're after one target and one target only, and it's not you. That good enough to show which side we're on?"

"So why don't you go after Hayek yourself?"

The arm dropped. "Life as a top bureaucrat is as political as elected office. There's just one rule to riding the Washington bull. Fight the battles you can win."

"I don't get it. All the manpower and connections at your disposal, and your best hope is the greenest guy in Congress?"

"It's not as crazy as it sounds," Welker replied. "Our first alert on Hayek came from somebody else without any logical connection to the financial community. A nobody acting as messenger for a group called Sant'Egidio. Does the name ring a bell?"

"Let's take this outside. I hate hospitals. They smell like bottled death." Bowers led them into an evening mist too fine and windless to be called rain. "Here's the thing. We know Hayek has been involved in some nastiness south of the border. But there's nothing concrete we can pin on him."

"Mexico?"

"Farther down. Doesn't matter. What I'm saying is, Hayek is tainted, but also very careful. We know for certain he's not colluding with any of his Wall Street brethren. We also know he's being flooded with funny money, enough so he's started a second fund. But none of it traceable to anything illegal. Remember, there's nothing illegal about betting against the market."

"But that's not what you think is going on here, right?"

Bowers' spectacles glistened like glass flowers, hiding irises of angry blue. "Would I be wasting my Friday night standing in the rain if I did?"

"Give us the ammunition, Congressman," the agent said. "We'll blast the guy right out of the water."

"We've heard that this Tsunami project might be aimed at crippling the U.S. financial markets," Wynn ventured. "But we don't have any proof. Not yet."

A swift exchange of glances, then Bowers allowed, "Hayek's crew has suddenly gotten very busy this afternoon, buying dollars with both fists." He shoved a card into Wynn's pocket. "Cellphone and home numbers are on the back. You've already got Welker's card. Stay in touch."

52

Saturday

THE TOP MAN IN Valerie's firm owned a riverside house he stubbornly insisted was in Georgetown, although both the state and city lines were set firmly on the wrong side of his property. He paid Glen Echo city taxes and drove a car with Maryland license plates, but declared with all the inbred stubbornness of his Deep South ancestors that someday he would set the matter straight. Whatever side of the line, the place was still a jaw dropper. Three acres, mostly of trees and ridgeline, overlooked the steep-sided Potomac. Upon this plateau rested a redbrick throne embroidered with pillars, balconies, chandeliers, heart-of-pine flooring, and original oils. One associate claimed to have seen a letter from the chairman to the architect approving an order for three thousand square feet of granite.

Valerie's wrought-iron chair was at one corner of the slate-and-stone veranda, an untouched drink on the table in front of her. All four senior partners were present. A bombshell she had promised, and a bombshell she was going to deliver. One big enough to require the privacy of an off-site meeting. "Yesterday evening I received information that should take down our principal opposition once and for all."

"That greenhorn congressman from Florida, what's his name?"

"Bryant. He was the CEO of a high-tech start-up. They sold out to the company formerly run by Jackson Taylor. Two weeks before the buyout, Bryant apparently used secret accounts in a Bermuda bank to purchase futures in Taylor's stock, which had been depressed by a major court case that looked like it was going against them. The case was resolved through the acquisition of Bryant's company. Bryant shared these profits with his sister. Very hush-hush."

"Dynamite," her immediate boss declared. "This will totally destroy the guy."

"There's a slight problem," Valerie warned.

"How slight?"

"The sister is Governor Wells' recently deceased wife."

"The one who was whacked by the Arab terrorists?"

"Yes."

"I don't like it." The top partner was three years from retirement and considered himself more of a mover and shaker than a mere lobbyist. He had the booming tone of an actor reading unfamiliar lines. "We're in this for the long haul. There's a difference between striking hard and hitting below the belt."

Valerie gripped the arms of her chair, her features set in the concrete of having been through this many times before. This was precisely the sort of imbecilic rubbish she had come to expect from their top man.

The others disagreed for her. "You weren't there for the meeting with AIM's representative. I was. They want to see this thing go away forever."

"Part of success in this business is knowing which trigger to pull," another agreed.

"They definitely do not want this baby to get out of the crib. Our job is to kill it in the cradle, before it can crawl out of committee."

Her immediate boss asked Valerie, "What else do you have planned?"

"Monday we're going after the political forces in the committee members' home states. My people will be contacting the top fund raisers, showing them just how important it is to call in their chits. We'll do the second round of meetings with the members themselves on Tuesday, if possible with a tame Treasury official in tow. The talking heads are getting their first strikes in tomorrow."

"When is the committee scheduled to vote?"

"Nothing's been slated, but this is being pushed hard. Our best guess is Wednesday."

The chairman declared, "I'm still not in agreement here."

"Your objection is noted." The youngest of the senior partners did not bother to hide his sarcasm. "But I say we hit them with everything we've got. This is a top priority from one of our biggest clients, and we've just been handed a silver bullet." He turned to Valerie. "You've got concrete evidence against Bryant?"

"I'm told it is being couriered up to me tomorrow."

"I say run it by legal. If they think it's solid, we should strike first thing next week."

Without another word, the chairman finished his drink, rose to his feet, and left the table. They waited for him to move out of range before the man slated to take his place said, "Way to go, Val."

"What's with the old man?"

"He sees everything these days through the lens of hankering after a cabinet appointment." The man next in line shrugged. "Val, you make this happen and there's a chair waiting for you in the boardroom."

"Wiping the floor with the man fronting our opposition," her boss agreed. "That's the way reputations are made in this town."

53

Saturday

A S BURKE WAS CHECKING into the Forex Dealers convention at the Breakers of Palm Beach, he witnessed two brokers go toe-to-toe over the hotel's one remaining suite. Framed notices stood to either side of the reception desk, announcing some of the goodies on offer. A wire service was hosting a daylong gambling cruise. Another welcomed every arriving broker with a half gallon of vintage Dom Pérignon. Dealing networks had set up six bars in the lobby and around the outdoor pool. Brokers spent the convention handing out Rolexes like candy. The air was full of false cheer and people determined to spend their way into a good time. Traders who made it to the top were paid to be instant and aggressive. Hit and pay, make and run. The language was physical, the tension constant.

Burke tipped a bellhop to carry his bags upstairs and began his first circuit. He was there to observe and be seen. He passed a table where five men were shouting over a female first-timer. College, they called the fresh meat. One of the men barked, "Deal you twenty-six, twenty-eight on the college."

"Hit you fifty," another called back.

The girl was doing her best not to look like a total turnip off the truck from Chicago, but she clearly did not have a clue to what the men were talking about. When she just sat there with her pasty little smile, the first dealer leaned over his floral-print belly and said, "Whattaya make me, College?"

"I—I'm sorry, I just wanted a drink."

"Drink, schmink. Look, Alfie here's got fifty thou you're either under twenty-six or over twenty-eight." When she faltered, he popped his fingers like castanets. "Word of advice, College. People figure if you talk slow you think slow. And if you talk quiet you ain't got power for the floor. So give it to us loud and now."

"Shout out the age, College," Alfie agreed. "Make me a happy man."

Burke walked away. Senior traders could never leave it behind. They were addicts looking for the next fix. The later the hour, the higher soared the bets. It was all about instant gratification. They'd bet on anything.

Two years earlier, when the Forex convention was in London, Burke had watched a group of traders go a hundred thou each over whose main course had the highest number of green beans. They'd slipped the maître d' five thousand dollars to play ref and count the stringers on each plate. Two guys tied for first and walked off with four-fifty apiece. It was all gone by the next day, lost to a female trader from Singapore who won the pool on how many towels were in the sixth-floor pantry. Twenty-two traders had taken that action, trooped upstairs, bribed some Chinese cleaning woman with a hatful of cash, crammed into and around the pantry, then watched and shouted as she counted the towels for them. The woman trader from ING Bank had woken up the entire floor when she won and shrieked and walked off with the convention's top draw of just under two million bucks.

That had also been the year the brokerage firms stacked their receptions like chips, so the traders could visit them all. The firms had drawn their times out of a brass champagne bucket, and moaned and argued over the placings but held pretty much to the schedule. The best by acclaim was the reception given by the French brokers, a Parisian saloon with can-can dancers that hadn't started until four o'clock the final morning. Which meant there'd been so many nightlong drunks they'd called the last breakfast buffet the Xerox convention, since almost everybody showed up wearing the same clothes they'd had on the night before.

As he headed for the lobby's rear doors, Burke caught the drift of a senior trader talking on the phone, ruining a minion's weekend. "If it breaks the year low, I don't want anything to do with the euro." A pause, then the words became a shout. "Look, I don't care what your analysts say. You've got your stop orders. If it hits the low, dump every euro in the bucket."

Burke entered the sunlight and walked toward the bayside pool, the banter splashing off him like rain.

"That guy runs a real book in London. A genuine triggerman."

"Hit and pay, that's what I told him. I've stuffed you. You owe me a name."

"All of a sudden, the guy next to me screams, Feds at ten o'clock! I felt the old ticker do a total freeze."

"I talked to my contact at Bubba, then the top guy at the Old Lady. They gave me nothing. I hit the ground running just the same. Was up half a big one by lunch."

Burke felt eyes on him from all directions. But he'd had a lifetime's experience ignoring those who assumed he was of a lesser breed. He seated himself at an empty poolside table, isolated by his own preference, there only because Hayek had ordered him to come. And waited.

It came as no surprise when the traders at the next table swiveled their chairs in order to include him in their conversation. "Where are all your boys, Burke?"

"I'm the token force this year. I guess you heard, we had a sudden inflow of new cash this week."

"So how are things around Hayek these days?" This from the top Barclay's New York trader.

"Busy."

"You guys missing Wall Street yet?"

"Like we would a boil."

There were rules of engagement to be followed in such an exchange. Power was tightly stratified among traders. Minnows talked to minnows, the sharks only with other sharks. Burke knew these guys were aware of Hayek's extraordinary Friday moves. But they could not say anything outright. It was like bidding in bridge. Everything had to be done in code.

The senior Dresdner Bank trader was from Singapore by way of Chicago, and known for his Cuisinart blend of accents. "We hear buyers started coming out of the woodwork late Friday."

Burke pretended surprise. "What's the spot?"

"Come on, Burke." The Barclay's senior American trader was an utterly hairless man who wore a straw boater to protect his pate. "Like you guys weren't nose down at the trough."

The Dresdner man pressed, "Dollars against euros, sterling, yen, anything so long as the position has them dollar long."

"The dollar does look pretty firm, doesn't it," Burke said.

But the cognac and the company had fueled the Dresdner man's ability to mask his worry with angry bluster. "It's a panic spree."

Burke smiled at the guy. "You're telling me you're long euros?"

"We're looking at a sure-fire arbitrage. I've told my guys it's a mopping-up exercise."

"Not me." Barclay's spoke to the Paribas guy but was eyeing Burke, hoping for a sign. "I told my people they better have their buyers locked in before they move. Either that or they'll be planted on the street."

"The dollar's overvalued, I'm telling you." This from Dresdner.

Burke smiled once more. "Then why are you sweating?"

"The heat down here stays cranked up to sauna, that's why. Look, have your guys call my guys. We'll take whatever you've got on offer."

The Barclay's guy moved in tight. "Unless Hayek is trying to form a bull corner on the dollar market."

"Cornering is illegal," Burke replied coolly. "The Fed would plant their inspectors in our front room and shut down our operation for the duration."

"So there's nothing to the rumor," the Barclay's man pressed, "that Hayek is holding some juicy big news, something that might really strike the market hot?"

"All I can tell you is what I've already said. The dollar is looking pretty solid from where we stand, and the current investment flow seems to be pushing it higher." Burke rose to his feet, gave the table a benign smile. "Think I'll go check out the action in the bar."

He took his time maneuvering through the tables, exchanged greetings with people he knew from previous conventions. Things were moving just as Hayek had predicted, and it was important for the gathered traders to see him and take note. All the while, Burke marveled at Hayek's plan. Currencies often made huge fluctuations in August and early September. The same thing happened between Christmas and the New Year, when the gnomes of Zurich closed down for their annual migration to Gstaad and St. Moritz. The financial press often assigned blame to whatever political or interest rate crises happened to be brewing. But the reason was far simpler: less liquidity. Fewer traders were exchanging less money. A relatively small amount of activity was therefore enough to cause a massive shift. Hayek's plan was to push the markets around, and do so violently. The best time to do this was when the fewest senior traders walked the floor. The senior traders were the ones allowed to trade the bigger positions. And come Monday, these traders would be on the third day of a serious annual binge.

Burke smiled to the palms and the manicured lawn and the blistering heat. One thing was certain. Hangover or not, come Monday the gathering would be swarming like a hive on fire.

54

Sunday

SUNDAY MORNING CARTER Styles picked Wynn up and drove him first to church with his family, then the three blocks from the church to their tract home on the outskirts of McLean. Carter's wife was a quietly intense woman who did statistical research for the American University science department and three local labs. The two Styles children were six and nine, and mercifully resembled their mother. Their home was a two-story brick cookie-cutter with a large fenced-in backyard full of swings and toys and an ecstatic golden Lab.

Carter tended burgers on the grill as he sipped a glass of iced tea and made short shrift of his background. "I was born and raised in Fort Pierce. Little town of about fifteen thousand, double that when the snow birds come flocking down. Sits between Vero Beach and Boca. Place is full of your basic hourly wage crowd."

"I know Fort Pierce."

"Sure you do. I was fourteen the year we finally crawled out of Vietnam. Spent my teenage years watching my hometown grow tumors. Fourteen head shops. Six Harley depots. Meth houses. Bars with bullet holes in the front doors. By the time I got out of college, I was just looking for a way to get even. Graham found me, pointed me in the right direction, told me which legs to bite."

Wynn squinted through the smoke of grilling meat, listened to the kids laugh and play tag with the dog, and watched Carter's wife talk over the fence with a neighbor. He knew there would never be a better time than this to unload. "The years before I was able to sell my business, Grant ran for Congress. Toughest race of his career. Only one he ever lost. Cost a ton of money. Sybel was campaign treasurer. Ended up she'd personally underwritten some of the debt."

"Oh, man."

Wynn nodded, seeing nothing but smoke and sunshine. "I set up an offshore account in Bermuda. We'd licensed a Taiwanese company to use our technology, and my share of the take never found its way home."

"Far as I recall, this is a totally illegal act you're describing to me."

"I used the funds to buy futures options on the company that was buying us out. Jackson Taylor's old company."

Carter was no longer tending the meat. "It just gets worse and worse."

"Made a bundle. Had the bank write Sybel a check. Never mentioned it was me, but she knew, and knew enough never to talk about it."

Carter glanced down, started sliding the burgers onto plates. "The account was in your name, is that what you're telling me?"

"Do I look that dumb? But somewhere there are bound to be records showing my signature on something." He waited for Carter to call the kids over, then said, "If you guys want me to resign, I'll do it tomorrow."

CARTER HAD TAKEN over the guest room for his home office, claiming it was the only way he could watch his kids grow. He found Kay at Esther's and had Wynn repeat his tale over the speakerphone.

Kay was silent a long time. "There had to be something."

"There usually is," Carter agreed.

"Grant had something he figured would tie you in a knot, so he appointed you like Sybel wanted. I never did like that man."

"There's something more." Wynn related the meeting he'd had in the hospital lobby.

"You went to see Nabil?" Kay sounded genuinely pleased. "He didn't mention that to me."

"The point is, the Feds left themselves the perfect out. If the press makes a big noise with this, the FBI will basically be obliged to open an investigation."

"Do you want out?"

"Not if I can still do some good here."

"Carter, what's your take on the situation?"

"I'm clear out of answers at this end, but my gut tells me we ought to stay with what we have."

"I'll think on it and let you know tomorrow." Kay sounded very weary. "A little clarity would be sweet just now. Very sweet indeed."

55

Sunday

JACKIE SPENT THE entire weekend searching through her textbooks, waiting for Eric's phone call, and picking at the scabs of old memories. She found nothing but futility and frustration on all counts. Eric neither called nor answered his phone. She drove by his development twice each day, walked the street, but saw only drawn curtains and a barking dog from two doors down. Each time she left a little more worried.

Her Saturday highlight was shopping for Millicent, her somewhat lunatic landlady. Jackie then had tea in the big house's moldy kitchen, drinking from a cup she hoped was stained with age and not encrusted dirt. The old woman made a little more sense than usual. She worried over Jackie back there with the moonbeams and the man in black, which Jackie assumed was a reference to the pastor's nighttime visit. Jackie gave the woman only half an ear while the rest of her brain replayed all the dusty textbooks she had perused. She finally returned home, weary from wishing she knew what she sought.

Sunday morning she paused in her research long enough to attend the Lutheran church. Dressed in her most conservative clothes, Jackie joined the crowd, sat through the service, and marveled at her actions. The people and the sermon and the singing and the way she was greeted afterward were all very welcoming. A small sliver of sanity inserted into her day.

When she returned home it was to find a terse message on her answering machine from Eric. "I got your messages and don't call me again. I don't know if they're listening and I don't want to know. I'm still searching. I'll be in touch."

Jackie entered her kitchen alcove and went through the motions of fixing her lunch. She ate with an old textbook for company, wishing the niceness could have lasted a little longer.

A hint returned that evening, when Wynn called to report, "I've had a very strange day."

"Tell me about it."

"I'd rather not. At least, not until we're together. Is that all right?"

She set aside the textbook, used a dishtowel to rub the dust from her hands, and walked out onto the tiny balcony. The evening sky was full of semitropical display. "Sure."

"How's your shoulder?"

"Better. And my leg. The stitches come out this week."

"Jackie, late Friday I got hit on by a guy from the Fed. He said Hayek was buying dollars with both fists."

She could almost hear her brain grinding into an unaccustomed gear. "Interesting."

"But that makes a mockery of your news, right? I mean, he wouldn't be digging himself in deeper if he thought the market was going to tank."

"Not necessarily. Hayek might try to set up a feeding frenzy. Imagine a thousand currency piranhas attacking the dollar and devouring it whole. The effect would be an economic H-bomb, demolishing every U.S. market—stocks, bonds, commodities, the works."

"But the Fed guy says he's *buying*."

"Just listen for a second, okay? Let's assume what we've heard is right and Hayek is going to play on a weakening trend. They'll want to be the first with unexpected news. It'd be something of a devastating nature, with a particular impact on derivatives."

"Some seriously bad news."

"Like an accounting scandal at Treasury. Or an industry bellwether declaring record losses for the quarter, so big it drags down the whole board. Something that has the foreign investors fleeing for a more profitable market."

"That could happen?"

"Sure. A foreign pullout sparked the crash of '29. No reason why it couldn't happen again. You know what the market calls foreign investors? Nervous money. They jump at shadows. A massive loss by one of their key investment accounts could have them bailing out in droves." She was talking faster now, her glances scattering green lightning around the treetops. "It would be a perfect setup. Currency traders move the markets every chance they get. This is highly unethical in, say, stocks or bonds. If he's caught at it, a trader can lose his license and in some cases go to jail. But in the currency market it's business as usual. Forex traders don't analyze trends and try to anticipate where the market is headed. This isn't a straight-ahead game, as the traders say. When they can, they *create* upheaval. Being the first with major news would mean they could position themselves for a huge push. If they're big enough, their goal would be not just to ride the market but to demolish it. Turn a slight downward trend into a full-fledged rout."

"You're telling me," Wynn said, clearly struggling to keep up, "Hayek could be buying dollars to heighten the market's swing?"

"See, you're learning. Say word gets out about Hayek and his dollar buys. Something this big is bound to be known. Hayek is a major force in the Forex markets. He's won time and time again, which means the other players watch him. They hear Hayek is moving in and buying dollars. Others would crowd in, gambling that Hayek is betting right. The market goes ballistic. People scramble all over the globe. The central banks call around, trying to find a reason for this. Nobody knows for certain, but rumors abound. And still the dollar keeps climbing. Okay so far?"

"You're telling me Hayek would do this just before the big news comes out, right?"

"Exactly." But even as she said the words, the niggling sense of a lost signal pushed her back inside. Jackie stood looking down at the pile of textbooks. What was she missing here?

Wynn said, "Which means we don't have more than a few days to find out what's going on."

"Less." She paced the apartment's tight confines, her brain shrieking. Where was Eric? "In this game, a few days are one step away from eternity."

56

Monday

A T TEN-THIRTY THE next morning, Wynn entered the Dirksen Senate Office Building and walked down to the meeting room. Eyes followed him constantly, but no one approached. He nodded to several people and did his best to pretend all was well.

Turning the final corner, he found Carter standing with Kay. As soon as he came into view, Kay spun around and walked away. Wynn's own tread turned glutinous, dreading the news that Carter waited to deliver—that he was on his way out, a liability they could no longer afford.

He did his best to feign ignorance by saying, "I'm getting the pariah treatment around here this morning. I assume that means something's happened."

"The House leader came out vehemently opposed to the amendment. Stated he was in favor of striking the entire appropriations bill if we tried to push it through as is."

"Not good," Wynn said, resigned to his fate and his farewell.

"He declared it would be better to let the government shut down for a while than watch this amendment grind our economy to a halt." Carter squinted as Kay had, like the place smoldered with the stench of a deal gone bad. "You know what that means?"

"I suppose—"

"Kay doesn't like doing this, but right now she's all out of options. You're going to have to play the sacrificial lamb. Let the press claw you apart."

Wynn tried to fit his mind around this news. "You want me to stay?"

"What, you thought Kay left me out here to swing the ax?" Carter grinned hugely. "You really want to stay around that bad?"

"Absolutely. If you'll let me."

"You're all right, you know that?" Carter motioned toward the meeting room. "Come on, let's go watch the fireworks."

But before they could reach the entrance, their way was blocked by a trio wielding tape recorders and press badges. The portly male struck Wynn as vaguely familiar. But it was the more angular of the two women who said, "Gail Treats with the *Washington Post*, Congressman Bryant. Could you spare us a minute?"

Carter started in with, "We're just about to—"

"It's all right," Wynn said. "There's time for one question."

"Thank you. The senior congressman within your own party has had some pretty harsh things to say about your so-called Hutchings Amendment. Do you have any comment?"

"Our economy is in serious trouble," Wynn replied, weaving together points from the files. "We just don't know it yet. Hedge funds and the derivative traders in our major banks are getting away with financial mayhem. Today our system's governing bodies operate according to what I call the New Orleans Theory of Finance: Let the good times roll."

"What about—"

"The past several administrations have been real friends to the status quo. This bunch is no different. The Treasury and the Fed have both taken revolving-door policies to Wall Street. They come in, they club around, then they return to the domain of big bucks and fast living. This has resulted in an accident waiting to happen. The excesses of these huge equity funds need to be reined in. That is what our amendment proposes to do. No wonder they're rolling out the big guns against us." Wynn turned away. "That's all the time I have."

The portly man called out in an aggressive English accent, "Would you care to comment on the accusations that you are guilty of insider trading?"

Wynn had no choice but to turn back. "I know you from somewhere." Then he remembered. "Sure. The British embassy reception for the new ambassador."

"Excellent memory, Congressman. The question is, how selective is it?"

"The ambassador's aide warned me about you. She didn't mention you were a paid stooge."

The reporter swelled like a ripe plum. "I resent—"

"I don't know exactly what information you have, but I can assure you any such accusations are totally without merit." He switched his attention to the *Post* reporter. "The important thing is, something good is turning into something bad. The people who have profited from putting our economy at risk will do anything and everything, including slurring my good name through planted accusations like this, to halt this vital legislation."

When he was through the door and inside the committee room, Wynn cast Carter a sidelong glance. His aide was smiling again. "What's the matter?"

"Nothing. Not a single solitary thing."

"I just gave them what you fed me."

"Not just." Carter waited for Wynn to take his seat, then leaned over and said, "For a second there I could've sworn I was listening to a real pro."

57

Monday

THERE WAS AN osmosis quality required for top Washington lobbyists, an ability to read the political winds and react accordingly. Any lobbyist who waited until results were official was doomed to banishment and life in the wastelands beyond the Beltway. Valerie walked into her office that morning and instantly scented the change. People she had seldom spoken with were coming up, searching her out, trying to attach their careers to her ascending star. Two of the four senior partners made a point of stopping by the downstairs chamber that had become her team's ops center. Supposedly they just happened by, as though they made the light-years journey between floors every day.

Two hours later she climbed the stairs and found her boss and the firm's incumbent chairman huddled in the doorway to the boardroom. It was a perfect place for Valerie to declare, "We've completed our straw poll of committee members."

Both of them grinned, discerning the news before she spoke. "Home run for the home team."

"That's the way it looks to us."

"Come on in here," the incumbent said. He gestured toward one of the suede-and-chrome chairs. "Try this on for a ride."

"I've been in here before, thank you very much."

"Not as a partner, you haven't." He patted the seat back and said to her former boss, "Is that corner suite ready?"

"Her name's not on the door yet, but I doubt she'll mind."

Valerie slid into the seat, sighing ecstatically. "Nice." It wasn't her own firm, but there were advantages to having company along for the ride. Especially at a moment like this. "Very nice indeed."

They took the two chairs to either side. "So the holdouts have come through."

"They've said.as much." She gave the chair a little swivel. "We're ahead by one vote for certain, possibly as many as three."

"Val." The incumbent leaned forward. "Given the situation, we'd like you to bury the personal stuff on Bryant."

She halted in midswing. "What?"

"The senior partner is weighing in on this pretty heavily." Her former boss was apologetic but firm. "He sees his chance of a top-level appointment going right down the drain if this is ever traced back to us."

"Which it would be," the incumbent intoned. "There is only one place this could have come from, that's what they'll say."

She saw it then. The careful maneuvering, the friendly probes. Setting her up so she revealed the situation before they struck. Being handled by pros. "I suppose I have no say in this matter."

"You said it yourself, Val. This thing is won." He used his most soothing tone. Stroking out any hard feelings. "Something like this you can just tuck away, save it for the next time you get Wynn Bryant in your sights."

But this was personal, she wanted to shout. She wanted to watch Wynn Bryant bleed. She'd already planned to record his resignation off C-Span, toast his departure for weeks to come. "I've already put out a couple of leads."

The two men exchanged a swift glance. The incumbent said evenly, "Don't feed them any more. We'll just have to hope they don't come up with enough meat to carry it forward."

"The half-life on something this big must be a thousand years," her former boss agreed. "And the old man won't be around here to stop you next time."

58

Monday

A T SEVEN THAT evening, traders finally began straggling off the Hayek Group's trading floor. Eric was among the first to leave. The swelling to his forehead and lip had gone down over the weekend, and the traders were now too busy to rib him any further. The common wisdom was that he had struck a doorpost hurtling from a forbidden bedroom. Eric said almost nothing, kept to himself, and avoided Colin. Which granted Colin the excuse not to confront his pal with what he knew. And worse, what he suspected.

Around ten, the paper shrapnel cleared and the senior traders left the pit. Colin was still in his cubicle, a lonely circle of light in the midst of a dark fluorescent night. He remained because he could feel the storm gathering, and because he had nowhere else to go. At home, Lisa's absence felt too much like personal deprogramming. The best of everything had been lost along with her, every day's clarity erased. He had tried to rewrite his memories of the whole affair as just another warped and twisted mind game imposed by a merciless reality. But it did not help. Nothing did.

Alex swung around the corner with the ease of a man too tired to care whether or not he was welcome. He slumped into the visitor's chair and announced, "If Hayek is right, we're going to clear six months' profit off this battle. If he's wrong, they'll sweep me out with tomorrow's garbage."

Colin used his well-chewed pen to point at the central screen, on which he had thrown up the floor's highest camera, the one showing the upstairs balcony. "It's empty now, but they started showing up about noon."

"I saw." Alex leaned over, squinted into the screen, and asked, "How'd you do that?"

"Tapped into the security system. They walked around, made themselves comfortable, checked the monitors, spent a couple of minutes grinning down and watching you guys kill yourselves."

"Which means either they weren't in on the action, which I doubt. Or they'd set their dollar positions hours ago."

Colin said nothing. Just sat and chewed on his pen and watched the empty screen.

Alex eased himself slowly back, testing each muscle in turn. "Hedge funds run off information. We're hunters and gatherers. I use brokers who give me fresh data, and give it to me first. We bring all this information into one place, and a small group of us makes the decisions. Only nine of us really pull the trigger. Nine senior traders. Seventeen billion and counting on the balance sheet. A lot of ammo." A pause, then, "You see where I'm headed with this?"

"I really don't know anything more," Colin replied solemnly. "If I did, I'd tell you."

"So you're not part of this new team who might be running an inside feint on us."

"Not a chance."

"What about Hayek's personal stuff, can you get in there?"

"Out of the question. He uses a special coding system, one-timers off an electronic encryption pad. The man is supercareful."

Alex backed off a notch. "You're what they call a hacker, am I right?"

"Since the very beginning," Colin affirmed, not minding that it was finally out in the open. Wishing he could trust this guy fully. "When I went over to the other side and joined Hayek, I became what is known as a white hat."

"Hayek's bound to have something on you," Alex guessed with a trader's intuition, far beyond the realm of normal logic. "He'd never just up and give his electronic security to a guy off the street, no matter what credentials he carried."

Colin had known it was bound to come, had imagined the moment and the response. He did not hesitate. "FEMA."

"What?"

"Federal Emergency Management Agency. If the Afghanis ever manage to sneak in a nuclear bomb and plant it in Times Square,

FEMA will be the people to pick up the pieces. If California finally gets hit by the big one, same thing. They've written up reams of contingency plans for everything from terrorist attacks to an attempted military coup to aliens landing on the White House lawn. That's their job. Imagine the worst that can happen, then find solutions."

"So?"

"I got caught taking a peek."

Alex grinned for the first time that day. "No way."

"Utterly real, I'm afraid. They had an invisible firewall. Lit me up like a Canaveral launch. I was arrested, fingerprinted, photographed. The works. A full dose of reality. Grim and horrid."

"And Hayek bailed you out?"

"In a manner of speaking. He sent his security man, Dale Crawford. I was nol-prossed, which means no record. Hayek won my undying loyalty."

"No kidding, alien invasion contingency plans?"

"So I've heard. I wasn't able to see for myself, and after they caught me I was left wondering if anyone has ever really been inside." Colin began the process of cutting off his electronic bits and pieces. "Whatever the case, FEMA remains one of the dream sites."

"Like the Everest of hackers."

"Precisely. Every conspiracy nut in the universe wants a look into their files. Not just to study the eventualities, you understand. FEMA reportedly keeps tabs on what has actually happened. They're supposed to have records on all sorts of supersecret events."

"*X-Files* come to life," Alex said.

"I suppose it was inevitable they would be well protected. Actually, much better shielded than the Pentagon."

"You've hit Defense?"

Colin rose to his feet and flipped the light switch. "Perhaps I should stop there."

Together they headed for the rear entrance. Alex held his briefcase with two fingers of one hand. His jacket was slung over his other shoulder. His hair was as limp as his tie. "I haven't felt this tired since the day my ex took me to court. Hayek placed us at the very core of an active bull market. We talked the market up five percent in less than ten hours. Biggest short-term dollar rise in over a year. Everybody's watching us. The brokers, the Street, everybody. I've got dealers I haven't heard from in years calling me out of the blue, asking why I wasn't there for the

Forex convention this weekend, talking to me like I've been lost in the Sumatran jungle and all of a sudden they want to play my best pal."

"Which means everybody's looking to hear what big news Hayek is holding," Colin surmised. "That doesn't make sense to me. If it was big enough to talk up the dollar, how could he keep it quiet with the whole world sniffing around?"

"Listen to you." Alex pushed through the doors and entered the parking area. "A backroom geek figures it out after I've spent all day hammering on the other senior traders, getting nowhere at all. All they want to know is what bonus they're clearing off this deal."

Alex twisted his neck back and forth, hearing it creak. The moon was brilliant enough to outshine the yellow lights rimming the parking area. Cicadas played a summertime chorus in the empty lot across the street. Alex murmured, "Almost looks normal."

"Whatever that is," Colin agreed.

"I tell you something, sport. A couple of billion put the other way, a flash of bad news, and you're going to see people start dumping dollars, stocks, bonds, the works. We're talking full-scale panic."

Colin found himself not merely listening to Alex's words. Suddenly he heard not with his ears alone, but rather with an auxilliary system that did not belong to him at all. He felt another's presence, gentle as the breath that no longer sighed on his cheek, and it stopped him in his tracks.

He searched the night, saw nothing but softly rattling palms and pools of light in an asphalt sea. He was missing something. The message had not come in words but rather in a whisper of wind. Colin asked, "What would happen?"

The yellow streetlights turned Alex's features metallic and impossibly hard. "The market would panic in stages. First there'd be this flurry of reverses. The Fed would probably intervene at that point, and hopefully I'd be proven wrong."

The night became still. The cicadas' concert drew to a hushed close, the wind halted. "And if the Fed didn't move?"

"Ninety-nine times out of a hundred, it would. Buy a little, shove interest rates up a notch, sometimes just a good word is enough. You know, Big Brother is watching and all is well. But if the news were bad enough, then maybe the Fed's nudges might be overridden. Then there'd be the risk of the dollar sliding down to the panic stops."

"The what?"

"Every spot desk has what are called panic stops. Usually it's the lowest position that currency has hit in the previous twelve months. If the dollar ever gets to that point, the traders would automatically get out of every dollar position they held. It's called puking your positions, and it is a horrible thing to observe. And rare. I've only seen it twice, the day Reagan was shot and then the day Soros and his crowd broke the pound."

"But what *happens?*"

"Everybody in the business holding serious dollar positions has computerized stops in place. All these stops create an artificial floor. The instant the dollar touches that zone, the market would be flooded with sell orders. The dollar would shoot down a further ten, fifteen, even twenty percent."

Colin wanted to turn and shriek to the night that he was not the person to receive any such message, not with silence, not with wind, not even with Alex's words. He just did not know enough. "But it would be corrected, right? The Fed would just do more to prop up the dollar."

"The Fed *can't*. The market's gotten too big, too powerful. The day Reagan was shot, within ten minutes they had closed markets all over the world. But those ten minutes were enough for the dollar to lose eighteen percent of its value. Why? Because all those spot positions are *electronic*." Alex studied the asphalt at his feet. "Now imagine what would happen if they didn't know the cause of the slide. The President getting shot, that's a clear signal, something that will make people act fast. But what if it took them three hours to respond? Or three days?"

"The dollar would collapse," Colin said, still not seeing.

"Not just the dollar. Investors would pull out from every dollar position they held. Stocks, bonds, futures. Every market in the U.S. would drop into oblivion. There would be a full-scale destruction of the American economy."

The whisper came again, this time clear enough to turn him around.

He watched as night shadows congealed into a dark, swiftly moving shape. A black automobile shushed forward, a glimmer of oncoming death.

Colin shouted, flung his arm around Alex, and leaped forward. Together they fell behind the fender of a parked Mercedes.

As they struck the asphalt, the automobile hit the opposite fender and broke the bumper loose in a shower of sparks and shrieking metal. Despite the noise, Colin heard yet again the silent whispers, the voices from all the untried paths, the ones telling him it was not over yet.

He wrapped his arms around the sprawled senior trader and rolled, pulling them both as close to the Mercedes' undercarriage as they could go. The attacker's motor raced, the bumper tore free and clanged onto the pavement. There were two brilliant flashes and quick bangs. Then a whanging sound by Colin's ear. Then the car raced away.

Gingerly the pair of them raised up, searched the empty reaches, saw only the splash of streetlights and empty asphalt. Alex gaped about him, and demanded, "Were they after me or you?"

"Use your cellphone," Colin said. Feeling lightheaded. More. Almost light of heart as well. "Call the police."

Alex bent over and fumbled with numb fingers at the latches of his briefcase. He hesitated long enough to search the darkness once more and ask, "What should I say, we were attacked by a phantom locomotive?"

"Mention the gunshots," Colin replied. "That should get them here in a hurry."

59

Monday

THE NIGHT WAS humid and close. Heat lightning flickered occasionally, faint skyborne reflections of the neon clamor. Kissimmee was alive with a crowd that either could not afford or had no interest in the Disney world order. Eric sat in a rental car, far to one corner of the bar's parking lot. Just being there caused the gradually healing welt on his forehead to throb.

Once more the bevy of cars were parked in the handicapped zone, five of them this time, including a showstopping Lamborghini Diablo and a Mercedes 500 SEL custom convertible. Eric had come prepared for a long wait. There was no telling when the traders would emerge, probably not for hours. They had been forced to forgo the Forex convention. Like his own colleagues, they were probably determined to party with violent abandon. Eric understood them with an insider's bitter wisdom. These traders would get off on the bar's edgy danger, especially as they had bought themselves a measure of safety. They impressed the girls with their hundred dollar tips and tasted the peril like just another drug. They were a macho crowd. Almost all traders were. The floor's tension was an impossible opiate. They required somewhere loud and close to the edge to forget, even for a few hours.

Traffic along the eight-lane Highway 50 had thinned out and the clock's dial had lost all meaning by the time the traders finally straggled out. Eric watched them play the doorman like a muscle-bound joker. He saw the tension in the bouncer's shoulders, observed the clenched way he pulled his face into a smile when they handed him a two hundred dollar tip. The dregs of Eric's thermos were bitter with memories of his own similar stupidities.

He followed them along the strip. They were flying now, revving engines at the stoplights, shouting and calling back and forth between cars. Two ladies they had picked up at the joint displayed the stoic boredom of women who had seen all there was to infantile behavior. One of the cars peeled off and headed back toward Orlando. Eric decided to follow the others.

They pulled into a Denny's and made a clamorous entry. At least most of them did. One head remained visible in the back of the open-top Mercedes.

Eric waited until he could see the traders causing mayhem in the restaurant before cautiously approaching the car. The top remained down. The guy in the back was a total stranger and snoring gently. Heart in his mouth, Eric slipped his hand into the guy's jacket. Nothing on the first side. He held his breath and reached over, peeling back the other lapel. The wallet slipped out easily. He raced back to his car.

The problem with long computer entry codes was that they were almost impossible to remember. Especially now that they were changed every quarter. Hayek's system also denied code holders the privilege to personalize access. Some versions used fourteen-digit strings but were capable of being rewritten within six hours of every quarterly change. But Hayek's security program was not so flexible, which meant most people kept a written reminder close at hand.

Eric found the slip of paper sandwiched between two credit cards. He copied down the string of letters and numbers, then replaced the paper back into the wallet. He rose from his car and checked the parking lot. His blood congealed and his heart entered overdrive when he realized the guy's head was no longer visible.

Eric sprinted back to the Mercedes. The car was empty. Crouching low, he moved closer to the glass front wall, and searched the inside of the restaurant. He wasn't absolutely certain, but he didn't think the guy was among the traders carousing at the tables.

Eric spent frantic minutes searching the lot. Nothing. He crawled back to the Mercedes just to be certain the guy had not somehow reappeared. Empty.

Keeping at least one car between him and the windows, he slipped around to the entrance. The gray-haired woman on cash-register duty started to greet him, when from inside the restaurant there came a crash of dishes, and a great shout of laughter. Grimly she slipped her key from the register and hurried back. "Wait right here, please."

Eric hustled toward the washroom and pushed through the door.

The guy from the convertible eyed him blearily and slurred, "Don't feel so hot either?"

"Excuse me?"

"You're all bent over." The guy rolled his forehead against the ceramic tile. "Where'd the music go?"

"Here, try washing your face. That always works for me." Eric eased the guy toward the sink, slipping the wallet back in the process. He turned on the cold water and stepped back.

"Can't focus 'thout the music." The guy splashed his face, then raised his head and stared into the mirror. "Do I know you?"

"Not a chance."

"You look like somebody." He gave a bleary grin. "Sure. You're all banged up."

"Slipped in the bathtub."

"Nah, it's something else." Doused himself a second time. "Give me a second."

"Sorry, wrong guy." Then the outer door squeaked. Eric took another step backward, entered a cubicle, and shut the door. Heard the new voice say, "Tony, hey, what are you doing in here?"

"There's somebody in there, I know him."

"Forget it, man, he's not one of us." The voice was familiar. Not shouting, but Eric knew it instantly as the guy who had sicced the bouncer on him. The trader Colin had attacked. Brant somebody. Eric crouched lower and heard, "Look at you, man, you're a mess."

"But I was talking with somebody."

"Forget him, I tell you." There was the sound of towels being pulled out of the container. "Here, dry yourself off. Okay, good, now let's go join the party."

"Is the music gonna start again?"

The guy barked a hard laugh. "Sure man, sure. I'll have one of the little darlings sing you a song. You'll like that." The door closed.

Eric waited through three tight breaths, then slipped out and raced into the night.

60

Monday

EVENING'S APPROACH FOUND Jackie wondering if perhaps the search of her old university books was merely a quest for fables. Eric's silence only compounded the lack of solutions. And she missed Wynn. The fact that she was even admitting to such an emotion left her battered by all that might still happen.

She carried her laptop out into the darkness and softly closed the balcony door behind her. An earlier rain had cleared, leaving the air warm and windless and filled with the chorale of tropical springtime. The surrounding Florida oaks were twisted Chinese etchings upon a wash of stars and moonlight. Jackie turned her chair so that she was staring out over the treetops toward the north. All evening she had heard hints of churchbells fading into the distance. Now she sat and sipped at her mug and mourned how time and distance were already blurring her Roman memories. The questions she had asked herself in Rome and the faint awakenings of new hope were too fine to let slip away. She flipped open the cover of her laptop and began a new file. One she simply called *Essential.*

She stopped only when fatigue stripped her words of meaning. The wind rose with the night, whispering in the language of trees and night-birds that such thoughts were too vital to be addressed with a sleepy heart. She closed the laptop, stretched, and felt as good about the hour as she had in a long time. She was not finished. In fact, she had scarcely begun. But admitting there was reason enough to remember, and to question, was the biggest step she had taken in years.

□ □ □ □

JACKIE WAS SO dead asleep, she thought at first the sound came from thunder. Then the house trembled about her, and once again she was faced with a fear she could not handle. Terror tossed her from her bed and slammed her into the side wall with the accuracy of a catapult. She tumbled to the floor and landed hard on something plastic, cracking it into shreds. She shook the stars from her eyes and crawled to her kitchen, where she pulled a drawer down on top of her, making all the noise of a construction site in full swing. Which left her no choice but to scream, "I've got a gun!"

"Stop, hey, no!" The shadow silhouetted against the dawn screamed almost as loud and certainly as high as she had. "It's me!"

"Eric?" She managed to scramble over close enough to see the young-old features through her screen door. Relief surged into an anger so strong she could have stabbed him through the wire. "Do you have any idea how you just scared me?"

"Join the club. Put down that knife, will you? And let me in."

Her fingers made hard going of the hook. "You've got it?"

"Where's the letter from Shane?"

"Wait a second." She turned on the light, walked back to her desk, and pulled out the envelope from beneath her laptop. On the floor by the alcove she saw the shards of what had formerly been her cellphone. "You really have the code?"

"Put down that knife, okay? Yeah, I've got it." He flapped open a sheet of paper, his features bloodless. "But this is it, right? No more contacts, no changing your mind. I don't ever want to see you again."

"Yes." She made the exchange. Studied the scant notations. "This is all I need?"

"Long as you know what you're doing." He opened the envelope, gave it a quick read, and said bitterly, "If the drunk remembers me or that other guy puts two and two together, I'm dead meat."

"What are you talking about?"

"Never mind. What's important is I don't have to see you again. Am I right?"

"Far as I'm concerned, it's over."

"You won't tell Hayek?"

"Not a word."

"Right." He started toward the door, then added, "The numbers may be coded. You know, the first three digits one number forward, the next three back. That's what I do. And be careful when you access the computer, it may have a silent alarm that goes off if the wrong codes are put in. We had a guy use the previous quarter's code once. Security swarmed."

Jackie followed Eric outside, watched him tumble down the stairs and hurry away. She lowered herself onto the top step, massaging the place on her forehead where she had slammed into the wall. Like it or not, she needed to find herself a bolt-hole. A few more terror attacks like this and there wouldn't be anything left for Hayek to mangle.

61

Tuesday

THE NEXT MORNING, Colin arrived at Hayek's headquarters two hours earlier than normal. Vague desires and shattered dreams had chased him from his apartment and driven with him down gray and empty lanes. He sat in the parking lot and yearned for a world he had only known within Lisa's gaze.

The day had begun on a miserable note. Unable to sleep, he had done his regular scan of Havilland's files just before six, only to find himself assaulted from the most unexpected direction. Fury had launched him from his chair, leaving him pulling his hair and shouting silent epitaphs against Havilland, against Lisa, against this benighted place and time.

Jackie Havilland had opened a new file called *Essentials*. It was as if Lisa had reached across space and time to strike a final blow. Somehow Jackie Havilland had arrived at the same point as Lisa and begun to ask the same questions. He could not shrug this off as mere coincidence. The enigma could not be so comfortably dismissed. Fate's blind hand could not simply have plucked two such unlikely people and hurled them into the darkness, only to have them *both* come to the same conclusion. Colin had stared at the pilfered words on his screen and found pure agony in Jackie Havilland's desperate wish to hold this same impossible vision.

Now as he walked through the overcast dawn, he yearned not for whispers but the voice of a woman who once had spoken to him of timeless love. A voice so melodious it had merely to breathe into his ear for him to hear the chant of ages and music from the stars. Her absence left him confronted by his own emptiness in all its skeletal horror.

He was almost relieved to enter the front office and be confronted by a day already running at hypertense speed. Alex and the barrel-chested derivatives trader stood by the reception desk, talking with a gray-suited man Colin had never seen before. Every seat in the foyer was taken by senior traders. All eyes were on him. Tight gazes, tense features. Faces from the floor.

Alex waved him over. "Want you to meet Thorson Fines. Chief of the Capital Markets division over at First Florida. This is our resident e-guru, Colin Ready."

Without looking over, Thorson gave him the sort of onetime up-and-down handshake traders reserved for people not of their tribe, and thus below their contempt. "Right."

Alex kept him there because Fines wanted him gone. "We all got calls from the pickle woman. You know who I mean?"

Colin nodded. Hayek's secretary.

"She woke us up at a quarter to five. Wasn't it about then, Barry?"

"You got me," the derivatives man replied, eyeing Fines as he would a fish dead far too long. "All I know is, the phone sounded like the gong of doom."

Fines spoke up then. "What, we're filling in the backroom gophers now? Letting them know we're here on what I was told is highly confidential business?"

"Miss Prunella sounded like she'd been at her desk for hours." Alex ignored Fines' comment entirely. "The lady probably mainlines coffee at midnight, just keeps chugging along. She goes, 'Mr. Hayek will see you promptly at half-past six. Be ready.' As if I always go upstairs with my pants at half-mast. Ready for what, I ask her. But the old dear had already plunked down the phone."

Barry said to Colin, "Alex told us about your set-to in the parking lot last night."

"The kid here saved my bacon," Alex confirmed. "Got to see if I can't work up a special bonus."

"That's really not necessary."

Barry asked, "Did the lizard lady call you as well?"

"No."

"So what gives, you always show up this early?"

But the elevator doors opened then, and Hayek's secretary announced, "This way, if you would please."

Colin waited until the senior traders had filed obediently inside, then proceeded back through the trading room. A number of traders, no doubt alerted by their bosses, were already at their desks. They worked the screens and checked contacts in the Far East, where the markets had long been open. They shouted worldwide positions to allies at various stations about the floor. Already the entire building held the charged atmosphere of a day brought to the heated brink of storm and kept there far too long. The air was so filled with frenetic particles Colin felt ready to gnaw off his own limb, if only he could determine which one held him chained to this place.

Alex stopped by Colin's cubicle about fifteen minutes later. "Hayek heard about the attack in the parking lot. He wanted to make sure everything was still attached and in working order."

"That's why he called you in?"

"Partly. Also wanted to have us meet with Thorson as one of the clan. You understand?"

"All one big family."

"A family swimming in cash. We're getting another two billion today. Maybe more. Hayek makes the announcement like a king bestowing favors. Like the cash is all his."

"He wants you to buy more dollars?"

"My guess is, he's stoking up the market. But for what reason, I can't figure out. If we get hit by bad news, the dollar's so high investors will flee like lemmings and the markets will crash right through the floor." Alex was sheet-white with the coming strain. "When I mentioned the possibility, the guy actually laughed. It creaked from disuse."

"What do you want me to do?"

"How about a little backdoor op? Could you sneak into the glass cage upstairs and see what they're doing? Hayek kept Thorson in there after we were shown out. I tried to hang around upstairs, but Miss Prunella sent me packing."

"You want me to slip into their network," Colin interpreted. "And see if they're buying dollars like you are."

"Can you?"

"Not directly. But maybe I could tap into the outgoing call system, see who they're talking to. Give you some numbers for you to call yourself."

Alex nodded grim approval. "They got a name for that?"

"Sure. It's called phreaking."

"A couple of contacts will do. Just enough to make sure we're all working for the same team. Don't hang around long enough for them to get a line on you."

Colin was already moving, keying in, prepping the attack order. "Give me half an hour."

Forty-five minutes later, Colin passed through the rear trading floor door and entered a maelstrom. A shouting, screaming delirium. There were no individual voices, no clear words. None. Just one great solid howl.

Each trader held two phones and raged into mikes. Senior traders, unable to make themselves heard over the younger, louder voices made do with hand signals. Squawk boxes were turned on full, and the brokers were raging back at them. On the wall to Colin's right, the Bloomberg wire streamed fiery gold letters across a red-tide background.

He spotted Alex in the middle of the spots arena, pointing and chopping in six directions at once. Colin waited and hoped for a calm moment, but he was seeking sunshine in a tornado of cash.

Colin moved over to where Eric sat watching his screens and chewing his pen. Up close, the cut splitting Eric's eyebrow ran a red crease down his cheek and ended with the healing tear above his lip. The young trader emitted a tension that all the nonchalance in the world could not mask. His gaze skittered across the trading floor, the screens, the glassed-in balcony overhead. Colin asked him, "You've been sidelined?"

"Alex has me on euros to yen. Bottom of the day's feeding barrel. Look at them out there. I'm missing all the fun."

Colin had to shout to be heard. "So what's happening?"

"Dollar's flying, ready for a fall. Up two cents since the opening bell." He drew out his pen and inspected it for defects. "Poor old dollar."

Colin started to move on but had to fend his way around a trio screaming in midaisle. Alex moved up from the aisle's other end, shoved them apart, and shouted loud enough to semidull the frenzy in three sets of red-rimmed eyes. "You duke it out on your own time! Right now I want a price. Dollars to anything! Any price! Now move!"

When they swung back into position, he drew Colin over with a jerk of his head. "What have you got?"

"Nothing. I've got nothing." Colin hated having to admit defeat. "I tried every avenue I could. They've got the entire system blocked up tight as FEMA."

"They didn't catch you."

"No. I was careful."

Alex was talking loud, but the surrounding din swallowed his words almost before they reached Colin's ear. "I did some calling of my own. The guys upstairs are buying as well. But take a careful look."

Colin did so. Things were busy, but not chaotic. There was time for an occasional glance down below. He stiffened as he caught sight of the blond deadhead, the one who had planted a surveillance bug in his cubicle.

Alex scowled up at them. "Like vultures waiting for the kill."

THE CALL FROM the trading floor was so frantic Colin could not understand the problem, merely the urgent need. That it came at all was both good and bad. Good because it gave him the chance to rescue Eric. Bad because it started the clock ticking down to his own personal destruction.

He and another backroom techie made a frenzied effort to discover why the floor had suddenly lost contact with Bloomberg. The wire service was a key source, running approximately a half hour ahead of television news. The electronic read-board ran across the upper left wall, visible from every trading station. Anytime there was a significant development, the wire ran what was called a blast message, alerting the traders to breaking data. At least, that was the principle. In reality, multiple pages of information poured in constantly from the Bloomberg wire, from the television monitors tuned to the twenty-four-hour news services, from the phones, from the data passing across traders' screens, or shouted from one desk to another. The trading floor consistently ran one step ahead of data meltdown.

The junior techie held Colin's ladder and handed up tools as he refitted the jacks, which had somehow been yanked completely free. The floor gave him a raucous cheer as the news began racing again at normal speed. Alex then turned on the hoot'n'holler, the PA system that broadcast to the entire floor, and said what he did about that time every day, "All right, listen up, gang. Let's take a moment for the midmorning catch-up."

Colin tuned out the summary of currency positions and interest-rate spreads, followed by Alex's slant on what effect the current news would have on later-day positions. But every trader on the floor took careful notes, their attention focused on incoming ammo.

From his position on the ladder, Colin was the only person on the floor to spot the four faces moving to the balcony's glass wall.

One face belonged to the deadhead, Brant Anker, minus shades. Another trader stood to one side. Jim Burke, the Unabomber, stood beside the mystery trader. To the deadhead's other side was the senior security man, Dale Crawford. The unknown trader was pointing down at the floor and talking volubly. The security chief said something in response. Another security guard moved up alongside Crawford. All attention was focused upon one desk on the trading floor. Colin did not need to turn around to know what they saw.

Colin took it easy climbing down the ladder, not wishing to draw attention his way. He handed his tools to the other techie and said as calmly as he could manage, "Clear this up, will you. I've got something else to see to."

He strolled down the back aisle, taking it slow, ignoring the gradually re-amping noise from the floor. Eric did not look up at his approach. Colin used his body to block his motion from the balcony, as he jammed his thumb hard into Eric's side.

"Hey!" The guy turned around, to all the world just another trader whose world had narrowed down to four screens and three telephones. But the welt was still there on his forehead, the lip still bruised, the shadow ghosts still in his gaze. "What the—"

"Run," Colin said, notching his head a fraction toward the balcony. "Now."

Colin strolled over to the back door, then turned and shouted a silent scourge upon all the day. Eric still sat at his desk. The young trader stared dumbly at Colin. Colin glanced up and saw that the balcony was empty. He said to Eric and the enveloping chaos, "Worse and very much worse still."

Then he flew.

Had he more time to think things over, perhaps he would have done nothing at all. Just let Eric be trapped and flayed and tied to the sacrificial altar. But there was no time for anything then except action.

Colin raced back to his cubicle. He flipped open his box of auxiliary gear and set up an emergency firewall. Two rotating electronic eyes the size of matchboxes were perched on the cubicle's walls, angled so they monitored the aisles, the back passage, and the door to the trading floor. On his four monitors he threw up patterns designed for this very purpose, numbers and code in haphazard scrambles that would appear to the unknowing eye as work-in-progress.

Colin yanked out the fastest computer from beneath his desk and plugged in the latest of his acquisitions, a gift from a contact on the hardware side. The salesman had passed over top-of-the-line experimental gear in hopes that Colin would put in a good word when they next upgraded the floor. The new heads-up display looked like the bug-eyed sunglasses worn by the San Francisco deadhead. The heads-up was made for 3-D gaming. But the eye-level monitors were so finely calibrated he could read script. He coded in the entry pattern for slipping inside the company's maintenance computer. Then he overrode the security camera system and spied in on the trading floor. He cursed softly when the first thing he saw was Dale Crawford and another security guy entering the trading floor with Jim Burke.

Colin observed helplessly as they came at Eric from two sides, cutting off his escape. Eric watched their approach in helpless horror. Only when the security chief gripped him by the shoulder did he start screaming. The camera caught the open mouth, the terror-stricken eyes, the way Eric clutched at his chair, the desk, his neighbor. They ripped his hands away and dragged him across the floor. Burke shouted something, the words lost to Colin's silent vision. The other traders remained static, inert.

An idea did not take shape so much as explode into his brain. Colin flipped from the camera viewing the frozen-tundra display of the trading room floor to the one monitoring the reception area. He saw Eric's silent shouts and futile scramblings as Crawford and the other security goon held him and waited for the elevator. Colin worked at a blinding pace, keying in commands, finally finding a logical reason for all the hours spent wandering about the company's various systems.

He was there and ready when the elevator doors opened. His timing was exact, the seconds pared into careful instants packed with hundreds of heartbeats and dozens of breaths, as though he was amped to Eric's level. Not out there screaming and dragging his heels across the granite-tiled floor. But there just the same.

Dale Crawford stepped inside the elevator, trying to drag Eric with him. But Eric had managed to lock one arm around the reception desk's nearest stanchion. While the other guard sought to pry his fingers loose, Burke stepped into the elevator and pulled on one of Eric's legs, adding his muscle to Crawford's, trying to wrench Eric free.

Colin slammed the elevator doors shut. Hard.

Alarm bells went off in the distance. The doors opened back up at his command. Crawford had lost his grip and was leaning, stunned, against the elevator's back wall. But the Unabomber, who had also just been semimashed by the elevator doors, still had his hands locked around Eric's leg. So Colin ordered the doors shut again. Harder still.

The pretty Hayek receptionist, known for her icy demeanor and unflappable calm, was in full panic mode. She was up behind her chair, hair out at all angles, screaming silently. The elevator doors opened again, but only far enough for Burke to drop in a limp, defeated huddle. Colin swiftly reshut the door before the security chief could emerge, and sent the machine to the basement. And watched.

The single remaining guard was no match for a hyperamped Eric. The frantic young trader released his grip on the stanchion only to grab the brass trash can. He hammered the guard's blond fuzz. Then he did his best to rearrange the guy's upper mandible and nose and right temple. On the third blow the guard staggered back a step. Eric hurled the can at him and fled through the front doors.

Just in time. Burke and the security chief came racing up the stairs and were swiftly joined by two other guards. Burke was limping. He used the reception desk for support as they shouted at the guard who sprawled in the corner, too stunned from Eric's onslaught to respond. Then they turned to the terror-stricken receptionist, who pointed one trembling hand toward the front doors.

But Colin was ready for them. The doors were locked.

He watched them try to batter their way futilely through the bullet-proof glass, then turn and shout and point behind. Which gave Colin the instant required to strip off the display, pocket the tiny cameras, clear the screens, and join all the others standing at the entrances to their cubicles and watching openmouthed as the Unabomber and the

muscle came roaring by. They crashed through the back doors and careened out of sight.

Colin did not join in the subsequent chatter, however. He was under
no illusions. Sooner or later they would track him down. Just like Eric.
He returned to his desk and pretended to work. No question. He was
toast. It was just a matter of time.

62

Tuesday

KAY CAUGHT WYNN just as he and Carter were about to enter the committee room. "You heard anything from our Florida friend?"

"Not since last night." He refrained from adding that he had tried to call Jackie twice that morning. He had gotten nothing but a busy signal on her landline, and no connection on the cellphone. He was missing her mightily. "Why?"

"Just grabbing at straws. We're losing."

"But there's still time for a turnaround, right?"

"Time is not the issue here. We need a miracle, and we need it yesterday. Things are coming apart."

A voice called from behind them, "Kay, just a minute please."

The senator's expression hardened further. "This was not what I want right now."

Jackson Taylor was not a handsome man. Normally he affected enough polish to hide his natural state, which was that of a man who had bullied and blustered and fought so many corporate scraps they were stamped upon his features like pox. Today's rage made tatters of his facade, and lay bare the simian bulge to his cheeks and jaw. "You don't feel it's necessary to return calls from your own party chairman?"

"I apologize, Jackson. But we have been incredibly busy, as you well know."

Jackson halted Wynn's progress toward the chamber entrance. "Stay right where you are, please. I've got words for you as well." He turned back to Kay. "You folks were very eloquent about this cause of yours."

"Mr. Chairman—"

"Wait, now. It's my hand on the gavel, and I've got something to say. We've made a good-faith effort to help you out here. But this particular provision doesn't stand a chance."

"With respect, I disagree."

"Do you have the vaguest idea what kind of stink bomb you've let loose? How could you possibly expect me to support your position on this bill?" He swept his arm about, connecting with all the unseen foes. "The banks have all the clout in the world. We've got their lobbyists swarming around this place like a battalion of Gucci cockroaches."

"You don't need to support us, Mr. Chairman," Kay replied quietly. "Just don't get in our way."

"You're not hearing me, Senator. This issue is dead. I want you to help me bury it as quietly as we possibly can."

Kay's voice held desperate appeal. "The international banking business needs to be placed under tighter regulatory control. But the nature of the modern-day beast has changed. Finance has gone global. So the only way to control it is to do likewise. What better way than to tie it to debt relief, give these extremely poor nations a helping hand?"

"Spare me, okay? We're all done here."

"I'm not withdrawing the amendment, Jackson."

"Then we're burying you along with the proposal. I am siding with the opposition and readying an emergency spending measure to counteract the loss of the appropriations, at least temporarily."

"I think you're making a terrible mistake."

"That's your reaction?" He punched the sides of his hips instead of somebody else. "What happened to your political sense, Kay? I thought I could rely on you to see the light while you still could."

"Excuse me, Mr. Chairman," she replied stiffly, turning for the door. "I have a committee to chair."

Jackson Taylor waited for her to vanish through the door before turning his ire on Wynn. "Who's behind this madness of yours?"

"I should be asking you the same thing."

"You've succeeded in raising the hackles of some of our biggest supporters. You might be green when it comes to politics, but a guy with your experience ought to know you don't hang your top clients out to dry." He closed the distance between them, moving in near enough for Wynn to see the tiny flecks in his eyes, bloodstains from previous wars. "It's payback time for all the misery you put me and my company through. If I could, I'd sell tickets to the spectacle of watching you crash and burn."

63

Tuesday

ORLANDO WAS EXPERIENCING a foretaste of summer, a wet and sticky misery that sent the last snowbirds drilling their Buicks through the soggy air hanging over I-95. Rain was predicted for that afternoon, but Jackie knew the heat would not truly abate until the hurricanes of September. She was in for five months of growing certainty that Alaska might actually be a decent place to live.

Jackie worked at her dinette table wearing cutoffs and a tank top. Tension radiated off her in waves as strong as the heat. Her laptop was logged onto the Trastevere site, but so far her twice-hourly messages to the Boatman had elicited no response. The white screen was a major fear factor. She had no idea how to access Hayek's computers or run the code. She hated the fact that she had become so dependent upon a ghost, a guy she had seen only once, and who up to now had given her nothing but more mysteries and riddles. But there was no one else. What was she supposed to do, take this to her Washington pals, say she wanted to break into a hedge fund's mainframe with a stolen access code?

Jackie looked down at the book in her lap. She had been stuck on the same page for almost an hour. She was no closer to discovering why she had felt so drawn to the old textbooks. Three days of searching had done nothing but pluck away the scabs, leaving her dripping from the blood of old memories. To make matters worse, aftershocks from Eric's midnight appearance transformed every outside noise into an attack by goblins and fiends.

She slammed the book shut, reared back, and flung it crashing into the side wall. She leaped to her feet, kicked at the scattered books, and stomped across the room. Slamming open her screen door, she raised her fists to the dismal sky. "We're on the same team, right? How about a little help here?"

She lowered her fists as the back door to the big house creaked open. Millicent Kirby crabbed out, blinking in the light as if it were the first day she'd seen in months. Jackie sighed and made her way down the steps, calling ahead, "It's all right. I wasn't talking to anybody. I'm just having a tough morning."

The old lady waited until Jackie was standing by the rotting back stairs to ask, "Are the bad men coming back?"

Jackie did not have the strength to lie. "Maybe." She felt her insides clutch up tight with the fear of being asked to leave.

Millicent Kirby just plucked at the mole on her neck and stared at the heat-drenched day. "It's hard to be alone in the dark, isn't it."

WHEN THUNDER RUMBLED across the afternoon sky, Jackie re-emerged to commune with the storm. She leaned against the stair railing and flapped the sweaty T-shirt against her belly. She promised herself a good hard run once the lightning had passed and the rain settled down to a cooling drone.

Then she spotted the figure scampering down her drive. He ran like a skinny hamster, searching out the walls to a cage from which he had already escaped. Twice he paused to sniff the air, or so it seemed from where she stood. Jackie squinted as lightning blasted close enough for the sound to come with the flash, a great crackling boom that sent her tumbling down the stairs.

The young man cowered midway between the back of the main house and the garage, as though trapped in amber and not heavy rain-drops. Jackie saw no danger to his expression or the way he huddled under his jacket. He shouted at her, "Are you permanently deranged?"

Recognition of the voice with its slight accent flashed in time to the thunderbolt. And the storm became more appropriate still. "Boatman?"

"I've tried your phones for *hours*. Your landline was constantly busy and your cellphone is disconnected." His red-rimmed eyes were as devoid of color as the sky, his gaunt features held a waxy cast. "Tell me that wasn't intentional."

It was her own turn for rage. "Where have you *been*?"

"Busy. And believe me, you don't want to know more than that." He flinched, taking the rain as he would blows from above. "I hope your computer is functioning. I was forced to depart in a hurry. The only thing I carried with me was my phone. Which has proved to be of no benefit whatsoever."

"It's working."

"Excellent." He scampered forward. "Is there someplace safe where we can get to work?"

"I'm not sure. About the safety part, I mean."

64

Tuesday

JACKIE STOOD BY THE doorway, scarcely able to take in the fact that he was here and real and even named. "Let me get this straight. You were a hacker before you became one of Hayek's computer nerds?"

Colin Ready's hands flew through the process of establishing internet pathways on Jackie's laptop. "Corporations like to pretend they're totally secure. Bankers are the worst of the lot. They want the world to think they're absolutely invincible, never taking a wrong step. Well, we're the gremlins who pass on a much-needed dose of electronic truth. In a fair world, we'd be getting paid for doing mankind a service. But whoever said this world was fair?"

"Tell me," she agreed.

"I started hacking when I was twelve. Phreaking when I was fourteen. By then I knew I had to keep this second life separate. I worked hard at the mask called life, made it all the outside world saw. But inside I knew better. After my parents divorced I became a pawn in the battle they'd started before I was born. The outside world was compacted misery, as far as I was concerned. I'd get on a bus, spend an hour going five miles in city traffic, all so I could attend a school where the kids dreamed about dates so they could grow up and argue like my parents, or cars so they could drive and get stuck in more traffic. What kind of life was that? Then I'd go home, tap a few keys, and be exploring the other side of the world. Entering new universes. Building magic kingdoms of my own. Or best of all, sneaking through the enemy's minefields, killing their dragons, stealing the keys, and entering the secret domains. It was the only life worth living."

"What were you called? Your hacker name, I mean. Not Boatman."

"O-zone. What can I say. I was fourteen." Impatiently he ran his fingers impatiently about the edges of the keyboard. "This download is taking forever. I feel like I've moved back into the stone age, using a standard phoneline modem."

"It's all we've got."

"Then it will have to do." He started tapping keys. "We'll go in through a back door I opened weeks ago, preparing for this. I hacked into the Atlanta federal reserve bank."

"Tell me you're kidding."

"Not the money-control section. That place has guard dogs with titanium teeth. Just the external comm link. These drone machines disperse the daily Fed releases to all the regional banks. I was astonished at how lax their security was. Making entry was a piece of cake." His calm tone was utterly disconnected from the fingers tapping the board. "But the address is the same, which means any local bank will still recognize us as a signal from on high."

"This is a terrible idea."

"Relax. We won't go in directly. First we'll phreak our way around the globe, lay out a false trail."

When she remained standing with her arms clenched tight across her chest, Colin halted and looked up. "In or out. Now is the time."

"Can I trust you not to get us fried?"

He replied simply, "This is what I do."

"Okay. Fine." She pulled a chair over next to his. "I'm in."

"Right." He turned back to his boards. "First we need to phreak into a secure connection." He hesitated again. "Do you want to hear, or should I just go and do?"

"I'm in, I told you. I want it all."

"Okay. Like all computer skills, phreaking has evolved through a gazillion generations since the early days. We're not talking about just stealing phone time any more. Nowadays the phreaker is after non-traceability."

She watched things flicker across the screen as he typed, symbols she had never seen before. "This is Sanskrit you're writing?"

"Just a little code. Relax. Okay, now I'm dialing an 800 number I've already checked out. It's what we call a high-impact line. High impact means constant access, used by hundreds of people."

"Do you know who?"

"Sure." He let a little of his own excitement show through. "As far as the outside world is concerned, we're just calling the home office of the drive-happy people."

The computer chimed. He swung back. "Right. Now I'm downloading files I've stored on my own secure website. Once that's done, we're going to play a prerecorded tonal message using a digitized recording. The tones are actually a series of messages most often used by busy execs given codes to access the corporate 800 number for *outgoing* calls. Follow me?"

"Maybe."

"This company has perhaps a couple of hundred execs in the field. Any of them can call the company's 800 incoming number, punch in a code, and get an outgoing line on the corporation's trunk line."

"And save the company the cost of a long-distance call. Smart."

"Precisely." The computer screen lit up with the word *Linked*. "Now just to be certain, we're going to use this line to call another company." He pulled up a list, scrolled down until he settled on one, and said, "Hong Kong. Perfect. Right, we're through. And now one more time, how does Zurich sound to you?"

"Amazing."

"We're ready now. Hidden behind three companies' phone networks, the messages traveling ten thousand miles in each direction. Time lapse, just under five minutes. All while using a nonserver system that operates at a speed barely above snail mail."

"You're showing off."

"Maybe a little." His fingers were a maestro's blur. "We're going to the Atlanta federal reserve now. And . . . in. Their drone is excellent at following instructions. We'll have it call up the Hayek Group's mainframe." An instant later, the monitor displayed the Hayek logo, a golden phoenix rising from the flames. "I've often thought it would be a nice gesture to mankind if I changed that logo to a buzzard rising off a fresh carcass."

Jackie leaned over so as to study his face more closely. "Why do you hate him?"

"Suspicions, mostly." He held out his hand. "Let's have the code."

She unfolded the paper from Eric with the password. "Just suspicions?"

"Up to now. Maybe we can change that." He typed in the code, said, "We're in."

"What if they're monitoring this connection?"

"That's why we took precautions. We're on what is called a flash-link, utterly untraceable without raising flags. If they start hunting, the drone has orders that I inserted in an earlier foray. It will instantly sever connections and erase all related files." He was typing faster than he spoke. "Good old drone."

"Tell me about you and Hayek." When he merely kept at his work, she pressed, "This is very important, Colin."

"I met Lisa Wrede at a conference on computer security. She was a researcher at the Library of Congress. In her free time she worked for Sant'Egidio. At the request of Nabil Saad she began researching international hedge funds and currency traders. When she discovered I worked for Hayek, she wanted to break things off. Perhaps I should have let her. Life would certainly have been tons easier. But it was too late." His voice grew dim. "We argued all the time. She was constantly warning me that I would be toasted, circling the flame as I did. But I was too hooked on the life and the money and the thrill. Then it turned out she was the one who paid."

Colin's fingers slowed, then stopped. "They threw her off a roof. Hayek's men did. And it was my fault."

"You don't know that."

"I was the one who first mentioned the secret file called Tsunami." He forced himself to pick up the slip of paper and return to his typing. "We're in."

She drew in close enough to see both the screen and the rigid grip he kept on himself. "I'm so sorry about your Lisa."

"Thanks." A vein in his neck pulsed in time to her own racing heart. "Now let's focus on the attack, shall we?"

65

Tuesday

HAYEK'S SECRETARY WAS already gone for the day when Jim Burke knocked on the chairman's door. There was no sound from within. He entered, wondering what he would find. The trading floor might be filled with frenetic activity, yet up here the air was usually somehow purified, as if the King had found some way of crystallizing out the sweat and the fear. Today was different, however. The air smelled tainted with a dust so fine it coated his tongue before he even spoke. "Got a minute?"

Hayek's posture was no different. He stood at the window behind his desk, observing a tableau that on any other day would have been magnificent. The stone courtyard glistened with rain. The central lake shimmered with liquid fractures. The sky was deepest gray, except for one slit to the west where the sun lanced through. The surrounding clouds were liquid fire, and all the drops caught by the light became fairies dancing to thunder's tune. Hayek said nothing, merely swung one hand in a fractional motion, waving Burke inside.

"I have something for you." A strange choice of words. Like gift-wrapping a dagger. He motioned to the two people in the outer lobby. "Come on in."

Hayek stiffened as the San Francisco trader stepped inside. Ankers' habitual smirk had a pasted-on quality, as though borrowed from some better time. The head of security slipped in behind the trader and moved to a shadowed corner. For such a big man, Dale Crawford had an assassin's comprehension of stealth.

Nodding toward Anker, Hayek said, "I gave strict instructions for the entire team to be kept isolated."

"I asked him to join us. It was the only way." Burke waited, but the chilling force Hayek could bring to bear when contradicted did not arise. Burke said to the trader, "Tell him."

"We've been working for days to get inside Colin Ready's system. But his firewalls were too solid. We couldn't do a break-and-enter from outside."

"What is this insanity? You bring this man in to tell me one of the men responsible for computer security is doing his job?"

Burke hesitated. Not because of his own news, but rather because of Hayek's response. The bark was there, but not the fire. His trader's senses sorted through the change, both in the man and in the air. And came up with the only possible option. "You already know?"

"What is there to know, that Colin Ready works as a spy? We've been through this before. Did you think the Brazilians and the Russians and the Japanese would simply grant us their billions and walk away?"

But there was more. Burke watched as Hayek reached into his engraved gold case for a cigar and realized the chairman sought something for his trembling fingers to hold. For the first time since entering Hayek's world, Burke was afraid. He said to Anker, "Tell him."

Anker swallowed hard enough for Burke to hear. "Colin Ready left early today."

"Right after the incident with that young trader," Burke supplied.

"We circumvented his passwords and entered using his own system," Anker continued. "It took hours, but we finally did it. We found a message from Jackie Havilland. She claims to have one of our traders' access codes."

"I've already shut down the system," Burke said. "We don't know how long they've been in, or even if they managed to enter at all. But nobody and nothing can do it now. Tonight we'll reconfigure the entire system. Everyone will have new passwords waiting for them in the morning."

Hayek reached for his heavy desk lighter and made a ritual of firing up his cigar, inspecting the smoldering tip, blowing the smoke on and on for what to Burke seemed like hours. He then looked directly at Anker for the first time. "Not a word of this to anyone."

"N-no sir. I wouldn't dream—"

"Get out." He held Burke in place with a stab of the cigar. When Anker was gone, he continued, "You have the article prepared?"

"Ready and waiting."

"Plant it after the morning papers have gone to press, but in time for the news shows. They'll leap at the chance of breaking a story this big ahead of the newspapers." He glanced toward the corner where the security man still stood. "You have the woman's address?"

"Already checked it out," Crawford answered. "Just waiting for your green light."

"Do it."

Burke said, "I want to go with Crawford. I want to watch Colin and this Havilland woman pay." When Hayek did not respond, Burke licked his lips and took another tiny taste of the air. He found no comfort, no assurance. Only the dust of crypts. "You were right all along. The woman was poison."

66

Tuesday

WHEN THEY WERE in the car, Burke said, "Give me a gun." Crawford glanced over and gave his patented little smile, but said nothing. He was a strange sort of man, moving in whispers to match his voice. Unfazed by anything. Watching the world with the tight leer of one who had seen and done it all.

"What, you think I can't handle it?" Burke felt more than heat grip his gut. Anything that caused Hayek fear made serious tremors to his universe and had to be viciously stomped out. "I want—"

"It doesn't matter what you want." Crawford pulled the nonde-script Chevy into a busy service station and killed the motor. "Guns are for making statements. Guns leave messages."

"That's what we want."

"I was there same as you. I didn't hear the man say a thing about statements. Don't go getting slick on me, now. You hear what I'm saying?"

"These people are a genuine menace."

"Aren't they all." Crawford slid from the car. He started to walk away, then leaned back down and added, "Try to remember this is just a job. Nothing more. That's the way to stay safe."

Burke watched Crawford enter the service station and recalled the last time he had seen him in action. Burke had gone along against Hayek's wishes that day, not certain himself why he had wanted to be present. In fact, Burke had not been clear on why Hayek had wanted the job done at all. But when the order was passed on to Crawford, Burke had included the lie that Hayek wanted him there as a witness. Crawford had offered another of his tight-lipped smiles but said nothing at all. Leaving Burke with the sense that he knew more about what was going through Burke's head than Burke did himself.

That particular day had been the third annual march on the IMF and World Bank general congresses in Washington, D.C. As predicted, the protest had proved far more successful than the earlier marches. They had picked up the woman as she left her apartment that frosty spring morning, then used the cover of the city's chaos to drive downtown and enter the deserted underground garage of a hotel where Crawford had taken a room. From their rooftop perch they had watched the city become a six-mile-long street party. The police were on strict orders to maintain some semblance of control while not provoking any of the violence that had created such worldwide publicity in Seattle.

The marchers had taken the turning where Lafayette Park met Sixteenth Street. Then the leaders had turned to harangue the protesters and amp up the volume. Burke had stood at a slight distance, feeding off the actions, watching and learning. For the first time he had noticed how Crawford's eyes were a washed-out brown, like the man was sparse even with color. His smile was the worst thing about him.

Crawford was smiling then, as he held the woman there at the roof's edge. From where Burke stood, he could hear the crowd down below but could not see them. The lip of the roof protruded just far enough to block his view of the street. Lisa Wrede had shown remarkable poise for a woman on the brink of dissolution. She had refused to look directly at either of them, staring instead up at the sky with an intensity that for some reason left Burke shivering.

The rally cheered the spokesman with the bullhorn. From this height, the clamor sawed the crisp air, adding an extra force to the day's events. The drums and noisemakers and whistles all crashed and melded together, as though some feral beast crouched in the narrow stone cavern and roared for its next meal.

Crawford glanced at Burke and spoke to him for the first time. "Stand well back, now. We don't want them hippy-dippies seeing anybody but the missy here."

He then gripped the corner of the tape sealing her mouth. Burke heard the ripping sound, watched as Lisa Wrede winced but said nothing, as if she had already left such mundane things as momentary pain far behind.

Crawford cut her hands loose, then took a firm grip on her arms. He tensed so that his every muscle clenched tight, right up to the cords around the edge of his jaw.

Lisa Wrede continued to stare up at the sky, as though fascinated with the clouds.

The man moved in close enough to fill her vision with a pock-marked leer. "Be a good girl, now. Give us your very best scream."

She blinked once, and returned her gaze to the sky. In a small voice, she spoke then. Saying only, "Oh God, you are my God."

The words seemed to convulse Crawford, so that he recoiled from her rather than flinging her forward. Lisa Wrede flew out and over the lip.

Burke was himself drawn forward. He had a single momentary glimpse of the truly enormous crowd below. Then gentle fingers of air and wind turned Lisa Wrede about, so that she could glimpse the sky once more. Her clothes opened up around her, like shadows of unseen wings.

BURKE WATCHED CRAWFORD load two five-gallon plastic containers of gasoline into the trunk. The security chief then drove in a seemingly aimless pattern before halting a second time at another busy service station. When Crawford returned with two more filled canisters, Burke got out of the car. Crawford lifted them into the trunk and said merely, "Lot of old houses around Winter Park. Nothing burns fast as cured cypress."

Burke said nothing, his gaze held by what else the trunk contained. A thin leather satchel revealed a precision rifle with a long-distance scope, and a blanket was wrapped around three ax handles. Crawford gave him another of those tightly knowing smiles and said merely, "Can't hurt to be ready for whatever comes."

They parked down the street from Jackie Havilland's residence. The rain had stopped momentarily. All the world smelled of cool wet earth. Crawford led them unerringly around the main house and along the gravel drive. Silently Crawford directed Burke to walk on the grassy verge to mask their footfalls.

Burke stood alongside the lanky man and stared up at the garage apartment. Lights blazed from every window. He could distinctly hear two voices, one male, one female. A young man shouted the single word, "Amazing!" It was enough to identify him as Colin Ready. Burke started for the stairs.

Crawford stopped Burke with an iron grip. He walked over, pressed cautiously on the bottom step, then pulled back as soon as the old wood creaked. Crawford raised a warning finger at Burke before vanishing into the night.

Soon enough he was back with two canisters gripped in each hand. He refused to let Burke take one. Crawford sloshed gasoline all over the stairs, then reached as high as he could and set an open canister down upon the step. When the stair creaked faintly, the two men stared up at the backlit screen door, but saw nothing save the yellowed ceiling. The voices continued to chatter away inside.

Swiftly Crawford poured a trail of gasoline around the base of the walls. He pitched the liquid up and over the two shed doors, then moved around the corner and emptied the final unopened canister directly beneath the narrow balcony. Burke nodded understanding. The man had directed the second flash point below the only other avenue of escape.

Crawford pulled Burke back to the steps, reached into his pocket and handed over a book of matches. The man reeked of gas. Burke would have to light the fire.

Burke's heart hammered as hard as it ever did on the trading room floor. Another high discovered. He flicked a match and sent it flashing onto the stairs.

The flames started with a quiet little whoosh, a tiny puff Burke felt as much as heard. No heat, just a soft light that danced about the shed, moving so easily it was hard to realize just how fast the flames were spreading.

Crawford punched his shoulder, jabbing a finger at the night and the street. Burke shook his head and turned back to watch the flames.

Crawford gripped his arm and tugged. Burke ripped his arm free and kept his eyes on the fire.

Crawford hissed once, then turned and ran.

An instant later, Burke heard a car motor start and tires squeal. But he did not turn away. Already the flames were growing so hot he had to back off, drawing into the shadows now cast by the surrounding trees. Then the fuel canister at the back of the house caught with an enormous *whoosh*. Flames shot up higher than the roof. From inside, voices rose in alarm. Burke moved farther into the grove. He heard a siren in the background, then another. He continued moving away, but not too fast. He stumbled over a root and almost went down. Still he kept his gaze upon the apartment. Waiting for the screams.

67

Tuesday

THE DAY WAS so busy Wynn could not keep up, not even with himself. Radio, television, newspapers, magazines—he refused no one. The unaccustomed nature of the task left him shattered, even when he was merely adding his own punch to lines from the files. Carter's features became folded in upon themselves with worry, and the other staffers eyed his appearances with genuine anxiety. He took it as a compliment and soldiered on.

Several times during the day, the question was raised, had he broken the law? Wynn brushed it aside, insisting they remain focused on the Hutchings Amendment. To his surprise, they did not insist, leaving him with the impression that they were chasing nothing more than unsubstantiated rumor. So far. He spent the afternoon waiting for the incoming stealth missile, the one that could not be deflected.

But when Kay called at half-past six, it had not yet arrived. "You've decided it's a good day to die, is that it?"

"Just doing my job."

"Your job," she replied, "does not include digging your own grave with reporters for pallbearers."

"I heard the party chairman this morning, same as you."

"So?"

"There's so much heat riding on this thing now, somebody is going to take a fall. I'm setting myself on the pedestal, giving everybody an easy target."

Kay said, "For once in my life, I am truly at a loss for words."

Wynn managed a smile. "I never knew painting myself into a bull's eye could be so tiring."

"Look, why don't you join us over at Graham and Esther's tonight, give me another chance to find the right words and thank you."

He was still smiling when Carter opened the door and asked, "Are you in for a call from the fibbies?"

"This one and nothing more. I need a half hour to camp out on the sofa." He reached for the phone. "This is Wynn Bryant."

"Agent Welker here, Congressman. We've been following up on bringing your sister home. It looks like they'll release her remains sometime next week. Our people in Cairo insist it's not possible to be any more precise than that."

Wynn rubbed his face. *Remains.* "Thank you."

"I can't tell you how sorry I am. I just wanted you to know we haven't dropped the ball."

"I understand."

"Do you mind if I hit you with something else?"

"Everybody else has taken a swing today. You might as well go ahead."

"I've heard from our friend at the Fed. Hayek's group has placed themselves in an incredible position, buying dollars. We're talking mountains of greenbacks."

"You can't arrest them?"

"It's not illegal to own dollars, last time I checked. We were just wondering if your insert had anything for us."

"She's not an insert, and I can't reach her."

"If you like, we could send a couple of agents by, make sure she's okay."

Wynn hesitated, then decided it was time for drastic action. "Her name is Jackie Havilland." He read off her address and phone numbers. "You'll let me know what you find out?"

"Soon as we know something, I'll be in touch."

WYNN STRIPPED OFF his jacket and tie in one continuous motion. He stretched out on the sofa, comforted by the sounds of his office winding down. People talked, phones rang a final time, a staffer answered with his name. The noise granted him substance and a place where he belonged. At least for another few days.

He had no real sense of falling asleep. He knew where he was the entire time, lying there on the lumpy leather sofa, the slick armrest hard against the back of his head. He could even feel the rise and fall of his chest. But a patina gradually spread over him, staining him the same arid yellow as the ambassador's window back in Cairo.

The scene unfolded, not against his closed eyelids but rather across all his other senses. Gradually he listened and heard the wind pick up, until it was howling through his office as loud as it had upon their return journey through the Western Desert. The windstorm blistered his unprotected skin with lashings of sand. An ocher-and-orange storm bellowed just overhead.

The wind heightened further, until its lament shrieked and sobbed and cried words he could almost understand. A desert dirge filled his nostrils and covered his body with desiccated tears. The weight upon his chest increased until it grew hard to draw breath. He struggled, but he was pinned down now, trapped and unable to move or even weep. As he lay and wished for the strength to find a place safe from the storm he would always carry with him, he felt a liquid red burning upon his hands. The caustic blaze spread up his arms, across his chest, his face, his eyes, his heart.

"Wynn?"

He gasped, or thought he did, and found himself sitting up even before he had fully opened his eyes. Gradually the sands departed, and the howling wind diminished. Carter stood in the open doorway, watching him anxiously. "Are you sure you're up to going by the Hutchings'?"

In response, he rose and slipped on his jacket, stuffed his tie in his pocket, and brushed at his sleeves. Slapping away not dust but rather the impression that lingered from his dream. When it did not depart, he motioned for Carter to lead them out. Resigned to the fact that he would remain ever scalded by his sister's blood.

The taxi ride seemed as endless as the surrounding night. Carter spoke several times, but the words became lost in winds that still whispered and threatened. Every time Wynn blinked his eyes, he could feel the desert grit grinding away, streaking his vision and choking off his air.

When Esther opened the door for them, Wynn slipped by both her smile and her welcome and entered the crowded living room. There were at least a dozen people scattered about, many of whom Wynn recognized from the committee hearings. Graham's wheelchair was in its usual spot, the sofa alongside still dimpled from where Esther had risen. Wynn walked over and sat down.

Up close, Graham looked truly ravaged. But the eyes were brilliant, the strongest light in Wynn's entire day. Esther sat down at Wynn's other side and slid over the box of tissues. "You need to use these every once in a while and clean his face. Swallowing is such a struggle."

On the opposite sofa, Kay sat surrounded by officials and staffers. When Wynn looked over, she asked, "You all right?"

"Sure."

"I heard one of your interviews on the way over. CBS used it as their lead story, that and how the financial markets are going ballistic. The banks' spokesman did everything but blame you for the bubonic plague. You sounded very solid by comparison. Very sane."

A young woman in one of the dining room chairs said, "If I read this correctly, Senator, I'd say we should hit them head-on. Explain that the currency traders acting for hedge funds and private equity funds are the ones imperiling the financial health of our nation. Not us."

Kay exchanged smiles with Carter, two people who had been at the game for a very long time. She said, "Tell her for me."

"Your ideas are fine," Carter said. "But they won't wash."

"It's all too far away," Kay agreed. "None of this really concerns the average person. That's why the banking lobby's managed to wreak as much legislative havoc as they have."

"Our only hope," Carter said, "lies in finding something that will put a local face on this thing. Something that defines a threat people can point to and say, this could cost me big time."

"Other than a severe recession," Kay added. "Or a meltdown of our banking system. Let's try to avoid both of those."

Wynn turned his attention back to the figure in the wheelchair. Graham reached out the one hand still mobile, a trembling leaf fighting his own storms. Wynn gripped it very gently, and allowed his hand to be drawn back over to rest upon the wheelchair arm. He could feel every bone beneath Graham's skin. But there beside this man who could do little more than sit and wait for death to strike the final blow, Wynn found peace. The winds stopped their whispered wrath. He could swallow down the sorrow born of all his futile days, and breathe free.

The phone rang. Esther rose to answer. The talk swirled. Beyond the window the night glowed with tiny lights that came and braved the darkness for a time, then departed. Wynn stayed where he was, listening to all the lessons the old man left unspoken.

"Wynn?"

Esther gazed down at him, both hands clutching the phone to her chest. "Something terrible has happened."

68

Tuesday

O UR AGENTS FOUND the house by the light the fire made
against the rain." Agent Welker sounded grim as the news he carried, hard as the night. "The old place went up like a torch. Rain was
hissing and dancing off the roof. The local cops stopped a lone male
driving a Chevy with stolen plates. Turns out he smelled like he'd
bathed in gasoline. Had quite an arsenal in his trunk. He refused to supply any ID. They're holding him on suspicion of arson."

The room around him was a single set of eyes, silent as the grave.
"What about Jackie?"

"I'm sorry, Congressman. I really am. The agents tried to make it
up the stairs. The place was a furnace. These are good men, believe me,
I checked. If they say they tried, that's what they did."

A chiming came from where his jacket was slung over the sofa
back. Wynn gestured at the room, urging someone to pick up his phone.
Carter was the first to move. "I understand."

"Apparently the agents heard music and they think a voice. But
who was actually in there, we won't know until the firemen finish going
through the ashes."

Carter stepped over to him and said, "It's Jackie."

The agent heard that. "You've got the woman on another line?"

"Hold on a second," Wynn said, trading phones. "Are you all
right?"

"Barely. We almost had a heart attack. We were just working away,
minding our own business, then whoosh. The whole place went up like
a bomb."

Jackie did not sound the least bit worried. In fact, if Wynn had to
put a name to her tone, it would have been elation. "Where are you?"

"Millicent Kirby's upstairs front room. We wanted to go to a hotel but Millicent wouldn't leave her house. We knew they were on to us soon as they cut our feed into Hayek's mainframe. But we had enough by then. Almost everything, in fact. Colin just did these huge dumps. Basically ever since then we've been trying to figure out what it is we're looking at."

"You're not making any sense, Jackie."

"Colin is a genius. He rewired my phone so it played over my stereo, we left on all the lights, then worked up here with his cellphone dialed to my apartment number. We could hear ourselves talking from the back porch. Brilliant." She paused to cough. "Millicent hasn't been up here in twenty years. We've had sneezing fits that've lasted for hours. The place smells of mildew and cat pee and we can't get the window open. It's awful."

"I know this woman?"

"She's my landlady. Crazy as a loon. But a sweetheart." A voice spoke behind Jackie. She seemed to stifle laughter as she went on, "Colin says I need to get to the business at hand. Don't mind me. I'm giddy over not being a crispy fritter. Not to mention what we've discovered."

The phone in Wynn's other hand began squawking angrily. Wynn said, "Hold on one second." He took the other phone, said, "Ask your agents if there's a woman named Kirby living nearby."

Welker said tightly, "We've got a felonious situation on our hands, and you want them to play twenty questions?"

"She's Jackie's landlady. Jackie says she's hiding upstairs with somebody named Colin."

"Who?"

"I have no idea. Oh, and tell your men the Kirby woman is apparently not entirely sane."

A huffing breath, then, "Why should she be any different?"

Wynn returned to the cellphone. "What have you discovered?"

"Oh, man," Jackie replied. "This is sweet. It really is."

69

Wednesday

WYNN WAITED UNTIL five o'clock the next morning to waken the Fed official, Gerald Bowers. It had taken Jackie and Colin that long to sift through all the data and come up with something that resembled a case they could walk around with. Show to people, convince others they weren't totally off the wall. Add to that another half hour it had taken to explain it in single syllables so that Wynn and Kay and Carter could understand.

But when he got the Federal Reserve Bank official on the line, Wynn stared down at the pages in front of him as if they contained the cuneiform scribblings of some alien race. Which is why he woke the man up with, "Sir, I have reason to believe that the nation's financial system is going to be attacked this morning."

"It happens every day at nine, Congressman." The man croaked a tune that truly fit his appearance. "The moment Wall Street hits that morning bell."

"No sir. This is something different. At least, that's what we think. Or thought." Wynn looked helplessly across the room. The Hutchings parlor was much the same as it had been upon Wynn's arrival. Graham was lying down in the other front room, but the last time Wynn had checked, the old man's eyes were open and fully alert. One staffer had surrendered to fatigue and was sacked out on the floor by Graham's bed. The tables were littered with papers and coffee cups. The air had the stale quality of gritty exhaustion. "Somebody come help me out here."

Carter merely smiled. Kay watched him with the grim satisfaction of seeing an acolyte come into his own. "You're doing fine."

"Thirty seconds," Bowers finally growled. "Then I'm hanging up only long enough to call Welker and have him lock you in a cage."

"Too late. Welker is on the FBI jet they've sent down to collect Jackie and Colin."

The voice on the other end sharpened a notch. "Who?"

"They're supposed to be arriving at National about seven," Wynn said. "Why don't you come join us. Hear this straight from the horse's mouth."

"And why on earth should I do that?"

"Because," Wynn announced. "They've located Tsunami."

THE RAIN PASSED with the dawn. Not that Jackie gave it much notice. The FBI formed a three-car convoy in Millicent's front yard. Two men with shotguns stood sentry at either end of the porch. Welker waited in the front hall as first Jackie, then Colin, used the downstairs bathroom, showering under a trickle of rust-colored water, trying to scrub away the fatigue and the fear.

When Jackie came out of the back room, her wet hair was plastered to the same shirt she had worn the previous day. And all night. It was all she had. Everything else had gone up in the backyard bonfire. Welker paid her clothes no mind whatsoever. He glanced at his watch and said once more, "We really need to be going."

"Almost ready." Jackie slipped by the agent and walked down the back hall. Millicent was in the same place she had been since the agents stormed her house. "Are you going to be all right?"

"Mrs. Kirby will be fine," Welker replied, stepping in behind her. "We're stationing an agent here on permanent watch."

"I wasn't talking to you," Jackie said, seating herself beside Millicent, taking her hand.

"Ms. Havilland, we need to be leaving *now*."

Jackie massaged Millicent's hand, shifting in her seat until she was as close as she could get to the center of the woman's roving gaze. "You remember how you told me you were afraid of being alone in the dark? This nice man will be around just to make sure that doesn't happen."

The gaze might have been as scattered as sunlight on windswept waters, but the voice was all there. Soft and precise and terrified. "They're going to put me in a home."

"Not a chance in this world."

"You don't know. They'll watch me and they'll see what they want to see."

"Millicent, look at me." Jackie waited until the woman had brought her gaze under some semblance of control. "How would you like me to move in upstairs?"

The fragile shoulders lifted a fraction. "Live with me?"

"It won't be all the time. I don't know where I'm going to wind up after this, but I doubt it will be here." Jackie pushed away thoughts of any future beyond the next few hours. "I've got some money coming. At least, I think I do. We could have some people come in, build me a little apartment I'd use whenever I'm in town. Would you like that?"

The tiny woman used her free hand to wipe shaky streaks down both sides of her nose. "We could be best friends."

"That's exactly right." Jackie rose, then bent down and kissed the top of Millicent's head. Her hair felt like spun glass. "I'll be back as soon as I can."

She turned to the FBI agent and gave a little nod. Welker lifted his wrist to his lips and said, "Heads up. We're moving."

70

Wednesday

BURKE STUDIED THE dawn beyond his window. The rain had passed with the night, and the sun rose within a pristine sky. He reached for his phone and dialed Hayek's private line. The hand holding the phone stank of petrol and charred wood. He had showered four times after finally arriving home and still could taste the fumes.

The man answered himself. "What is it?"

"I'm just making sure," Burke replied, "you want me to go ahead as planned."

"Yes, Burke. I want you to do exactly as we discussed. Make the two calls. Report back to me. Now precisely which portion of this did you not understand?"

"But Crawford hasn't checked back in. Which means he might have been arrested. And we still don't know what Colin Ready managed to steal or whether—"

"Fear, Burke. When you begin to question the course of events, remember that. The greater their terror, the larger our gain."

The words were the same, but not the power. Burke had the impression that Hayek himself no longer fully believed what he was saying. "I'm sorry, I don't—"

"Chaos. Turmoil. Frenzy. That is what we are after here. Remember this at all times. Our success will be determined by one thing. The market's level of panic." When Burke did not respond, Hayek continued, "War is won not merely by force. They must hear our approach like drumbeats from the forest shadows, and fear what they can neither see nor understand. That way the battle will be decided before we even commit our forces."

Burke cut the connection. He went through the motions of following Hayek's orders, trying to stifle the argument he could not bring himself to present to his boss. That they were overextended, dangling on the precipice. And the unknown was still out there, the menace still not entirely checked.

He dialed Thorson Fines' home number. When the man answered, Burke said, "Be ready to start buying more dollar-long contracts."

"But the new money hasn't arrived."

"It will."

"When?"

"This morning." Burke almost added, soon as the markets crash. But there was no need to reveal his hand. "Right after the markets open. Five billion will be transferred straight into your accounts. Remember, use Interbank only. Fully leveraged. Max out every credit line."

Fines hesitated. "So it's really happening?"

Burke hung up the phone. He said to the empty office, "I hope so."

He unlocked his lower drawer and brought out the secret folder. The phone was answered by a voice more wheeze than sound. "Harris Forex."

"This is Burke."

A swift intake, then, "Back in five."

"Make it less." But the man had already hung up.

When Burke's phone rang, he took a long moment and breathed hard before answering. It was not a big step in and of itself, except for the fact that he was afraid. Of what, he could not say. He was doing as he always had, following his master's directions. But today the fever was not present, and he saw his actions with the cold clarity of one who was utterly divorced. Or perhaps one who had already lost. Still, he had no choice. So he answered the phone with a simple, "Yes."

"Okay." The sound of heavy breathing signaled a swift dash to a pay phone outside the building. "I'm here."

"It's a go."

The breathing stopped, then restarted. "Go?"

"Exactly as we discussed."

"And the money?"

"As promised, the second half will be paid upon confirmation that the insert has gone as planned."

"I can only write the pieces and put them out, I can't guarantee the papers or television will carry the spots."

Burke started to say that it wasn't the papers he was concerned about, then decided that was one point he definitely did not need to pass on. "Do what you can."

71

Wednesday

THE FBI JET LANDED at National beneath a dawn hammered from blue and palest gold. Jackie had spent the journey reviewing the data with Colin, going through it all one more time, committing as much of it as possible to memory. But now, as she watched them taxi away from the main terminals and over to where a convoy of dark cars and gray-suited officials awaited them, she found it hard to conjure up her own name.

It helped marginally that Wynn was the second person up the stairs, behind the welcoming agent. He gave her a hug fierce enough to still some of the jitters, at least momentarily. "You okay?"

"No."

"You look fantastic."

"No I don't. I'm wearing the same clothes I've had on for thirty-six hours, I haven't had a decent night's sleep since I left Rome, and I'm so full of burned coffee they could plug me into the airport system and light up a runway."

The cleft of his chin turned ax-blade deep, his smile was that big. "I'd say that pretty much sums me up as well."

She reached back into the plane and pulled Colin through the door. "This is the man himself. Colin Ready, meet Congressman Bryant."

The young man stammered, "I'm not certain I'm ready for all this."

Wynn nodded agreement. "Who is?"

A voice from down below shouted, "I'm waiting!"

Wynn stowed his grin away. "Heads up."

Jackie glanced over his shoulder and saw a man who made Carter Styles look good enough for the cover of *Vogue*. "Who's the frog?"

"Gerald Bowers, Federal Reserve Bank." Wynn gripped her hand and led her down the stairs. "This is not turning out as I'd hoped."

The man waiting for them danced on the tarmac like an overhot junebug. He could not keep still, not even as his eyes tracked Jackie's progress over toward him. "Let me see if I've got this straight. You called me in the middle of the night to say I've got to shut down the nation's entire financial system because of *her*?"

"If you'll just—"

"Hang on, I'm not done here. You claim Hayek is planning to push our financial markets into meltdown, and your only basis for this pronouncement is a hacker and a lowlife flunky who've committed a serious felony by breaking into a fund's trading system? How on earth do you know Hayek didn't just plant the data, waiting for them to sneak in and steal it?" Bowers choked on his rage, then shouted, "Whatever those jackals in Congress end up doing to you isn't nearly enough!"

Jackie slipped her hand out of Wynn's, and closed the distance between them. "It so happens that I'm not the lowlife in this picture, bub."

The man turned a choleric purple. "Young lady, get out of my face or I'll have these agents introduce you to the local penal system."

She moved in closer still, forcing him to stare up or back away. "You try that condescending tone with me once more, and I'll use your tie for a noose."

Bowers rounded on Wynn. "This is our contact? This is the star lead? A woman with no credentials you've got the hots for?"

Jackie reached over, gripped the little man's lapel, and swung him back around. "If you'd manage to *shut up* and *listen* for *two seconds* you might learn something you can *use*!"

Wynn offered, "Why don't we all ease off a notch here."

Jackie ignored Bowers' futile slapping at her grip, and kept him drawn in close. As the agents hustled toward them she hurried to say, "We know the data wasn't planted because we used a trader's own entry code to tap into Hayek's mainframe!"

Two sets of arms pinned her and dragged her back. She might as well have been chained to stone peaks. She shrieked at the man, "Hayek isn't running two funds. He's got *three*."

"Wait. Let her go." Bowers shrugged his jacket straight. "What are you talking about?"

"First you tell these goons to back off!"

"It's all right, gentlemen. We all just got a little carried away." Bowers took a single step forward. "Three funds."

"That's right." Jackie turned and called back up to where Colin still stood in the doorway of the jet. "Get on down here!"

He showed no interest in budging. "I'm just fine where I am, thank you."

"Colin Ready is the one to explain the details. I just interpreted what he found."

"Let's just stick to you for the moment." Another cautious step. "Three funds."

"As far as I can tell, it's the old shell game. Hide the pea with sleight of hand, right?"

A trace of the man's bullish nature resurfaced. "We're talking billions of dollars here, young lady."

"The name is Havilland," Wynn snapped. "Use it."

Jackie took small comfort in Wynn's presence. "Hayek supposedly has all his resources committed to the dollar, and he's bought billions."

"Correct." The bank official showed the root cause of his ire, drawing out a handkerchief, wiping his hands, massaging the cloth until it knotted up and disappeared. "We can't even determine how much he has acquired. But what makes it worse is how the entire market has followed suit."

"Which is exactly what he planned. Today Hayek is planning to dump his dollars. Soon as the market opens. All of them."

Bowers' face resembled a drain whose plug had been ripped away. "He'll be massacred."

"Not," Jackie replied, "if he has another team waiting in the wings to buy them back."

THE K STREET CLOCK ticked to a faster beat than the rest of Washington. By the time the Beltway and local Interstates experienced their daily dose of gridlock, most of the lobbyists had been at their desks for several hours. Even so, Valerie hired a caterer for this particular dawn conference, since many of the senior figures in attendance were unaccustomed to the rigors of K Street attack mode. Behind the boardroom table ran a buffet of smoked salmon, eggs Florentine, baskets of fresh bread, whipped butter, fruit salad, and stacked briquettes of filet mignon. She waited for the team to settle down, then said, "Last night I was invited to a function at the Press Club. They were doing a charity roast of the Vice President. Midway through the evening, I was cornered by Senator Alfons."

She resisted the urge to beam, their response was that strong. Hands up and down the table were trapped midair by the news. Senator Alfons of New York was one of the President's staunchest allies. New York was also key to the President's chances of reelection. She reveled in the spotlight of anticipation a moment more, then announced, "Alfons is coming out against the amendment."

"All *right.*"

"This is dynamite," another agreed.

"The timing could not possibly be better," Valerie went on. "So far as we know, the committee will have a vote on the bill this very morning. Before they meet, we need to muscle our way into as many offices as possible. The Department of the Treasury, the Council of Economic Advisers, and the White House staff. They all need to hear the same message—this amendment critically damages America's sovereignty, and backing it will do irreparable harm to the President's chances for reelection. The President can't afford to come out on any side but the senator's."

"Anybody who votes for this thing," her former boss predicted, "will earn themselves a one-way ticket back to Iowa."

Valerie leaned back, sipped from her cup, smiled at chatter she scarcely heard. The senior partner seated midway along the table gave her a fraction of a nod. Things were definitely going her way.

"HAYEK IS PLAYING a high-finance version of the old shell game," Jackie repeated, swiveling around in her seat so she could take in Wynn and Bowers in the back. "Switching the pea around in plain sight, but moving back and forth until the placement is lost."

She pointed behind them, to where Colin rode in the next car. The snarled traffic had them jammed in so tight she could see the worried pinch to his pale features. "Colin Ready told me how Hayek had built a second trading floor above the main one. He brought in this new team everyone hated, then seemed to climb down again and move them over to this bank he had acquired. At least for a while. But both funds kept growing at this incredible rate, and this week Hayek tells them the bank doesn't have enough room, they had to bring these new guys back over. But with both funds awash in new money, who's going to complain?"

"Hayek's ownership of First Florida has not been officially confirmed," Bowers said, his bark muted but still in place.

Jackie paused long enough to give him a look, then continued, "It wasn't until last night that it all finally fell into place. I've been wracking my brains trying to figure it out. Then it hit me. Something Colin said sparked it off. How there was still activity going on over at the bank. A *lot* of money being kept in abeyance. Not even listed on the books. Held in offshore accounts, just waiting for Hayek to give the word."

"You've lost me," Wynn confessed.

"It was a trick perfected by Rothschild. Back in the early 1800s, he was the king of the European financial world. Whatever he said basically was followed by the entire market. Just before Napoleon's defeat at Waterloo, all the banks were wondering if this was the end. Rothschild said nothing, but word spread that he was selling. We're talking serious panic, getting rid of everything he owned, switching to gold bullion and diamonds. Exactly what you'd expect if you had to flee a nation about to lose a war." Jackie squinted tiredly into the rising sun. "The markets just tumbled. But what they didn't know was Rothschild was secretly buying everything back at fire-sale prices."

Bowers demanded, "You're telling us Hayek owns a *third* bank?"

"He doesn't need one. A huge trading floor is required to handle different kinds of trades, and do them fast. But if all you're handling are forward contracts through the Interbank, a handful of traders could dispose of billions in a matter of hours."

Bowers leaned forward, snarled at the driver, "Can't you make this traffic get out of our way?"

Agent Welker was senior enough to remain languid in the face of Bowers' ire. "Sir, unless you're in the President's own convoy, the only way to get the Washington rush-hour driver out of your way is with a gun."

Bowers drummed on the window, ground his teeth, finally decided, "We've got to act. I don't like it, but we can't take the chance you're right. I'll have my people start gathering a team. But we can't hit the markets based on this kind of evidence. We'll just have to wait and see if Hayek starts dumping dollars."

Jackie's eyelids felt coated with shards from the hourglass of lost sleep. "We might have something more. One question first. How has the market responded to all this publicity over the current legislation?"

"Frantic. Terrified. Think of oil dropped on a red-hot skillet."

"There was something Colin found, or a part of something. We were halted before we could download all the files. They shut down their outside access. But what we came across got us wondering."

As Jackie outlined her fears, Bowers received the information as he would news of his own demise. He spent a long moment massaging his chest, then kicked the front seat. Hard. "Shoot somebody if that's what it takes. But get us into the city *now*."

72

Wednesday

S O MANY OF THE things Colin told me last night I just couldn't draw together," Jackie was saying. "Hayek is one of the world's most successful currency traders. He lives and breathes controlled risk. The only way to manage risk is through calculated logic. But there wasn't a logical explanation I could attach to so much of what Colin uncovered."

Wynn switched his gaze back and forth between Jackie and Bowers. The Fed board member's demeanor had undergone a drastic change. Bowers now watched Jackie with something akin to awe. "Give me a for instance."

She was seated in the Fed's basement command center. The walls of the windowless chamber were lined floor to ceiling with monitors, television screens, computer towers, cables, keyboards, dials, servers, and the hum of collective tension. The room was packed. Two local techies remained, both now operating under Jackie's instruction. Colin sat beside her. Arrayed on the long bench before them were four LCD monitors and two keyboards. Colin looked fairly comfortable for the first time since their arrival at National. He kept his attention fastened on the incoming data, leaving Jackie to deal with the suits.

Bowers was seated to Jackie's other side. Wynn stood with the rest of the team, an amalgamation of senior staffers from both Treasury and the Fed. Kay Trilling and Carter stood across from him. The two Fed techies squatted between the bench and the walled array, watching and adjusting. With the sound muted to bare murmurs, the screens showed all the morning talk shows, plus MSNBC, BBC World News, and CNN. The Reuters Board and Bloomberg streamed their constant flows of data. Colin's monitors scrolled with fast-breaking news. The wall clock read eleven minutes to nine.

"According to Colin, Hayek was reportedly sitting on a story so big it would rock the markets worldwide when it was released. But there were two problems with this. First, nothing that big could be sat on for weeks. Minutes, maybe. If he was lucky perhaps a whole day. But weeks?"

"It happens," Bowers said. "Not often. And not likely. But it could."

"Maybe," she said doubtfully. "But then there's the other factor."

"Which is?"

"Timing. How could he control the exact moment when the news broke? This isn't something Hayek is *hoping* would happen when he wants. He is *certain*. He's committed *everything*."

Bowers shifted nervously. Hating to have to ask, "So what conclusion did you draw?"

"Hayek," Jackie replied, "is going to plant a false lead."

The crew around Wynn shifted and murmured. Wynn was relieved when Kay saved him from having to ask, "Explain that to me, please."

"High-stakes trading has bred a number of parasitical offspring. One is real-time journalism. Before, the wire services ran to a very few feeder organizations, most of them news groups in themselves—television, newspapers, weekly journals, the financial trade press. Which meant anything major received off the wires was rechecked and usually redrafted before going out. But all this changed with the explosive growth of Forex and derivative trading."

Wynn observed a few of the team between him and Kay turn and ask one another who this woman was, seated there in her sleeveless high-neck cotton top and form-fitted black jeans. Jackie was the only one wearing anything other than standard bureaucratic gray. He saw the shrugs and astonished faces, caught sight of Kay giving the back of Jackie's head a look of pure approval. He wanted to reach down, sweep her up, hold her for days.

"Bloomberg is the leader in real-time journalism," Bowers agreed, directing his words to Kay. "They've seen their subscribers expand by two thousand percent in just ten years. Nowadays they employ nine hundred and fifty people in seventy-nine bureaus. They compete head-on with the more established wires of Dow Jones, Reuters, AP, Bridge News."

"They all sell the one thing that has value in the trading world, speed." Jackie seemed unaware of how fatigue was beginning to slur her words, or how the strain on her features was spreading to her voice. "The race is constant, twenty-four hours a day, sprinting around the globe in time to continental trading hours."

"Financial wire services generally receive news releases fifteen minutes prior to general distribution. To a trader armed with fresh data, these fifteen minutes are an eternity," Bowers agreed. "Senator, wouldn't you prefer to sit down?"

"I'm fine where I am, thanks." She asked Jackie, "So what does this have to do with Hayek?"

"The problem with real-time journalism is the crush of data. News flashes can't always be checked prior to initial release. The time it would take for a wire service to call and confirm a breaking story means that someone else might carry the scoop. Too many lost scoops, and the wire service would be draining customers and income like a sieve."

Bowers moaned one word, "Emulex."

Jackie nodded agreement. "Last year, a news flash was released over the wires claiming that Emulex's CEO had been forced to resign and the company would be restating its earnings. The story was later proven to be a total fabrication, brought on by a hacker who had sold the stock short. Even so, Emulex stock fell through the floor."

Wynn watched the shock register around the room, the sudden heightened tension, the newfound reason to watch the screens. Bowers leaned forward and said, "Young lady, would you possibly be interested in a job with our organization?"

Jackie's mouth opened, but no words came. She glanced back at Wynn, her gaze fawnlike with fear. He could do nothing but smile, urging her to move forward and accept what was already unfolding. Hoping only there would still be room in her life for him.

Colin saved her the need to respond by saying, "Heads up, everyone."

Jackie swiveled back around. "Who is it?"

"Harris. New kid on the block. Lower level of coverage, which means lower salaries. Perfect." Colin leaned forward and asked one of the Fed's techies, "Can you set a trolling signal for the word *Cisco*?"

"No problem."

Bowers exploded from his chair. "What are you telling me?"

"Harris has a flash release," Colin started, but was cut off by the MSNBC announcer's voice suddenly shouting at full volume, "This just in. We have an unconfirmed report that Cisco Systems' chairman is expected to announce this morning that their quarterly earnings were grossly overstated, and in fact the company is now facing a loss greater than its year-to-date profits."

"There goes the Nasdaq," the woman beside Wynn exclaimed. She caught sight of Wynn's confusion and explained, "Ever since Microsoft went head-to-head with Justice, Cisco has been the Nasdaq bellwether."

Bowers was already on the phone. "Get me the Nasdaq chairman." Then, "I don't care what time it is, and I don't care what you have to do to get him. Find him *now*." He stabbed the connection shut, looked back to where the Treasury guru stood, and asked, "Are we in agreement on this?"

"Unless we can get official confirmation that this news is for real, absolutely."

Bowers pointed at his people among the crew. He had aged a decade in the previous few minutes. "Check this out."

Colin pointed at one of his screens. "We're receiving another flash."

"What now?"

"Harris again." Colin spoke to the techie poised in front of him. "Chase Manhattan."

The woman beside Wynn muttered, "There goes the Dow."

It was CNN this time, announcing in grave tones, "We have just received a wire report that Chase Manhattan's Japanese arm, the recently acquired Bank of Sapporo, has admitted to previously undisclosed Forex losses amounting to . . ." The announcer squinted over the paper in his hand. "In excess of six billion dollars. Which is more than twice the entire bank's last-year profits."

The woman beside Wynn added, "The dollar is going to bomb."

Bowers said to an aide, "Get your team to work. Place calls out to the entire Interbank network. Neither Hayek nor First Florida are to receive credit. None. Any purchase they want to make requires a hundred percent up-front payment. Then inform Hayek that we are sending in the inspectors."

The aide fled. Bowers said to the room at large, "We can't close down the foreign exchange markets. They are too big and too global. If the gamblers can't place their bets in New York, they'll send them to

London. So we have to hope that cutting off his Interbank credit will at least slow him down."

He lifted the phone. "I need you to connect me with the President. Yes, now. Tell him we are facing a potential crisis."

"Jackie." Wynn leaned over. Asked softly, "Tell me what's happening here."

She turned only slightly, her attention held by the monitors. "What is reality in economic terms is less important than what the market *thinks* is real. Or, even more important, what the market thinks will be real *tomorrow*."

"So?"

"Most economic pundits think a downturn is under way. The most likely scenario is what the economists call a soft landing. Economic growth declines slightly, remains relatively stagnant for a time, then gradually picks back up. Such contractions are all part of a normal economy. Okay so far?"

"Yes."

Up close she bore stains deep as bruises beneath her eyes, at the edges of her mouth, upon her temples. She reached for her cup, grimaced at the taste of more cold coffee, drank it anyway. "But if pressure is precisely applied, the soft landing could be turned into a suicide leap. A twenty percent decline in the Dow would be enough to make the international investors panic and start dumping—the same scenario that brought about the Black Monday surge at the beginning of the Great Depression. These same pundits predict anything over a fifteen percent slide in the value of the dollar would have the fund managers racing for the safety of international waters, spurring a panic-driven spree of diving stock and bond prices and an uncontrolled fall of the dollar. Whoever bet against the lemmings would make a killing."

An aide raced back into the room shouting, "Cisco denies the whole thing. Chase too."

Bowers had straightened as much as his paunch and bowed shoulders would permit. "Mr. President, I am calling to inform you that we are shutting down the markets. Yes, sir. All of them."

73

Wednesday

BOWERS INSISTED THAT the press gather in the Dirksen committee room. Kay then placed Wynn next to her own chair, the place of honor normally reserved for the committee's senior congressman. But the other members made no objection to being moved down a rung. Not after Bowers began with an announcement that every financial and commodities market in the United States had been shut down temporarily, that warrants had been issued for the arrest of Pavel Hayek, and that all assets under Hayek's management had been frozen.

The television lights were hard on them all, exposing every line, every fear. Jackie leaned on the back wall beside Carter. The two of them looked like walking wounded. Wynn felt no better. As Bowers started his wind-down, Wynn quietly confessed to Kay, "I can't do this."

"Too late for withdrawal symptoms," Kay's mouth scarcely moved. "Get ready to go sing your song."

"You'd be much better—"

"It's your baby, Wynn. You named it. You rock it." The edges of her mouth rose slightly. "Just think of it as probably the most important moment in your entire life. That ought to help."

Bowers turned to the committee chairman and took his cue from how Kay raised her gavel and pointed it at Wynn. "I am now going to turn these proceedings over to Congressman Bryant, who will endeavor to tie this unfolding crisis into the legislation presently under consideration before this committee."

As he rose, Kay reached over and tugged the hastily scrawled pages from his hand. "I'll take those."

"What are you doing?"

"Saving you from coming across like you're reading somebody else's letter." She glared away his objections. "You know this stuff, Wynn. Now get up there and give it to them."

Wynn stumbled and would have gone down, sprawled flat in front of all the world, had not a pair of hands been there to steady him. He arrived at the podium, stared at the bare polished wood, gave a tight shrug of resignation. Given his current state of mind, the notes probably wouldn't have helped.

He looked up, confronting a sea of faces and camera flashes and the glare of television lights. He did his best to meet them all head-on. "In the period just after the Second World War, officials from Britain and the United States developed what is today known as the Bretton Woods Accord. This was an international effort, advanced by two key Western powers, intended to ensure that the Great Depression's devastation would not ever recur.

"This accord gave governments the primary responsibility of managing their own financial systems, and stripped from the banks the power to regulate themselves and print their own money—two principal reasons why the Depression happened in the first place. Naturally, the banks and the other financial powers of that day were vehemently opposed. But the officials responsible for drawing up this plan managed to convince their respective governments. They explained that without such restraints, the financial institutions would hold the power to sway public policy toward increasing their own profits, even when it damaged the public good. Not only that, but there was a very real threat that the banks would grow in size and influence until governments were held accountable to them, rather than the other way around."

Perhaps it was a trick of the glare, or maybe just the effect of strain and fatigue. But the cluster of lights seemed to gather into one flashing illumination. A single brilliance that dominated his vision, blotting out all else, giving him the chance to hear himself and know what needed to be said. "Over the previous two decades, financial institutions have led a two-pronged attack against these laws, seeking to destroy the regulations that were set in place to protect us. They have beggared the laws themselves, until the loopholes are so great they can act with impunity. And they have replaced the printing of money with something just as lethal—a collection of high-risk notes that go under the collective heading of derivatives. Banks have exceeded the ability of any one government to control them, and they call this progress. They wreak havoc with the economies of nations and call it globalization.

"The Hutchings Amendment intends to meet this threat on two fronts at once. In a concerted action similar to the original Bretton Woods Accord, a group of some two dozen nations are together enacting new laws. A global body will oversee international currency transactions, instituting a level of sanity to these activities. Any nation that does not enter into this agreement will find its financial institutions unable to do business with the member countries. Furthermore, a tax will be levied on every currency and derivatives trade, not so large as to halt the flow of genuine business but enough to stifle this wild tidal flow of risk. And the proceeds of this tax will go toward ending the stifling burden of debt carried by the world's poorest nations."

Only when Wynn paused for breath did he realize he had said enough. A more experienced politician would have found a way of ending on a stronger note. But when he blinked the lights separated, the faces all stared up at him, and the only thing he wanted was to be away.

By the time he had returned to his seat, he was certain he had blown the whole thing. But before he could apologize, Kay reached over, gripped his hand, and squeezed hard. With her free hand she raised the gavel, rapped the table and announced, "This committee is hereby called to order. The chair is open to motions to proceed on a vote on the appropriations bill."

Wynn drew strength from the hand upon his own, and said, "So moved."

"Second."

"Moved and seconded." She raised Wynn's arm with her own, so that the cameras and the photographers' flashes caught the senator and the congressman seated there in grim satisfaction, their hands raised above their heads, as Kay declared, "All those in favor of the bill's passage out of committee, including most especially the provision known as the Hutchings Amendment, say Aye!"

74

Wednesday

HAYEK'S DRIVER WAS busy polishing the Bentley when Burke drove up. The circular drive was shaded by cedars planted to form a sentinel line down the crushed-seashell lane. Morning's light spilled through the high cedars and formed a complex pattern on Hayek's lawn. Hayek's realm was as perfect and orderly as ever. Only Burke was no longer fooled.

The muscled young man who opened the door showed him straight into the breakfast room with its polarized view of the paddocks and the fields beyond. At his approach, Hayek looked up from his *Journal* and said merely, "Another coffee for my guest, Samuel. And a fresh cup for myself." He waved Burke into the wrought-iron chair next to his and said, "Have you seen the day's top story? Apparently those imbeciles in Brussels are going ahead with a European army. Led by the French, no less. Who have gloriously illustrated their fighting ability in two World Wars."

Burke remained standing. "Our Interbank lines have been chopped off. The markets have shut down. Our news items have been denounced. The Feds are flying inspectors down from Washington."

Hayek seemed not to have heard. He frowned and searched the empty doorway, then lifted the little silver bell and shook it vigorously. When no one appeared, his scowl deepened. "That young man is history."

"You're leaving, aren't you?"

"I beg your pardon?"

"All this is over. You're leaving the United States."

Hayek looked at him for the first time. "And if I am?"

"Take me with you."

The smile came and went so swiftly Burke could only take it for silent assent. But before he could respond, a voice from behind them said, "Afraid it's too late for travel plans, gentlemen."

Burke turned and confronted the senior spot trader. Alex was flanked by two swarthy men, still in their gray blazers. He could only gape.

Hayek, however, responded more coolly. "It was you all along. Of course."

"Always wanted to run my own fund," Alex replied. "The Brazilians and their new Russian partners have got to park that money with somebody. Why not me?"

He motioned the two goons forward. "I'm pretty certain they'll get their job right this time."

EPILOGUE

WYNN DID NOT realize he was holding Jackie's hand until the memorial service was drawing to a close. The Melbourne park was so full and the wind so strong the words spoken by Sybel's daughter were almost lost by the time they reached him. But he had no interest in moving closer. Surrounding him there at the back of the crowd was a second group of mourners. They were poorly dressed and seared by winds far fiercer than those rushing through the gathering. But these were Sybel's people, and Wynn found comfort in standing among them to say his own farewells. Along the park's far side, others unpacked a memorial feast for those Sybel had considered her special clan.

As people began drifting away, he felt Jackie's eyes on him. He said, "It all began right here."

She smiled so gently he could feel the comfort in his bones. "You need to make peace, Wynn." When he did not move, she added, "Your sister would want this."

He stared over her head up to where Grant stood surrounded by the better-dressed flock. "I'll do it when the cameras aren't watching. Besides, we need to be going."

They drove to the prison in silence. Wynn glanced over from time to time but could read nothing from Jackie's expression. Only when they turned off the Beeline Expressway and pulled into the prison parking lot did she say, "Do you mind if I watch from out here?"

He scanned the almost empty lot. Atop the chain-link fence, the razor wire danced and shivered in the wind, the sunlight glinting along its surface like sudden bolts of current. "Not at all."

She started to reach for him, then redirected her hands to tightly clasp her chest. "Thank you, Wynn."

The warden was there in the gatehouse and greeted him with, "An honor to meet you, Congressman. You're all signed in, and the people are already assembled, so let's move ahead, shall we?"

Wynn followed the warden down the path and into the concrete hall. All the tables had been pushed to the sides, save one down the center where a group of four people sat. In front of them was a lone man in a small plastic chair. He tossed nervous glances at Wynn and the warden, then returned his gaze to the assembled four.

"Shane Turner, you have been called before this exceptional meeting of the parole board. At the express request of Congressman Bryant, we are granting you a conditional release based on good behavior."

Wynn studied him as he would a new opponent, and saw a too-handsome man in prison blues who could not believe his own ears. The spokesperson went on, "You will spend the next ninety days in a halfway house, then be placed on strict probation for the next three years. You must find gainful employment outside the financial arena. You must report to your parole officer on a weekly basis." A pause, then, "Do you have any questions?"

THE WHITE HOUSE meeting was arranged by Polk Hindlestiff, professional kingmaker. His chair in the hallway outside the Oval Office was intentionally distanced from the AIM officials and the lobbyists who had hired him. His attitude, spoken and silent both, showed them a snobbish disdain. The two senior Wall Street bankers who headed up their little group glowered and bit off tight words of protest. Valerie did not need to approach them to know what was being said. After all, they had paid Hindlestiff forty-five thousand dollars, and all he had done was make a couple of calls. But apparently forty-five thousand dollars was not enough to purchase the old man's respect.

Valerie paced as far down the hall as the Secret Service agents allowed, then turned and stalked back. Finding herself along on this little jaunt only deepened her wounds. She hated how she had been not just thwarted but vanquished. Being this close to the flame branded her with everything she had almost grasped.

The Secret Service agents alerted them by stiffening to sudden attention. The President came striding down the long hallway, leading an entourage made up of his chief of staff and three more agents. He acknowledged the man who had brought them together with, "I didn't know you were in on this, Polk."

"Only marginally, Mr. President."

The man's almost apologetic tone once again provoked the bankers. Valerie's boss stepped forward before the pair could demolish the moment even further. "Mr. President, we are extremely grateful for this moment of your time."

"A moment is all you've got."

"Yessir." Clearly this was as close to the Oval Office as they were going to come. "We have prepared documents that will show clearly what a terrible mistake it would be to sign this legislation into law."

"I don't need to see your papers to tell you how I read this," the President replied. "You folks have showed up here today because you want to hand me a live grenade. And I'm here to tell you that I'm not accepting it." He waited long enough to be assured he had finally silenced them, then added, "Now that this is taken care of, Frank here will offer you a bone. I advise you to take it and run. Good day to you."

When the President had disappeared around the corner, his chief of staff opened his arms in grim welcome. "Why don't we step into my office."

He did not seat himself, however. Instead he leaned against his desk, crossed his arms, and said, "The President is going to sign this legislation, and that's all there is to it." One upraised hand was sufficient to silence the bankers' objections. "You've had your word with the President, now you've got ninety seconds with me. You want to rant, that's your choice. Or you can listen up and hear how things stand."

When he was certain they were going to keep their protests leashed, he nodded. "Fine. This appropriations bill is a crucial piece of legislation, and several of the riders attached to it are vital components of this administration's goals. Not to mention the fact that Hayek has made your entire industry out to be an enemy of this entire nation."

"If you'll just give us a second, sir, we can explain—"

"Don't even start. The nation is not in any mood to listen, so neither are we." When they had subsided once more, he continued, "Now then. If your lot can be on its best behavior for a year or so, next term you can pressure your allies in Congress to back a repeal. The

President gives you his word he won't stand in your way. You'll have a level playing field. But you'll be acting under the spotlight of international attention."

He indicated the meeting was over by pushing himself off the desk. As they began filing out, the chief of staff patted the top fund manager's shoulder, a recognition of his campaign funding potential. "Just make sure you back all the right horses between now and when Congress reconvenes. We'll make this happen. You can count on it."

WYNN HEARD THE PRISON GATE clang behind him and took a free breath. He walked to the car to find Jackie cutting the connection on her cellphone. He asked through the open window, "Anything wrong?"

"Colin's been offered a job with some group that does internet monitoring for the fibbies." Jackie's face had grown pinched during Wynn's time inside. "He wanted my advice."

Wynn climbed into the car. "It's done. Shane is to be released on parole." When she did not turn from watching the sunlight and shadows dance upon the windshield, Wynn asked, "Do you regret doing this?"

"Maybe a little." Her reply was a sigh, not of fear but release. "Could we leave here, please?"

Wynn drove them back to the Beeline, hesitated only a moment, then pointed the car eastward. Toward Merritt Island, the ocean, and home. A rising wind turned the marsh grasses and palmetto stands into silver blades, framing lakes the color of hammered tin. Clouds raced one another across the blue horizon, and not even the packed highway could overtake the perfume of storm and sea.

Jackie continued her silent perusal of the clouds and the light. Wynn's nerve held until they approached the toll booths. After he paid, he pulled over to the side of the highway and asked, "Where exactly are we headed, Jackie?"

She slid across until she was more in his seat than her own, as though she had been waiting all along for him to make this exact move. "I guess sometimes the only way forward is by finding space for the impossible."

Wynn nodded slowly, glad she could put words to concepts that remained for him only half formed. Jackie seemed pleased with his silent assent, for she wrapped one arm around him and used the other to finger-trace the hair off his forehead. "Do you know a place that rents sailboats?"

"Down on the coast, sure."

She kissed him then. Just a brushing of lips, the moment too full for anything more. But she must have felt the current too, for she shivered slightly in his arms. "I think it's time you had your first lesson in how to ride the wind."

ACKNOWLEDGMENTS

As anyone familiar with the Forex trading world will appreciate, the majority of my contacts spoke with me on the condition of strict anonymity. But I must thank them nonetheless. It was both heartening and frightening to discover quite a number of traders and investment banking executives who not only shared my concerns, but could clothe them in the reality of today's international derivatives market. I must thank the executives of Bank of America's investment banking division who helped by teaching, by making connections, and by shepherding me through their trading floors. Also I am most grateful to the traders on the newly computerized LIFFE exchange in London, who took time from incredibly hectic trading days to help a novice learn which questions needed asking.

Robin and Darryll Bolduc are both former Forex traders with major banks. Robin now operates a Forex fund of her own, and Darryll has recently begun law studies. They spent three days walking me through the murky labyrinth of Forex trading, helping to name the specters. In researching every book, one source always proves particularly invaluable. Robin and Darryll patiently supplied the answers I was desperate to find.

Timothy Canova, Assistant Professor of Law at the University of New Mexico, was my first source on linking the new banking situation to the arena of legislation and law. Conducting good interviews requires knowing what questions to ask. His expertise prepared me to approach time-starved officials on Capitol Hill and sufficiently impress them with my background knowledge for them to walk me through the halls of power.

Congressman Joseph Pitts and Congressman Dave Weldon were

most kind to aid me in my work. Heartfelt thanks must also go out to their incredibly capable staff, most especially Stuart Burns, Stephen Piepgrass, Bill Wichterman, Brian Chase, Jimmy Broughton, and J. B. Kump.

Not surprisingly, all but one of the K Street lobbyists with whom I spoke did not want to be identified. Nonetheless, I was amazed at how open and aboveboard they were about their tactics. Tim Powers, principal at Podesta, is a most erudite political strategist, and the time I spent with him was a fascinating tutelage in Machiavellian tactics. I must also offer heartfelt thanks to Douglas Domenech, Director of Government Affairs at NCHE, and Mike Ferris, Director of HSLDA. Retired Justice Daniel J. Monaco also took patient care to walk me through the process of dismantling existing laws through amendments to priority legislation.

Some people are much harder to thank than others, usually because they have affected me so deeply. Ziki Zaki is one such individual. A lady of many accomplishments, Mrs. Zaki has done everything from running the Egyptian operations of an American mainframe computer company to operating one of Cairo's leading art galleries. Nonetheless she took the time to open her home and her life to me, shepherding me about Cairo and unlocking a thousand doors. All the while I was taught from her store of wisdom, as she tried to show me the city through an Egyptian's eyes. Many of the recollections found within these pages are in fact her own. To her, her husband, Hussein, and her daughter, Magda, I offer my humble thanks.

Sameh Mina has been a friend for more than twenty years. He is one of those most subtle of men, who teaches most clearly through example. His friendship remains a godsend.

In the very early days of my business career, while working in Africa more than twenty years ago, I was fortunate enough to be befriended by the Middle East director of a major British bank. Cyril Price took a naive young American under his wing, and in so doing saved my professional hide a dozen times and more. Since then, he and his wife, Nancy, have become two of my very closest friends. I remain indebted to them both, as ever.

Two other people whose memories of Cairo provided a background to scenes are Dr. Mohammed A. Allam, the American University vice president, and Dr. Tim Sullivan, university provost. Their frank discussions and very deep insights proved both beneficial to my work and personally very enriching. It was an honor to meet both these fine gentlemen.

Dalia Mabrouk is Public Relations Specialist at the American University of Cairo. She managed to share a remarkable enthusiasm for the region and its heritage. Professor Nazli Shabik is an Egyptian born in America, who returned to Egypt at the tender age of fourteen. She now teaches English and composition at the American University, and was most kind in sharing her early experiences of Egypt; it was these valuable lessons which helped to shape the world Sybel knew.

David Ballard is Press Attaché at the United States Embassy in Cairo and kindly took time the day before his U.S. departure to walk me through the compound's structure and explain how a visiting freshman congressman might expect to be treated.

To my newfound friends with Saint Egidio, I can only hope that you find this book to be a worthy effort.

The more I work with Doubleday and Waterbrook, the longer grows the list of those to whom I am truly indebted. Profound thanks must first go to my editor and friend, Eric Major. I also wish to thank Steve Rubin, Michael Palgon, Elizabeth Walter, Harold Grabau, and Dan Rich. I stop here only because to continue would lessen the importance that must be given to the above names, and the innumerable ways they have helped and taught and directed. Thanks also to the outside editor who is becoming a fast friend as well as valuable teacher, Judy Kern.

Finally, my lasting gratitude goes to my wife, Isabella. Her wisdom and influence can be found on every page, both of this book and of my life. She is a true partner.